Praise for the
Time Rov

✠

SOJOURN

Time Rovers ~ Book 1
Winner of Seven National Awards

"Sojourn is a rare, well-researched and entertaining tale of time travel set against the backdrop of Victorian England and the Whitechapel Murders."
– *Casebook: Jack the Ripper*

"Oliver's first Time Rovers book is a spellbinding, multi-layered mystery with a bit of romance that will delight fans. She's done her research, skillfully recreating the sights and sounds of Victorian England with perfect detail, and she's equally adept at fast-forwarding into the future. Strong characters and realistic dialogue add to this exciting page-turner."
– *Romantic Times BOOKreviews*

✠

VIRTUAL EVIL

Time Rovers ~ Book 2

"Oliver is a first-class storyteller, able to bring the past to life with atmospheric suspense... Readers are in for a gripping adventure."
– *Romantic Times BOOKreviews*

"Virtual Evil is a sensory overload of spine-tingling adventure and mind-tickling wit."
– *Fantasy BookSpot*

Madman's Dance

Time Rovers ~ Book 3

JANA G. OLIVER

Save a Tree Program

At Dragon Moon Press, our carbon footprint is significantly higher than average and we plan to do something about it. For every tree Dragon Moon uses in printing our books, we are helping to plant new trees to reduce our carbon footprint so that the next generation can breathe clean air, keeping our planet and its inhabitants healthy.

Madman's Dance, Time Rovers~Book 3
Copyright © 2008 Jana G. Oliver
Cover Art © 2008 Christina Yoder, Dragon Graphics and Lynn Perkins

ISBN 10 1-896944-84-1 Print Edition
ISBN 13 978-1-896944-84-5

Time Rovers® is a Registered Trademark of Jana G. Oliver

Dragon Moon Press is an Imprint of Hades Publications Inc.
P.O. Box 1714, Calgary, Alberta, T2P 2L7, Canada

Dragon Moon Press and Hades Publications, Inc. acknowledges the ongoing support of the Canada Council for the Arts and the Alberta Foundation for the Arts for our publishing programme.

The Alberta Foundation for the Arts
COMMITTED TO THE DEVELOPMENT OF CULTURE AND THE ARTS

Alberta
COMMUNITY DEVELOPMENT

Canada Council for the Arts   Conseil des Arts du Canada

Printed and bound in Canada or the United States
www.dragonmoonpress.com
www.timerovers.com

In Memory of
Jeremy Beadle, MBE
Raconteur, Ripperologist & Humanitarian
The world is darker without you

ACKNOWLEDGEMENTS

My heartfelt gratitude to authors Donald Rumbelow (*The Triple Tree: Newgate, Tyburn and the Old Bailey*) and Stewart Evans (*Executioner: The Chronicles of James Berry, Victorian Hangman*) for their incredible body of work. Keats' Newgate saga took on a life of its own because of their meticulous research. Also, a tip of the hat to Neil Hanson for his riveting book, *The Dreadful Judgement*, which provided excellent fodder for the 1888 conflagration scenes.

And my thanks to:

Adrienne deNoyelles, my incredible editor, and Gwen Gades, my very patient publisher.

L.W. "Lynn" Perkins and Christina Yoder worked together to created the fiery cover art and design. They caught the essence of the story perfectly.

Robert Anderson, whose generous donation to the UK 2007 Jack the Ripper Conference netted him the pivotal role of... Robert Anderson. I had merry fun with this gent!

Nanette Littlestone, who finds the mistakes in my manuscript even though we're always right on deadline.

Ally Ryder, who has a fantastic ability to see the holes in any plot.

Tony Saladino, who continues to teach me the wonders of Chen Style *Tai Chi Chuan*.

Bob Hinton, who gave me good advice on period firearms.

And finally, my gratitude to the intrepid members of my critique group who frequently remind me to add more "visuals": Dwain Herndon, Nanette Littlestone and Aarti Nayar.

"AS FLIES TO WANTON BOYS, ARE WE TO THE GODS;
THEY KILL US FOR THEIR SPORT."
— WILLIAM SHAKESPEARE

PART ONE

CHAPTER ONE

Wednesday, 24 October 1888
London

Even emptiness has an echo.

She heard it in her mind, fighting for primacy. As time passed and the fire in her head dimmed, she became aware of movement. Creaking leather, the sharp click of horses' hooves. Each jolt of the carriage set off new reverberations in her head, causing her stomach to churn. Someone was talking. It only made the echo worse.

An eternity. The movement stopped. More voices. She felt someone help her to the ground and then walk her forward. Each step felt as tenuous as the last. She kept her eyes jammed shut. It hurt less that way.

"Stairs here," a deep voice warned.

She forced open her eyelids to find herself dwarfed by an immense stone building. Huge alabaster columns loomed upward into the night, so tall she couldn't see the tops of them. The columns spoke of strength, of permanence.

She pulled free, wanting to touch one. It was cool. She laid her left temple against it, relishing the sensation. It numbed the pain.

"Miss?"

"Leave her be for the moment," a voice commanded. It was the one that had been with her since the emptiness began.

Eventually, she straightened. The inferno between her eyes reignited, causing her stomach to heave. She vomited near the base of the column. Couldn't they hear the roaring? Why didn't it hurt them like it did her?

Someone handed her a piece of cloth, a handkerchief. She wiped her face with it and then clutched it to her chest as she was led inside.

There were more voices. They rose and fell like the wind on a winter's night. As they talked, she tied the handkerchief into knots. Knots were real.

Brain fever. Laudanum. Papers. Committal.

She bowed over, the storm in her head raging anew.

"Name?" an older woman asked, looking down at her like she was a lost child.

"Doe…Jane Doe," her companion replied.

Dr. Alastair Montrose gingerly splashed his face with cool water from the basin, cleansing away the soot. Then he leaned closer to the mirror, studying the effects of the warehouse fire. His eyes were puffy and bloodshot; his nostrils stung with every breath and his cheeks were splotched with red where falling embers had scorched them. The suit was ruined, the shirt as well. There were even abrasions on his palms, courtesy of his dive for safety when the rum barrels exploded.

Given the magnitude of the blaze, he'd gotten off lucky.

But what of Jacynda?

Even now, he could still hear her frantic cries from inside that warehouse as he fought to tear open the locked doors. Hours later, when the fire had died down, he and Reuben Bishop had found a charred corpse amongst the ruins. It was not that of a slender female: a fact that gave Alastair cause for rejoicing, although it felt heartless.

The question remained—what of Jacynda?

Reuben observed him from a nearby chair, his feet propped on another. "At least your eyebrows are still there," he commented casually. "I think your moustache took the worst of it."

Alastair studied his reflection again. "Indeed." It was a measure of his mentor's decency that he was trying to lighten the moment.

"Personally, I would be devastated if anything happened to mine," Reuben joked, running a finger along his upper lip. That was a given. Reuben sported a moustache that would turn any woman's head, along with sandy hair that made Alastair's brown hair seem dull by comparison. He cut quite a figure for a man who spent most of his time conducting post-mortems.

"I'll loan you one of my suits," Reuben offered. "It won't fit, but at least you'll not smell like one of those fellows in the Fire Brigade."

Alastair delivered a wan smile. "I appreciate that."

"Put some ointment on those palms," Reuben advised. "They look rather nasty. I'd offer you some, but I don't have any. The dead don't seem to require that kind of care," he added with a wink.

"No, I suppose they don't," Alastair replied, betraying a hint of a smile at his boss' characteristic black humor. He took his time patting his face dry with the cloth. He knew Reuben wanted the whole story, but he didn't know where to start. He dropped into the chair near the kitchen stove. The room was chilly, lit by a single gas lamp on the wall. He took a sip of brandy. The liquor burned his raw throat, making his eyes water. He blinked to clear them.

"In the past," he began slowly, "I've spoken to you of Jacynda Lassiter."

Reuben nodded, his face brightening. "Ah, yes, the adventurous American who has captured your heart." His jubilation instantly withered. "Good God, she wasn't in that blaze, was she? Was that why you were so keen to ensure the corpse was a male?"

Alastair nodded, shifting his attention back to the brandy. "The last I saw her she was inside the warehouse, near the doors. We'd discovered a body and I had gone for a constable." He put the glass down, struggling to keep his voice from breaking. "I should never have left her alone."

"You did everything humanly possible to save her. Your injuries attest to your courage."

Alastair was not so sure.

"How did the fire start?" Reuben asked.

"I have no notion," Alastair replied with a distracted shake of his head. "There was a lantern in there, maybe it tipped over."

His host put down his glass, then tented his fingers in thought.

"Hmm...Tell me more about the corpse you found."

Alastair took a deep breath. "His name was Hugo Effington, a warehouse owner who lived in Mayfair. He'd been stabbed, a single thrust between the ribs that must have nicked the heart. When I returned with the constable, the doors were locked and the building ablaze." He added, "Jacynda has been investigating Effington for some time."

"Why would she do that?" Reuben asked.

"It all began with an attempted assassination at a dinner party earlier this month. Effington was the host."

"Who was the intended target?"

"It's hard to tell. The Prime Minister was in attendance as well as the Prince of Wales, amongst other dignitaries."

"Why in heavens were they there?"

Alastair's eyebrow rose. "I don't follow."

"You say this Effington chap was a warehouse owner, no doubt a prosperous one to live in Mayfair. While I understand that the prince loves a party as much as anyone, still it's a bit...down market."

"I hadn't thought about that."

Reuben chortled. "Of course, if Effington has a wife or daughter who's a beauty that would explain it. The prince is always looking for a new conquest."

Reuben tended to view most matters in terms of human frailty. "Mrs. Effington *is* quite handsome," Alastair allowed.

"Aha!" his mentor exclaimed. "I knew it."

"Jacynda foiled the assassin. From what Chief Inspector Fisher told me afterward, she just leapt on him before he could shoot. Knocked him to the floor. She has been involved in the case ever since."

"You make her sound like a professional sleuth."

"In many ways, she is. She told me that she works for the Pinkerton National Detective Agency."

It was a passable fib, one that he knew Jacynda used with others. Far better than attempting to explain to his mentor that she was a time traveller from the future.

"How did you meet this remarkable person?" Reuben quizzed.

"She was rooming at the boarding house for a time. I treated her for an illness. I found her quite…unique." *Irrepressible, quick-witted, and prone to occasional oaths.*

Reuben's face burst into a smile. "I must meet this woman. What verve!" Then the smile dimmed as he added, "Of course, her boldness is what put her in the middle of that fire."

She's not dead. She can't be.

"I haven't seen any mention of this botched assassination in the newspapers. Certainly such an event would have been hounded into the dirt by the Fourth Estate."

"It was kept very quiet."

"It won't be when the fellow is brought to trial."

"That may not happen. He…vanished from his jail cell the same night he was arrested."

Reuben snorted. "Now you're sounding like a Penny Dreadful."

Alastair looked away, unable to explain further. He had no idea if his friend knew about the Transitives, the shape-shifters who could mimic any form. Or the Virtuals, who seemed invisible. How easy it would be to shift into nothingness, wait for the cell door to open, and take a quick stroll to freedom…

"What sort of man was this Effington?" Reuben quizzed.

"He was an arrogant bully, one of Nicci Hallcox's paramours. From what I gather, he was being blackmailed by her."

"Like most of London, it seems. She had a vast number of men in her bed. If the calling cards we found in her room are any indication, she was well connected in society."

"No doubt blackmailing every one of the men she'd seduced," Alastair added darkly.

Reuben shook his head. "I still do not understand why Chief Inspector Fisher summoned us to the murder scene rather than one of the Home Office coroners."

"Sheltering my friend Keats, no doubt. He's very fond of him. Fisher hopes that he will someday take his place at the Yard."

"Well, that's not likely to happen now," Reuben mused. "Even if your friend comes forward and is found innocent, his behavior has tainted his reputation."

Unfortunately, Reuben was correct. Keats' decision to remain on the run was at odds with what was expected of a detective-sergeant of Scotland Yard.

"I am astounded at how his life imploded," Alastair observed. "One moment he's a rising star, and then the next a wanted man."

"Fate can be very cruel to the best of us," Reuben observed.

Alastair had been so proud of his friend that night in Green Dragon Place. Keats' daring attempt to arrest a dangerous Fenian anarchist had resulted in his recovery of a wagonload of stolen gunpowder. The papers had lauded his triumph. Now he was known as the Mayfair Slayer.

How quickly they'll turn on you.

"It's pure fiction to believe that he would spend a night in sexual congress with that Hallcox woman and then strangle her in an insane rage," Alastair protested. "Keats would never do such a thing."

There was the creak of the kitchen door. A woman in a navy blue dressing gown entered the room, her hair lying across a shoulder in a long black braid.

"Reuben?" she said. "I didn't hear you come in." Then she stared at Alastair, mouth agape. From what he'd just seen in the mirror, he couldn't fault her.

"I'm sorry we woke you. Sometimes I forget how loud I am." Reuben gestured toward Alastair. "This is Dr. Montrose, my new assistant, the fellow I've been telling you about. Alastair, this is Mrs. Henrietta Forrest, my housekeeper."

"Madam," Alastair replied politely, rising, though it wasn't required. The housekeeper quickly regained her composure.

"Dr. Bishop has spoken very highly of you, sir." Before Alastair could respond, she asked her master, "Do you wish me to light a fire? Perhaps some tea?"

"No, I think we're just fine. The brandy is sufficient to cure our ills." He turned his attention to Alastair. "You, however, are running on sheer nerves. I prescribe rest and a good meal. I have a comfortable guest room that you are welcome to use. When you rise, we will have a hot breakfast. Henrietta is an excellent cook."

"I don't wish to be a burden," Alastair began, touched by the offer.

"If you were, I'd just chuck you out the back door. Besides, my guess is your day is going to be a full one. If you return to your boarding house now, you will get no peace until the coppers have asked every question they can put to you."

"I suspect you are correct."

Reuben clapped his hands together. "So that's the plan. Henrietta, please light a fire in the guest room and, ah, leave him one of my suits, will you? His appears to be a loss."

"Certainly, sir." Then she was gone.

Alastair opted for praise. "A very handsome woman," he remarked.

Reuben stared into his drink, his expression melancholy. "She is." He blurted, "We are lovers. Does that arrangement shock you?"

Alastair finished off the liquor before answering, taken aback at Reuben's personal confession. "I had a similar arrangement when I was in medical school, though we were not in love. We saw it as being to our mutual benefit."

"Precisely! Unfortunately, being smitten complicates the issue." Reuben rose in a fluid motion. "Now come along. I'll show you the way. Sleep as long as you like. I'm sure if the coppers want to find you, they'll pound on my door."

—

Satyr was uncharacteristically late for the breakfast appointment with his superior. That made him irritable. He grumbled at the hansom driver for the length of time it took the man to make change, and then stalked into the dining room on Rose Street, the usual meeting place. The staff immediately gave way as he entered the private room in the back. To his annoyance, the Ascendant was already well into his meal, a newspaper open at his elbow.

He noted without amusement that the leader of the Transitives still insisted upon the same "presentation," as they called it. Satyr had repeatedly suggested that he shift form. What was the point of going *en mirage* if you did not alter your appearance every now and then? Changing some slight aspect kept your enemies off guard. Satyr employed that strategy, shifting hairstyle or eye color at whim. You did not become Lead Assassin by being lazy.

His superior looked up. "Ah, there you are, Mr. S." He gestured with a fork toward the newsprint. "It appears you had an eventful evening, so I will forgive your tardiness."

Better that you do. Satyr removed his hat and coat, placing them on the chair nearest the door. He rang the bell near his plate. A deferential waiter appeared instantly.

"More sausages, please." The Ascendant had eaten the majority of them, and the remainder would not be hot. Sausages had to be the proper temperature or there was no reason to consume them.

His superior was studying the newsprint again. That was just as well. Satyr was not in the mood for light conversation. Where once there had been a respectful give-and-take between them, he'd noted a change in his leader's recent behavior. More authoritative, with an inclination to meddle.

"Your sausages, sir," the waiter announced, setting a colorful Majolica bowl in front of him.

"Thank you. That will be all." The door closed behind the servant as the mouth watering aroma of spiced meat filled the air. Satyr repressed a sigh of appreciation.

"Well?" the Ascendant inquired, looking up from his paper.

Satyr ignored him, forking three links onto his plate and then carefully replacing the lid on the bowl.

"You are very subdued this morning," the Ascendant probed. "Did something go wrong?"

Satyr paused in his precise dissection of a sausage. "No, matters went very well. I dispatched Effington inside one of his warehouses and then burnt it to the ground. Very satisfactory."

"Yes, so I see," the Ascendant replied, gesturing at the paper. "There is a particularly lengthy article about the fire and the discovery of the corpse."

Satyr did not reply, savoring the taste of the hot pork. He knew what was coming.

"I trust there will be no repercussions of last night's activities?"

"None."

"No witnesses?"

Satyr's hand tightened on the knife. "No."

"What of Miss Lassiter? I do not note an article regarding her demise."

"That situation is under control."

"Is she alive or dead?"

"Depends on how you look at it."

A grunt of disapproval. "Satyr, you are my Lead Assassin. I would expect such distraction from one of your juniors. I have repeatedly asked you to remove this person, and you are ignoring my orders."

"I am not distracted, sir. Miss Lassiter is dead, at least in the mental sense."

"I am not in the mood for cryptic games!" the Ascendant snapped.

Satyr deliberately placed his knife on the table to avoid employing it on something other than the food. Then he looked deep into the Ascendant's eyes. To the man's credit, he didn't look away. His predecessor had always blinked. That one hadn't lasted long.

"At present, Miss Lassiter's mental capacity is that of a child," Satyr explained, holding his irritation in check. "She has no memory to speak of. She doesn't even know her own name."

The Ascendant settled back with a frown. "How did you accomplish this?"

"I do not reveal my techniques, sir. You know that."

The frown deepened. "You assure me that she is no longer a threat."

"No threat at all."

"Why didn't you just kill her?" his superior demanded.

"This seemed a better solution."

"Where is she now?"

"In Bedlam."

"Under her own name?"

"I am not stupid, sir," Satyr hissed.

"Well, of course not. What if she regains her memories?"

"Highly unlikely." He snatched up his knife and attacked the links with considerable annoyance. "If she does, I'll promptly cut her throat."

"No need to be petulant. My concern lies with the safety of my plan."

"Your plan, as much of it as I am able to fathom, is on track, sir. Effington is dead. By serendipity, Detective-Sergeant Keats is the lead suspect in Nicci Hallcox's murder, and the explosives are secure. I'd say you're worrying too much."

The Ascendant tossed his napkin on the table and rose. "I sense you are going to be difficult this morning, Mr. S., so I shall take the remainder of my breakfast at my club. When you cease being so tedious, feel free to join me again."

The moment his superior was out the door and on the street, Satyr felt his appetite fade. In the end, he couldn't cut Miss Lassiter's throat or pierce her heart like he had Effington. *That* killing had been righteous; hers would have been heinous. It would have been like crushing a rare butterfly just to know what it felt like.

His hand sank into a pocket and retrieved the silver tube, the device he'd used to render her a huddled, blank-faced bundle of humanity. He turned it, studying how the light from the gas lamps glinted off the shining surface. Such a simple instrument to cause such destruction.

An odd sensation stirred within him. Remorse? He doubted it, yet there was a tight band around his throat just the same.

CHAPTER TWO

Detective-Sergeant Jonathon Keats sat in the dining hall, just one of many laborers enjoying the substantial food at cheap prices. Of course, he wasn't there in any official capacity. To the locals he was known as Sean Murphy, and while one eye was on the newspaper, the other searched for anyone who resembled a constable. Caution had quickly become second nature.

With the babble of voices, Keats found it hard to concentrate on his paper.

QUESTIONS ARISE REGARDING MAYFAIR CASE
DID SCOTLAND YARD SHIELD ONE OF THEIR OWN?
KEATS STILL ON THE RUN
REWARD OFFERED!

As if I ever would have had relations with such a despicable woman. The thought was repulsive, enough to make him regret the meal he'd just eaten. In his opinion, Nicci Hallcox was not a beauty, even *en mirage*. If anything, it was that she represented all that was dark within the human soul. Yet for many, he had to concede, that darkness was an irresistible lure.

As it happened, Nicci considered his revulsion to be a challenge. The last time she'd suggested he spend a night in her bed, she'd dangled a most appealing bait: information about the cache of stolen explosives Desmond Flaherty had so boldly carted off. Instead of taking that bait, Keats had stomped off, swearing he'd find the explosives without her help. In doing so, he'd fanned her wrath and that of her drunken butler.

My first mistake.

There was the scrape of a chair on the wooden floor as a dockworker seated himself farther down the long table. "I heard some toff got burnt up," he remarked before tucking into his food.

The fire in Wapping was on everyone's lips. Any blaze that started within a warehouse was of interest in the docks. Keats busily scanned the newsprint until he found the article. To his surprise, he noted his best friend, Alastair Montrose, had been present.

Probably trying to find me. A pang of remorse shot through him. The last few weeks had seen their friendship grow as they'd stood by each other in their darkest hours.

If only I could send him a note, let him know what has happened. But he dared not. Inspector Ramsey, in particular, would be watching the doctor closely, no doubt monitoring his mail for just such a letter.

The article went on to suggest that the sole victim was none other than Hugo Effington, the warehouse owner and well-known bully.

Keats let out a frustrated sigh. Another avenue of enquiry dead. Literally. Effington's many warehouses made likely hiding places for the stolen explosives. Although Nicci had probably known for sure, Keats hadn't been willing to pay her price. Now she was dead as well, strangled by someone who had visited her later that very night. Nicci's butler had testified at the inquest that her last visitor had been Keats, but it could have been any Transitive mimicking his form.

No one would believe that at that very moment he'd been squaring off with five Fenians, been knocked senseless, and then transported into the countryside packed in a coffin, of all things. It sounded absurd. If someone had told Keats such a yarn, he would have laughed heartily as he hauled the miscreant to the clink. Instead, it was his head on the block and his career in tatters.

Folding the paper, he tucked it under his arm with a frustrated sigh. "Ready?" he asked his companion.

Clancy Moran nodded, pushing his bulk away from the table. He had burly arms and a strong body, courtesy of years of work on the docks. His brown hair was unruly, sticking out from around his cap.

"Sounds like a bunch of hogs at the trough in here," he remarked.

"Hey, watch your mouth!" someone growled.

Clancy glared at the offender, who paled and stammered an apology. Moran was not someone to be trifled with, and most of the dockworkers knew it.

"That's better," Clancy replied, sending the man's hat spinning onto the floor. "Got no manners, do ya?" The fellow pulled on a weak grin and then tucked back into his food, sensing it was prudent to play the fool.

Clancy had told Keats there was a job for him, one that didn't involve heavy lifting. Until his broken rib healed, that would be the only kind of task he could handle. Besides, Moran wasn't going to let him get too far out of his sight. Not with the bargain they'd struck.

"What did you say I'd be doing?" Keats asked as soon as they were outside.

"Tallyin' goods. Someone's got to count all them barrels and such."

"How'd you get *me* the job?" In the last few days, neither of them had been able to find much work. Suddenly, Clancy had them both employed.

"I called in a few favors. This place just lost a man."

"Lost?" That didn't sound right.

"He left Rotherhithe all of a sudden," Clancy added, a mischief in his voice. "Truth be told, I had a kindly word in his ear."

Keats groaned. It was clear: Clancy had threatened the clerk. The Fenians were respected in the docklands, and few would cross them. Clancy Moran was one of them, but at the moment he was Keats' protector. The lure of the sizable reward kept the big man at his side, at least until Keats could locate the explosives. Then he'd turn himself in and Clancy would get the reward money to start over. It was ironic: a copper being protected by the very sort of man he was sworn to arrest.

Noting his disapproval, Clancy added, "Stop grumblin'. It's the best way I can keep an eye on ya. If someone else turns ya into the rozzers, they get the money. Remember, that's our deal."

"I know, but..."

In an effort to console himself, Keats' thoughts drifted to the night before. His mind's eye still lingered on the curve of Jacynda's calves as she'd removed her boots in his room. He recalled the rising desire between them, the potential of energetic lovemaking, what would have been the final consummation of their ardent feelings for each other.

Then it had all gone wrong, so horribly wrong.

"Ya all right?" Clancy asked.

Keats nodded, not wanting to explain. Instead, he went in a new direction.

"The newspaper said that Hugo Effington was inside that warehouse that burned last night."

Clancy raised a bushy eyebrow. "Hell ya say. Well, I won't be sheddin' no tears, that's for sure. Nasty bastard. I heard he hit a foreman once, split his head right open with one blow. Poor fella didn't die. Best if he had."

"What had he done?" Keats asked.

"Asked about a wagon that came in the night before. He thought somethin' was a bit dodgy about it. Effington hit him without a by-yer-leave."

What was Effington so desperate to keep hidden?

Explosives.

"Do you know the fellow's name?"

"Dillon, or something like that. Some said he's not been right in the head ever since." There was a hopeful pause. "Effington burn to death?"

Keats gave his companion a curious look. "No. The papers say he was knifed first, right in the heart."

"Surprised they could find it," Clancy remarked with a laugh. "Pity. A bastard like that needed a taste of hell afore he died."

"The Devil wouldn't want him. Too much competition."

Clancy eyed him. "Yer a cynical one, aren't ya?"

"Can't be anything but," Keats remarked. "You think we can find this Dillon, the one Effington hurt so badly?"

"Why?"

"He might know something about Flaherty."

Clancy nodded. "I like how ya think. Come along, let's have ya meet yer new boss. And don't go chappin' my ass if I don't move fast enough to suit, ya hear? Those barrels are heavy."

—

This day began like all the others: the grate of the bolt on the cell door, followed by the sound of metal bowls sliding across the stone floor. The food held no interest. Others would eat it.

She closed her eyes and returned to the wasteland of her mind. Little snippets of images and sound floated by, erratic clouds pushed by a light wind. A man's face. He kept saying a word she couldn't understand. Another face, warm and smiling. The smell of sheep. Something blue with legs.

Her head still throbbed, though the place near her temple was less sore now. She'd hoped that as the pain dulled, answers would come rushing back, that she would know who she was, what she was doing here. Wishful thinking. Asking her cellmates did little. One of them didn't know her name. The other demanded her boots in payment for any answer.

She'd never been brave enough to ask any of the attendants. Most of them frightened her. If she admitted to them she didn't know who she was, they'd never set her free.

If she could just remember her name. That would be a beginning. Once she knew her name, she could start to find the other missing pieces. There were so many of them.

What she'd discovered so far was of little comfort. The solid stone walls around her belonged to a mental asylum called Bedlam. Tormented shrieks rent the air at all hours. All mad people here, one of her cellmates had told her.

"Little miss?" a voice called.

She opened her eyes. One of the attendants, the nice older one, stood inside the door, his hands full of empty bowls.

"Did ya eat?"

She shook her head.

He sighed. "Ya got someone to see ya, missy."

A woman entered the cell, then halted in front of her. The visitor knelt and peeled back the light veil she was wearing. Her eyes were hazel, and her hair brown, with some gray at the temples.

"My God," she whispered. She hesitated for a moment. "Do you know how you got here?"

"No."

"Do you know who you are?"

"I, ah..." She shook her head. "Do you?"

The woman leaned closer. "Yes."

A thrill of hope rushed through her, even as she worked to tamp it down. "I won't give up my boots," she declared, fearing some trick.

"No, you keep them. You'll need them." She leaned even closer and whispered, "You are Jacynda Lassiter."

Jacynda? "Why don't I know that?"

"You've been hurt. Now repeat the name to me."

She couldn't. She'd forgotten it already. Tears threatened to flow.

"Jacynda Lassiter. Now you say it."

She did. The next time she tried, it was gone.

"I know it's hard." The woman rummaged through a pocket and retrieved a piece of paper. She tore off a small section and handed it over. "Can you read it?"

She studied the finely printed letters and sounded it out. "Ja...cynda Lass...iter."

"That's it," the visitor affirmed, smiling encouragingly.

She pointed to another word. "What's this one?"

"Cynda. Your friends call you that. Now keep this paper safe. Repeat the names over and over until you know them without looking. You must eat and—" a pause and the voice lowered, "find a way out."

"I don't know how," she wailed.

Her visitor took hold of her shoulders. "Now listen to me. If you stay here, you will die. Do you understand?"

She nodded. "Can't I go with you?"

"No. You have to find your own way out. Eat and survive. It's very important for all of us, Jacynda Lassiter."

The woman lowered the veil, then knocked on the door. It swung open, courtesy of the attendant. A moment later, the door bolted behind her visitor. The cell felt empty now. She'd liked the nice woman.

SHE LOOKED AT the paper and sounded out the letters. "Jacynda Lass... Lassiter." The kind lady had given her a name. It might not be her real one, but she'd claim it anyway. She knew no other.

"YOU WILL SEE she eats?" the woman asked as they walked along the lengthy corridor toward the entrance. On the left side were countless cells, each harboring a lost soul.

"We've been tryin', but she says she's not hungry," the attendant replied. "She says a lot of odd things. Thinks we make her sleep on straw 'stead of a bed. Says that there are two others in there with her and one of them's tryin' ta steal her boots. Says she's been here for days. Only just came ta us last night." Then he looked chagrined. "Course ya'd know that, bein' family and all."

The woman nodded. "You will watch out for her, won't you?" she asked.

He thought for a moment and smiled. "I'll take her to Mad Sammy. If she likes the little miss, she'll watch over her. No one crosses Sammy."

A matching smile blossomed on the woman's face. "That sounds like a very good idea."

—

By the time Alastair reached Pratchett's Bookshop, it was nearly eleven. He entered through the back gate and made his way down the passage to Jacynda's rented room, his pulse racing with uncertainty. When his knocking brought no response from within, his heart sank. Perhaps the owner of the building had seen her this morning. That's all Alastair needed: confirmation she was still alive, somewhere. Better yet, he wanted to hear Jacynda's tale in person, while thanking God for her survival.

Mr. Pratchett looked up as he entered the shop, a welcoming smile in place. It seemed genuine.

"May I be of service, sir?" he asked brightly. Then he stared at Alastair's face. It was a common reaction. The fire had not left him in good shape.

"I am Dr. Montrose and—"

"Oh, very glad to meet you!" Pratchett bustled out from behind a sizable stack of books. He was all of five feet, though not rotund like some of that height, his eyes clear and radiating a zest for life. "Miss Lassiter has spoken of you in such glowing terms I feel I already know you," he enthused.

"How kind," Alastair replied. "I knocked on her door, but she does not seem to be in."

"I haven't seen her since yesterday. She does keep odd hours."

"Yes. May I leave my card so that you can let me know if she does not return? She wishes me to keep track of her things, you see. She is often required to…um…leave London at short notice."

"I already have your card, Doctor. Miss Lassiter gave it to me some time ago. I must say, she leads a very active life."

"Indeed she does." *Beyond your wildest imagination.*

"I've got a spare key for you. She said you should have it."

The man dug under the counter and produced the item. "Oh, I almost forgot. She ordered a book for you. It came in just last evening." More excavating produced a tome. He set it on the counter like it was fine crystal. "It's about forensic science. She said you were quite interested in that field."

"I most certainly am." Alastair stepped forward. *"Post-Mortem Examinations: With Special Reference to Medico-Legal Practice."* He caressed the spine, deeply affected by the gesture. In the midst of all her difficulties, she had thought of him. This was his very first forensic text, a worthy start to what he hoped would become a personal library someday. Although being a doctor and a newly minted forensic pathologist didn't pay that much, he could still have dreams.

"She already paid for it," Pratchett informed him. "I doubt she'll mind you collecting it today. I'll wrap it up, if you like."

Alastair nodded, still astonished at Jacynda's generosity. Yet it was not the first time she'd been so thoughtful. In weeks past, she had provided him with a substantial sum to support his medical work amongst the poor. That gift had given him hope for the future.

With a rustle of paper, Pratchett expertly encased the book in brown wrapping and then tied the package with twine.

"Have they had any luck finding Sergeant Keats?" the bookstore owner asked.

Alastair was jarred out of his reverie. "Pardon?"

"Keats. The wanted man. I noted he is a friend of yours. There was some mention of it in the papers. I've been following his career since he arrived at the Yard. Well, him and others." Pratchett looked chagrined. "You see, I always wanted to be a copper, but my ancestors were all stubby, so I failed to meet the height requirements." He paused for a quick breath before rattling on. "I don't believe he did it for a second. Only ignorant men throw away a promising future over *that* sort of woman."

"I agree."

"I'm willing to wager he's on the trail of the murderer," Pratchett surmised. "It'll make great reading in the newspapers when he finally catches his man, and a comeuppance for those who look down on his stature."

Alastair couldn't help but warm to the bookseller. "Did you read about the inquest?"

"I did. That's how I learned that the sergeant is a short fellow, like me. Do you know that the editor of the Pall Mall Gazette wrote an article in his paper about that very thing?"

"No, I was not aware of that."

"He says the reason they can't find the Ripper is because the constabulary has no room for *clever little ferrets of men in the London detective force.* I totally agree with Mr. Stead on that point. Why should height be a barrier to detection?"

"I agree. Well, hopefully Keats has his day in court."

Alastair picked up the parcel. "Do you mind if I check Miss Lassiter's room?"

"Not in the least. If she's trusted you with a key, I shall as well."

"Thank you."

Jacynda's room looked untouched. The bed was made, the fireplace cold. The edge of her Gladstone peeped out from under the bed frame. He nudged it farther underneath with his boot. Then he sat on the foot of the hard bed, cradling his head in his hands. The scene came back to him with vivid clarity: the smell of the burning tobacco, her pleas for help as her fists hammered on the warehouse doors. Smoke pouring out around the hinges as the rum barrels exploded like cannon fire.

You cannot be dead.

CHAPTER THREE

2057 A.D.
Time Protocol Board

T.E. Morrisey noted with displeasure that the meeting was being held in a private room inside the Time Protocol Board complex. That meant there would be no public record. Furthering his irritation was the stipulation that his assistant and legal advisor, Fulham, not be admitted.

"Just a friendly chat," one of the board members had remarked with false bonhomie. "*The Genius* needs no legal representative."

Morrisey detested that label. Though he held a score of patents and had created the *Fast Forward* software that powered the time immersion industry, he didn't consider himself a genius. He just paid attention, noting things that others missed. Like this room, for example. It was decorated in what Miss Lassiter might call Corporate Dull. No elegant artwork on the walls, tatami mats on the floor or a waterfall gracing a corner. In Morrisey's eyes, the room had no soul. It mirrored its owners.

Most of that was the fault of the current chairman, Marvin Davies, a sixty-something career politico with a penchant for bad haircuts. If they could manipulate DNA to create the perfect politician, Davies would be the result. He had little to no knowledge of time travel, which set the standard for the other five members of the board. M. A. Fletcher, the one board member who actually knew something of the industry, was noticeably absent. That was the most striking change since Morrisey was last here.

First came the warm, caring approach. They'd offered him tea served by a very attractive young Asian woman. He'd taken the tea and ignored the physical bait, irritated they knew which buttons to push.

Then they'd asked him a myriad of questions, all the while apologizing for wasting his valuable time. Just a few more, they'd said, and then you can get back to the strenuous work of managing TEM Enterprises.

When Morrisey hadn't provided the answers they desired, a nod came from Davies. The gloves were quickly tossed aside.

"Defoe? Where is he?" one of the board members demanded.

"I have no idea," Morrisey replied, his clipped British accent providing a civilized contrast to those around him. It was a bold lie. Harter Defoe, his partner in TEM Enterprises and the world's first time traveler, was currently recuperating in Morrisey's private quarters. He would stay there until his bullet wound healed, or he was discovered. With a Reasonable Force Warrant in effect, Harter was definitely a wanted man, though TPB insisted it was only to protect Time Rover One, as he was called.

Chairman Davies stirred to life. "Why did you allow Lassiter to transfer to 1888 against our orders?"

"She returned to finish the job." *And to fulfill her bargain with the Government.* They'd been threatening a decade-long prison term if she didn't dance to their tune.

In Morrisey's opinion, her illegal actions were humanitarian—smuggling tomato seeds to the Off-Gridders, those who lived outside of society. Her lawbreaking had kept a number of them from starvation. He thought she deserved a medal, not ten years in a jail cell.

But that wasn't the only sword hanging over her head.

"Lassiter's *latest* TPB hearing resulted in a sentence, Mr. Morrisey." Davies tapped the holo-keyboard on the tabletop in front of him. "Let's see—six months' incarceration, mandatory treatment for her behavioral problems, and revocation of her Time Immersion license, all for violating time directives."

"Returning my nephew's ashes from 1888 is hardly a crime," Morrisey replied. She'd risked her life and her career to bring Chris home to his family. It's why Morrisey had gone out on a limb for her.

And will continue to do so.

"She was specifically ordered not to. Lassiter has a long history of flaunting the rules." Davies looked up. "By letting her return to 1888, you helped a fugitive escape."

"Escape?" Morrisey replied. "No indeed. She will return once she's finished her tasks." Another falsehood. At least he hoped it was.

"Her Open Force Warrant is still in effect," Davies announced.

"I am aware of that." He was still incensed that TPB would issue such an abomination in the first place. An OFW was a no-holds-barred retrieval. As long as the fugitive returned to 2057, it didn't matter in what shape: alive or dead. If Jacynda had to stay in the time stream to avoid a grave, Morrisey would see to it.

"Did the Government have something to do with this?" Davies quizzed.

Dodging the question, Morrisey replied, "Miss Lassiter returned to the nineteenth century because of the *disconnect* between 1888's recorded history and what was happening in real time. That's a Rover's job, gentlemen. No one knows '88 as well as she does."

After a quick glance toward the other members of the board, Davies shifted in his seat. "We know about the disconnect. It's not a major concern, at least not so important as to allow a fugitive to run amok in the time stream."

Not a major concern? That's not what they'd been saying awhile back. "The disconnect is more pronounced than you may realize," Morrisey hedged, testing the waters.

"Not according to our engineers," Davies shot back. "They assure me it will adjust once Lassiter is no longer in the time period."

That was a new one: a Rover destabilizing the time stream. They had to work extra hard to come up with that.

Davies leaned over the table, adopting a let's-be-reasonable expression. "Come now, Mr. Morrisey. I respect your concern for an employee, but this Rover has gone too far. After she returned to 1888, she assaulted one of our contract employees. She is out of control."

"That is a matter open for debate."

"According to Copeland's report, he was trying to execute the Open Force Warrant issued against her."

"I do suspect the word *execute* is appropriate here."

"Absolutely not. He says *she* pulled a gun on *him*."

That wasn't what he'd heard from Harter. The bullet in his friend's chest had been courtesy of TPB's henchman, though apparently they weren't aware of it.

"You must recall her and Defoe immediately," Davis ordered.

"We've lost contact."

"Then perhaps we should amend Defoe's RFW and make it Open Force. He is as much a threat as the other Rover," Davies argued.

Morrisey's temper flared. "Harter pioneered this technology. He *is* time travel. Without him, you wouldn't have this job, Davies."

"And I am grateful," the man replied dismissively. "If you think you've gone unscathed, we will be drawing up charges for willfully disregarding our orders. If Defoe and Miss Lassiter return to 2057 immediately, we won't file those."

"She still goes to jail?"

"Of course, with time added on for her assault against a TPB employee. She's up to three years and counting."

No deal. "I really do not know where she is," he repeated.

"Well, then, you're in it deep, aren't you?" Davies replied, a note of glee in his voice.

That pretty much summed it up.

—

Wednesday, 24 October 1888
London

As Alastair neared the archway that led to the Metropolitan Police Headquarters, he felt he was crossing into another world. He always had that sensation. He'd not been in London in '84 when the Irish anarchists had placed a bomb in the public restroom beneath Special Branch's office, but he'd read the newspaper accounts. There had been many injuries. Fortunately, no one had died. Now, as he walked toward that particular building, he wondered what it must have been like in the minutes after the bomb exploded. "What gall," he muttered.

Would Flaherty attempt that again? Considering the three wagonloads of explosives the anarchist had stolen, he could bring down the entire building. If not for Keats' keen sleuthing abilities, Flaherty would still be heavily armed. In early October, Keats had noticed a wagon in Whitechapel and shrewdly deduced that underneath the casks of rum were hidden barrels of gunpowder. As usual, he'd been too eager. Though badly outnumbered, he'd confronted Flaherty and his men, refusing to wait for additional constables to make the arrest. Alastair could still hear the thud of the punches as they landed on his friend, the shouts from the onlookers, the two-tone police whistles shrilling in the night air.

In the end, the police had secured the wagon, but the cost had been unfathomable. The fight had left Keats with a broken rib and a brutal head injury, which rendered him incapable of shifting form. If Jacynda hadn't treated him with whatever fantastic medicine they had in her time, he could easily have died. Now the Hero of Green Dragon Place, as Keats was once called, was reviled as a murderer. The two accounts did not square.

Once Alastair offered his calling card and explained the purpose of his visit, a constable trotted off to Chief Inspector Fisher's office. Alastair chose a bench and settled there, resisting the urge to open the parcel and dig into the book. Hopefully, he would not be here long; he just needed to explain the events of the previous night and his involvement in the discovery of Hugo Effington's body. Scotland Yard would expect such a report, if only to ensure they did not turn their eyes in his direction when it came to the murder.

The last time he'd been here he was full of hope, sure that the evidence he'd uncovered would overturn Keats' arrest warrant. It had not come to pass, even though he had proved that his friend was too short to have murdered the Hallcox woman. The legal machinery, once in motion, was very hard to stop.

"Doctor?" the constable called, waving him up the stairs.

That came more quickly than expected. Alastair squared his shoulders and marched upward.

"Ah, Dr. Montrose," Fisher greeted, rising from behind his desk. Keats' superior was immaculate, his beard and moustache well groomed. He was always that way, no matter the time of day. The instant he saw Alastair's ravaged face, he winced. "Please sit. We have some matters to discuss."

The other man in the room wasn't someone the doctor relished. Inspector Hulme, the local inspector in charge of the Hallcox murder investigation, eyed him glumly.

"Doctor," he muttered.

Alastair nodded in reply. Fisher leaned forward, his eyes full of morbid curiosity. "You are definitely singed around the edges, Doctor."

"To be blunt, it was a hellish night."

"So I hear," Fisher replied. "I must thank you for coming to us. You were not at your boarding house this morning, and your landlady was unsure of your location."

"I stayed the night with Dr. Bishop. I was too exhausted to return to my own bed."

"I see. Do tell us what happened, will you?"

Alastair related the evening's events, or at least the parts he thought the police might accept. Telling them that Miss Lassiter was actually from the future would only earn him ridicule and render his other testimony suspect. He hardly believed it himself at times.

"What of the fire itself?" Fisher quizzed.

"I have no notion how it began. I went to fetch a constable and when I returned, the building was ablaze."

"Where is Miss Lassiter now?" Fisher asked.

"I am not sure. She does tend to wander," he remarked, hoping with all his might that it was true this time.

"Indeed. What were you doing there?"

"I was looking for Keats." *As you asked me to.*

"So why was Miss Lassiter there?" Hulme jumped in.

Alastair had wondered how long the inspector would hold his silence.

"She was particularly interested in Effington, ever since the assassination attempt at his party. She'd heard that he was skimming goods off the top of his customers' loads and hiding them in one of his own warehouses. She wanted to investigate the claim."

Hulme scowled. "I suppose it never occurred to her that there is a paid constabulary in this city."

The doctor swore he heard a chuckle from Fisher.

"Miss Lassiter is single-minded, Inspector," Alastair explained. "Once she has the bit in her teeth, there is no means of stopping her."

"I will vouch for that, Hulme," Fisher added. "I've spoken at length with the woman, and she is quite tenacious."

"So it seems," Hulme grumbled.

"Is she still residing at the Charing Cross Hotel?" Fisher asked.

"No," Alastair replied. "She's staying in a room at Pratchett's Bookshop in the Strand."

"Why?" Hulme challenged.

"You'll have to ask her."

"From what I gather," the chief inspector interjected, "they're still digging through the remains of the warehouse, but they have not found any further corpses."

"Thank God," Alastair murmured.

"Did you kill Hugo Effington?" Hulme asked.

Alastair's eyes widened. "No."

"Set fire to the building?"

"No. Why do you think I would do such things?"

Hulme only smirked for an answer, making Alastair's gut churn. *Does he know about what happened in Wales?*

"We put these sorts of questions to anyone who may have been at the scene of a crime, Doctor," Fisher remarked.

"Even when you know what the answer will be?"

"Of course. Sometimes you receive a reply that surprises you," the senior officer replied. "Who do you think might have killed him?"

"Given his egregious behavior, Effington no doubt had a long list of enemies. I would hazard that it was someone very familiar with human anatomy. As best as I could tell from a brief inspection of the corpse, the blade went neatly between two ribs at the precise level to impact the heart."

"A doctor?" Hulme quizzed.

Alastair gave him a sour look. "Or a professional assassin."

"There are a lot more of the former around than the latter," Hulme replied.

"I requested a copy of the post-mortem results this morning," Fisher cut in. He offered the doctor a few sheets of paper.

Alastair scanned the notes from the local coroner who had performed the post-mortem. "*Lack of soot in the lungs indicative of death before the fire, pericardium pierced by a single incision.*" He dropped the papers on the desk. "As I expected."

Hulme extracted his notebook and flipped a page. "I understand that you and Miss Lassiter escorted Hugo Effington's wife to Southampton on the eighteenth. Is that correct?"

"Yes."

Hulme continued, his tone gruff. "You were involved in this woman's surreptitious departure from England, though you knew I was investigating her supposed suicide."

Alastair felt like he was in the dock, facing a jury. The questions carried that sort of edge. "I cautioned her on that point, but she refused to go to the police. She was terrified of her husband, and said that was why she made it appear as if she'd killed herself."

"How convenient that terror has been removed, and she has the perfect alibi—she was on a ship bound for America."

Alastair opened his mouth to protest, and then shut it.

"No defence of the widow, Doctor?" Fisher asked, leaning forward.

"No," he replied abruptly. "I do not have enough information to say either way, though I doubt that she would be so bold as to hire someone to kill her husband."

"Perhaps," Fisher conceded. "Nevertheless, my years as a copper have taught me many lessons, one of which is that women are a mystery. They appear as innocent as children, though I believe they are the more cunning of the species. They often employ that childlike innocence to rally our noblest male instincts in their defence."

"So you maintain that you had nothing to do with Effington's death?" Hulme pressed.

Alastair's jaw was firmly set. "Yes."

"I am given to understand that Mrs. Effington has accused her husband of physical cruelty," Hulme went on.

"There was evidence to support her claim."

"Bruises?"

"And old scars."

Hulme's eyes narrowed. "How do you know that Mr. Effington delivered those blows?"

"I accepted her word on that point. How did you learn all this?"

"Mrs. Effington sent me a cable once the ship was at sea. She said you had documented evidence of her husband's abuse."

"I do. It's at the boarding house. I will send it to you."

"Do so. She also instructed me to speak with her lady's maid, who provided a few details."

Alastair couldn't resist bearding the lion. "Have you questioned Mrs. Effington's paramour yet?"

"Paramour?" Hulme retorted.

"Mrs. Effington admitted she had taken a lover, a gentleman by the name of Reginald Fine. She said he is a solicitor."

The inspector's face darkened. "I'll track him down and see if he has an alibi, and have another talk with the maid while I'm at it."

"Excellent," Fisher said. "Any notion of where Keats is, Doctor?"

Alastair shook his head. "I might as well be looking for a ghost."

"Or Flaherty," Fisher replied. "Anything else, Inspector?"

Hulme shut his notebook and stuffed it into a pocket, frown firmly in place. "That's enough for now," he said, rising. "Good day to you, sir." He didn't bother with the courtesies when it came to the doctor.

Hulme pushed past a constable in the doorway, who then stepped forward to place an envelope on Fisher's desk. "From Sir Charles Warren," he intoned gravely.

Fisher nodded. "Ah, yes, the daily missive. Thank you, Constable." Once the door closed, he grimaced. "These are never good news," the chief inspector confided, pushing the envelope aside like it was a ticking bomb.

"Was there something else, Doctor?"

"Yes. I have learned that one of Effington's maids disappeared right after Desmond Flaherty stole those explosives. "

"From what source did you hear this?"

"Miss Lassiter."

Fisher's brow furrowed. "Yet you didn't think to mention this information in front of Hulme?"

"No. There are ... mitigating circumstances."

"Such as?"

"She is Flaherty's daughter, Fiona. According to Mrs. Effington, a mysterious gentleman named Mr. S. would call at their home to speak to her husband. She said the man wore different *disguises* each time. The girl vanished right after one of those meetings."

Their eyes locked. "Could he be one of your kind?"

"I fear so," Alastair replied, though he hated admitting it. Fisher was already leery of the Transitives as it was. "According to Mrs. Effington, her husband was one of Miss Hallcox's clients. She was blackmailing him. Perhaps Effington knew something about the location of the explosives, which is why she dangled that bait in front of Keats."

"If he'd fallen into the trap, Miss Hallcox would own him for life."

"Precisely."

Fisher walked over to the window and stared down at the street. "Given that the Hallcox woman was involved with Effington, it is quite possible she *did* know Flaherty's location. Keats should have brought her in immediately."

"And risk censure for attending one of her parties, even by accident?" Alastair protested. "You saw the list of men who were bedding her. Almost without exception, those calling cards we found in her bedroom represent powerful people who do not want to risk exposure. Either way, Keats would have been made the fool."

"Better a fool than a condemned man," Fisher shot back. "Damn and blast! We are missing a very large piece of this puzzle, Doctor. My twenty-two years on the force tell me there's another player in this game, one who's way ahead of us."

"Perhaps it is the man who was visiting Effington."

Fisher turned. "In *disguise*, no less."

Alastair didn't reply, unsure of what to say. Fisher had no direct knowledge of Transitive politics. For an Opaque, as the non-shifters were derisively called, he knew too much already.

"I will see what I can learn from my... *kind*," the doctor said, rising.

"That would help. I deeply appreciate your candor, Doctor. Keep me apprised of anything you hear. If we're lucky, these are no more than overly ambitious anarchists."

"And if we're not?" Alastair asked.

Fisher turned his back on him, resuming his post at the window.

"One thing is very certain, Doctor. Blindness always comes at a very high price."

CHAPTER FOUR

2057 A.D.
TEM Enterprises

Morrisey waited patiently as Harter Defoe adjusted the Thera-Bed controls with considerable care. His usually sharp gray eyes were dull, his face sallow. He'd always seemed so robust, but the bullet wound in his chest had drawn down some of that vitality.

"Did it fall out like I thought?" his friend asked.

"Yes," Morrisey replied, pulling up a chair. "Davies was in fine form, as usual. They want Miss Lassiter back immediately, and they'd love to get their hands on you, old friend. If I give them what they want, they won't file charges."

"Well, then, I'd sell us out if I were you," Defoe joked.

Morrisey chuckled. "And listen to you bitch for eternity? No thank you."

Defoe issued his own cautious chuckle in deference to the healing wound. "So they still don't know I'm here, or that I'm wounded. That's a miracle, of sorts."

"Loyal employees are an imperative in this business. Did you know that Fletcher is off the Board?"

"You're kidding? I thought she was there for life. She was the only sensible one of the bunch."

"There's a decided lack of good sense on the Board at present."

"So what's Davies' take on the '88 mess?"

"He doesn't think it's a big deal. They believe that if Miss Lassiter returns to '057, all will be well."

Defoe snorted. "From what you've told me, this isn't just a ripple."

"Not at all. This is something much bigger."

"So what is really happening?"

Morrisey laid it out in plain language. "A Victorian's timeline has been completely hijacked, and if the new thread continues, Sergeant Jonathon Keats is going to hang for a murder that never occurred in the original timeline. Should the new thread gain precedence, it will continue to ripple forward, altering history."

Although time usually mended itself rather quickly in Morrisey's experience, this wasn't history skinning a knee; this was a life-threatening hemorrhage.

"What a mess," Defoe grumbled. "Did Lassiter do this?"

Morrisey frowned. "I'm not sure. I think she had some impact on Sergeant Keats' timeline, but it should have mended itself."

"Any word from her?"

"No," Morrisey admitted. "She does go off-leash on occasion, but I would have thought she'd have contacted us, if nothing more than to check on your condition."

"I told her to leave me there."

"What, so you could die a hero?"

"Don't start that crap," Defoe shot back, glaring. "I get enough of it from the Vid-Net news reporters and all those damned time groupies. Lassiter was just reducing her debt. I've saved her enough times."

"For which I thank you."

Defoe gave him a puzzled look. "You're a lot more hands off when it comes to the employees, especially the women. Why the change?"

"Before Chris left on his last trip to '88, he asked me to watch over Miss Lassiter should anything happen to him."

"Do you think your nephew knew he was in danger?"

"No, but he was unusually solemn. Something seemed to be weighing on his mind."

"How did you know I was in 1888?" Defoe asked.

"An educated guess. You once said you wanted to see Richard Mansfield's performance of *Dr. Jekyll and Mr. Hyde* at the Lyceum Theater. I figured once you'd done that, you'd remain in London for a while. You were always fond of that era."

"Very clever." Defoe went quiet for a time. "When I met Chris that night, he told me about Guv's offer. They wanted me to keep an eye on things, work for them. They were worried about what TPB is up to."

"I suspected as much."

Defoe winced when he took too deep a breath. "I'm sorry…"

"What?" Morrisey asked, momentarily confused.

His friend looked him straight in the eyes. "After Chris… I'm sorry we ever figured out how to time travel. We should have left the fourth dimension alone, Theo. Who the hell did we think we were? Gods?"

"Not gods. At least not me."

Defoe smiled wanly at the jest. "It's too late now. Just like Pandora's Box. We've got people jumping all over the centuries, doing this and that. I'm surprised it hasn't gone wrong before now."

"We'll fix it, Harter. Then I think maybe we should step back from this. Let Guv take it on."

"They'd be as bad as TPB," Defoe protested.

"I don't know. I don't sense Davies has a conscience, but every now and then I swear I see the glimmer of one in Senior Agent Klein."

"That's a disturbing thought." Defoe fussed with the sheet for a moment. "How much trouble would you be in if Klein learns I'm here?"

"From Guv, not much. I think TPB is a bigger threat at present."

"Then give me a few days, and let Klein know I want to see him." He adjusted the controls, upping the amount of painkiller. "I'm going to rest now."

"I'll stay until you're asleep."

Morrisey waited until the patient's breathing was deep and regular. The blue line on the Thera-Bed had advanced considerably during the day, heralding his friend's continued improvement.

Thank God for that. I can't bear to lose you as well.

—

Wednesday, 24 October 1888
Bethlem Royal Hospital

The new cell was much like hers, only the occupant was very strange. Why had the nice man brought her here?

"This is Mad Sammy," the attendant explained. Then he lowered his voice, "Whatever ya do, don't make her angry, ya understand?"

Cynda nodded and the door swung shut behind her. The woman in the corner jutted out her neck and glared at her. They eyed each other. When the other woman didn't speak, Cynda pulled a bit of leftover bread out of a pocket and offered it to her. Nothing happened. She took a few steps forward and held out her hand. The woman snatched it from her like a feral child.

Then she began to sing. The voice was low, with an earthy Irish accent. It sounded like a lullaby. Entranced, Cynda went to the far side of the cell, settling against the wall, knees to her chest. She drifted with the voice. It made her head hurt less. In her mind, she heard another voice singing along, and saw the face of a woman with brown hair. She had no notion who the woman was, and that made her sad.

When the song trailed off, a flitting gray figure scurried toward the other woman. It was a mouse, a baby one. It paused, whiskers testing the air. Then it inched closer.

The woman crooned, "Come here, little one." She laid bread crumbs on her palm and then extended it flat on the stone floor. The little mouse hopped up and began to daintily nibble on the food.

Cynda smiled in wonder. "So small."

The odd woman's face turned toward her, neck extending. Her eyes narrowed.

"I had a pet mouse once," Cynda said, then blinked in confusion. Where had that come from? She tried to remember the creature, but nothing more came from her ravaged brain.

"Ya'd feed it?" Mad Sammy asked.

Cynda nodded.

The eyes grew less cautious. "There's another one," she said, pointing.

A fuzzy gray face appeared from under the bed. It was bigger than the baby one. Cynda broke off a piece of bread and placed it on her palm like the other woman.

Whiskers twitched.

"I won't hurt you," Cynda murmured, captivated by the creature. It worked its way toward her, one cautious scurry at time. It climbed up onto her hand, claws resting on her flesh. The mouse picked up the piece of offering and began to eat, rotating the bread after each nibble.

Cynda beamed. When she looked up at her companion, Mad Sammy gave a jerky nod of approval.

"Ya'll do," she declared. "Ya'll do."

The sharp rap on Alastair's door didn't sound like his landlady, but nevertheless indicated someone of authority. He rarely had visitors late in the evening. His interest piqued, he cracked open the door. His hunch was correct: Chief Inspector Fisher waited in the hallway.

"May I come in?" Fisher asked.

Caught off guard, Alastair could only agree.

Fisher hoisted a chair. "Your landlady advised me you only had one." He moved in as if he were a relative, setting himself close to the hearth. Then he examined the room. "Intimate," he observed politely.

That was an understatement. All of ten-by-ten, the room contained a single bed, chair, a washbasin and wardrobe, all jostling for space with his medical books.

Alastair angled his own chair toward his visitor, leaving only a few inches between them. It was uncomfortably tight.

"Has Keats turned himself in?" he inquired hopefully. He could think of no other reason for this unprecedented visit.

"No. Instead, I received a letter at my home this evening. It is a rather remarkable one. I felt you should see it." Fisher retrieved a folded stack of papers from his jacket. "I will admit to being stunned upon reading this. Keats has an alibi, did you know that?"

"Then why has he not come forward?" Alastair asked, astonished.

"It's the nature of the alibi that is the issue. These…" Fisher waved the many pieces of paper, "comprise a private letter and a police report, if you can believe it. He's on the run for murder and he's still filing reports, just like he's on duty."

"Sounds like Keats." Alastair accepted the papers, straightening them.

"Before you delve into all that, you might as well know: Desmond Flaherty is his alibi."

Alastair's mouth dropped open. "But…how…that's absurd!"

"Indeed. After Keats visited Miss Lassiter at the hotel on the night of the murder, he went into Whitechapel. He was promptly accosted by Flaherty and a few of his men. Instead of cutting him up…well, read it for yourself. It is no less improbable on paper."

Alastair skimmed through the documents. Smudge marks immortalized Keats' thumbprint in grime. The penmanship was uneven, as if he didn't have a desk, but wrote on whatever surface came to hand. The first page was a letter to Fisher, apologizing for the trouble he had brought upon his superior. The next few sheets comprised a detailed summary of Keats' whereabouts from the night of Nicci Hallcox's murder until he realized he was a wanted man. The last page was a summary of what he'd learned about Hugo Effington and the possible connection between the warehouse owner and Desmond Flaherty.

By the time he finished the pages, Alastair was despondent. Keats, blinded by his duty to capture the anarchist, had put himself into the noose. Instead of recovering from his injuries in the safety of his rooms, he'd been snooping in Whitechapel—a fact that had allowed someone to frame him for murder.

"What an idiot," Alastair muttered. "If he'd only listened to me." He found the chief inspector watching him intently. "If you arrest Flaherty, can the Yard bargain with him in order to obtain his testimony?"

Fisher leaned back into the wooden chair. "If we do, it will look as if we'd forced him to testify to save Keats' neck. It will only work if Flaherty comes forward voluntarily and we have evidence to substantiate his testimony."

Which will never happen.

"Someone must have seen them in Whitechapel," Alastair complained. "You can't have…" he flipped through the pages again, "five Fenians in an alley accosting a man without someone noticing. And this coffin Keats mentions, where did that come from?"

"That is yet to be determined."

"Why not put a knife into him, or beat him senseless like the last time?" Alastair persisted. "Why go to all the trouble of hauling him out of the city?"

"It is a puzzle," Fisher replied. "I'll put Ramsey on this tomorrow morning, but I doubt he'll learn much. No one's going to talk to save a member of the Yard, not when Flaherty's involved."

Alastair handed the correspondence to the chief inspector. "Where was this mailed?"

"Wapping. The postmark is from last night."

Jacynda. When he'd encountered her in Wapping the previous evening, she'd just mailed a letter—perhaps this very one, which meant she knew where Keats was hiding. Had he told her of his alibi? Why hadn't Keats shared this information with him first?

Fisher rose and tidied up the pages, putting them back into the envelope. He tucked it away inside his coat and then let his hands drop to his sides.

"I have held hope in my breast since this first happened, but every day makes it worse. There are even calls for my resignation."

"You cannot resign," Alastair protested. "Keats must have a champion."

"That is all that keeps me in place."

Alastair rose and offered his hand. "Thank you for sharing this information, Chief Inspector. I deeply appreciate your courtesy."

They shook hands solemnly. "I felt of all people, you should know. Keats fought for you when it looked as if you had blood on your hands. I know you will do the same, even if I'm not there to help him."

Fisher retreated down the stairs, his shoulders hunched, appearing older than his fifty-plus years. In his distraction, he'd left the spare chair behind— not like him at all.

What must it be like for the man? He'd painstakingly groomed Keats to take his place in the years to come. Now that dream was over, snuffed by the sergeant's relentless drive to exceed his superior's expectations, to make the grade. In his own way, Fisher had aided Keats in his destruction.

There are no winners here.

After he closed the door, Alastair sat next to the fire, trying to stave off the chill in his bones. His eyes drifted shut as he pulled Desmond Flaherty's face from memory, letting the image flood through him, pushing through the shakes and the queasiness in his stomach. When the sensation faded, he studied himself in the small mirror above the basin.

The face of the anarchist stared back. He closed his eyes and shifted back into his own form. This time, the sensation wasn't as bone-jarring. Instead, it felt right.

Until now, he'd never viewed the ability to go *en mirage* as a blessing, rather a blatant invitation to evil, a point Keats and he had argued repeatedly. He'd had no notion that the Transitives existed before Marda's death. He had simply held the woman he loved while the ability crossed to him with her last breath. The Transitives had a name for it—the *Rite de la Mort*. His life had changed. That was many years ago and he'd steadfastly resisted the urge to indulge his "curse," as he called it.

Alastair had risked his career and even his life to hold that line. In the end, the other Transitives had won.

But not for the reason they might believe.

—

Thursday, 25 October 1888
Scotland Yard

"It's a load of bollocks," Inspector Ramsey fumed, tossing the papers on his superior's desk with disgust. "Keats is a damned liar. Flaherty would cut his throat right off, not stuff him in some box and ship him across the country like a bunch of apples."

Fisher retrieved Keats' report, organizing it into a neat stack, unruffled by Inspector Ramsey's outburst. "I know how much you detest the sergeant, but the fact remains he is one of us. To that end, you will conduct the most thorough investigation of your career. Do you understand?"

Ramsey's face flushed with anger. "Sir, I—"

"What if this load of bollocks, as you call it, is the truth?"

Ramsey settled back against the chair. It gave a decided squeak at his weight. "If he's guilty…" The inspector paused and shook his head. "Bloody hell."

"If he's guilty, then that's his fate. But by God, Ramsey, it just doesn't feel right."

"You're too partial to the little bugger. It clouds your judgment."

Fisher's moustache twitched. "I admit it, I am partial to Keats, but that doesn't explain why my gut has been in a knot since this started."

Ramsey looked away, then down at his boots. "I…oh, shite," he muttered under his breath. He looked up. "I don't like it either, sir. It puts us all in a bad light. Keats is a swaggering little gnome, but he wants your job and he damned well won't get it by strangling some pox-ridden tart."

"Blunt as usual, but correct. I want you to do two things: verify the validity of Keats' alibi, and ask around about Inspector Hulme. Something's off there. I suspect he's holding back on the investigation."

"Why?" Ramsey challenged. "What would it gain him?"

Fisher drew forth a single sheet of paper and handed it over. "This is the list of men who left their calling cards at Miss Hallcox's residence. The dates are when we believe they partook of her *custom*. She may well have been blackmailing all of them."

Ramsey studied the list, then whistled. "There's a load of toffs here."

"That's my point. Important people know how to pull strings. It's how you remain important."

"This didn't come out in the inquest."

"We were not allowed to mention it. Find me the truth, Ramsey. I'll live with it either way."

Ramsey returned the list. When he rose, Fisher added, "Oh, one other thing. Police Commissioner Warren has saddled us with some American reporter. He's here in London doing a piece on Scotland Yard."

"Damned poor time for it," Ramsey observed.

"I pointed that out, but Sir Charles disagreed. Vehemently. Let's see, I have the man's card … here."

Ramsey took it, looked at the name and snorted. "Robert Anderson?" he read with a smirk. "We already got one, and ours is a Sir. Don't need another."

"Common name, apparently," Fisher replied. "Warren wants the world to know we're going about this case totally without prejudice. I was against the notion, but I was overruled, yet again."

"Can't someone else squire this fellow around?"

Fisher looked him straight in the eyes. "There's no one else I'd trust with this, Inspector."

"You always say I'm too blunt. I could say something wrong and it'll end up in the newspaper."

"I've been given permission for this man to be fully involved in *every* portion of this investigation."

Ramsey stared in horror. "What? Is Warren mad?"

"Very likely. So take this Mr. Anderson everywhere. Let him hear it *all*."

"I don't know if that's a wise idea, sir."

"Don't worry, it'll be my head on the platter, not yours."

"But—"

Fisher leaned forward. "It doesn't matter, Martin. I'm not going to be here much longer. Warren is just looking for a reason to send me packing. We've never seen eye to eye. If my career is at an end, I want the truth out there for once."

Ramsey grunted. "I don't think they want to know the truth, sir."

"That's entirely possible. Either way, take this Anderson fellow under your wing. Show him what he needs to know. I leave it up to you."

A resigned nod. "Where do I find him?"

"He'll be at the Clarence at one sharp. I have no idea what he looks like. Warren didn't bother to tell me that."

"I'll find him. Reporters all look the same."

"If you find Keats, kick him in the arse for me, will you?"

Ramsey nodded, a smile lighting up his face. "With pleasure, sir, right after I give him a swift one of my own."

Then the man was gone, his heavy boots thumping on the stairs.

Fisher's eyes fell upon Warren's latest note. He reluctantly slit it open. It was almost a twin to the one he'd received the day before, and the day before that.

He skimmed the message, pulling out the relevant passages. "Dismayed at my lack of progress. Wishes to see me promptly with a full report." He crumpled the paper and tossed it toward the fireplace. It slowly unfurled, mocking him. With a low sigh, he collected his bowler and headed off for yet another dressing-down.

What had his wife said over breakfast? "Let them sputter, J.R. They are in no better position than you. Only you can solve this case, and they know it."

Fisher smiled. Jane loved him so much, she never gave an inch.

In the courtyard, the Rising Sun was bustling like any other pub in London. Maybe when he got back from Whitehall, he'd have a pint, even if he was on duty. What would they do? Give him the sack?

He laughed at the thought, and began to whistle as he headed for the far gate.

CHAPTER FIVE

"So what do you think?" Reuben asked, circling around the center of the room, arms extended like a dervish.

"Ah…I…don't know," Alastair sputtered. One moment they'd been discussing a peculiar set of post-mortem findings, and then the next, his fellow physician had hauled him to this house and proclaimed it should be *his*.

Reuben abruptly halted. "There are two floors, three bedrooms, a large room near the kitchen for a cook or housekeeper, and an additional room next door that the tenants used for their shop. It's not fancy, but the furniture comes with it and it's near the train station."

The furniture was decent, the location ideal. Still, that didn't help Alastair understand what his mentor was up to.

"Reuben, I can't afford a house," Alastair protested. "I've some money, but—"

"How much?"

That was a rude question, at least from anyone else but Reuben Bishop. "About three hundred pounds now."

"Three hundred!" the man shouted. "I thought you were impoverished."

Alastair flooded with embarrassment. "Well, one hundred of it is from the Wescombs, to fund my work amongst the poor, so that's not really mine, you see."

"And the other two hundred?"

"Jacynda gave it to me to help me build my practice, but I prefer not to spend it on my personal expenses."

Reuben shook his head in dismay. "Good Lord, you must have Scottish blood in those veins."

Alastair bristled. "As a matter of fact, I do. Why does that matter?"

"I'm not asking you to *buy* the bloody place, you know."

Alastair cranked an eyebrow upward. It was one thing for Lord and Lady Wescomb to act as his patrons, but Reuben's intentions were confusing him.

"Oh, dear," the man groaned. "Here's the truth: I'm a right bear as a landlord and Henny…Henrietta is very particular that my investment properties remain in good condition. Finding suitable tenants is difficult."

"Why do you think I would be suitable?"

"You just would be. Now come, come, I haven't shown the best part yet." Reuben beckoned him forward, then unlocked a door and pushed it open. The room smelled stale. "Don't mind the odor. A bit of scrubbing will do wonders."

It was actually two rooms. The front was rather large, opening onto the street. The other room was a bit smaller, but still quite adequate.

"Do you see what I mean?" Reuben prompted, his eyes aglow.

Alastair walked around the main room, letting his enthusiasm off its leash. "Big enough for a waiting room, and this…" he noted, moving into the smaller space, "is ideal for a surgery and an office."

Light clapping came from his companion. "So when do you wish to take possession of your new home, Doctor?"

Reluctantly, Alastair shook his head. "I dare not. For all I know, Flaherty's warning is still in effect. He was furious I came to Keats' aid that night in Whitechapel, and he may well bomb the clinic if it reopens. If you're concerned about your property, my tenancy could easily bring it to the ground."

"Then don't open the clinic until Flaherty is caught. It will take some time to get matters in order anyway."

"He may still seek personal retribution," Alastair protested.

"Then wouldn't it be better to be in your own home than in a boarding house? As I see it, if he were going to harm you, he would have done so by now. It's been a fortnight, at least."

"I know, but... I have no equipment. I sold my benches." Alastair wandered out into the bigger room again, his mind suddenly churning with possibility.

"You have that hundred quid from the Wescombs. You could use it here," Reuben prompted. "I know they'd approve."

What is happening? He didn't dare think of—

"How much?" Alastair asked, astonished.

Reuben grinned. "Twenty shillings a week. I won't need a deposit, and I'll help you get the equipment at the best prices available."

Alastair cocked his head. "Why are you doing all this for me?"

Reuben's enthusiasm fell away, replaced by a thoughtful expression. "I had a wise advisor when I was first in practice. He helped me find my way. His only stipulation was that when I found a promising new doctor, I should aid him in the same manner. That's the debt I'll expect you to repay down the line."

"Who was this kind soul who gave you a start?"

"A physician in Edinburgh."

"He must be very proud of you."

"I think he is, but he's not said a word. Dr. Bell is not—"

"Bell? Dr. Joseph Bell?" Alastair exclaimed. "But he's one of the leading—"

Reuben put his hand on Alastair's shoulder. "Yes, that's the man. One sharp-eyed, hard-edged fellow, but he taught me the profession. I'll do the same for you, if you're willing."

"My God," Alastair whispered, humbled. Reuben was offering him the world.

"As I remember, my reaction was precisely the same."

"I'll accept, but only if you'll introduce me to the fellow," Alastair replied, grinning. "I've always wanted to meet him."

Reuben guffawed and they shook hands heartily. "I've already written him a letter making that very request. Come on, we'll sign the papers and then have a celebratory luncheon. You can move in tomorrow. Henny can help you find a maid-of-all-work or a housekeeper, if you wish."

Alastair hadn't even considered that. A house needed someone to watch over it. The solution came instantly.

"No need," he told him. "I know the perfect person, if she'll accept."

⸺

"Anderson?" Ramsey called out.

The reporter had brown hair and a crisp moustache. He looked up from the notebook he'd been studying and issued a quick nod. There was a pint in front of him, but Ramsey didn't spy any of the telltale signs of a heavy drinker. Not all journalists would pass muster in that regard. Or coppers, either.

"I'm Inspector Ramsey." He didn't bother to sit. There was too much to be done for them to be chatting about the weather. "Let's get to it."

"As you wish, Inspector." The man rose, tucked away the notebook and left the half-pint of ale on the table. Most of his ilk would have gulped it rather than waste the booze.

Ramsey waited until they were on the street to open his barrage. "I hear I'm stuck with you on the soles of my shoes until further orders."

"Yes, you are."

"How'd you manage that one?"

"I know people."

"Warren?"

A nod. "I wrote an article about Sir Charles' exploits in the Sinai. He thought it flattered him."

"Did it?"

"Not really. The folks in Chicago want to know what it's like in London, so I've been here since the second Ripper murder."

"If you want to know about *him*, you have to talk to Inspector Abberline."

"I already have. Now I'm interested in the Yard's latest case."

Ramsey groaned. "Everybody wants to know about Sergeant Keats." He halted abruptly. "It's like this, Anderson. We've got a mess here. The last thing I need is a reporter dogging my heels, but if Warren says you're with me, that's the way it has to be. In return, I expect only one thing."

"Which is?"

"Honesty. Call it straight. If Keats killed that woman, he swings. If not, we're barking up the wrong tree and it would do no good to hang an innocent man while the real murderer laughs at us."

"Is Keats innocent?"

"That's what I have to find out." Ramsey hesitated for only a moment before detailing the sergeant's alibi.

Anderson mulled on the information as they continued down the street.

"It sounds fantastical," he noted after some time.

"I agree."

Anderson arched an eyebrow. "I understand that you and Sergeant Keats have an adversarial relationship. That, in fact, you detest each other."

Ramsey eyed him. The reporter seemed to be very well informed for someone hailing from Chicago. How much had Warren told him?

"We can't stand each other. Been that way since the first time I saw the little runt."

"What if he murdered that woman?"

"Then everything I've worked for over the past fifteen years goes to hell. It throws mud on all of us, don't you see?"

They paused at an intersection, waiting for a lorry to pass.

"I'll keep an open mind, Inspector," Anderson replied.

"Good." Dodging between a hansom and a brougham, Ramsey followed up with, "Do me a favor, will you?"

"Which is?" Anderson said, hurrying to catch up.

"Remind me to do the same."

"My chest is much better," Mrs. Butler said. She was sitting at the flimsy table in her minuscule hovel she and her son called home. "I'm coughing less and I don't have to take that medicine you gave me."

"Excellent," Alastair replied, pleased his treatment had a good result. Chest infections were often fatal. "I have some news of my own," he began.

Then he blurted it all out in a rush, though he'd not intended to. He still didn't believe it himself. As he gave Mrs. Butler time to gather her wits, his mind flashed back to their initial meeting. In truth, he'd met her son first, as the lad lay in a street with a broken leg. His tending the boy had cost him his position with Dr. Hanson, who had long frowned on his charity work. Despite Hanson's theory that the poor were indolent and gin-soaked wretches, he'd found Mrs. Butler to be a hardworking woman. She'd already lost a husband and two other children to illness, and that had bred a tenacity for survival.

"You bought a house?" she asked wistfully.

"No, no," he replied. "I'm only a tenant. I cannot afford a house of my own."

She stared at him with open-mouthed incomprehension. The concept of possessing even enough funds to rent a house was beyond her ken.

Davy, now all of twelve, understood immediately.

"You need a maid," he said brightly.

Alastair beamed. The lad was always quick on the uptake.

"Actually, I'll need a housekeeper, and I want you, Mrs. Butler, if you're willing."

Her eyes widened further. "Me?"

"Yes. The house is very pleasant. Eight rooms, plus space for my clinic. I know your health is not strong enough to handle everything, so I will allocate funds to hire a maid-of-all-work to do the heavy tasks."

Mrs. Butler blinked, her mind clearly awhirl. "A whole house? Near the train station?"

"Yes. Reuben... Dr. Bishop assures me that most of the street's residents are of a decent nature. I would not bring you or your son into a situation that was not to your liking."

Mrs. Butler's attention roamed around the one-room Bury Street hovel in which they lived. Mold laced its way down one wall, and the single broken window had a rag stuffed in it to keep out the cold. Loathsome things lived inside the walls. Alastair could hear shouts from some brawl above them.

"You make it sound like a palace," she said dreamily.

"To me, as well," Alastair replied, though in truth he had grown up in a house much like the one he'd just rented. "You will have Sundays off. I promise you will find me not a demanding master."

"I…"

"Mum," Davy urged. "We can't stay here. Not with the landlord pushin' you all the time."

"Your landlord has been bothering you again?" Alastair asked, hackles rising.

"He's always sayin' he'll lower the rent if she goes with him. When she tells him no, he raises it again." The glower on Davy's face told Alastair that one of these days the landlord would find himself on the wrong side of the young man's fists.

"All the more reason you need to move, Mrs. Butler. I am offering you thirty-five pounds per year, room and board. You will have your own room, which is much bigger than this one."

"Thirty-five," she repeated, astonished.

"All right then, make it forty," Alastair responded, feeling generous. "I will pay the first month in advance, as I know you will have expenses for the move."

"Dear God, that's a fortune."

"Well, what do you say?" Alastair pressed.

Mrs. Butler wrapped her son in a tight embrace. "Yes."

Then she broke into tears.

—

The moment the transfer effect began to stabilize, Copeland knew he'd find the Ascendant on his knees, head bowed reverentially. What else would a Victorian make of those whirls of light and that odd sound, especially if he was at all religious?

He couldn't restrain a grin. *Damn, I love this job.*

Sure enough, there was Hezekiah Grant, prostrate in awe as if his visitor were a god or something. From Copeland's perspective, Grant had three things going for him. First, he lived in an unstable time period. Second, he was the leader of the shape-shifters. Third, he was a very pious man—too pious, some might say, with a tendency toward fanaticism. Thanks to a few examples of technical hocus-pocus from the twenty-first century, Grant was now absolutely convinced that he was receiving visits from the Archangel Michael. His ego already oversized, Grant had no trouble believing that he, alone, was the recipient of God's most senior messenger.

What a sucker.

"Have you done what God asks of you?" Copeland boomed.

Trembling, Grant nodded furiously. "In all things, Most Holy Messenger."

"Tell me."

"I have ensured the explosives are divided amongst the warehouses so they will not be found before the Day of Judgment, just as you instructed."

That would please Copeland's new bosses. They demanded results. Failure, they said, wasn't an option. He liked it that way. Davies and his TBP cronies had been too skittish to really turn him loose, let him use that street knowledge he'd picked up over the years. They'd never understood his particular talents. His new bosses did.

"The w-warehouse owner is dead, as you commanded," the Ascendant stammered, evidently unnerved by the silence.

"Well done," Copeland said, throwing the man a rare verbal bone. Pulling his strings was so easy. Step by step, he'd guided Grant through the theft of the explosives and their distribution. When the plan reached fruition, the shifters would take the blame, along with that Fenian.

"What of the Devil's servant?" Copeland demanded. "Is she dead?"

Grant's trembling accelerated. "No…no. She is in Bedlam," the man murmured, still on his knees. "Insane, I hear."

Bedlam? Endorphin Rebound finally got her. He let loose a laugh, causing Grant's eyes to snap upward in surprise. Apparently, archangels weren't known for their humor.

"God's wrath has fallen upon her," Copeland announced with relish, staying in character. "We have no mercy for those who side with the Devil."

The Ascendant nodded enthusiastically.

"She must die before the Sabbath. Do you understand?"

Grant's eyes widened. "But the Lead Assassin—"

"Is standing in our way!" Copeland bellowed. "Go around him!"

"As you command, Most High Messenger," Grant said, his forehead touching the carpet in humble obeisance.

Copeland smirked, knowing it wouldn't be seen.

Just kill the bitch, will you?

✢

CHAPTER SIX

"I expected something more posh," Ramsey complained as he took a visual inventory of Keats' sitting room. Two chairs, a couch, small writing table, and a bookcase. Decent condition, but not new. No obvious signs of wealth.

Disconcerted, he moved to the window and looked out onto the street below. "Nice view," he muttered.

"Why did you expect anything different?" Anderson inquired, still hanging back by the door.

"Keats' family has a bit of money, from what I hear. I figured he lived better than this. Looks like any other sergeant's rooms, except they wouldn't have all those books."

Anderson edged inside. "Are you saying that police officers don't read?"

"No," Ramsey responded curtly, suddenly aware of the trap opening up in front of him. "I'm saying that most coppers don't have time to sit on their bums in front of the fire."

"You think Sergeant Keats was derelict in his duties?"

"I don't know that for sure. Always had a hunch, you see."

"I thought inspectors kept a tight rein on their detectives," Anderson declared.

"They do, but when it came to Keats the chief inspector gave him all sorts of liberties."

"Why do you dislike the man so much?"

Ramsey's nose wrinkled. "He's the sort I used to beat up when I was a lad. You know, the short, whiny ones."

Anderson raised an eyebrow. "That's it? The only reason you dislike him is because he's short?"

The inspector's bravado deflated. "Not really. I've always had to work for everything I got. For Keats, hell, it just seemed to always go right for him, like he had some guardian angel watching over his sorry arse."

"The sergeant has had some successes."

"Yes," Ramsey admitted grudgingly, "he has. And he's sure to wave them under my nose every time he can."

"If he did kill that Hallcox woman, what would be the motive?"

Ramsey scoffed. "Simple. He jumped in bed with that tart, and she laughed at what he offered her."

"Does that happen often?" asked Anderson, his face all innocence.

"Not to me," Ramsey replied with a manly grin. "Let's see where he hides the posh bits." The inspector made it as far as the small room off the hall and then stopped.

"What in the hell?" He pushed inside and lit the gas lamp. Tiny colored pins littered maps that were attached to three of the four walls. "I thought he was winding me up."

"Pardon?" Anderson asked from the doorway.

"The sergeant said he'd comb the newspapers and put pins in maps so he could see if there was a pattern to the crimes." He moved closer and tapped a thick index finger on the map of Whitechapel. "Damn, look at this. Robberies, indecent acts, murder. He's got it all."

"So that's why there's a large stack of papers by the chair in the other room," Anderson observed. "Quite a useful tool."

Ramsey shook his head. "A waste of time, I think." He bent over and riffled through the contents on the desk. Nothing promising. A check of the drawers revealed the usual detritus of life: paid statements from a tailor and a cobbler, old letters from Keats' family. Nothing that pointed toward blackmail or the desire to throttle the woman in Mayfair.

Ramsey frowned. "He's a short little bugger. Where would he hide things?" Certainly not up high. He bent over and dug under the desk. Nothing. Running his head underneath the top revealed a small shelf concealed behind the wooden façade.

"I thought so. So what's this?" He opened the book. "A diary." With a disapproving chuff, he retreated to the sitting room for better light, pushing past the reporter along the way.

"Anything of interest?" Anderson inquired.

Ramsey flipped through the pages. "His last entry is on the twelfth. Says he went to Nicci Hallcox's house."

"The night before was she was killed."

Ramsey nodded. He squinted at the writing. "*Her butler lied to me and said there was no gathering in progress. I was very afraid for Jacynda's safety. Their perverted behavior sickens me to the core. I would have arrested them all, but heaven knows who they really were. Given Nicci's licentiousness, any one of them could be a lord, a judge or a clergyman. Nicci was of no help in regard to Effington, only interested in pressing her lurid attentions upon me.*

I fear I shall never find Flaherty before he employs those explosives. That will taint the Yard's reputation further and may well cost Chief Inspector Fisher his position. That would be a great loss."

Ramsey closed the book and said nothing for a time.

"Not what you expected?" Anderson observed quietly.

The inspector shrugged, suddenly uncomfortable. "Don't know," he muttered as he stuck the diary in his pocket.

The sergeant's bedroom revealed no surprises. His clothes weren't expensive, he hid nothing under the mattress, and his wardrobe was obsessively tidy. A picture of a woman hung on one wall. Given the resemblance, probably his mother.

"Bloody waste of time," Ramsey grumbled as they headed down the stairs to the street.

—

Friday, 26 October 1888
Rotherhithe
My God.
Keats shot Clancy a look. He received a nod of understanding in response.

Effington's former foreman, Dillon, was slumped in a chair near the fire, one side of his mouth slack. A line of spittle dribbled from the corner. His hand on the opposite side of his body was clenched into a permanent fist, the arm now useless. Each breath required a thick rasp of effort.

The man's wife glared at them from across the tiny room. It'd taken all of Keats' charm to gain them admittance. The room was chilly, the fire subsisting on only a few chunks of coal. The woman wore no coat, rubbing her hands up and down her arms to forestall the cold. Her husband had a threadbare blanket over his shoulders. The story was plain to see: everything they'd had was gone, pawned for food and warmth. All because the man had dared to ask Hugo Effington a question.

Keats felt the anger stir in his soul, his bones. It was fortunate the bully was dead.

"Why are ya here?" the woman asked warily.

"We're wondering what it was that caused Mr. Effington to do this to him," Keats replied as evenly as he could.

The name evoked an immediate reaction from the crippled man. His eyes rose and his mouth worked without producing any sound.

Keats knelt next to him. "I'm sorry for bothering you, but I have to know what happened that night. What made you ask Effington about that load?"

The man's eyes grew wide, but the mouth wouldn't work right. "Bl…bl…"

"Ya'll not get much," his wife said.

"Was it in barrels?" Keats asked.

The man reached over with his good hand and gave Keats' arm a squeeze.

"Yes," the wife translated.

"Was the top of the load rum?"

Another squeeze. *Yes.*

"What about the bottom ones?" He immediately cursed himself. The poor wretch couldn't answer such a complex question. "Were the bottom barrels different?"

Squeeze.

Gunpowder?

"Do you know Desmond Flaherty?"

Squeeze.

"Was he there?"

A nod this time.

"Stttttopped…"

"What? I don't understand."

The man's wife cut in, "That Flaherty fellow kept him from bein' beat to death."

Keats shifted his questions to the wife. "Do you know where this warehouse was?"

"Near the docks, that's all I know. They brought him home on a piece of planking."

"Effington is dead. Someone killed him."

There was a thick wheeze. The drooping corner of Dillon's mouth vainly tried to angle upward into a pathetic smile.

As Keats rose, he pulled out all the money he had, about two quid. He placed it in the woman's hands. "We did not come to visit you, do you understand? If Flaherty learns what we're about, there could be trouble."

The woman nodded, her eyes riveted on the coins in her hands. "I never seen ya."

"Good." Keats placed his hand on the man's shoulder. "Thank you, sir."

The barest of nods was the only response.

"I don't think Flaherty did that poor blighter any favors," Clancy observed once they were on the street. "Livin' like that..." He shook his head in dismay.

That could have been me.

Flaherty had taken after him with a vengeance the night Keats had discovered the wagonload of gunpowder, striking him a horrific blow that had ended his ability to go *en mirage* and nearly cost his life. That rage hadn't been there when they'd next met in Whitechapel. Flaherty had appeared weary, unwilling to kill him though the anarchist had ample opportunity. Then there was Dillon. Why would the anarchist get involved? That was out of character for a man who'd cut Johnny Ahearn's throat.

"Something's changed him," Keats murmured. *But what?*

—

Cynda's visitor didn't look familiar. He wasn't young or old, but he looked fuzzy around the edges. She blinked her eyes to clear them. Still fuzzy.

"Do you know me?" he asked. She shook her head. His face seemed to fall. "It's a sad day when you don't know your own brother."

Brother? Did she have one? Cynda frowned, picking through the clouds in her mind.

"Jane has always been very simple, and we've been embarrassed about how far she'd fallen. She was on the streets and..." he trailed off.

"Ah," the attendant responded, nodding sympathetically. "She'd be easy pickin's for some of them out there."

"I'm afraid so."

"Still, you've come for her, and that speaks well of ya."

"Thank you."

Come for me? Cynda stared at him until her head began to hurt again. It was no use. She had no idea of his name. Still, maybe it was all right.

An attendant walked her back to her cell, saying something about papers to sign. She dug in her pocket for a handkerchief to wipe her nose. A flutter of white fell to the floor. As she picked it up, she remembered. It was the piece of paper the veiled lady had given her. She kept forgetting it was in her pocket.

"Jacynda…Lassiter," she whispered and then tucked it away.

The attendant returned. "Are you ready?"

Behind her was the man who'd come for her.

"It's time for us to leave, dear sister," he said.

Cynda stared at that unfamiliar face. It had a slight smirk on it. Or did it? It was gone in a flash.

Outside, a carriage waited for them. It seemed huge, all black with no markings. The driver eyed her, then turned away as if she was no longer of importance.

Not right. Cynda looked back at the big building. She'd miss the columns. As they'd walked toward the carriage, the new man hadn't let her touch them, saying that was ridiculous.

"In you go, sister," the man told her, devoid of emotion.

She thought of refusing, but what good would it do? Maybe the new place would be nicer. Maybe they'd help her get better.

"Where are we going?" she asked.

No reply. He pushed her into the carriage and she huddled on the far side, not liking him to touch her. The carriage rolled away the moment the door shut. She shivered in the cold. He wouldn't let the curtains be opened, and the dark frightened her. Once her eyes adjusted, she studied him. He seemed younger now, his hair a different color. How could that be?

The coach rolled on for a long time. She huddled to stay warm. He'd not offered her a coat or a blanket to cover herself. Even the people in the crazy place had done that.

"Where are we going?" she asked again.

"To the river."

"Why?"

"Because that's where we need to go."

A while later, the sound of the wheels changed. He drew back the curtain. "We're on the bridge now. Nearly there."

"Who are you?"

No reply. On instinct, she moved toward the closest door.

He launched himself at her in an instant, her neck in his hands, jamming her up against the side of the carriage. She flailed as his grip tightened.

"Just let…it…go," he grunted, bearing down harder. Black stars swirled in front of her eyes as she struggled to breathe, fingers clawing at his iron grip. She kicked at him, clipping a knee. His fingers loosened for a second, then redoubled in pressure.

Panic exploded within her. Another kick caught him mid-groin, and the air filled with blistering oaths. Cynda jammed a bunched fist into his midsection, as hard as she could. This time he released her, gasping for breath. His face changed as the white fuzziness around him faded.

Cynda flung herself at the far door and it swung open, revealing patchy darkness beyond. She wrenched herself free from the hands on her shoulders, hearing her sleeve rip. When she landed, the impact drove the air out of her. She instinctively rolled, fearing the carriage wheels.

Her head came to rest against a metal support, a gas lamp on the bridge. With a furious shout and the skittering of horses, the carriage screeched to a halt a few feet away. As she pulled herself upward, hands grabbed her from behind. She fought back, trying to keep them away from her neck. Too late, she realized the man's intent. With a grunt, he hoisted her in the air and heaved her over the side of the bridge.

Cynda sailed downward. The wind billowed her skirts and whistled in her ears. Acting on instinct, she tucked into a ball the moment before she struck the water, then sank into the freezing depths like a bedraggled mermaid heading for a muddy grave.

CHAPTER SEVEN

Why didn't someone help her? Furious, she struggled upward. With a tremendous effort she finally broke the surface, only to sink down. Lungs splitting, she clawed desperately toward the surface again. The second time Cynda breached the water, something jammed into her shoulder. She grabbed at it blindly. Shivering intensely, she clung to the wooden oar, trying to work her legs free of the cloth wrappings as the pull of the water worked against her efforts. A moment before she lost hold of her lifeline, hands pulled on her, drawing her up. She scraped across something and then flopped face down into the bottom of a boat.

"Why'd ya go and do that?" a rough voice asked. "If ya'd left 'er in there a bit longer, we'd 'ave got more brass tonight."

"Oh, hush up," a second voice replied.

Cynda focused on each breath. In...out. In...The breath caught and she choked, spitting up water in a heaving gasp, nearly causing her throat to spasm.

"That's it girl, ya keep breathing, ya hear?" the second voice commanded.

"Just clunk 'er on the 'ead with the oar. Does the trick every time."

"I can't do that."

The first voice swore. "And I thought we'd get another five shillin's." He spat into the water. "Maybe she's rich, and we'll get us a reward for findin' 'er."

"Not bloody likely. Give me that tarp, will ya?" Something heavy and rough enfolded her. "There ya are, girl. It's up to ya if ya live or die. I'm not God, so I got no say in the matter."

Cynda couldn't speak; her throat hurt too much. She focused on each breath as the watermen chatted back and forth. She finally caught their names: Syd and Alf. It'd been Syd who had suggested they hit her on the head with the oar. Listening to their conversation, it sounded as if they spent their nights hauling passengers back and forth across the Thames. Occasionally, they'd snag a body. Those were always worth money.

Her eyes blinked open when the boat landed.

"Is she still alive?" Syd asked.

Alf peered over at her. "Yup."

He spat into the water again. "Never get a break."

—

Saturday, 27 October 1888
Rose Dining Room

As usual, his superior was already in his chair, paper at his elbow, enjoying his breakfast. They'd traded terse pleasantries, and the food had arrived. Still, Satyr sensed that all was not as it should be.

"Are the buyers in London yet?" he inquired, swirling a bit of toast around the plate to capture the remaining bits of egg.

The Ascendant did not answer, but poured himself another cup of tea.

Satyr poured his own tea, to buy time. He always took it black. The darker the better. In fact, the dining establishment made a separate pot just for him as his superior had pronounced it unpalatable.

Satyr tried again. "Have our customers indicated how they'll remove the items from London without drawing attention?"

"That is not your concern."

Satyr's irritation rose. "On the contrary; as Lead Assassin, *everything* is my concern if it involves you, sir."

"The transfer is in hand," the Ascendant replied tartly.

"Do you need me there to ensure—"

"Not needed."

What is going on? Why am I suddenly of no importance to this project?

There was a tap on the door. The servers knew never to interrupt them unless they were summoned. Satyr was up and moving in an instant, vanishing into nothing as the knife came out of his pocket.

"Not to concern yourself, Mr. S. It is one of our associates." The Ascendant put down his cup. "Come!"

That was unwise. His superior had no notion who was on the other side of the door. To Satyr's surprise, the man who entered *was* one of his associates. Or at least he was presenting as such. The Lead Assassin remained vigilant.

"Ah, Tobin, there you are," the Ascendant called in a welcoming tone, beckoning the man forward. "Please come in."

Satyr returned to his usual form, eyeing the newcomer. Tobin was equally uneasy. He made the customary sweeping motion with his finger across his left wrist, the sign that he was one of the Seven.

Satyr closed the knife and dropped it back into his pocket. Secondary assassins were not invited to this breakfast meeting. That was reserved for the Lead Assassin only, a perquisite of rank.

"Sir," Tobin greeted, giving a slight bow. He repeated the gesture to Satyr, but the bow wasn't as deep as it should have been.

Currying favor, are we? The junior assassin was ambitious. Not necessarily a bad trait, but one that put Satyr on edge. There was only one position higher than Tobin's at present—his own.

"I trust you have good news for me?" the Ascendant inquired.

With another cautious glance toward Satyr, Tobin replied, "Yes, sir. She met her end last evening on Southwark Bridge."

She? "What is this?" Satyr asked.

"You seemed to have an issue with removing Miss Lassiter, so I asked Tobin here to tidy up the situation. And so he did. Well done, young man."

The flame of Satyr's anger ignited. Only the Lead Assassin was allowed to assign a contract to one of the juniors, as he was the best judge of which man and technique should be employed. How dare the Ascendant go around him as if he were some inefficient clerk? "Sir—"

"I know it's a breach of protocol, but I felt it necessary," the Ascendant replied. "So how did you do it, Tobin? Did you take my suggestion?"

Suggestion? Now he's dictating technique. This is outrageous!

Tobin, emboldened by the Ascendant's praise, explained, "Yes, sir. I bribed one of the staff who told me which inmates had been admitted in the last week. Once I knew which one it was, I left, changed forms and returned as Miss Lassiter's brother. I gave them false dismissal papers, after which she went meekly to her death."

Their superior leaned forward. "How did you dispatch her?"

"I lured her into a carriage and then strangled her. I threw her body in the river. It sank immediately."

"Splendid," the Ascendant remarked, raising an eyebrow in Satyr's direction. "According to the Lead Assassin, the lady was hard to kill."

"I did not find it so," the young assassin replied, offering Satyr a smug glance.

Liar. Satyr's face was a mask of calm. Beneath, lava boiled in his veins. "I will be filing a protest with the Twenty, sir," he announced. "Your actions are unacceptable."

"Oh, don't be a fusspot, Mr. S.," the Ascendant retorted with a dismissive wave of his hand. "I just needed to have a good night's sleep knowing the young woman is no longer a threat."

"You never said why that was the case."

"That is not your concern." At that, he rose. "Come along, Tobin, you can walk me to the cab stand. I want to hear all the details."

"Yes, sir."

Satyr remained standing long after the Ascendant and the junior assassin had departed, the lava in his veins now white-hot. The Lassiter woman was to be his kill, the crowning moment in his career, and at a time of his choosing. To have Tobin dispatch her was an insult to both him and the victim.

He forced himself to pour more of the dark tea. Fate had a way of turning the tables on men and their petty ambitions. A showdown was coming, and it would be his task to ensure he'd be the last one standing when all the scores were settled.

—

When Cynda awoke, the watermen were readying the boat for the day's work. They were on the shore. Cold, she edged closer to the fire as Syd watched her sullenly. He only had one arm and the other one ended in a hook. That scared her.

She yawned, letting the tarp fall away.

Alf turned toward her. "Here, girl," he said, offering her a cup of something hot. "Tea. It'll warm ya." She took the cup, watching the other waterman warily.

Syd shook his head. "Right quiet fer a woman. Most of them yammer yer ears off."

Alf nodded. "My second missus was like that. Yap, yap, yap. That's why I went to work on the water. She couldn't folla me there."

Syd burst out into laughter, then grew solemn. "What's yer name, girl?"

She tried to remember, but all she could think of was the handkerchief. Cynda set aside the battered tin cup and reached into a soggy pocket. Pulling out the white fabric, she stared at it. Why was it important? When she unfolded it, soggy pieces of paper clung to the inside.

She held the cloth closer to the fire, trying to understand. There were bits of ink still readable. She squinted at the writing.

"Ja…cynda," she said. The other pieces were too damaged to read. She tucked away the handkerchief and took hold of the cup once more.

"Well," Alf observed after taking a puff on his clay pipe, "I guess that's one way of 'membering who ya are."

"'Ow'd ya end up in the water?" Syd asked. "Ya jump in?"

She could still feel the smooth hands on her neck, the sensation of floating through the air. "He threw me in."

"Off that bridge?" Syd pointed upriver. She craned her head around, though to do so made her neck ache more. In the distance, a huge iron structure with three arches rose above the water. She recognized the gas lamps marching across it. Cynda nodded, turning her attention to the tin cup once again. The liquid inside was very hot and she blew on it to cool it. It tasted strong and sweet. She liked that.

"Who did that to ya?" Alf asked.

"Brother." *Not brother.*

"Well, 'ell," Syd said, shaking his head. "I don't fancy me family, but I don't try to kill 'em."

Alf spat on the ground. "Where do you live, girl?"

Scanning the shore, Cynda didn't see anyplace that looked like home. Then, in the distance, she saw a white fortress. It seemed familiar. "There," she declared, pointing. "I'll go there."

Alf followed her eyes and then laughed. "We got a Royal here, Syd. She says she lives at the Tower."

"She might; ya never know with that crazy German lot."

As they chatted back and forth about the eccentricities of the Queen and her brood, Cynda neatly folded the tarp and then handed it to Alf. He stowed it in the boat.

Syd unshipped the oars, one at a time. "Must be goin'. We're losin' money 'ere."

Alf gave her another long look. "Keep yerself safe, girl."

"If yer gonna keep talkin' all mornin', we're goin' to lose all the trade," Syd chided.

"I hear ya." Alf climbed into the boat and with swift strokes they moved away from the shore. As the craft caught the current, he turned and waved.

Cynda returned it. Once the boat became a small speck on the oily river, she sighted on the white tower and started walking along the Thames. Maybe she did live there. There was only one way to find out.

—

Jacynda's room was untouched, exactly as it had appeared earlier in the week.

"She hasn't been back," Alastair mumbled. Her body wasn't in the warehouse, and no one had seen her since the night of the fire.

Perhaps *they* came for her again. They'd done that in the past, but the last time they'd let her take her belongings. That was what made this disappearance different.

Alastair methodically checked the room, but all her possessions appeared to be in the Gladstone. Had she planned on leaving, or just never unpacked?

Curious, he opened it up, wondering if he might discover a clue as to her whereabouts.

A spare dress, some undergarments, which he set aside quickly, a brush, toothpowder, and socks. Inside one of the socks was a pocket watch. He opened it and gave the stem a wind. Nothing happened. Perhaps this one wasn't from the future. Just in case, he tucked it in his pocket to keep it safe.

Then he found a Vespa box. Why would she carry one? She didn't appear to smoke. Maybe women did in her time.

What an unholy thought.

More digging unearthed a strange stuffed animal. It was caramel-brown with black rings around its eyes and a long, angular body.

"A weasel?" he mused. It seemed an odd thing for her to carry across the centuries. Perhaps it had some hidden meaning.

The final item in the Gladstone was a small box with a hinged lid. Alastair wavered: this was something very private. Perhaps it was best not to pry too far into her personal life. Finally, he gave in to the temptation: he'd already violated her privacy by searching the Gladstone in the first place.

He opened the lid. Inside was a portrait that he remembered well—that of Christopher Stone in his coffin. Alastair had commissioned it so Jacynda would have something to remember her lover by after his violent and untimely death. It tugged at the doctor's heart that she carried it with her even now.

Stone had been a young man, perhaps mid- to late twenties. According to Jacynda he was a merry sort who could tell a good joke and had a sense of adventure. Alastair regretted he'd seen the man after his passing. With a troubled sigh, he repacked the case, checked the room one last time, and then headed for the bookshop to return the spare key. There was a finality to this task, weighing him down like a millstone.

CHAPTER EIGHT

If they wouldn't feed her here, she'd have to find her own food. Cynda spied the moldy potato in a bin behind a pub. It had black spots on it, but she didn't care. She dug the worst parts out with her fingers and ate it slowly. It tasted grainy, but was better than nothing.

She'd felt safe in the crazy place. The Mouse Lady had watched over her. There was no Mouse Lady here. Maybe the *not brother* who threw her in the river would find her. Throw her in again. She looked up, panicking at the thought.

When a portly man walked out of the rear of pub, Cynda shrank back, hiding herself behind a pile of planks. He belched and then unbuttoned his pants. A stream of urine hit the board fence. When he finished, he shook himself and went back inside.

Once the potato was gone, she rose. In the distance, something caught her eye. It was red, moving in the sooty breeze.

"Pretty," she said, clambering over the low fence. She heard something rip when her skirt caught. Looking back, she saw a small section of cloth trapped in the boards. She pulled it off and put it in her pocket, not sure why she did it. Her hand touched something else. She unfolded the handkerchief like it was a treasure.

The paper inside was still damp. "Jacynda." That was who she was. That was all she knew. She hid it away again and set her sights on the red shawl hanging on the line in the next backyard. A quick tug made it hers. It smelled clean. She wrapped it around her shoulders and continued on.

When someone brushed against her on the street, she jerked away, anxious. Just an old woman with a basket of apples. They looked so good. Maybe she could take one and the old lady wouldn't notice.

"Hey, girl," a man called out. "Pretty shawl ya got there."

"It's mine," she declared, looking around for a means of escape.

"I didn't say it wasn't," the man replied with a toothy grin. "Why don't we go into the pub? Have a drink and a laugh."

"No," she said, backing up. The leer on his face frightened her.

"Ya hungry?" he asked, moving in closer. "I got some food." He stretched out his hand, displaying a half loaf of bread.

Not right.

She fled before he could reach her.

—

Keats moved closer to hear the man's voice, he spoke so softly.

"It was that warehouse there." The watchman pointed, then spat on the ground. "Heard about Effington. Good riddance."

Clancy snorted his approval.

"Were you there the night Dillon was hurt?" Keats asked.

"Yeah." The watchman pursed his lips. "I never seen nothin' like that. Just hit him, no warnin'. Left him bleedin' like ya would a dog. Couldna cared less."

"Dillon asked about a particular load. Did you see it?"

The man nodded. "I saw the casks. Somethin' not right about them. Got no notion of what was in them boxes."

"Boxes?" Keats repeated, his pulse picking up like a hound sighting a hare.

"Yeah. Didn't have no markin's on 'em."

"I'd like to see them." *And Ramsey's face when I deliver them to Chief Inspector Fisher.*

"They're gone. Left a few nights ago with the casks."

"Flaherty took them?" Keats pressed.

"Don't know. I wasn't on duty that night." The man spat again.

"Can we see inside the warehouse?"

The fellow frowned. "Why do ya care about all this?"

"'Cuz of Dillon," Clancy replied. "He's bad off now."

"Yeah. I heard that," the man noted with a small shudder. "I'll take ya inside, but I don't want nothin' to do with that Irishman. That's pullin' the devil's tail, it is."

Keats took his time searching, though clearly the watchman wanted to be somewhere else.

"Ya think all of it was here?" Clancy asked.

"Not likely."

"I heard he had two loads of the gunpowder."

"He did, but I got half of it that night in Whitechapel. And a lot half load of rum," Keats replied. "It's how he hid it—rum on top of the load, gunpowder casks on the bottom."

"So what're we lookin' for?"

"Fenian fairy dust," Keats told him. That earned him a confused look.

It wasn't until they moved some barrels around that he found what he was looking for. Keats knelt and ran a finger through the black spot on the warehouse floor and smiled. *Gunpowder.* A bit farther away, he ran his hand over something else and sniffed it, then hastily wiped his hand on his coat.

When he stood, he wavered, dizzy.

Clancy grabbed his arm. "What's wrong with ya?"

"Dynamite. It gives you a headache if it's leaking. The nitroglycerine does it."

His companion frowned. "That's not good, is it?"

"No, it's not."

Clancy's frown transformed into a smile. "It'd be a right shame if Flaherty blew himself up, wouldn't it?"

"Yes, it would." *He'd take my alibi with him.*

—

Cynda stood on the shoreline, hands on her hips. Across the water were the gray walls. Inside of those was a tall white tower. Maybe it was like the other place. Maybe they had a Mouse Lady, and someone would feed her. But how would get she get there?

She pulled the shawl tighter, puzzling as to why she had thought she could cross here. There were only two stubby piers in the middle of the river.

Something was missing. She scratched her head, trying to make sense of the jumbled images floating through her mind.

A boat glided by and a waterman called out, asking if she needed a ride. That confused her. There should be two of them in the boat, like last night. She shook her head and continued to stare at the open air above the piers. Her mind came up with something stone, really tall. But what was it? Looking back up the way she'd come, she saw what was missing.

A bridge. Someone had stolen it.

"Miss?" It was a man dressed in blue with a tall helmet. He had a kind face, or she would have run away. "Are you ill, miss?"

Cynda shook her head and pointed toward the far shore. "I need to go…there."

"To the castle?"

She didn't think she wanted a castle. "Do crazy people live there?" she asked.

"Sometimes. Years ago, I heard."

"Not now?"

He shook his head and then pointed. "There's a subway over there, miss. It'll take you to the other side. Just mind your step on those stairs."

"Thank you." She set off in the direction he'd indicated. The longer she studied the white tower, the more it didn't seem right. It didn't have any of those white columns like the other place. Still, across the water felt right so she kept hunting for the subway the blue-suited man had talked about.

To her surprise, the subway looked like a little hut. When she stepped inside, she realized that inside the hut was a hole in the ground. A man came out of it, then another. *Subway.* Did she like those? She didn't know. This one had a stairway that spiraled deep into the earth. She started down. Each step increased her anxiety. Her heart sped up, her mouth went dry. A headache started up behind her eyes, thudding with each increasing heartbeat.

At the bottom of the stairs, she peered into the giant iron tube that stretched in front of her. It wasn't very wide. Though there were lights, it was hard to see because of the haze.

Under the river.

Condensation rippled down the walls as echoes assaulted her ears. Voices. Footsteps. She shivered, clutching the shawl tighter. She froze as a figure emerged from the mist. It was a man carrying a bag. Up the stairs he went, humming to himself. Then another man, this one limping with a cane. Then two women, their high voices resounding off the metal walls.

As she edged into the tube, the flooring flexed beneath her feet. She shrieked and fell against a damp wall. She could feel the wall bending toward her. Fear gripped her and she began to cry. The iron tube would smother her, drown her, or crush her to death. She could feel its menace, hear the water searching for a way to get to her.

She flew up the stairs, tripping on her skirts as she went.

Once outside, she sped away as if something would snatch her, hurl her back into the subway's mouth. Only when she was a safe distance did she sink to her knees, her chest heaving in panic.

Subways were bad. Very bad. There had to be another way across the river. If not, she'd swim it. No matter what, she had to get to the other side.

—

Fortified by a couple of pints of ale, Keats' headache had eased, but not the problem of how to find Flaherty.

"How'd ya know about the dynamite?" Clancy asked him in a low voice as they exited the pub.

"Worked for the railroad. Learned how to build tunnels."

"I guess if ya still got all yer parts, ya did all right."

"Wouldn't want to do it again. I was young and foolish."

"Like now?"

"Not so young, still foolish."

Clancy laughed. "Flaherty could have moved the *goods* anywhere."

"I agree. I think we might start on the second problem."

"Which is?"

Keats told him about Flaherty's daughter, how someone had taken her.

Clancy looked amazed. "Ya think maybe he's being forced to do this?"

"Yes."

"That's enough to make a man piss his trousers."

"Why?"

"Someone messin' about with Flaherty. I always thought he was the nastiest bastard in all London. Goes to show…" Clancy chuckled. "Ya got company, Sean."

"Rozzers?" Keats asked, looking around.

"No, it was yer girl. I didn't recognize her right off. She was headed toward the pub. Told ya she was a goer."

Keats turned, searching the street for Jacynda. "What is she doing here?" he grumbled, heading back the way they'd come.

Clancy shook his head. "If ya have to ask that question, *Sean,* I worry about ya."

CYNDA STOOD IN the doorway, drawn by the sound of people and the smell of food. The aromas made her stomach ache, but the noise was too much so she didn't go in. Why had she come here? Where was someone who could help her?

Outside, she found the stairs. These didn't plummet into the earth, but stopped at the river. The tide was coming in. Cynda gingerly descended to the water's edge and tried to judge the distance to the other side.

A wide stretch of dark water lay between her and her goal. At her feet were broken pots, pieces of rusty metal, a bottomless pail. Tying her shawl around her, she edged her way out across the short mud flat to the water. In the distance, she heard the solemn tolling of bells and the chug-chug of a steamer heading downriver.

As she walked, the river wormed its way into her boots. She shook her feet, first one and then the other, like a cat who hates getting wet. The ground was uneven, treacherous. The water dragged on her skirts and petticoats. Behind her she heard someone shout, but she ignored it, keeping the far shore in view.

The first shiver shook her thin body like a baby rattle. The image of cold water closing over her face came unbidden. She stopped for a second, wanting to turn back. The shivering intensified.

No. I have to go there.

As the water reached her waist, she knew this was wrong. The current was too strong, pulling as the wet garments made each step harder. Cynda tried to turn, but something had caught one of her bootlaces. She pulled hard, but it wouldn't give way. Frantic, she tried to wiggle the foot loose. When it came free, the current caught her and she flailed to regain her balance.

A hand appeared near her, and she grabbed it.

"Jacynda?"

She stared at the man. He was like the others, but his eyes looked familiar above the heavy beard.

"My God, what are you doing?" he asked.

She found her voice. "How do you know my name?"

Shooting a nervous glance at the growing crowd of onlookers, the man lowered his voice. "Why wouldn't I know your name? What's wrong with you?"

"Who are you?" she asked, still grasping his hand to keep from being pulled away by the current.

"I'm…" Another glance toward the onlookers. "a friend. Let's get you out of here. We don't a want constable bumbling into this."

She allowed him to put his arms around her waist and lead her to the shore. He seemed to know her, seemed to care. Not like the man in the carriage, the one who had said he was her brother.

"That one's not right in the head," someone said as they came ashore.

"If the rozzers get her, they'll send her to Bedlam."

No! She tried to pull free, but her rescuer held her hand firmly.

"I won't let them take you there," the man told her. "I promise."

She looked into his eyes and believed him.

CHAPTER NINE

What a damned nightmare.

They were going toward the north shore in a boat; Keats didn't dare hire a hansom or take the train. When he'd mentioned the Thames Subway, Jacynda had panicked and tried to run away. So he'd hired a waterman to ferry them to Wapping. Clancy had called Keats a damned fool for risking his life over a crazy woman. That hadn't set well. The Irishman was just worried about the reward money. Finally, Clancy had offered to deliver Jacynda to Whitechapel himself, but her level of trust was paper thin and only Keats seemed to be worthy of it.

Ramsey would be hunting him in Whitechapel; that much Keats would wager. Still, he saw no alternative but to deliver her into the doctor's hands. She was too incapable of rational thought, and there were too many who would take advantage of her weakness.

What if Alastair isn't home? What will I do then? He couldn't keep her with him, and in her condition he dared not leave her alone at the boarding house.

Keats slipped a look at his companion. Jacynda was asleep on his shoulder, a ragged and filthy mess. The filth could be cleaned away. It was her docile behavior that frightened him. This woman would never have confronted the anarchists that night in Green Dragon Place, thrown herself into the middle of an affray. Something awful had happened, something that had broken her fiery spirit.

By the time they reached Whitechapel, he'd formed a plan of action, one that he hoped would allay suspicion: he would send a street urchin to the boarding house to summon Alastair on a medical call. It might work, even if Ramsey had the place under surveillance knowing it was only a matter of time before Keats visited his friend.

That time had come.

"Just a bit longer," Keats urged. No reply. It was like walking with a lamppost for company. Jacynda's shivering was worse now as her clothes slowly dried in the night air. His weren't much better. He still felt water in his boots with every step.

It took considerable effort to find Alastair's new location.

"Of all the times for you to move house," Keats grumbled under his breath. They'd stuck to the back alleys, the passageways, and deserted areas, away from the main streets. It was a chore with Jacynda at his side. She moved slowly and just about everything frightened her.

Keats studied the front door of Alastair's new house like a copper. The doctor had chosen a good place to reside, though it was just too dangerous to march up and hammer on the door. With his companion in tow, Keats worked his way behind the building and was eventually rewarded by finding a back gate. There was a light in the rear of the house.

Who else would be there? Perhaps Ramsey had laid a trap for him. His blood chilled at the thought. There was no other option but to knock and ask for help. Jacynda had put her life on the line for him more than once. It was only right that he do the same.

"Stay here," he advised softly, pointing to a patch by the fence. It was dry and relatively clean. "I'll go see if Alastair's home." He gently pulled her shawl up, like a scarf. She obediently slid to the ground. Her acquiescence, though welcomed, was profoundly disturbing.

His heart hammering, Keats rapped on the back door. Footsteps came his way.

He shot a look back at Jacynda. She was right where he'd left her.

What if Alastair can't help her? What if she remains like this for the rest of her life?

The door edged open. Keats let out a sigh of relief when he saw the doctor's astonished face.

"I am in desperate need of your help, my friend."

Alastair's mouth fell open, then closed just as quickly. "Come in! Hurry, before someone sees you."

"One moment." Keats hustled into the back yard and helped a bedraggled figure to its feet.

Alastair bolted the door behind the pair of them and then ordered, "Go down the passage. Stay in the kitchen. There are no windows there."

"Is there anyone else in the house?"

"No. Mrs. Butler doesn't move in until tomorrow."

Keats helped the figure sit in a chair and then removed the red shawl.

"Jacynda?" Alastair said, astounded. She looked up at him with a lost expression, quaking intensely. "What has happened?"

"Some sort of mental collapse," Keats explained. "I found her in Rotherhithe wading into the Thames in some bizarre attempt to reach this side of the river."

"Why in the ..." Alastair knelt and took one of her hands. It was icy. "Help me move her closer to the stove. I'll make some tea." Once she resettled, he stoked the fire and put on a kettle, shooting occasional worried glances toward his guests. "You look awful," he observed to Keats.

The fugitive mustered a game smile. "I know."

"Apparently, you are still unable to go *en mirage.*"

"That continues to elude me." Keats removed his boots and set them near the stove, draping his wet socks over them. He wiggled his pale toes. "Ah. That's better."

"Fisher told me about your letter. Have you had any luck finding the Irishman?"

"Not a bit of it, though I am getting closer to the explosives."

"Then that's some good news. How are your injuries?"

"Healing. Still can't do heavy work."

Alastair knelt next to Jacynda, warming her hands between his. She looked toward him, confused. "Do you know who I am?"

A slow shake of the head. "Not ... right," she said, pointing to her temple. Alastair leaned closer, thinking what he saw was a smudge of dirt.

As he reached toward her, she shied backwards. "I won't hurt you." She closed her eyes as if anticipating great pain. Delicately moving her hair aside, he studied the round mark.

"What in the devil ..."

"There is blood on the back of her collar, as well," Keats added, shaking his head in despair. "I felt you were her best hope."

Alastair examined the wound at the back of her neck with great care, all the while feeling his anger rise. Leery of frightening her, he went clinical to keep his seething emotions in check. "She's been struck with something. It's not fresh, though. A few days old." He addressed Jacynda. "Who hit you?"

"Macassar," she said.

"What?"

"She's not made a great deal of sense," Keats explained. "I ask her questions and often she has no answers. She didn't remember my name or yours, for that matter, but she insisted she had to get to this side of the river."

"What's this?" Alastair carefully pulled her collar aside, making her tremble. He looked up, disgusted. "Thumb marks. Someone has attempted to strangle her."

"Good God," Keats murmured.

Jacynda looked up at the doctor as if he'd just appeared in the room. "Who are you?"

He groaned. "Alastair. Alastair Montrose. We met at the boarding house."

She shook her head, brows furrowed. Then she turned to Keats. "You?"

"Jonathon Keats. I'm with Scotland Yard. At least for the present." She gave another shake of the head. Keats' eyes filmed in sadness. "She wasn't this bad a few nights ago."

"When was that?" Alastair asked.

"The night Effington died. She found me in Rotherhithe. We went back to my room and—" Keats looked away, "she suddenly went hysterical, claiming that we were on a sinking ship. She said this temporary madness was because of her job, that she comes from the future. Quite impossible."

Alastair fixed him with a look. "Was that all that happened?" He asked evenly.

Keats nodded too quickly for Alastair's liking. Jacynda was rolling the edge of her shawl up and down in rhythmic fashion, watching them with childlike fascination.

The kettle's whistle cut through the air and Alastair found himself welcoming the distraction. He assembled the tea and returned with the pot, placing it on the table with two of the new cups Mrs. Butler had purchased. He'd expected happier circumstances for their first use. While he sliced the cheese, he debated. Even if Jacynda and Keats had become lovers, her condition rendered the question moot. There was no point in hiding the truth from his friend any longer.

"She did not lie to you, Keats," Alastair informed him quietly. "She is from the future."

"Nonsense!" the sergeant spluttered, hot tea splashing over the edges of his cup as he replaced it firmly on the saucer. "If she's going mad, just tell me. Don't cloak it as some ridiculous tale."

"It is *not* a ridiculous tale. I have seen her travel into the future."

"Nonsense," Keats repeated. In his distraction he was stirring the tea, though he'd added nothing to it.

"Remember that night when she was knifed in the alley, and no one could find her? She went to her time to be healed. The knife had slit her lung. She would have died here."

Keats' face darkened. "I simply refuse to believe that you—you, of all people—would accept the ramblings of an obviously misguided woman as truth. You're so under her spell that you don't know what you're saying."

"I saw the technology she carries with her," Alastair insisted, his voice rising. "It was no parlour trick."

Keats opened his mouth to deliver a broadside, then stopped. "My God, you're serious."

"If you handed me a Bible, I'd swear upon it." Alastair took a deep breath. "Her lover, Mr. Stone, was from the future as well. That is why she dared not go to the police. As she put it, how do you solve the murder of a man who hasn't been born yet?"

Keats rose from his chair and paced in the small room, his face wrinkled in thought. As he passed Jacynda, she shyly pointed at the cheese. He handed her some and she started to nibble on it, watching him the entire time.

Keats finally came to rest in his chair.

"This is too outlandish to believe," he declared with a shake of the head. "It *can't* be possible to journey through time." He looked back up at Alastair. "Can it?"

Sensing an opening, Alastair pressed his advantage. "Yet it is possible to send wireless messages through the air, to light whole streets with electricity. We even journey by train beneath London's streets. Feats that would have seemed remarkable to people a hundred years ago!"

Keats stared at Jacynda for a long time. She was nibbling on a second piece of cheese. "She gave me a list of Effington's warehouses. I wondered at the time how she'd gotten them all. It must have taken a great deal of effort to collect that information."

"Not with her contacts in 2057."

For a moment, it looked to Alastair as if Keats were coming to terms with the concept. Then he shook his head. "I cannot accept this. I admit that she acts in an unusual manner most of the time, but to believe it is because…" His brow furrowed.

"You know I am not given to exaggeration, Keats. Remember, I *saw* the technology myself. She used it on you after your head injury."

Keats stared at him. "I… remember feeling so cold. Like I was… Then I felt better, warmer. I thought it was because of the blanket." He glanced over at Jacynda again. The cheese plate was empty, and she was eagerly eyeing the teapot.

The sergeant issued a long sigh. "So, what is it like? Have we gained utopia?"

Alastair relaxed, despite the skepticism in his friend's tone.

"I sense that's not the case," he replied. "Although their medicine is infinitely superior, all is not well. Jacynda's job, as I understand it, is to keep time on track. They send visitors to different eras, and apparently some of them are inclined to meddle."

"So nothing much changes, then," Keats replied sourly.

"Not that I can tell. She has tenacious enemies. Mark my words, this—" he pointed toward the darkened circle at her temple, "is something far more unholy than a knock on the head."

"Something from her time?" Keats inquired, sounding curious in spite of himself.

"I fear so." Alastair offered Jacynda a cup of tea. "Here, it will warm you." She looked at Keats for approval. He gave a nod and she took the cup. When Alastair went to put his hand on her forehead, she shrank backward.

"I promise I will not hurt you," he repeated gently. She nodded and he touched her skin. "No fever, at least."

"That's a miracle," Keats remarked. "She was wet up to her waist. I had no way of warming her."

"River," she murmured.

"What?" Alastair asked.

"River. Cold. Threw me in."

Keats leaned closer. "Someone threw you in the river?"

She nodded and then pointed to her neck. "Brother."

"Your brother?"

"Not brother."

"Was it the same fellow who stabbed you?" Keats pressed.

"I doubt it," Alastair remarked. "He was found guilty of her lover's murder and is incarcerated in her time. At least that's what she told me."

"Lord, she has more enemies than I do." Keats watched her swirling the tea in her cup, entranced by the eddies. "How will you treat her?"

"I'm not sure. Perhaps her memory will return spontaneously, but I doubt it. I will consult Reuben. He may be able to offer some advice."

"At least she's off the streets," Keats allowed. He began to pull on his socks and then his boots. "I miss my good pair. These make my feet ache."

"While you're here, I should examine your rib, ensure it is healing properly," Alastair offered.

"No need. It's doing fine. I'd best leave. If Ramsey finds me on this side of the river…" Keats took down the last bit of his tea with a gulp. "Jacynda?" he said, kneeling in front of her. He took one of her hands and kissed it. "Alastair will take care of you. You can trust him."

She looked from him to the doctor and back. A nod.

Like a small child who has to be told what to believe.

The sergeant reluctantly rose. "At least that worry is resolved."

As they walked down the passageway to the back door, Alastair asked, "Do you need money?"

"No. I have an ample sum."

"Where are you staying if I need to find you?"

"Rotherhithe. I'm at Mrs. O'Neill's boarding house on Neptune Street. It's near the chemical works. I'm known as Sean Murphy over there. Send a note, rather than coming yourself. It's too dangerous for both of us."

"If I come, I'll be *en mirage.*"

It took a moment for that to register. "So I've finally pulled you down that road, have I?"

"Somehow, I always knew you would." They clasped hands and then Keats hurried across the yard to whatever fate awaited him.

THE NICE MAN with the beard had said she'd be safe here, that the new man would take care of her. She would just have to trust them. With nothing else to do, Cynda's eyes wandered around the kitchen. It was clean but sparse. There were a few dishes in the tall cabinet on the wall and only a teapot on the stove. It was so quiet compared to the crazy place.

The man with the brown hair returned. "I'll lay a fire in the parlour. It'll be more comfortable there," he told her. "I'm sorry, I just moved in. I don't have a lot of things squared away yet."

It sounded like this was important to him, but she had no idea why.

"I collected your Gladstone from Pratchett's when you didn't return," he continued, carrying a load of kindling into the next room. She followed him noiselessly as he dropped the wood into the hearth and then lit the gas lamps, one by one. "It's just there," he said, pointing toward a black bag sitting next to a chair.

Cynda studied it, running her hands over the leather. There was a long rent in the side of it. Then she pulled her hand back suddenly, a cold pang shooting through her chest.

She looked up at him. He was staring into her face, puzzled.

"Something…bad," she said, shivering.

"You were mortally injured when you were carrying it. Your lover's ashes were inside that Gladstone. You took him home with you."

"Lover?"

"You can't remember him, either," he murmured. "How much you've lost. Well, come here and watch me light the fire."

Cynda hefted the case and brought it with her. Sitting on the floor near him, she began to pull out the contents, one by one, like a child on Christmas morning. First, the clothes. She held a navy dress for a long time, eyes closed.

"Pretty," she whispered.

"Yes, especially when you're wearing it."

That only confused her. By the time he had the fire lit, she'd set the clothes aside and was holding the stuffed animal.

He looked over at it. "Is it a weasel?"

Cynda shook her head, hugging it fiercely, not knowing why it brought her such comfort. After she set it in her lap, she dug further into the case, pulling out a small box. She opened the top, peered inside and then slammed it shut.

"Sad," she said, pushing it away on the floor. "Can't."

The man looked like he understood. "You may not remember Mr. Stone's name, but you still feel his loss." He waved her over to the couch. "Come here, it's too cold on the floor for you. I'll fetch you a blanket."

When he returned, she was clutching the stuffed animal in her arms again. It felt good to pet the top of its head.

"Jacynda, do you know who I am?" the man asked.

She nodded. "Fred."

The hope in his eyes evaporated. "No, I'm Alastair. I'm a doctor. Do you remember me now?"

"No." The pieces in her brain just weren't coming together. She could see images, places, people, but they made little sense.

"My God," he murmured. His voice sounded different now, as if there were small pebbles in it. "What have they done to you?"

Her stopped petting and moved her finger upward to the side of her head where the strange mark resided. She tapped it a few times.

"Will it get better on its own?"

She shrugged.

"Damn them," he muttered.

She started at. Something wasn't right.

"I apologize. I'm sounding like you now." Then he paused. "You remembered I don't swear, at least not often." A smile grew on his face. "I would think that a good sign." He pointed toward the animal. "You say that he is not a weasel. What kind of creature is he, then?"

She frowned. "Fer... fer..."

"Ferret?"

"Yes. It's a fer...ferret."

Heartened, he returned to another question. "What's your name?"

The handkerchief came to mind. Cynda pulled it out of her pocket and extracted the damaged piece of paper.

"Jacynda," she announced. When he reached for it, she hid it away. She trusted him, but it was the only thing that told her who she really was.

"Where did you get that?"

"At the crazy place. A woman gave to me."

"But how did they know your name?" He frowned. "Someone had to tell them. Who brought you there?"

"Macassar," she replied, pointing to her head.

"I'm sorry, I'm as confused as Keats about this." He tucked the blanket around her. "I think it's best we remove your boots. Your socks are probably wet, and that will not do a thing for your health." She leaned over and watched him unlace each of them. When he removed the second one, a single coin fell to the floor.

He laughed. "I'd forgotten—you store your money in the most improbable of places." He picked it up and showed it to her. "It's a shilling."

"I didn't know," she whispered. "I was so hungry."

The man's humor withered. "How long have you been on the streets?"

"Ah... don't know," she told him. "There was a man... I ran away from him. He wasn't right."

"Good," he said, nodding. "Trust your instincts. That's the best protection you have right now. Now tuck your feet under the blanket. They're very cold."

She did as he asked. He placed her boots and damp socks near the fireplace. Sitting on the couch with her, he opened up a book and then displayed it to her.

"You bought this for me, though I doubt you remember that now. It has proven very helpful. Thank you."

She had no idea what he was talking about, but it seemed to make him feel better. As she held the little animal she stared at the fire. It made her warm and drowsy. Every now and then, the doctor would look over at her then return to his book.

"Just you and me tonight," he informed her. "Mrs. Butler will move in tomorrow morning. She will be a great help."

"Who?"

He shook his head, dismayed. After a few more minutes, he thumped the book shut and set it aside. Cautiously, she leaned against him and he tucked her under his arm. He would make a good brother, she thought. He'd never try to hurt her. Try to throw her in the river.

"Go ahead and sleep. You're safe here," he whispered.

Reassured, she nestled closer.

CHAPTER TEN

Keats cut south toward a landing where he could hire a waterman to take him to Church Stairs. He kept looking over his shoulder, expecting to hear a shout or a police whistle at any moment. Once he was in Rotherhithe, he'd be fine.

Only a few more days. Find Flaherty and the explosives, then everything would fall in place. The charges would be dropped and he might be able to resume his career, though there would no doubt be disciplinary action for his egregious behavior. Hopefully, they wouldn't bust his rank.

When he reached the landing, he saw a waterman returning across the Thames, oars breaking the surface in long, sure strokes. Keats tugged up his collar, trying not to look nervous.

Speed it up, will you?

The boat was forty yards from the shore when he saw the constable. The fellow was swinging his lantern around, hunting for something.

Me.

If he moved from his spot, it would look suspicious. Gritting his teeth, he forced himself to stay put. The boat glided toward the shore as the constable tromped on. It would be too close for his liking. In the dark, he saw a second boat approach the first, causing it to stop. The two watermen began to chat about whatever was on their minds, a waiting customer be damned.

Talk to him later! He had no choice now and turned away, intending to skirt along the river's edge and cross using the underwater tunnel.

"Sir?" a voice called. It was a second constable and his bull's-eye lantern caught Keats straight in the eyes, blinding him.

"Constable," he acknowledged, shielding his face.

"What's your business, sir?"

"Goin' cross the river to my wife and bed," he replied, pushing the working-class accent to the hilt.

"What were you doing in Whitechapel?"

"Lookin' for a job. T'ain't any to be found."

Behind, Keats heard the first constable approaching. He was trapped between them.

"Ya need a row across, mate?" a voice called. The waterman had finally arrived.

Keats turned away from the glare of the lamp. "I do."

"Then get aboard," the fellow called. Keats made sure not to hurry, moving more like a tired man might rather than one fearing arrest. Behind him, the two constables talked amongst themselves.

As the boat steadily moved away from shore, Keats allowed himself to relax. Finally, he could no longer resist and he looked back over his shoulder at the constables. One was waving his lantern, like he was signaling someone. Keats turned toward the far shore. Another lantern swung in reply.

They'd figured out who he was, but too late. "Let's land a bit further upstream," Keats suggested.

"Prince's Stairs?"

There was a police station near there. "No, Cherry Garden Stairs," he replied.

"Cost ya extra."

"I'm good for it." Keats leaned back in the boat.

Too close.

A few minutes later Keats heard the sound, but tried to ignore it. There were a number of steam vessels on the Thames, he assured himself. It could be any one of them. The noise continued, rising in intensity. When the boat's bow chugged out of the darkness, it angled to cut them off from the far shore. Keats swore under his breath. The constables had signaled a launch.

The waterman shot Keats a questioning look. "I can cut 'round 'em, try a run down river."

Was it worth the risk? Could they escape? He only needed a few more days…

"Don't bother. It's not worth the risk to you and the boat."

The man shipped the oars.

"If you have any sense, you'll claim you recognized me right off and were going to turn me in once you reached Bermondsey. That way, you might be able to collect the reward."

"Reward?" the man repeated eagerly.

"It's a large one. Seventy-five quid is the last number I heard."

Realization dawned as the waterman gave a low whistle. "Yer that copper they're looking for." Keats nodded. "That's a right fair number. Did ya do it?"

"No." *Which is why I am the unluckiest man in all of Christendom.*

As the launch drew nearer, a familiar voice bellowed across the water. "Thought you'd get away, didn't you, you little gnome?"

Ramsey. Keats groaned aloud. Why couldn't it have been the two constables? *The Ram,* as he called him, would make this arrest a personal triumph.

He waited until the launch pulled up alongside, sending the small boat rocking precariously. "You're a bit late," Keats called out, issuing a wink to the waterman. "This fine gent had already nicked me."

"Ah...I spied him right off," the man shouted.

Clancy was right: he won't collect a bit of brass out of this.

"We'll sort the reward out later. Now get your arse up here, *Sergeant.*" Ramsey turned to a trio of Thames constables and barked, "Got some chains on this boat? I want him secured. He's a wily one. If he gets loose, I'll have every one of you up on charges."

What an overbearing sod. He's playing it to the hilt.

Keats grasped the rope lowered over the side of the launch. Then he remembered his damaged chest.

"I'll need some help. I've got a busted rib."

"Fish him up!" Ramsey ordered. "He's a light one. Shouldn't be any trouble."

One of the Thames constables snagged onto Keats' shoulder on the affected side. He winced at the sharp bite of discomfort.

"Easy, please."

As he tugged upward, the constable whispered, "The guv'ner 'ates ya summat fierce. What'd ya do to 'im?"

Through a grimace, Keats confided, "It would take too long to explain."

Once on the launch, he tried to stifle the pain in his side.

"You all right?" Ramsey asked.

"A bit sore, that's all."

"Is that the rib that was broken during your altercation with the Fenians?" a man asked. Keats eyed him warily. He didn't look like a policeman.

"Yes. And you are?"

"Robert Anderson. I'm with the Chicago Herald." He had a notebook in hand, pencil at the ready.

Oh, Lord.

"Sergeant Keats, do you have a comment for our readers?"

To hell with the lot of you. Instead, he replied, "Nothing that is printable, sir."

He peered into the dark water. He could cast himself overboard and might actually make it to shore. Or drown under the weight of the chains.

"I wouldn't suggest you try jumping," Ramsey advised cheerily, "though it would save the Crown a lot of money."

"Then it would be my civic duty, wouldn't it?" Keats snapped.

"No," Ramsey barked. "Stay put. You move and I'll have them chain you to the deck."

So this is it. He'd failed. Flaherty was still free and he was the one in chains. Still, deep down, a part of him felt immense relief. He no longer had to look over his shoulder in fear of his fellow coppers. No need to listen in on every conversation in case someone had recognized him.

He sagged in the chains. "How did you find me?"

The inspector beamed. "De-duction. That's what you're always spouting, isn't it? I have informants too, and one of them saw you in Whitechapel tonight. I knew you were hiding in Rotherhithe, so it was only a matter of waiting until you tried to return. You wouldn't dare take the train, so that left the river, one of the bridges, or the Tower Subway. I had them all covered."

"Well done," Keats muttered. *That's exactly how I would have handled it.* Silence fell for the remainder of the journey. The inspector looked infinitely pleased with himself. The reporter remained quiet, studying Keats and making notes in his little book. No doubt it would be quite a coup—an American newshound present at the daring capture of the Mayfair Slayer.

It wasn't until Keats was manhandled into a carriage that his superior dropped the pleased-as-a-peacock attitude. Ramsey hauled himself into the conveyance and slammed the door with more force than necessary. He pounded on the roof and the carriage rolled off.

"Why do you have a reporter with you?" Keats asked.

"Warren's orders. I don't like it, either." A pause. "Why in God's name didn't you turn yourself in?"

"Flaherty. I was getting close to both him and the explosives."

"You're not the only copper at the Yard, gnome."

Keats glared. "I am not a gnome, sir. I am a *detective-sergeant*, at least until such time as they give me the sack."

"Fisher tells me that Flaherty's your alibi. If that's the truth, you're already on the gallows."

Keats nodded. "I know." *That's just what you're hoping for, isn't it?*

"Who killed Effington?"

"Could have been anyone. He'd been skimming off the top of every load. That adds up to a lot of enemies. It might even have been Flaherty himself."

Ramsey leaned back. "I want you to tell me everything that happened from the moment you arrived at the tart's house that night. I want to hear all of it."

As if he cares. "If you're keen to know my story, then I suggest you read the letter I wrote to Fish—"

He found himself pinned against the back of the carriage by two massive hands. "I don't care what you told Fisher. I want to hear it from you. Got it?" Ramsey growled.

Keats managed a weak nod.

The big man's face split into a triumphant grin. "You know, I think you look more like a scared rabbit than a gnome."

"Note where the rabbit has his knee," Keats replied coolly.

Ramsey's eyes roved downward, judging its proximity to his groin. He laughed and the hands retreated.

"So tell me this amazing tale of yours, *Sergeant.*"

After a deep breath, Keats began his report, skipping any mention of Clancy Moran. It took as long as the trip from Wapping to Leman Street Police Station, even though he'd pointedly left out his visit to Alastair's this very night. Ramsey had only said he'd been spotted in Whitechapel, not at the doctor's. Hopefully, that would spare his friend any further trouble.

Much to Keats' surprise, Ramsey didn't interrupt once.

"Helluva story," the inspector remarked at the end.

"Try living it."

A snort returned. "Why were you in Whitechapel?"

The lie came easily. "Looking for Flaherty."

"You didn't mention his daughter in your report to Fisher."

"Learned that after I posted the letter."

"You honestly believe that someone has him by the nads?"

"Yes."

"God, what a cock-up," Ramsey muttered. As the carriage drew to a halt, the inspector adjusted his coat. "Let's get you into a cell and I'll send word to the chief inspector that you're safely in custody."

Keats remembered the headlines, the drubbing Fisher had taken on his behalf. "How's he doing?"

Ramsey's expression flattened. "Looks a decade older. Your little crusade is going to cost him his job."

"That shouldn't trouble you," Keats shot back. "You're next in line."

"Won't trouble me in the least, if you're guilty."

If? Perhaps there was hope for him yet. "Just find the damned explosives."

"And save your life?"

Keats shook his head. "Not likely. Flaherty will be buying the first round the morning I swing."

Ramsey opened the door and grinned ghoulishly. "Who knows, I might buy the second one."

Bastard.

Sunday, 28 October 1888
Spitalfields

"I concur with your findings: a slight concussion, but nothing to the extent that would cause such issues with her memory," Reuben replied, stepping back after his examination. Jacynda watched him placidly, the stuffed animal in her hands. "I know this is a delicate subject, but have you determined if she has been...violated?"

"Mrs. Butler did not mention anything untoward after she helped her bathe this morning. I specifically asked her to be observant for any unusual signs. I was concerned that if I had another physician conduct such an intimate examination, it would frighten Jacynda even more."

"I agree." Reuben looked back at the patient and winked. A wink returned. "I am so sorry I didn't meet her before this," he remarked regretfully.

There was a pounding on the front door. Alastair opened it before Mrs. Butler could even exit the kitchen. It would take some time to realize he had someone *to do* for him. The young messenger held a telegram. Alastair dug a few coins out of his pocket and traded them for the paper. A quick glance proved it was from Lord Wescomb. The first line confirmed the worst.

Keats in custody.

"Oh, dear God," he murmured. It was plain to see—his friend had been found because he'd brought Jacynda to Whitechapel.

"Alastair?" Reuben probed. "Bad news?"

"It depends on how you look at it," he replied, handing over the telegram. As he sank in a chair, a tide of emotions battled for supremacy. Keats would be safer in custody. And yet...

"They'll move him to Newgate at the first opportunity," Reuben observed, dropping the telegram on the small table by the door. "I've never been inside there. I can only imagine what it's like."

"I had hoped he would find Flaherty, secure his alibi."

"And then you wouldn't have to testify?"

Alastair looked up at his mentor, chagrined. "Yes. That sounds so selfish."

"Not really. You will state the truth, and that's all you need do."

Alastair rose, his unease translating into motion. "I shall visit Keats as soon as possible, see how his wounds are healing. I did not have the chance last night."

Reuben raised an eyebrow. "Aiding a fugitive is frowned upon by the constabulary, though I heartily approve in this case."

"He brought Jacynda to me for treatment. He risked everything for her."

"Not the actions of a murderer, I would say," Reuben observed.

"No." Alastair looked toward the patient. "Thank you for examining her."

"Wish I'd had better news."

The instant Reuben stepped outside, he smiled in approval. "Cleanest steps on the block. I knew you'd be the ideal tenant."

—

Keats held his breath as Chief Inspector Fisher entered the cell. He'd been dreading this since he'd read of Nicci Hallcox's death. From the moment he'd joined Scotland Yard, there'd been a sort of synergy between him and his superior. Master and eager pupil. The first rift appeared when Fisher learned about the Transitives, that his sergeant was one of them. Now there was a wide gulf between them. Nearly all of it was Keats' fault. After a quick look in his direction, the chief inspector scrutinized the room, as if he'd never been in a cell before. Then his superior began to pace, a sure sign of emotional turmoil in this most controlled of men.

This was going to be worse than Keats had imagined. He straightened his collar and cuffs like he was up for inspection, even though he was wearing clothes fit for a dockworker and then cleared his throat. "How are you, sir?"

The chief inspector's gaze moved toward him, examining him with as much intensity as he had the cell. "I've been better, Sergeant."

"Sir, I—"

"Why in the hell didn't you turn yourself in, man?" Fisher exploded. "Do you honestly believe you are above the law?"

Taken aback at his ire, Keats could only sputter, "No, sir, I'm … I'm not. I felt I was the best choice to find Flaherty."

"That's nonsense! While you were playing copper, the press hammered home your guilt. By now everyone has heard of the Mayfair Slayer and believes he's good for the rope."

"You honestly think I'm capable of such an obscene act?" Keats demanded, his heart thumping wildly in his chest.

The chief inspector turned away. A rough shake of the head. "No, I don't. I think your only crime is being an overzealous fool." He turned toward Keats. "It wouldn't have been easy to sort out if you'd come in the moment this happened, but now it's damned near impossible. Evidence is disappearing and—"

"What evidence?"

"The pawn ticket you were issued in Ingatestone, the one they found in your suit when they arrested you. Hulme claims it has gone missing. He also says he wasn't able to find the pawnshop owner."

"What in the hell is going on?"

"Pressure. Pressure unlike anything I've ever seen. It's being brought to bear on all of us. There are those who do not want to see you acquitted, Sergeant."

Keats looked away, wrestling with his emotions. "That is clear enough."

"I expected far better of you, Jonathon. You have sincerely disappointed me."

That cut like a razor. All he'd ever wanted was to make this man proud of him. He'd done everything to that end, and now he was being taken to task for trying too hard. His anger mushroomed, sweeping aside all thoughts of caution.

"And I expected better of you, sir," he said sarcastically.

"What do you mean?"

"Why did you bring Dr. Bishop into this case? Why not let the Home Office coroner deal with it? They're impartial enough."

When Fisher made no reply, that goaded Keats on. "Now Alastair's involved, and you know his record—that death in Wales. The Crown Prosecutor will have a merry time with that, the evidence be damned."

"It's not for you to question my decisions, Sergeant."

"In this case, I shall. It's my neck in the noose. So why did you involve Dr. Bishop?"

"I trust him."

"That's it? I would have thought the same of any of the others. What about all those lectures you gave me about impartiality, sir? It appears your decisions are just as erratic as mine."

His superior glared at him. "There is more at stake here than your life."

"Your job, perhaps?" Keats chided. "Don't worry, Ramsey'll be there to take over. He's just been waiting for both of us to stumble."

"How dare you believe this is all about my position!" Fisher snarled.

"In the end, that's all that matters, isn't it?" Keats replied. He strode to the cell door and thumped on it, eager to end this torment. A jailer appeared almost instantly. "We're through here," Keats barked.

His superior passed him on the way out the door. As he heard Fisher's footsteps retreating down the hallway, Keats cursed under his breath.

He had failed not only himself and the Yard, but the one man who meant everything.

CHAPTER ELEVEN

Ramsey glowered as he jotted a line in his notebook. They'd visited every coffin maker they could find in Whitechapel. All claimed they could account for each piece of stock, and none employed a large Irish fellow who might be a Fenian.

"No luck so far," Anderson commented, surveying the scene around them. "Your job reminds me of mine. I spend the entire day wearing down my boot leather while people lie to me."

Ramsey snorted. "People in Whitechapel are closed mouthed. Jesus Christ himself could appear in the middle of Commercial Street, and no one would claim to have seen him. Well, except the toolers. They'd have his pockets picked in no time."

Anderson gave him a bemused expression.

"It'll happen some day, mark my word," Ramsey added. "Best not to put that in your paper, though."

"Agreed. So now where do we go?"

Ramsey flicked open his watch. That attracted the interest of a grubby boy loitering nearby. The copper shook his head at the pint-sized thief who scooted off in search of a less savvy victim.

"Let's find some food and then we'll do the rounds of the pubs. See what we can hear."

"Surely they know you down here," Anderson protested. "They wouldn't talk to a cop."

Ramsey eyed him. "You've done some studying on me, haven't you?"

Anderson nodded. "You used to work at Leman Street Station. You spent a number of years in the Whitechapel district before you moved up to the Yard."

"Like Keats. He started in Arbour Square. Those are rough patches for new coppers."

"You both survived."

Ramsey grunted. "Tomorrow, we'll go north to Ingatestone, check the sergeant's alibi in that part of the country."

"You actually expect to find a coffin in the middle of the forest?" Anderson asked.

"I once found one lying in the street with a gent in it. He'd been dead for a very long time, they said, at least one hundred years. Now how in the hell he got out of the ground, we never did find out."

"So what'd you do?"

"Had him reburied and threw a wake. That's about the only thing the Irish get right."

"You don't like them, do you?" Anderson quizzed, his pencil suddenly appearing in his hand, the notebook open.

The inspector didn't hold his tongue. "I don't like any of 'em—Irish, Hebrews, Germans, Poles, Russians," he paused for effect, "even Americans, not if they're making plans to bugger up my country. Now if they're here to earn a few quid, raise their families, go to whatever sort of foreign church they go to, I'm good with all that. They start making explosives and spouting nonsense about revolution, and they become my enemies."

"That seems pretty simplistic."

"Coppers like it simple. We leave the politics and all that shite to the highborn. We just get on with the job."

"Did Sergeant Keats *get on with the job*, as you say?"

"Yes. He's a sharp one. Got up my nose every time he could."

"Did you do likewise?"

Ramsey laughed. "Of course. That's what inspectors are supposed to do." He set off walking. "Food first. Oh, and mind that notebook and pen of yours."

"Why?"

"They'll steal you blind here, right down to the clothes you were wearing the day you were born."

"Sounds like Chicago," Anderson replied, carefully tucking away the items.

"Then you'll feel right at home," Ramsey shot back, leading the way.

—

"There's a little inflammation, but less than I thought there'd be," Alastair replied, gently examining the healing rib. The bruises had faded to a dull gray-green.

Keats observed his efforts solemnly. "Is Jacynda any better?"

"No. Still very quiet and unsure. Mrs. Butler plans to take her to the market this afternoon just to get her out of the house. She's not hard to manage, just very docile."

"So very unlike Jacynda," Keats replied.

Alastair nodded. "You can put your shirt back on."

As Keats slowly worked his way into the garment, the doctor packed his bag. Noise from the jail filtered into the cell.

"Your head wound has healed very neatly," Alastair reported, feeling some positive news was needed.

"Probably the vicar's salve," Keats remarked. "He seemed very proud of it." When he saw the doctor's puzzled expression, he added, "I met him and a very pretty lady named Lily when I was staying with the bums on my way to Ingatestone. The vicar was very... gregarious."

Alastair clicked the bag shut. "I'll go to your rooms, obtain a change of clothing and toiletry items."

"Thank you. Pull out my new suit. I just got it from the tailor. I never thought I'd be wearing it at my trial."

There was an awkward pause.

"They'll move me in the next day or two. I'll be at Newgate."

"I'll be there. If you need anything, send me word. I mean that."

Keats nodded. "Fisher came to see me this morning."

"How did it go?"

"Very poorly. He's furious at me for being an idiot."

"It is hard when a father sees a son headed in the wrong direction."

Keats looked up at him. "He has become my father in many ways, and I have let him down."

Alastair placed a hand on his friend's shoulder. "Keep hope. We'll get this sorted." He saw the empty look in the sergeant's eyes.

He doesn't believe a word I've said.

—

"Is this like Chicago?" Ramsey asked as they entered the Britannia.

Anderson glanced around the pub. "Exactly, except I can't understand what most of these folks are saying."

Ramsey cracked a smile. "You should hear them when they're not drunk. It's worse."

The publican promptly served up the pints they'd ordered. Ramsey shoved the coins across the bar and gestured for Anderson to pick up the ale. He trailed after the inspector as they went on the hunt for a free table.

"This'll do," Ramsey said, settling his bulk so he could watch the door.

"Do you honestly expect someone to come up to you so openly?" Anderson asked after a sip of his pint.

"That's not how it works. The people I need to talk to will see me here. If they have anything to tell me, they'll find me later in the evening. It's like being a whore, you see. You advertise your wares and then wait for the punters to come to you."

"You're a very colorful fellow, Inspector."

The cop's attention moved to him. "You're the same, Mr. Anderson, though you look otherwise." He scrutinized the man's face. "There's more to you than what you're telling Warren."

"Such as?"

"I sent a cable to Chicago. The Herald never heard of you." Ramsey waited for the reaction.

A nod of respect came his way, along with a faint smile. "Why did you think to check?"

Hard to rattle. He'd be a good one in a fight.

"I checked because I'm a copper. Warren, he's a military man. He doesn't expect people to lie to him." Ramsey leaned over. "So who the hell are you?"

"Robert Anderson…Pinkerton Agency," the man replied. "I have a letter of introduction in my pocket, if you need it."

"No. That fits. Course, I'll be checking that as well. Warren know who you are?"

"Most certainly."

"So why are you nosing around London?"

"Explosives."

Ramsey stiffened. "That's our job."

"It is, but we've heard there is a chance some of that missing dynamite might end up in New York or Chicago."

"Not everyone's happy in America?" Ramsey smirked.

"No, they're not. It won't be the Irish, of course. We're a safe haven for them, but there are others who love to see our country in revolt."

Ramsey sucked down more of his ale. "So what those newspapers articles you're supposed to writing?"

"I send the stories to a reporter who *does* work for the Herald. He files the articles under both our names, but collects the money."

"That doesn't trouble the newspaper?"

"Not really, as long as they get a good story."

"What about your bosses?"

"They're fine with the arrangement."

"Sounds like a right mess," Ramsey commented, his eyes roaming over the patrons. "I'll have to tell Fisher."

"I expected that," the man replied. Anderson leaned back in his chair, his eyes roaming over the pub's patrons. "Anyone look promising?"

"A couple. We'll finish off these pints and then go for a stroll. You posh detectives, you know how to defend yourselves?"

"Yes."

"Good. Problem with displaying our wares is that not everyone just wants to talk to us."

After they'd drained their drinks, Ramsey set off at a brisk pace, causing Anderson to hustle to keep up with him. "After we're done, we'll have to go a bit before we can catch a hansom," the inspector advised. "They don't like coming into this part of the city."

"I can see why."

The inspector swept his eyes over the street, trying to see it from the American's point of view. Costermongers, newsboys, whores, a flower seller or two, a few shady characters lounging in the doorways, sizing up potential marks.

Heaven. At least to a copper.

After a series of twists and turns, Ramsey shot down an alley. It was grimy, like most of them.

"Now what?" Anderson asked.

"We wait."

"I liked it better in the pub."

It wasn't long before a figure edged down the passageway, constantly looking over his shoulder.

Ramsey stepped forward. "Keep watch for us, will you?"

"As you wish," Anderson replied, moving a few steps away to give the illusion of privacy.

"Copper," the man mumbled.

"Evening, cheesemonger. Any word?"

The man shook his head. "Nothing. It's quiet right now."

"Quiet in a good way or…"

Another shake of the head. "People are scared."

"Because of our Irish friend?"

"No."

That surprised Ramsey. "Someone new in town?"

"No. Has something to do with those explosives."

"Flaherty has those," Ramsey said, testing the waters.

A shake of the head. "I've heard rumors that he doesn't."

Then Keats was right. "Anything else?"

"That's all I got."

Ramsey offered a coin. "If you hear anything more, let me know."

With one last look at Anderson, the informant slipped into the shadows.

Ramsey grumbled, "You think you know all the rats, and another crawls out of the woodwork."

"This alley is rank," Anderson commented, twitching his nose.

"They don't stink in Chicago?"

The edges of the fellow's mouth tugged slightly upward. "No, we pave them in gold. I thought everyone knew that."

Ramsey laughed. "Shite is more likely. I heard about your big stockyard."

There was the sound of footsteps as a snaggly-toothed man emerged out of the shadows.

"Oy, it's that rozzer come to spy on us."

"Old Dan. Been a while, hasn't it?" Ramsey looked over at Anderson and gestured toward the newcomer. "Dan here went to Pentonville Prison for robbery. Twice." He lowered his voice. "Keeps making the same mistakes. He's not quick on the uptake."

Old Dan snorted. "Yer the copper who put me there. Whatcha doin' on my patch?"

"London is *my* patch, gents. Maybe someone didn't you tell you that."

"Ya think ya own it all, don't ya?" The man spat. "I hates rozzers. Same with me mates here." Three other men emerged out of the shadows.

Ramsey laughed. "Is this enough like Chicago for you, Mr. Anderson?"

"Just like home."

The inspector put his hands on his hips. "It's this way, gents. You walk off and we call it even. You mess with us, you go to the clink. You might even end up with something broken. That would be a shame, though I certainly won't cry about it."

"There's four of us. We like those kinds of odds, rozzer," Old Dan replied.

As the toughs moved forward, the inspector squared off, raising his fists. Anderson just stood there. The moment one of them came into range, his hand flicked out and caught the man across the neck. The fellow was down in an instant, moaning in pain.

The inspector's face broke into an ecstatic smile. "Last chance, gents. You can walk away right now, or you're up for a proper kicking."

HALF AN HOUR later, they were in a hansom heading toward the Yard.

"What was it you did back there?" Ramsey asked incredulously. "I've never seen someone dropped that fast!"

"Posh detective secret," Anderson replied with a rare grin. "Can't share it with you."

The inspector guffawed. "I deserved that. I about split a gut when they took to their heels."

"It'll make a good article for the paper. Of course, I'll say you dropped the man instead of me."

"No. Tell it like it happened." Ramsey switched back to business. "Keats' arraignment is in the morning. Once that's done, we'll take a day in the country."

"After Whitechapel, it'll be a nice change," Anderson replied.

"Anything is a nice change after this sewer."

CHAPTER TWELVE

Alastair stood across the street, gathering his courage. Tonight, he would be taking an extraordinary gamble. The Artifice Club was a large, five-story structure with Doric columns. Inside were a series of rooms housing various gentlemen's clubs. The Conclave was at home in #8, which for some arcane reason shifted locations within the building on a daily basis.

Of the four members, Alastair was the most junior. George Hastings, nominally the leader of the group, ruled mostly by an overbearing attitude. His lackey, Edward Cartwright, always sided with him. Then there was Malachi Livingston, the man Jacynda believed was from her time.

Alastair shivered, focusing harder on the image he presented. People walking by would see a middle-aged man, well dressed in top hat and cape. They saw what he wished them to see. Nevertheless, even the shifters were not immune to discovery. He'd have to surrender his outer garments to the room steward, so he had purchased them just this afternoon. Tomorrow morning, he would resell them, hopefully not receiving the worse end of the bargain.

As he waited, he realized how far he'd fallen. He had intended only to use his ability for Keats' benefit, but now it was for Jacynda's. Tomorrow, it might be for someone else's. Each step took him further down a road he'd never intended to travel.

Though he hated to admit it, this deception was a matter of necessity, even were it not for Jacynda's condition. If Livingston were absent from the club for too long, they'd vote a replacement, most likely another one of Hastings' toadies. Hastings was not known for rational decisions: he'd hired thugs to destroy Alastair's clinic when the doctor refused to follow The Conclave's orders. Ironically, that had led to the doctor's new situation with Reuben Bishop. Nevertheless, Alastair certainly wasn't about to thank the old warhorse.

He'd always thought The Conclave was the power structure in the Transitive community. Now he saw it more as a decoy, a lightning rod in case someone needed to take the blame. It was Livingston's view that the Ascendant pulled George Hastings' strings. In return, Hastings appeared important to those who didn't know the truth. It was all a game, like some amateur séance designed to awe the gullible.

I almost fell for it.

Alastair took a deep breath and strode across the street. If Livingston were inside the club, it would be awkward. If not, he would preserve the man's position and might learn something of value during the encounter.

As he entered the antechamber, Ronald, the eighth room steward, snapped to attention. "Good evening, Mr. Livingston," he greeted with a polite smile.

"Good evening, Ronald. I trust all is well," Alastair replied, working hard to sound just right. Other Transitives could mimic voices with ease. He was too unseasoned to do it unconsciously.

"Very well now that you've returned," Ronald said. "I trust you had no difficulties?"

"Only urgent business matters," Alastair replied, offering his hat and cape. "Is the doctor here tonight?" It would be the kind of question Livingston would ask.

"No, sir, he's not."

"Pity. Hastings and Cartwright, then?"

"As usual, sir." Ronald gave him a penetrating look that made Alastair uncomfortable. As the steward opened the door, the doctor prepared himself for the show.

"Ah, there you are Livingston," Hastings called out, spewing a plume of cigar smoke into the air. "I wondered where you'd gotten to." He sat on the far right, brandy and cheroot in hand. Cartwright was working on his crossword puzzle, brows knitted. He looked up, gave a nod, and then resumed his efforts.

Moving purposefully, Alastair settled into Livingston's preferred seat. Ronald offered brandy and a cigar.

"Cigar only, thank you." It took enough effort to hold Livingston's form without adding liquor to the mix. The required level of concentration was wearying.

"So where have you been?" Hastings inquired.

"Business," Alastair replied, taking a few puffs on the cigar. It was of excellent quality. He'd never understood where the money came from for these indulgences. Who paid for all the fine furnishings, the leather chairs, the food, alcohol, and Ronald's attentive service? Though modest in size compared to many of the gentlemen's clubs in London, this room was certainly top-notch. Lord Wescomb, even the Prince of Wales, would feel at home here. Yet no one ever asked for any fees.

Probably best not to know whose pocket we're picking.

"The doctor hasn't been here, either," Hastings observed.

"No doubt embarrassed by our chess games. I always let him win, and I think he knows it."

From the heartiness of Hastings' laugh, it was clear that he hadn't a clue this wasn't Livingston. Alastair felt a thrill of exhilaration.

The moment Ronald retreated to the antechamber, Hastings leaned forward in his chair.

"We have a problem, one we could not address with the doctor present."

"Which is?" Alastair pressed, relishing this moment.

"Sergeant Keats is up for murder," Hastings informed him. "He's in custody. From what I hear, he will be found guilty."

"You sound so sure of that."

"He *will* be found guilty," Hastings repeated. "That makes it very dangerous for us."

Cartwright flicked his eyes back and forth between the pair of them, but said nothing.

"Why is that a danger?" Alastair asked, his hackles rising.

"If he is found guilty, there is nothing to prevent him from revealing our secret to save his own skin."

Alastair took another long puff on the cigar, just like Livingston. "You believe he will offer that information in trade for commutation of his sentence to a lesser penalty?"

"Or his freedom," Hastings said, shooting a look at Cartwright and then back to Alastair. "He must not be allowed that opportunity."

Hastings was coldly proposing Keats' death, yet again. He had done so in the past, but had been voted down. To calm his burgeoning anger, Alastair blew a smoke ring and then instantly regretted it. Had Livingston ever done that? *Well, too late now.* "Your worry is admirable, but misplaced."

"Why?" Hastings protested. "He can prove we exist."

Might as well let the cat out of the bag. "On the contrary. I have it on very good authority that Keats is no longer capable of going *en mirage.*"

"How do you know that?" Cartwright asked.

"I know many things, gentlemen," he declared, adopting Livingston's authoritarian tone. "The injury the sergeant took that night against the anarchist rendered him Opaque, as it were. He cannot shift."

Hastings frowned. "We're wagering our existence on some rumor."

Alastair shook his head. "It is not a rumor. Dr. Montrose told me in strict confidence."

"And yet you share it with us?" Hastings challenged.

Alastair shrugged, as if it were of no import.

"Keats could heal," Cartwright began.

"No, he will not." The doctor tossed the cigar stub into the fire. "We are free of this danger, gentlemen. If we intercede, we risk revealing ourselves."

Hastings gnawed on his cigar stub. "It may well be beyond that point, to be honest. I was only informing you as a matter of courtesy."

"Courtesy?" Alastair rose, dusting off a cuff as he'd seen Livingston do more than once. He pitched his voice perfectly. "It would be best for you, Hastings, and for The Conclave, that the sergeant is left alone. He cannot reveal our secret if he cannot prove it. If he attempts to do so, he will sound mad to his keepers. As I indicated the last time we spoke of this matter, I will take it very seriously if anything should happen to the man."

Hastings was staring at him intently. "Why?"

"Because if you'll stab him in the back, eventually you may do the same to me." Alastair took a gamble. "Warn your superior that it is not in his best interest to pursue this."

Hastings looked away. "I can't do that," he muttered. "He'll have one of his assassins after me in a flash."

So it is the Ascendant who holds the ring in your nose.

"Better one of them than me, Hastings," Alastair replied, putting just the right amount of malice behind the words.

He swept out of the room as Livingston would have done. He could hear hushed voices behind him. His threat had hit home.

As he donned his cape and hat, Ronald gave him an approving nod. Though the door was closed, the steward bent forward and whispered,

"Well done, Doctor."

"How—"

"The top hat. Mr. Livingston's is from Oxford Street. Yours is decidedly not."

"Oh." Recovering, Alastair slipped Ronald a generous tip. "Do you have any notion where he is?"

"No. I've not heard anything of him."

"When he does reappear, give him this, will you?" Alastair handed over one of his personal cards. "It's my new address. I must speak with him on an urgent matter."

"Most certainly, sir." Ronald's voice became louder. "Good evening, Mr. Livingston."

"Good evening, Ronald."

ALASTAIR MADE IT only a block away before he found a dark corner and shifted to his own form. While the ordeal left his stomach churning, the weariness resolved more quickly than he'd expected. After flattening the top hat and wrapping it in the cape, he headed home. In the morning he would speak to Lord Wescomb about the threat to Keats' life. In some perverse way his friend might be safest in a prison cell.

—

Monday, 29 October 1888
Old Bailey (Central Criminal Courts)

The report of Keats' arrest had spread quickly, through the newspapers and by word of mouth. Alastair was not surprised to find the courtroom filling rapidly with an audience eager to see Keats in the flesh as he made his plea. It'd be worse when the actual trial began.

They love a show.

As he jostled forward in the crowd, he heard a voice call his name. For all the noise, it was remarkable he could hear it. He turned and was rewarded with a sight he'd never expected.

"Evelyn?"

She stood apart from the crowd, clad in an emerald-green dress edged in beige lace, her brown hair arranged stylishly under a matching hat. Behind her, he noted another woman. Her lady's maid.

Up close, Evelyn Hanson looked more careworn than before. That wasn't surprising, given that she'd been compelled to break two engagements within the span of a few months. Evidently, each personal disappointment had exacted a heavy emotional toll. When he finally reached her, he hesitated, unsure of how he might be received.

When he finally reached her, he hesitated. What would her father think? Although Dr. Hanson recently had given him permission to see Evelyn again, his former employer had been the one to quash their engagement in the first place.

It would not hurt to be courteous. He owed her that much.

Alastair took her gloved hand and kissed it. Looking upward, he was pleased to note a subtle smile poised on her face.

"What brings you here?" he asked.

"You," she replied simply. "I read of your friend and knew you'd be here to support him. I thought you might like support of your own."

She doesn't hate me. Relief washed over him. It could so easily have proven the opposite. He'd openly challenged her father about who should be deemed worthy of medical treatment, and the vehement argument had led to Dr. Hanson quashing the engagement.

As if that weren't enough, Alastair had dashed Evelyn's future with her subsequent fiancée, by confronting the young rake and warning him that he might have contracted syphilis from Nicci Hallcox. Lord Patton had refused to be examined for the disease, seemingly unconcerned that he may pass the infection to his future wife. To Alastair's surprise, Evelyn had sundered *that* engagement on her own.

"Alastair?" she nudged.

"Sorry, I was thinking about...all that has come to pass between us," he said.

"I hold no anger for you over Lord Patton," she told him, as if divining his thoughts. "How can I dislike a man who saved my life?"

He felt humbled. "You have no idea what this means to me."

"Perhaps I do."

Too overcome to speak, he offered a smile and guided her to seats in the spectator's gallery, her maid trailing behind. The moment they were settled, there was a clamor. The doctor swiveled and watched as his best friend made his way into the dock. Keats was clean-shaven and wearing the suit Alastair had fetched for him. A rattling of chains accompanied the prisoner's every move. The doctor could feel his stomach turning. *This must be hell for him.*

"He looks so calm," Evelyn murmured.

"I suspect he has no other choice," Alastair replied grimly.

Keats saw them at that moment, and the ghost of a smile appeared. He did look better than the night before. The doctor gave a reassuring nod and it was returned.

When the time came, Keats stood with a clank of chains.

"Not guilty, my lord," he announced to the judge, his voice sure and strong.

"Not guilty? That's a crock. He done her for sure," a gent commented two seats away. "He's a rozzer. He didn't think he'd get nicked."

"Shoulda stayed in Whitechapel," another weighed in. "They'd-a never bothered him if he'd choked some whore down there."

"Mind the lady," Alastair warned through gritted teeth, fighting back the urge to confront whoever deemed his friend capable of such barbarian conduct. The coarse man muttered a half-hearted apology, but didn't retract his statement.

There would be no use arguing with any of them. They'd already convicted Keats. If hangings were still public, they'd be there, drunk as lords, to watch his friend twitch at the end of the rope.

With a sick anger lodged in the pit of his stomach, Alastair watched the inevitable play out. The court moved swiftly: Jonathon Davis Keats was remanded for trial for the murder of Nicola Hallcox.

With every step in this case, he'd hoped reason would prevail. What was Keats thinking? A quick look up to the dock yielded no answers. His friend's face was unreadable.

The courtroom emptied rapidly. To her credit, Evelyn had remained throughout the entire ordeal, one time taking his hand for comfort. Having her here with him had made the horror bearable. When they reached the street, he turned to her. He had many things he wanted to say but reined himself in. He dare not in such a public venue.

"Would you...like to go for some tea?" he suggested.

She shook her head. "I must go home."

Alastair's hopes crashed to earth. She had only been here to comfort him, nothing more.

She adjusted her arm in his. "My father's carriage is just there," she said, gesturing farther down the street. They strolled toward the conveyance.

He took a gamble. "I would like to see you again, Evelyn, if you are agreeable." The seconds ticked off. He heard none of the commotion around them, his attention riveted on what her answer might be.

"Perhaps we can go walking in Hyde Park tomorrow afternoon," she offered. "Would that suit?"

"Of course," he replied, before even considering his schedule. "May I call for you at...ah...two?"

Another smile appeared, this one much more reminiscent of when he'd first met her. "Yes. I would like that, Alastair."

They reached the carriage and he handed her inside. After her maid was settled, Evelyn called out, "Tomorrow, then. I am looking forward to it."

As am I.

———

"Quaint," Anderson noted, looking around the main street of Ingatestone. They stood in front of a chemist's shop. A sign in the window advertised Thermogene Medicated Wadding for all nature of chest ailments.

Ramsey took a deep breath. "Clean air. Not like London."

"Or Chicago," Anderson responded.

"Another nice thing about the country is that people pay attention, and they like to talk. If anyone saw Keats up here, they'll want to jaw about it. It makes them famous, you see. They actually saw a killer."

"Or an innocent man," Anderson corrected.

After asking a helpful citizen who seemed impressed that they were from London, they found the local sergeant at his post in front of the dining hall. His hair was combed back, his moustache bushy. From the bulging of his coat buttons, apparently he was inside the establishment more than was prudent.

"Inspector Ramsey, Scotland Yard," the inspector intoned. He offered one of his cards. The copper waved it away. "Need to ask you about the fellow who's up for murder in London. Sergeant Keats says he was here in Ingatestone the middle of this month."

"Heard about all that," the man replied. "What you want to know?"

"Did you see the sergeant that day?" Ramsey asked, his notebook out.

"I probably wouldn't have noted him. We get strange characters through here, what with the rail line and all. As long as they're not up to mischief, I ignore them."

"I see. Where are your pawn shops?"

The sergeant listed them off as Ramsey noted them. There were two.

"Did you or one of your constables go into the woods with Inspector Hulme to try to locate a coffin?"

"Who? Oh, that one. No, he didn't go nowhere. Sat in the pub all evening."

"Doing what?" Ramsey pressed.

"Nothing. Didn't drink much, just a couple pints. Nursed them all night. Then he got on the train back to London."

"Anything else you can tell us?"

A shake of the head.

"Then thank you for your time, Sergeant."

"All I got," the man said.

They finally tracked down the newspaper boy. He didn't remember Keats, but then he didn't seem the brightest of Ingatestone's population. The eel-pie seller didn't remember the sergeant, either.

"This isn't a good start," Ramsey commented, studying the list of pawn shops.

"Maybe he did make it all up."

"Could be, but why go to all that effort? It's too bizarre a tale."

It wasn't until they reached the second pawnbroker that someone recognized Keats' photograph. He was seventy, if a day.

"I saw the gent. He pawned his boots here." He looked down at the inspector's card. "Never thought I'd ever talk to someone from Scotland Yard. Wait til I tell my missus. She'll not believe it."

"When did he pawn them?" Ramsey asked.

Muttering under his breath, the old fellow shuffled off, then returned with a ledger that looked as old as he was. He cracked it open and ran a bony finger down the columns of surprisingly neat writing.

"Wednesday, the seventeenth of this month, in the morning." He looked up. "I keep track. Never know when it'll be important."

"Did he pawn anything else?"

"No, just a pair of boots. Excellent condition. I gave him top price. I could tell he hadn't been down for long."

"Down?" Anderson asked. "What do you mean by that?"

"Down on his luck, if you know what I mean. He'd been living rough, but not as long as some of them I get in here. His suit was dirty, but the cuffs weren't frayed and his boots were almost new. He had that stunned look when life takes a bad turn. The ones who've been down for a time don't have that anymore. They expect it to be bad."

"Did he say anything?" asked Ramsey.

"He was right sad to pawn them. Said they were the best he'd ever had and once he got some money from his family, he'd be back. Keen not to lose 'em."

"Did he buy another pair?"

"Right y'are. Sold him an old pair to tide him over. Nothing like the ones he pawned, I can tell ya that."

"Do you still have those boots for sale?" Ramsey asked.

"I'm wearing 'em."

"They're evidence. We'll need them for the trial."

The man's face fell. "They're right fine boots."

Ramsey dug in his pocket. "I'm willing to buy them from you."

"You got the pawn ticket?" the fellow asked. "I like to get them back. Keeps my records tidy."

"No, it went missing somehow." Hulme had never explained just how that had happened.

A shrug. "Well, I supposed it don't matter. You got something better than a pawn ticket," he said, pointing to the inspector's card.

The old man shuffled off again across the wooden floor. He returned in his stocking feet and placed the boots on the counter. "Fit me right perfect. I tried 'em on the moment he left. Needed a bit of cleaning, they were muddy and such, leaves stuck to the soles. They're a good pair, that's for sure."

"Leaves? Like he'd been in a forest?" Ramsey quizzed.

"Just like that." The fellow consulted his ledger and quoted the price. The inspector handed over the coins.

"Did this man have any injuries?" Anderson asked.

The inspector cursed to himself for not asking the question first.

"Yes. A bruise on his left chin. Nasty one. He said he tangled with a big Irishman."

Ramsey and his companion traded looks. Keats had said he'd been struck a blow. "Has anyone else been to talk to you? Another inspector from London?"

A shake of the head.

Why hadn't Hulme followed this lead? It was easy enough.

"You have a card, sir?" Ramsey asked. "We may need to call you to testify."

The bony hand produced one. "I'd love to come to London. Never been there before." He grew pensive. "Did that copper do what the papers say?"

"We're not sure," Ramsey replied, tucking the merchant's card in a pocket.

The old man shook his head. "I've seen lots in my time. Mean ones. They have that look in their eyes, cut you for a farthing. This one didn't. He looked lost, if you know what I mean."

"Yeah, I do."

CHAPTER THIRTEEN

Alastair floated home, barely aware of his surroundings. His heart warred over the joy at seeing Evelyn again and the cruel reality of Keats' future. His euphoria faded at the realization that he was no closer to finding Livingston. Unless Jacynda had dramatically improved during the day, there was little he could do to help her.

Mrs. Butler was drying the last of the new dishes and placing them in the Welsh dresser. "She doesn't say much," his housekeeper observed when he'd asked about their guest's welfare. "Just does whatever you ask her. Not at all like she used to be. Simple, if you get my meaning."

"Yes, I do." Alastair knelt next to Jacynda's chair. She studied him in return.

"Good afternoon, Jacynda." A nod in response. She did look better. Her hair was clean and clothes fresh, though he could still see the bruises on her neck. "Did you have a good day?" Another nod.

"Fred," she said, pointing to the stuffed animal in her arms.

"That's his name is it?"

She nodded. "I saw some sheep today."

"You like sheep?" he asked, reminded of similar conversations he'd had with his sister when she was a young child.

"I think so. They're wooly. They smell." She wrinkled her face in thought and then shook her head like a stray memory had wandered through her mind and then promptly got lost again.

Mrs. Butler was watching the exchange closely. "Are you sure you still want me to go out tonight?"

Alastair rose. "Most certainly. You and Davy deserve some time off after all the work on this house. I'm sure he'll enjoy the lecture about the Antarctic. He seemed quite interested when I mentioned the penguins."

"It's just that the house isn't—"

"It's so much better than when I first stepped inside. You have done wonders. You can't work day and night, or your health will give way again. Go out and have a good evening."

"What about her?" Mrs. Butler asked, looking toward Jacynda.

"We'll be fine. I am hoping to hear back from a specialist in brain diseases. I sent him a letter this morning. Perhaps he can find a way to help her."

"That would be a godsend. Well then," she said, putting down the last dish, "I'd best be going. I'm to meet Davy at the lecture hall."

Alastair beamed, pleased at how matters had fallen out. "Enjoy yourself, Mrs. Butler. Have a late supper if you wish. You can afford it now."

She shook her head in wonder. "I can't quite accept that yet."

"You will, in time."

At his request, Jacynda dutifully followed Alastair and then snuggled on the couch. He covered her lap with a blanket. In the distance, he heard the kitchen door close as Mrs. Butler hurried off to meet her son.

The parlour was even tidier tonight. Mrs. Butler had put the maid-of-all-work on her knees, scrubbing the floor for all she was worth. Even the rugs looked as if they'd been given a good beating.

"Another quiet evening," Alastair mused. He could get used to this if his companion were more like her old self. They'd grown closer during all the events of the last few weeks. They'd shared their secrets and found a common bond. They might have shared this house together as husband and wife.

But not now.

There was a playful giggle from his companion. Jacynda was playing hide-and-seek under the blanket with the stuffed animal. If she was a child, it would have been amusing. Instead, it broke his heart.

He recalled his encounter with Evelyn, how unsure he'd felt around her. It'd never been that way, but he sensed she'd changed since the summer. There was an edge to her now, a tenuous self-assurance. He'd seen only a glimmer of that during their engagement, but now it seemed stronger. He wondered where it would lead.

Weary of brooding, he opened up the evening's paper and read the account of Keats' indictment while his companion stared into the fire. What was she thinking? Did she realize how much of her memory she'd lost?

"Would you like me to read to you?" he asked.

She nodded eagerly and he set about relating various short articles to her. The first was about the preparations for Bonfire Night.

"Have you ever seen fireworks?" Alastair asked. Jacynda shrugged. "Then we shall have to ensure you do."

A knock on his front door, hard and heavy.

"Sounds like a copper," he grumbled, rising.

Only one was a police officer—Inspector Hulme—and the other a nattily dressed man with piercing eyes and mutton-chop sideburns.

"Doctor," Hulme said curtly. "I understand that Miss Lassiter is here."

"She is," Alastair responded just as curtly, not inclined to be polite.

"We need to speak to her."

"And you are?" Alastair asked, eyeing the other man warily.

"Wilfred Arnett, Crown Prosecutor," was the tart reply. "I am in charge of the case against Detective-Sergeant Keats."

"I see. Come in, gentlemen."

Jacynda was still staring at the fire. When she looked up at the men, her eyes went wide.

"Do be cautious, she is not of sound mind at present," Alastair warned.

"Wescomb said something to that effect," Hulme replied. He moved forward only a few paces and then stopped as she physically shrank from him.

"Miss Lassiter, I need to ask you a few questions about Sergeant Keats."

"Who?" she asked, eyes darting from him to the other man in bewilderment.

"Keats. You know him."

She shook her head.

"Now see here, Miss Lassiter—"

She skittered off the couch and ran to Alastair's side, hiding behind him like a toddler would when confronted by a big dog.

Arnett stepped forward, frowning. "What's this, then?"

"Miss Lassiter was assaulted," Alastair informed them. "She sustained a head injury and lost her memory. She has no idea who Keats is, or I, for that matter. All your questions are a waste of time and will only frighten her further."

Arnett looked down at her. "What are those marks on her neck?"

"Someone tried to strangle her."

"Who?" Hulme demanded. Jacynda did not answer. "If this is a trick, I shall file charges," the inspector threatened.

"It is not," Alastair replied hotly. "Have your own physician examine her. He will concur."

Arnett sighed. "No need. She was a better witness for the defence in any event. Let's go, Hulme."

Then they were gone.

"Well, that went better than I thought it would," Alastair remarked, closing the door and bolting it.

He found Jacynda back on the couch, clutching the ferret tightly to her chest. She jumped when he re-entered the room.

"They're gone."

"Not nice."

She has that spot on.

He knelt in front of her, taking her hands, his depression deepening. What if she never regained her full faculties? What if her people did not come for her? How would he care for her?

Jacynda pulled her hand free and tugged playfully on his pocket watch chain. He unclipped it and handed it to her. A pleased expression settled on her face as she began a deliberate winding pattern with the stem. He remembered the sequence from when she communicated with the future. She repeated it over and over, peering at the watch face, as if expecting something to happen.

"Not right," she said, giving the watch a sharp shake, as if it were malfunctioning.

I wonder...

Alastair hurried up the stairs, two at a time, and then extracted her own watch from the bureau drawer where he'd hidden it. As he clattered back down, caution rose. Maybe he shouldn't let her touch it. What if she accidentally sent herself somewhere unpleasant?

He sat on the couch and watched her repeated efforts, then copied the winding pattern. Nothing happened.

I was a fool to think otherwise.

He dropped the watch in amazement as a red glow appeared above it. When Jacynda's hand reached out to touch the dial, he pulled it back.

"Best not. I don't want you disappearing on me."

She glared at his interference. It was the first sign of anger he'd seen in her. When she pointed at his lap, he issued a gasp. The watch had generated an illumined grid of letters. It reminded him of the keys on the typewriters the clerks used. He stared at the image above the pattern of letters. It hung in the air without any visible means.

"Incredible."

He gingerly moved the contraption, placing it on the seat of a wooden chair and then drawing the chair closer. There was a slight noise and a word appeared in the air without any prompting.

Password?

Of course, they would want some security for this remarkable technology. A wild notion leapt into his head—perhaps he could communicate with Jacynda's contemporaries and they could tell him how to treat her.

This time when she reached toward the watch, he didn't stop her. She didn't attempt to touch it, but instead pressed one of the illuminated keys. An F appeared in the air.

"Go on," he urged. "Don't think about it, just put in the letters."

She looked down at the stuffed animal and frowned. She tapped the stuffed animal's head and gave him a distressed look.

"Fred?" Alastair prompted. A shake of her head. "Weasel?" Another shake. "Ah, ferret?" he tried. A quick nod.

Her finger typed an E, then an R. The letters appeared one by one. Then she stopped, bewildered.

"Ferret has two *r*'s," he informed her. That just confused her. "Let me." He tapped on the red square and an R appeared in the air.

"How remarkable," he murmured. He typed an E, followed by a T. "Now what?"

She cuddled the stuffed creature closer, rocking back and forth in agitation. Alastair resisted the need to swear openly. They were so close.

"Fred," she said.

Not knowing what else he could do, he typed in the word. Nothing.

"I'm sorry, I don't know what to do."

The words tore through him. He was supposed to help her, but he was powerless, an infant in the face of such advanced science. It was agonizing. He had long worshipped technology; now he only felt the need to curse it.

Alastair peered at the board, trying to sort through the keys and what they might mean. When he'd been in the bank setting up his account, he'd watched a clerk using a typewriter. It had fascinated him. When the fellow reached the end of a page, he pressed a lever that returned the carriage to the other side of the paper. What if this device required something similar to send the message into the future?

With a nervous wince, he pressed the key with a reverse arrow, praying it didn't make the watch disappear.

Another odd noise.

"Is that good?" he asked.

The air screen typed *Logged On.*

More letters, typed rapidly now. *Cyn? Where have you been?*

"Ah … ah ….oh my God, it worked!" Hands shaking, he began to type, praying that whoever it was wouldn't grow tired of waiting for him to reply and shut down the connection.

jacynda very ill need help

Nothing happened.

cyn?

Alastair remembered the strange key and pressed it.

Who are you?

montrose

A long pause. As each second ticked off, Alastair's panic rose tenfold. "Come on, talk to me!" he pleaded.

Dr. Montrose?

yes. "This is good. They remember me."

Jacynda leaned against him, staring at the words in the air.

"Pretty," she said, waving her hand through the letters.

"They'll help you," he offered, trying to sound reassuring.

She gave a firm nod that bolstered his spirits.

Send her here.

It was what he'd feared from the moment he'd seen the strange mark.

promise to treat her, he typed.

You have our word.

They'd given their word before, and it had been like gold. He had little choice but to comply.

tell me how

He did as the typed instructions required, closing the connection, securing the watch to her wrist and then placing it in her hand. She looked at him inquisitively. The trust in her eyes was like a bayonet to his heart. What if he were sending her into the arms of her enemies?

There was no other option. "You're going home," he informed her solemnly.

"Home?" she repeated, looking puzzled.

"Your friends will help make you better."

He threw her possessions into the Gladstone at a furious pace, snapped it shut and set it on her lap. Right before he closed the watch cover to trigger the transfer, he brushed her cheek with a kiss. Her innocent smile made tears bloom in his eyes.

"Even if…" he nearly choked on the words, "even if you never remember me, I will always care for you." He snapped the watch cover closed and staggered away a few paces, fists knotted.

She studied him with a sober expression, as if she knew how much this hurt.

The halo effect was brilliant, nearly blinding him. He saw her mouth open in astonishment, and then she was gone. He knelt, touching the floor where she'd been. Nothing of her remained.

And Keats thinks this is just nonsense.

Out of the corner of his eye he saw the stuffed ferret. It had fallen on its side, misplaced in the rush. He scooped it up, tucking it under his chin and letting his tears fall with abandon.

CHAPTER FOURTEEN

2057 A.D.
TEM Enterprises

Cynda landed hard, the wind knocked out of her. Her chin was resting on a chilly surface. It wasn't wood like the floor in the nice man's house. She inched a hand out. Flat…bump…flat…bump. Like mountains and valleys made out of solid metal. She kept moving her fingers farther away, touching the elevations and the depressions, trying to make sense of them. Then she encountered an obstruction. White, something hard. She tapped the end of it.

"Cyn?" a voice called.

The sound rattled around inside her head. She kept tapping the tip of the…shoe. A hand appeared and touched hers. She yanked hers back.

"Miss Lassiter?" another voice sounded, this one filled with authority.

She raised her chin to find two men staring at her. One had a long, gray-streaked ponytail that draped across a shoulder. His round glasses reflected the bright lights in the strangely shaped room. The other was dressed in black, with a dash of silver at his temples.

She focused on the one with the white shoes. He looked familiar. A name came to her tongue, but then it darted away.

"Is this a crazy place?" she asked through cracked lips.

"What?"

The other man cut in. "This is TEM Enterprises, Miss Lassiter. We were told you were ill. What is wrong with you?"

She shook her head, which made things worse. Shapes floated in front of her eyes like half-formed ghosts. Maybe they *were* ghosts. Where was the man who'd taken care of her in the old place? He would help her.

"Not right," she said, trying to rise to her knees. Hands caught her a moment before she sank into the welcoming oblivion.

—

Senior Agent Klein didn't fit the surroundings, but then few people did. Theo Morrisey's private solarium was a reflection of its owner: unique. Stocked with rare tropical plants and butterflies, skittering geckos and a small colony of hummingbirds, it was not the ideal place for a senior Government spook to interrogate someone.

Which is exactly why Harter Defoe had chosen it.

"Talk to me," Klein ordered, unconsciously tracking a hummer as it zipped mere microns over his head. "Tell me what's going on so I don't feel tempted to throw your ass in jail."

Defoe carefully spread his hands, mindful of his healing chest wound. "On what charges?"

"Removing your ESR Chip, for one. That's a Class 3 Felony. Traveling with a cloaked interface, a Level... hell, you know the regs better than I. You created them."

"Some of them," Defoe corrected. Time Rover One, as they called him, had not been responsible for the Essential Subject Record Chip rules. He detested the notion that someone knew where he was at any given moment because of a piece of hardware imbedded under his skin. "So what do you want to know?"

"Let's start with your chest wound. Who gave it to you?"

"Someone who works for the Time Protocol Board."

Klein perked up. "How do you know that?"

"Lassiter told me. When I got the drop on him, he was about to kneecap her." He grimaced. "Unfortunately, he scored the final shot."

Defoe altered his position in the chair to ease a cramp in his back. It didn't help. He'd been in the Thera-Bed too long. He wished the spook would wrap up the questions and leave.

"TPB hasn't said a word about the shooting," Klein remarked skeptically.

"They might not know. Lassiter bashed the guy on the head and sent him home before he knew he'd hit me."

Klein frowned. "Why would a TPB goon risk shooting you just to get Lassiter?"

"Perhaps he did not recognize me," Defoe offered.

The senior agent's frown deepened. "Or he thought he was looking at someone else."

"I don't know what you mean," Defoe replied. He wasn't about to confirm that he was a shape-shifter to a senior agent of the Government.

"Yeah, you do, but we'll leave it at that for the moment."

Klein leaned forward, unaware that a yellow-throated day gecko was eyeing him like he was a savory snack. "Here's the situation: TPB is hiding something. Something big. They circled the wagons when Davies moved up to the chairmanship position. We need to find out what they're up to."

Defoe let out a slow breath, trying to short-circuit his anger. "You got Morrisey's nephew killed over some damned interagency rivalry?"

"Nothing that petty. Stone was the third one we've lost."

"I haven't heard a thing about this."

"You haven't been around to hear it," Klein shot back.

Defoe huffed in frustration. "The lag was getting to me. I needed some time off."

"We figured as much. When one of our people said they'd caught a reading of your ESR Chip in 1888, we decided it was time to let you know what was going on."

Should have removed that damned thing years ago.

Klein rocked back in his chair, causing the gecko to sprint away. "To some extent this is a private battle between Guv and TPB, but there are bigger implications."

"That isn't comforting," Defoe grumbled. The Time Protocol Board was stocked with ambitious politicians. The Guv folks were the spooks, answerable only to themselves and the current administration. It was a toss-up as to which was worse.

As if reading his mind, Klein said, "I know you don't like us. No one likes us. But right now we're the lesser of two evils."

"Not a very compelling sales pitch."

The agent shrugged. "It's the way things are. What we know for sure is that people are in the time stream who aren't on record as being there. TPB is looking the other way. We want to know why."

"Like Chris Stone's killer?"

"Dalton Mimes is a good example," Klein acknowledged. "He hitches a ride along with his psychiatrist brother to 1888, but no record is made of his journey. TPB doesn't blow a cork about that when it comes to light. Why?"

"Morrisey said it was some deal Time Immersion Corp. cooked up to save themselves from bankruptcy. Once they went under, TPB didn't care."

"TIC wasn't the only one hiding the transfers," Klein informed him. "Time In Motion is doing the same thing."

"They've always been a front for the Board's behind-the-scenes deals," Defoe replied.

"Too easy of an explanation." Klein glared at the dragonfly perched on his arm. He shook it off. "Why the hell are we in here? There are things flying all over the place."

"They don't bother me," Defoe fibbed.

Klein's eyes narrowed. "I spent some time with Mimes. Nutty bastard. He says he was in '88 to frame some Victorian for the Ripper murders and make a freakin' fortune. He's very pissed that someone hasn't sprung him from the asylum. It's as if he thought that was a forgone conclusion."

"So he got stiffed. That's life," Defoe replied, wondering where this was headed.

"Mimes' attempt to screw with history isn't the big story here. What's troubling me is that he was willing to leave his brother behind in an asylum." Before Defoe could say a word, Klein cut him off. "I know he was bagging his sister-in-law. Still, it doesn't wash for me. Not everything boils down to sex and jealousy."

"Precious little in my experience."

Klein looked him straight in the eye. "What bothers me is that quid pro quo Mimes was expecting. When he realized I wasn't there to bail him out, he blew his cork. He claims he wasn't the only person involved in the death of Morrisey's nephew."

Defoe's chest tightened. "He could be lying."

A shake of the head. "Chris Stone's watch registered an ESR Chip right before he died. It took some doing, but we finally tracked the reading back to someone under contract with TPB. Ex-military prick named Copeland."

Defoe froze. "Tall, arrogant, dark-haired?"

Klein nodded.

Oh yeah, he remembered the bastard. Too busy trying to shoot Lassiter, Copeland hadn't seen him coming. There were advantages to being invisible. Unfortunately, TPB's hired gun won the round anyway. *But not the next.*

"He's the one who shot me," Defoe said.

Klein nodded. "I suspect he's good for the other deaths."

"So why isn't he in jail?"

"TPB denies it all, refuses to recall him."

"Then turn one of your people loose on him."

"I've lost enough already," Klein answered bluntly.

"But you're willing to put Lassiter and me on the firing line?"

"I judge it's worth the risk." Klein dropped the attitude. "We know you've had some contact with the Futures."

How the hell do you know that? Morrisey wouldn't have told them. Buying time, Defoe hedged his reply. "Futures?"

"Don't go coy with me. We know they've been snooping both in our time and in '88. I don't trust them. We have no idea of their agenda."

"Their agenda is simple: keep us from fornicating *their* future."

"Did they give you any details?"

"Not really." In truth, they'd said enough to scare the hell out of him. In five short years, laws would be passed to interdict Transitive behavior. The shifters would begin to fight back three years after that. It all went south from there.

Klein didn't need to know all that.

A hummingbird careened past them, pursued by another at top speed. Defoe let the seconds spin out, weighing his options against his conscience. He'd been at Chris' high school graduation and his graduation from the Time Immersion Academy. The kid had been first in his class. He shouldn't be dead. He should be settling down, marrying, having kids so Morrisey would have someone to spoil.

His eyes locked onto Klein's. "Okay, you got me. How do we reel Copeland in?"

To his credit, Klein passed on looking smug. "Go back to '88 and keep digging. The key is hidden there somewhere."

They heard a series of beeps as the outer door opened, followed by barely audible footsteps. The Guv agent went on the alert.

"It's Morrisey," Defoe said. No one else moved that quietly. Sure enough, his friend appeared at the entrance to the solarium, face shrouded in concern.

Defoe straightened up, his chest complaining at the sudden movement. "Do we barbarians at the gates?"

"Not yet, but I suspect TPB will be here soon enough," Morrisey replied, giving Klein a quick look. "Miss Lassiter has just returned from '88. Her mind didn't make the trip."

—

Cynda blinked open her eyes. It took awhile for her to realize she was in a new place. She found a man peering down at her. It wasn't the one with the odd-sounding instruments who kept asking her about her brain. The other man, the solemn one who wore all black, stood nearby, watching her intently. A third hovered near the door. She didn't like the looks of him.

"Do you remember me?" the first one asked.

She shook her head carefully, so as not to trigger another headache. The bed she was lying on seemed to help that, which didn't make any sense. The bed in the other place hadn't. The solemn man had said that the blue line on the bed needed to be longer before she could get up. She checked it again. It hadn't changed. Still, she liked the color blue.

"Do you remember falling into the river?" the man asked.

A stray image appeared. It was of rotting fish. She shook her head.

"Do you remember me being shot?" Another shake of the head. "What do you remember?"

"Mice. In the crazy place."

"The what?"

"I think she means an asylum," the solemn man explained. "We found a scrap of paper in her pocket. It had her first name written on it. Miss Lassiter said a woman gave it to her. I believe it's the only reason she knows her first name. She certainly does not remember Mr. Hamilton, and they've been friends for over a quarter of a century."

"What could have caused this?" the first man asked, his face pale now.

"The physician isn't sure, but he did find a circular pattern on her left temple that looks like a scorch mark," the solemn man continued. "He has no idea what could have caused it."

"Null Mem," the man near the door murmured.

"What?" the first one demanded.

No reply.

"Spill it, Klein."

"Not here."

CHAPTER FIFTEEN

They retreated to a quiet room. Only after Morrisey had instituted the complete security shield would Klein do anything more than grunt.

"What's going on?" Defoe demanded. "Why is she that way?"

The agent issued a thick puff of air. "A few years ago, the Government sponsored an experiment, a new treatment for schizoids and psychopaths, the most violent ones. It was called Null Memory Restoration. In layman's terms, NMR *reboots* a person's mind, causing almost complete memory disassociation."

"Why would anyone want to do such a thing?" Morrisey asked, mystified. "Our memories are what make us human."

"The theory was simple: clear out the old memories, rebuild the brain to a new set of specifications, and these crazies would become productive citizens. If it worked, you wouldn't have to warehouse them in prisons and asylums." Klein scoffed. "It was pure bullshit of course, but that was the plan."

"Did it work?" Morrisey asked.

"From what I can tell, the project failed. NMR treatment was abandoned about four years ago."

"Is it reversible?"

Klein shrugged. "Some of the patients never did retrieve their memories or progressed much further than a precocious child. Those who did recover their memories got worse...more violent."

Morrisey slumped in his chair. "My God."

"This has to be TPB's doing," Klein said. "When they couldn't kill her, they did the next best thing. She's gotten close to something they want hidden." His eyes moved toward Defoe. "Both of you did."

"I'm going back to '88," Defoe declared.

"You can't. You're not well enough," Morrisey protested.

Defoe rose, cautiously testing his endurance. His chest responded with spike of pain, but it wasn't as bad as the day before. It would have to do.

"Klein is right. It's time for me to leave. TPB will come for Lassiter. It's best I not be found."

"You're not well enough," Morrisey repeated, more emphatically this time.

"I have a safe place I can hide while I regain my strength. The longer I'm here, the more danger for you. We've been damned lucky so far."

Morrisey opened his mouth to object, but Defoe waved him off. "Go find me a set of Victorian clothes, will you? Whatever is happening is in '88. I need to be there."

WHAT WAS LEFT of Jacynda Lassiter peered up at him quizzically.

"Pretty," she said, pointing at the flower on his lapel.

Defoe slowly tugged the bloom off his Victorian cutaway coat. "This is for you," he said, voice quavering.

She took it. After a deep inhalation, she frowned.

He leaned closer, intrigued. "What is it called?"

"Ah...ah..." She shook her head. "I can't remember."

"That is a rose."

She took another sniff and shook her head, as if something weren't right.

"Do you remember who did this to you?" Defoe asked.

"Macassar oil," she said.

That brought an instant look of puzzlement. "I'm not wearing any."

"That's her reply whenever we ask that question," Morrisey explained. "I have no idea what it means."

She handed back the bud. "Not right."

Defoe smiled wanly. "That's correct," he said indicating the flower. "It should have a pleasant scent, but this one doesn't."

She winced and bit her lip.

Morrisey bent over her. "Is your head hurting again?" A slight nod. He adjusted a setting on the Thera-Bed. "Just sleep. It'll feel better when you awake."

She murmured to herself as her eyes closed.

Defoe looked up at his closest friend. "They've declared war, Theo. She's one of ours. So was Chris. This has to stop."

Morrisey nodded with grim determination. "And so it shall."

KLEIN WAS WAITING for them when they exited the room.

As Defoe reattached the rose to his lapel, he observed, "She's not entirely gone. For God's sake, don't let TPB near her. They'll destroy what's left."

"If she's judged to be incompetent, they'll appoint a guardian who can send her anywhere they want," Klein replied. "To an asylum. Maybe to prison, if they get a sympathetic judge."

"I won't let that happen!" Morrisey flared.

"A guardian. What an excellent idea, Senior Agent Klein," Defoe replied, winking at his friend. "I'm sure you'd be willing to help Morrisey make that a reality. Consider it a trade for my assistance."

Klein frowned, unaware of what had just transpired. "What do you have in mind?"

Morrisey nodded, suddenly catching his friend's drift. "A little sleight of hand," he said. "I need to communicate with someone Off-Grid."

"Who?"

"Miss Lassiter's father. I'll ask him to appoint me guardian until such time as she becomes fully functional."

"That could be a lifetime job," Klein said.

Morrisey's expression dimmed. "I'll accept that."

The agent flicked his gaze toward the closed door. "I'll get the clearances. That lady had stones. Now…"

"Nothing," Morrisey said. "That's the official line, no matter if she gets better or not."

Their eyes met. Klein's mouth twitched upward into a cunning smile. "That will be the official line." The agent strode toward the main entrance. Morrisey's assistant, Fulham, fell in step with him.

Morrisey's tone shifted the moment the Guv agent was out of earshot. "You sure you want to leave right now?" he asked his friend.

"No choice."

On Morrisey's orders, there was no chron operator present in the chronsole room. A moment before Defoe entered the time pod, they embraced, Morrisey taking great care not to cause any discomfort.

"Be careful, Harter," he said. "Keep in contact. Your interface isn't traceable."

As Defoe knelt in discomfort, awaiting the transfer, Morrisey's slender fingers tapped across the keyboard. Their eyes met. "Find the man who did that to Miss Lassiter and make him pay."

Defoe smiled. His friend might be a software wizard, but he had the heart of a samurai. "You got it, Theo."

Morrisey triggered the time pod door. A moment later, Harter Defoe, the greatest of all Time Rovers, vanished into the past.

As if on cue, Fulham appeared at the chronsole room door.

"Representatives of the Time Protocol Board have arrived. They know of Miss Lassiter's return. They've brought two security guards with them to arrest her."

He'd expected this: the interface that sent Jacynda home *was* traceable. "I wonder what took them so long."

Like the last time they'd visited the compound, the Time Protocol Board's minions were still using the aliases Smith and Jones. That continuing discourtesy had riled Fulham, especially since he'd been unable to ascertain their real names. Then there'd been a tussle about the security guards they'd brought along.

"No weapons inside. That's the rule," Fulham repeated.

"The guards won't be unarmed," Smith replied.

"Then they stay here, in reception."

"We have an order from—"

"Take it or leave it, gentlemen," Fulham barked.

Watching the verbal fireworks via a Vid monitor in his office, Morrisey cracked a smile. Mr. Fulham, like most clerks of the legal variety, possessed a nearly inexhaustible amount of patience. When it was gone, things got intense.

Smith finally acquiesced. It was either that or barge into the compound with armed guards. That faux pas would end up on the Vid-Net News. Fulham would see to that.

By the time they convened in the conference room, everyone was on edge. Smith and Jones parked themselves in the chairs at the end of the conference table, the two guards standing behind them, beefy arms crossed. A nano-drive skidded across the length of the table in Morrisey's direction. He trapped it under his palm without looking down.

"That's an Open Force Warrant for Miss Lassiter's arrest," Smith said. "We're here to execute it."

"I am aware of the conditions of an Open Force Warrant, Mr. *Smith*," Morrisey replied, keeping his voice level. "Miss Lassiter is in no condition to travel."

"On what basis do you make that claim?"

"She has sustained severe psychological trauma with resultant amnesia," he said, ensuring the diagnosis sounded as clinically cold as possible. The detachment was for their benefit. Fury still churned in his gut.

"*If* that is the case, our doctors will treat her," Jones replied.

"She is my employee, and will remain in my care." He couldn't do much for Jacynda's damaged mind, but at least he could keep these jackals from removing her from the compound. Once she entered the prison system, he might never get her free.

"She has a cell waiting for her, Mr. Morrisey. She is a threat to—"

"Miss Lassiter is no longer a threat to anyone, except herself. She has the mind of a child, gentlemen."

He retaliated with his own nano-drive, moving at lightning speed across the desktop. Jones tried to catch it, but missed. It tumbled into his lap.

"That's her medical report. Ask Chairman Davies how a discredited twenty-first century technology can be used as a weapon in the nineteenth. I'll be awaiting his answer."

He was out the door despite their vigorous protests. He needed time to get things squared away, and challenging TPB head on was the best way to slow the beast.

His seething resentment banked when he entered her room. Jacynda was asleep, curled up like a lost waif, with no notion that the world was full of people who wanted to harm her.

Ralph Hamilton, her best friend, sat near the bed.

Morrisey cleared his throat. "How is she?"

Hamilton turned the Thera-Bed's monitor in his direction. Her vital signs were good, her EEG still registering as aberrant. The physician had added another parameter: mental age. She was currently at just over five years old.

"So what the hell happened to her?" Hamilton asked, voice lowered to keep from waking his friend.

"What I am about to tell you must go no further, do you understand?"

There was a brusque nod. Morrisey explained as best he could, mindful of the years of friendship that stood between Hamilton and woman in the bed. As he spoke, the expression on the chron operator's face went from shock to righteous anger.

Hamilton leapt to his feet. "Dammit, this is your fault," he hissed, pointing an accusing finger. "You shouldn't have let her go back the last time. You knew they were trying to kill her."

"It was her decision."

"The hell it was. You could have ordered her to stand down, but you didn't. It's *all* your fault." Hamilton stormed out of the room.

You may well be right.

The chair still radiated warmth from the man's lengthy vigil. Now it was his turn.

—

Sunday, 28 October 1888
New York City

Harter Defoe took another deep whiff. Every place has its own particular scent, and this one didn't match with his desired destination. He'd asked Theo to send him a few blocks away from Adelaide Winston's house where he intended to throw himself on her mercy while he healed. And yet he smelled fish. His ears picked up the sound of something motorized, grinding away on a heavy load. That didn't track. Adelaide's posh neighborhood was noticeably absent of winches. He glanced down at the interface. It was blank. That was odd. He gave it a shake. Nothing changed.

The last thing he needed was equipment malfunction. He'd shaded the truth with his old friend: it was still too soon for him to be traveling like this. The wound hurt more than he'd admitted and his strength had yet to fully return.

Grumbling under his breath, he picked up the suitcase, adjusted it to reduce the throb in his chest, and set off down the alley. When he reached the next street, he knew he was out of position. A short walk down the pier was a massive steamship, passengers streaming up the gangplank.

He made for the closest newspaper boy. As he dug in his pocket for a coin, the masthead caught his attention. *The New York Times. October 28 1888.* Wrong place, wrong date.

I don't need this right now.

"Sir?" an eager lad called out. He was dressed in a messenger's uniform. "You Mr. Defoe?"

The hairs on the back of his neck rose. No one of this century called him that. Warily, he replied, "Yes?"

"Delivery for you, sir."

Defoe took the proffered envelope with a sense of foreboding. Digging out a coin, he realized it wouldn't do. "I'm sorry, all I have is British money."

"That's all right, sir. I've been paid."

"By whom?" By the time Defoe posed the question, the messenger had already scurried off into the crowd along the pier.

The envelope contained a First Class ticket to London dated that day. It was for the steamship further down the pier, which departed in two hours.

Annoyed beyond reason, he returned to the alley. This had to be Morrisey's doing— a means to ensure Defoe had time to recover from his wound.

And you think I play God.

As soon as he was alone, he opened the interface and began the winding procedure. A moment later, he was gone. Then he was back. To the same location. He repeated the maneuver. And returned to the exact same spot.

"Morrisey, I swear I'll—" Just then, his interface lit up and glowing letters marched across the dial.

The time has come.

This wasn't Morrisey's meddling, and for once he wished it was.

Knowing it was useless to try to transfer again, Defoe put away his interface, picked up his lone piece of luggage and headed for the ship. He was out of commission for a week, subject to First Class pampering that would rival Adelaide's.

I hope you idiots know what you're doing.

CHAPTER SIXTEEN

Monday, 29 October 1888
Newgate Prison

Alastair had never been inside the prison before, but it was as bleak as he imagined. The moment the cell door opened, Keats rose from his bed, smiling when he recognized his visitors.

"Welcome to my new home, gentlemen," he announced, gesturing broadly. "It's not quite as grand as I'd hoped, but it does rival my shabby room in Rotherhithe."

Alastair immediately took Keats' hand and clasped it between his. "Good God, my friend, I had never thought it would be like this."

Keats' bravado faded. "Neither had I."

"I asked for you to be put in your own cell," Wescomb explained. "I felt you would be safer that way."

"Thank you, my lord. How bad is it?"

Wescomb didn't hesitate. "It appears formidable. The butler is the lynchpin of their case. I hope to pound home the fact that he's a drunkard and that he harbored ill will toward you. Other than your calling card, the Crown has no other evidence you were there."

Keats retreated to the bed. "Sorry, I have no chairs," he said, keeping his back to them to allow himself time to regain his composure.

"Where would the killer have obtained your card?" Alastair asked.

"Oh, anywhere," Keats replied absentmindedly. "I am very free with them."

"Did you leave one with Miss Hallcox the night of the party?" Wescomb asked.

"No," he replied, turning back. "I wanted no trace of me to remain in that household."

"Have you seen the card, my lord?" Alastair asked.

"I have not."

"Surely Fisher would know my card," Keats insisted.

"Nevertheless, I think it would be of value to have someone examine it. I am leery of leaving anything to chance."

"Excellent idea. I shall arrange it." Wescomb tugged on his waistcoat out of habit. "I do have other unpleasant news, Sergeant. Your trial has been scheduled for Wednesday next."

"Wednesday?" Keats repeated incredulously. "Keen to get it over with, aren't they?"

"I sense that, yes," Wescomb concurred with a grim nod. "All I can offer are my best efforts."

"In all honesty, my lord, I could not hope for a more spirited defender."

"Alas, that spirit must be tempered in some regard. I shall present your case with extreme care. If I portray Miss Hallcox as a scheming woman inclined toward blackmail, it will only give the Crown Prosecutor further ammunition as to your potential motive. I have asked Kingsbury to help me with this matter. He is a very able assistant. He often sees things I miss."

"I leave it in your hands, my lord."

"I advise you to get your rest." As Wescomb reached the door, he turned. "If you need anything else, or think of something that may sway matters in your favor, send word immediately."

"Thank you, my lord."

The moment the cell door closed and the footsteps echoed away, Keats turned to Alastair. "How is Jacynda?"

"She has gone home."

"You mean…?" Keats began.

"Yes. They gave their word they will care for her."

"You actually talked to them?"

"Not directly. It was through their marvelous technology. You should have seen it, Keats. Remarkable!"

The wonder in his friend's voice sounded genuine. "I wish I had. At least she is safe." When Alastair didn't reply, Keats pressed. "She is, isn't she?"

"I believe so," the doctor sighed. "Her sudden disappearance has required me to claim she's been sent away, to a specialist in brain diseases. Mrs. Butler accepted the lie, but I'm not so sure if the Wescombs will."

"Lady Wescomb will probably want to visit her."

"That is my concern. Unfortunately, this means Jacynda is unavailable to testify on your behalf."

Keats gave a dispirited shrug. "It wouldn't matter. If she were still of right mind, she would only say that I was at the hotel until about half past nine. I could have easily returned to Mayfair and throttled Nicci with time to spare."

"She would at least have been able to indicate your mental state, that you meant Miss Hallcox no harm."

"I did not tell Jacynda of my decision, nor where I was headed. I didn't want a lecture." Keats sank onto the bed. "Now that I think of it, better a lecture than being here."

When the cell door closed behind his friend, Keats swung himself into the bed and stared upward at nothing. The trial would last two or three days and then his life would rest in the hands of twelve men. If they acquitted him, he would need to rebuild his reputation and his career. If he were found guilty, they would hang him after three Sundays had passed, as was the law.

Twenty-one days in which to regret he'd ever met Nicci Hallcox.

—

"A senior official from the Home Office is waiting in your study, your lordship," Brown announced the moment Wescomb entered the front door.

"Why is he here?" he grumbled, taking the proffered card. "It's like I'm some prize hunting dog they can whistle to their side any time they desire. I grow very weary of this."

"As you say, my lord," Brown replied tactfully.

Wescomb had barely placed his valise on his desk when his visitor delivered his broadside. For a few seconds his lordship thought he'd misheard. Then the stipulation clicked into place.

"That is not a condition, but a death sentence," he protested.

The senior official shook his head. "It is not as grave as you make it out."

"It is imperative the truth be revealed in court."

"Your concerns will be noted, my lord, but it is our position that the public not be aware that explosives are still in the hands of anarchists. It will cause a panic, especially with Guy Fawkes Day approaching. We cannot risk that."

"The explosives are the primary reason Sergeant Keats put himself in jeopardy, why he risked his career and did not turn himself into the authorities," Wescomb argued. "If I am not allowed to submit that point for the jury's consideration, then my case is as gutted as a fish at Billingsgate Market!"

"I know it's a blow, but even the Prime Minister agrees—no mention of the explosives may be made, except those that were confiscated last month."

"Good God," Wescomb muttered. "You wouldn't even have those if it weren't for Keats. The Crown's gratitude is as thin as a beggar's shoe leather."

"He has only himself to blame for being in the dock," his visitor replied, his expression as unfeeling as his words.

Lord Wescomb stared. "You can't honestly believe he killed that woman?"

"Guilty or innocent, it really doesn't matter. Our concern is that the public not be exposed to anything that might generate a panic."

The fellow paused at the door to Wescomb's study. "There is one other matter…"

Wescomb glowered. "And that is?"

"It has come to our attention that a number of prominent men were involved with the victim. The mention of their names in open court would be quite damaging to their reputations and…to those within the government. You are to steer away from revealing the identities of those whose cards were found in the victim's possession."

Wescomb's mouth fell open in astonishment.

"Lest you believe we have unduly hamstrung your case, I have already spoken about this matter with the Crown Prosecutor. He will hew to the same restriction. So it is even ground for both parties."

Wescomb rose. "Why are your masters trying to kill this man?"

The emissary's face turned grave. He opened his mouth and then closed it.

"Why?" Wescomb challenged.

"In truth, I have no idea, my lord."

The moment he was alone, Wescomb headed for the drinks cabinet. Very soon Sephora would appear at the door to his study, asking what the commotion had been about.

How do I tell her that I've lost the case before it has even begun?

A few minutes later, a light tap on his door.

"John?"

"Come in, my dear," he answered. He felt the need to refill his whiskey, but it would make no difference.

His wife was clad in one of his favorite gowns—the one that looked like violets in the spring. It fit her perfectly, contrasting with her silvered hair. She had been a beauty when she was young. She still was.

"What is wrong?" she asked, gliding to a chair. "What did Home Office want?"

"For me to allow Sergeant Keats an unfettered walk to the gallows."

She froze. "Why in heaven's name would they wish that?"

"The word has come down that I am not to mention the names of those degenerates whose cards were found in Miss Hallcox's possession. Nor am I to mention that there are still explosives at large. Can you imagine such a thing?"

Sephora frowned. "But those are key points of your defence. You must be allowed to introduce an element of doubt, that her murderer could be any number of men given the woman's sordid behavior."

"Well, that defence is now useless."

"But…that's ridiculous!"

"I know. The butler may be a drunkard, but he did see someone in Keats' form heading toward his mistress' bedchamber. It had to be a Transitive, though it is appalling to think that one of us committed such a vile crime," he replied.

Sephora fussed with a stray string on her cuff.

"I'm sorry to distress you so, my dear."

"This, on top of what has happened to Jacynda, is almost too much to bear," she said. "I intended to visit her, but this morning I received a message from Dr. Montrose. She has left London, for treatment."

Wescomb gave into temptation and returned to the drinks cabinet for more whiskey.

—

2057 A.D.
TEM Enterprises

Boredom quickly set in. It'd been a day or so since the man with the flower had visited her and asked all those questions she couldn't answer. The physician had been to see her, but he just muttered under his breath and made a lot of noises with his instruments.

Cynda studied the blue line on the machine. It was longer now. They told her that was a good sign. She swung a foot over the edge of the bed. Maybe they had a Mouse Lady here and she could follow her around. She'd like that.

When her feet touched the floor she waited for her head to pound, but it didn't. Just a dull ache. The cold metal on her left wrist did bother her, so she gave the band a solid tug. It didn't come off, and just continued to blink.

Chilly, she pulled the blanket off the bed and wrapped it over her baggy top and pants. As she approached, the door opened on its own. She stepped back, and it closed. Forward, and it opened. She laughed and clapped her hands. This was fun.

Once through the door, something beeped and the thing on her wrist vibrated. She jumped back at the sensation, frantically jerking at the band. It was blinking more rapidly now. Maybe she should go back to the bed. Then it settled into a steady rhythm and the vibrating stopped.

She stuck her head out of the doorway again, looking both ways. No one challenged her, not like at the other crazy place. In fact, there was no one around at all.

Cynda headed down the hallway, dragging the blanket behind her. She paused near a window and stared out at a large courtyard bathed in brilliant sunlight. There was a wooden building in the middle of it, surrounded by white sand. At the very tips of the roof were strange figures with long tails.

"What are you?" she whispered. She wandered along until she found a door. It opened automatically. This time she wasn't surprised when the band on her wrist vibrated.

"Come off," she demanded, pulling on it. It wouldn't budge. That would have to change.

Once outside, she tilted her face upward and sucked in the sun's welcoming rays. This felt right. A cloud marched by. It was big and looked like a... She groaned. The word wouldn't come. So many of them didn't.

Lowering her eyes, she saw the sand. It reflected the light in a myriad of different colors, like a... Another word gone. She stepped onto the white surface. Something was wrong.

She took another step. Nothing happened. That puzzled her.

"Miss Lassiter?"

She turned, bulldozing sand with her toes. Behind her were two men: the one with the ponytail and the solemn one. Had the thing on her wrist told them she was here?

Cynda pointed at the wooden structure and stuck out her chin defiantly. "I am going there."

The solemn one nodded his approval. "Spend as much time as you wish. If you want food, we will arrange to have it brought to you."

She turned her back on them, intent on her destination.

"Do you think she knows what happened?" the other man asked.

"I doubt it."

It didn't matter if they talked about her. She just liked being outside. There was white sand that didn't act right and a lot of blue above her. That was good. She sat on a square pillow, pulling the blanket around herself to keep warm. When she looked back, the men were gone. She sighed in relief. Closing her eyes, she thought of kittens and string.

When it began to turn dark, the solemn one, the one who said his name was Morrisey, came for her. "Time to call it a day, Miss Lassiter."

"Jacynda," she corrected proudly. That she could remember.

She rose stiffly and followed him. When she stepped off the sand, she abruptly halted. "What are they called?"

He turned around. "Pardon?"

She pointed upward at the creatures on the building. "Those."

"They're celestial dragons."

"Cel…lestial dragons," she repeated. "Do they eat people?"

"They won't hurt you, if that's what you're worried about. They guard the temple and whoever is inside it."

She liked that idea. "What did you say your name was?"

"Morrisey."

"I'm Jacynda," she announced.

A bemused smile. "I know. What did you think about while you were sitting out there?"

"Kittens."

He gave her an odd look. "Why kittens?"

"They chase string."

"Did you used to have a kitten?"

Did I? "I don't know," she admitted. "What are they again?"

It took him a moment to recall her question. "Celestial dragons."

"I like them."

"I'm glad to hear that. Feel free to ask me anything you wish."

As they walked, she pondered that offer. "Was I always like this?"

"No, you weren't."

"What happened?"

He hesitated and then suddenly veered toward the sand again, gesturing for her to follow. Kneeling, he scooped up a white handful. "This is what your mind used to be like." He spread his fingers, letting the sand drain out in rivulets. When nearly all of it was gone, he closed his fingers again, stopping the flow. "You've lost a lot of your memories and your ability to connect objects with their names."

She looked at what was left in his palms. It didn't seem like much. "Will it get better?"

"Maybe."

Cynda turned, studying the structure behind them. "Why do they live up there?"

This time, he knew what she meant. "I don't know," he replied, dusting off his hands as he rose. "Maybe they like it there."

"Do they have one of these on them?" she asked, holding up her wrist to expose the blinking band.

"No. You're only wearing that because we're afraid you'll get lost."

"I won't," she assured him. "I know where I am."

He looked genuinely puzzled. "You do?"

Cynda nodded. "I'm here," she declared, gesturing toward the ground. "Where else would I be?"

He smiled, although his eyes still looked serious. "How Zen. Come along, you need your rest."

Cynda kept looking at the dragons over her shoulder as she followed the one named...whatever it was. She'd come back in the morning. Maybe the dragons would talk to her then. She bet they knew things no one else did.

CHAPTER SEVENTEEN

Wednesday, 31 October 1888
Old Bailey (Central Criminal Courts)

With Keats' name in nearly every newspaper, it wasn't surprising most of London's underworld was here. The criminals wanted a front row seat for this one, a rare chance to see a copper sweat.

From his position in the dock, Keats had a clear view of the courtroom. In front of him was the chair from which the judge would make his pronouncements and sum up the case for the jury. To Keats' left was the jury box and to his right the spectator's gallery. It was filling rapidly. He recognized some of the faces: petty thieves and confidence men he'd arrested, a few of the prostitutes, a forger, and some of the local toughs.

Then he heard the catcalls start up.

"'Ey rozzer, bet ya wanna be up 'ere now, don't ya?" A chorus of laughter. "They'll 'ave to cut the rope mighty short for that one."

In reality, the rope would have to be longer because of his slight weight. Keats inwardly grimaced: knowledge was not always a good thing. He stiffened his resolve, if nothing more than to uphold the reputation of Scotland Yard.

Just in front of the spectator's gallery was where the barristers sat. Robed and wigged, Lord Wescomb would be to the left of the long table, the Crown Prosecutor on the right. Just behind the barristers sat the privileged witnesses and visitors. That section was already crowded. He saw familiar faces, and that cheered him.

Alastair was talking animatedly to another man, most likely Reuben Bishop. Seated a short distance away was Lady Sephora Wescomb. Her anxiety was displayed by the constant fussing with the strings of her reticule. The Chief Inspector sat next to her, pointedly not looking in Keats' direction. In the second row was Keats' cousin Roddy, dispatched by his grandparents to provide daily reports on the trial's progress. His usual gay demeanor was missing. When Roddy peered up at him, Keats gave a slight smile, hoping to allay the young man's fear. It proved futile. Roddy had always looked up to him, called him a hero. Now he saw that even his cousin's feet were made of clay.

Keats tugged on his coat sleeves. The action did nothing to obscure the chains at his wrists. Every movement generated a rattle. It was humiliating and the extra weight made his healing rib ache. How many men had he put in this very dock? How many had been innocent?

Why should my fate be any different?

"ARE YOU PREPARED if they call you as a witness?" Reuben asked, keeping his voice low.

"Yes, I am," Alastair replied resolutely.

Lord Wescomb leaned closer, clad in his black robe and horsehair wig. "They will try to ignore the scientific evidence. Most likely they will go after you as Keats' friend. Perhaps even mention your past brush with the law."

Alastair gave him a sharp look. "My past has no bearing on—"

"Come now, Alastair, don't be naïve!" Wescomb replied. "The Crown Prosecutor is particularly known to go for the jugular. If he can plant a seed of doubt that you tampered with the evidence, that you're not a man of your word, all the rest will mean nothing."

"So what do you propose?" Alastair asked, acidly.

"I will stress that neither of you knew that Keats was the prime suspect when the chief inspector summoned you to the scene of the crime, and that you did your duty without bias."

"Does the chief inspector know this?"

"Yes. He agreed to it."

Reuben shook his head. "Fisher is destroying his career."

"Perhaps, but at this point we're only worried about Sergeant Keats."

"I will do my best," Alastair pledged, still frowning.

"Whatever you do, refer to Mr. Justice Hawkins as *my lord*. It's a term of respect. The justices are rather prickly about that."

"I shall."

"And do rein in that temper of yours. Now is not the time for emotional displays."

Chastised, Alastair murmured, "Yes, my lord."

"BE UP STANDING!" a strident voice cried out. The courtroom rose as Justice Hawkins entered. With a rustle of his red and black silk gown, he settled into his chair. The room returned to their seats.

Keats braced himself for what would come next.

The Clerk of the Court cleared his throat and read out the charges.

"Jonathon Davis Keats, you are indicted and also charged with willful murder of Nicola Therese Hallcox on the 13th day of October instant. Are you guilty or not guilty?"

Keats rose with a clatter of the chains. He ensured his voice was firm and penetrated to all parts of the room. "Not guilty, my lord."

There were boos, but a few cheers came from the spectator's gallery, requiring Judge Hawkins to voice his disapproval. That surprised Keats. He'd figured everyone was keen to see him hang. Confounded, he lowered himself into the chair.

He made a study of the men who would hold his life in the balance. The jury was a mixed lot, both young and old. Only a few of them were staring up at him, the rest at the Crown Prosecutor, who cut a striking figure in his black robe and wig.

"You may proceed, Mr. Arnett," the judge commanded.

Arnett rose. "May it please you, my lord, members of the jury, I appear in this case with my learned assistant, Mr. Daniel Pryor, for the Prosecution. The Defence of Sergeant Jonathon Keats will be conducted by my learned colleagues Lord John Sagamor Wescomb and Mr. Herron Kingsbury."

"Just so," the judge replied, nodding his approval.

To Keats' relief, Wilfred Arnett was not as long-winded as most. As Arnett laid the case before the jurors, the summary leaned heavily on Keats' moral downfall, which led the prisoner to strangle Nicci Hallcox after what the prosecutor supposed was a night of unrestrained sexual congress.

The image made Keats queasy. He had never found Nicci of interest in that way. If anything, he'd always had the strong desire to boil his skin after coming in contact with her.

Arnett paused dramatically for emphasis. "We shall see that one of the motives for this horrendous crime lies within the victim herself."

Syphilis. Wescomb had said he'd hoped Arnett would go that way rather than toward blackmail. Keats wasn't sure if it would make any difference. From what he'd heard from his lordship, Home Office was applying pressure, insisting that certain topics were off limits during the trial. Wescomb had promised to work around those limitations as much as possible, but the blunt truth was that his barrister was already hobbled.

Much of the Crown's case hinged on the butler's testimony. Wescomb, in particular, was hoping to tear that to shreds during cross-examination. In the end, it might come down to the world learning about the existence of the Transitives or one detective-sergeant going to the gallows to preserve that secret.

That's no consolation.

Keats struggled to catalog every detail as Arnett continued, but his mind easily wandered. Who had been the killer? Was he in this very room, watching while gloating over his fortunate escape?

The first witness was called forward to the witness box. After the inspector held the Bible and swore the oath, Arnett began to build his case.

"Inspector Hulme, you are local inspector in "C" Division, are you not?"

"Yes, sir."

"Tell us your actions on the night of the crime."

"I was called to the Hallcox residence at Half Moon Street at approximately one in the morning on the fourteenth of October this year."

"What did you discover at that address, Inspector?"

"The deceased, Nicola Hallcox, lying on her bed."

"Who found the body?"

"Her lady's maid, Miss Ellis."

"At what time was the body discovered?"

"Approximately half past midnight."

"And the manner of death?"

"According to the post-mortem, Miss Hallcox was strangled with the cord from her dressing gown," Hulme replied.

"Was there anything else about the scene that you found unique?"

Keats set his jaw. He'd already heard the details from Wescomb. To look away might indicate to the jury that he was responsible for such a horror.

"She was…unclothed and her hands were placed on her breasts. Her legs were parted and—" Hulme halted abruptly, took a deep breath and then continued, "and a fireplace poker was lying on the bed, pointing toward her female regions."

There were gasps throughout the courtroom.

"What does it indicate to you, Inspector?"

"An extremely disturbed mind."

"Sexual deviancy, perhaps?" Arnett asked.

Wescomb rose. "Your lordship," he protested, "my learned colleague is leading the witness."

The judge nodded sagely. "Indeed you are, Mr. Arnett."

"As your lordship pleases," the prosecutor conceded.

"With due respect, your lordship," Wescomb continued, "unless Inspector Hulme is an expert in deviant sexual behavior, his opinion is hardly worthy of speculation."

"Certainly it could be argued that a police officer has daily contact with just such behavior," Arnett retorted.

"He well may come in contact with it," Justice Hawkins replied, "but that does not make him an expert. I am in the company of criminals every day, however I certainly wouldn't be inclined to consider myself an expert safecracker or forger." Justice Hawkins peered down at Hulme. "Confine yourself to the facts, Inspector."

"Yes, my lord," Hulme replied with a deferential nod.

Arnett smoothly transitioned to the next question. "Was there any sign of a struggle or disarray in the room?"

"None."

"What did that indicate to you?"

"That the victim knew her killer, and that he overpowered her before she could cry out."

"At what point did you summon Chief Inspector Fisher from Scotland Yard?"

"After I found the prisoner's calling card tucked underneath the deceased's jewelry box. I then spoke with the butler. He admitted that the prisoner had been the last to see his mistress alive."

Wescomb rose. "My lord, that is conjecture on the butler's part."

"The jury should make note of that fact." The judge gestured to the prosecutor. "Proceed, Mr. Arnett."

"Why did you feel the need to summon Chief Inspector Fisher? Have you not handled murder investigations in the past?"

"I have, sir," Hulme replied brusquely. "I thought it proper that the chief inspector be made aware that one of his sergeants might be involved in this matter."

"What did you do while you awaited his arrival?"

"I sent for the coroner, continued my inspection of the murder scene, and spoke with the witnesses."

"Ah, yes, the coroner. We'll get back to that. What did the butler," Arnett consulted a paper, "what did Mr. Landis tell you about the prisoner's *numerous* visits prior to Miss Hallcox's death?"

Wescomb shifted positions, indicating his displeasure.

Hulme flipped a page in his notebook. "Mr. Landis stated that the prisoner arrived at the house on the evening before the crime and then twice on the night Miss Hallcox was murdered. On that particular evening, the first visit was at quarter past eight. During that time, the prisoner had a verbal confrontation with the mistress of the house and left 'in a fine fury,' as Mr. Landis put it. The prisoner then returned at approximately quarter of eleven. He did not make his presence known, but ascended the stairs directly to Miss Hallcox's bedroom."

"When did the butler say he left?"

"Sometime before half past twelve, when the lady's maid went to check on her mistress."

"He did not see the prisoner depart?"

"Initially, he said he did. During later questioning he admitted he was otherwise engaged."

"Did you visit the prisoner's rooms?"

"Yes."

"Did you find anything of value there?"

"I found a set of lock picks."

"Are those standard issue for a detective-sergeant?" Arnett quizzed.

"Not that I am aware."

Keats perked up. The lock picks were a gift from the night he'd caught Fast Eddy Klein removing a king's ransom in diamonds from a Hebrew jeweler in Whitechapel. The criminal had promised to retire if Keats would let him go. Keats hadn't, but after Eddy finished his sentence, he'd delivered a new set of lock picks as a memento of his last caper, and even shown Keats how to use them. Last he'd heard, Eddy was in Paris, living a gentleman's life of leisure.

While I'm in the dock.

Realizing he'd been woolgathering, he pulled himself back to the present. Arnett had seated himself. Wescomb rose, adjusting his embroidered waistcoat. Keats felt his breath catch.

"Inspector Hulme, during your investigation did you discover anyone else besides the butler who witnessed the prisoner's arrival or departure from Miss Hallcox's home on the night of the murder?"

"No."

"Really? No jarvey or someone on the street, a neighbor perhaps?"

"None."

"Not even another member of the domestic staff?" Wescomb pressed, raising his voice in surprise.

"No."

"How remarkable. You would have thought someone would have seen the sergeant, admitted him to the house."

"None of the servants claim they did."

"I see. At any time did Chief Inspector Fisher interfere with your investigation?"

"Only in the matter of the coroner. He insisted I summon Dr. Bishop to conduct the post-mortem."

"Did he state his reasons?"

"No, he did not."

"Other than a preference for Dr. Bishop, was there any other interference?"

"No."

"What did Chief Inspector Fisher do when he realized that his sergeant might be involved in this case?"

"He immediately sent a constable to the prisoner's rooms, but the prisoner wasn't there."

"What were you doing while you were awaiting that report?"

"The chief inspector insisted we interview the butler and the other servants, yet again."

"What did you learn during this second interview?"

"It was at this time that Mr. Landis admitted that he had not seen the prisoner leave the house."

"Did you smell liquor on Mr. Landis' breath?"

"Yes. Quite a lot of it, actually."

Arnett rose. "My lord, certainly it could be argued that he sought the comfort of a stiff one to steady his nerves, given the brutal murder of his mistress."

"So it may be," Wescomb conceded graciously. He turned his attention back to the inspector. "I understand a collection of calling cards were found at the scene."

Hulme's face went ashen.

"My lord," Arnett began, issuing Justice Hawkins a concerned look.

"I shall confine my questions to the nature of the cards, not their owners, your lordship," Wescomb replied.

The justice eyed him. "Ensure that you do so."

Wescomb returned his attention to the inspector. "The calling cards. Who discovered those?"

"Dr. Reuben Bishop."

"Where were they found?"

Hulme looked uncomfortable. "They had been hidden in a false bottom of the deceased's jewelry case. I … did not think to look there."

"Didn't you have the maid verify if any of her mistress' jewelry had gone astray?"

There was a lengthy hesitation. "Ah, no."

"Why not?" Wescomb challenged. "Certainly you would wish to ascertain if the murder may have been committed during the course of a robbery?"

"I did not think a member of Scotland Yard would resort to petty thievery."

"And yet he may resort to murder?"

Hulme's jaw tightened.

Well played!

"Why do you think Miss Hallcox concealed the calling cards? Most of us are proud to display such items if they involved *important personages*. We even place them in plain view on our mantels so others may see who have visited us."

"Tread carefully, Lord Wescomb," Hawkins warned.

"I shall, my lord."

Hulme ran a finger under his collar. "The lady's maid said Miss Hallcox collected them from her… admirers," he replied, directing a worried look to the judge.

Wescomb flipped a page of notes. "Your report states there was a *stack of cards*. Just how many comprise a stack, Inspector?"

"In this case, forty-six."

Wescomb appeared shocked, though Keats knew his lordship was already aware of the number. "All men?" Another nod. "It would appear that the deceased was a very *social* lady, wouldn't you say?" There were titters in the crowd.

"I guess so."

"Perhaps any one of those men may have had reason to end her life. Did you interview *any* of these forty-six potential suspects?"

"No."

"Why not?"

"The butler said he saw the prisoner go up to his mistress' room. I thought it a waste of effort to interview those who had not been present in the house at the time of the murder."

"So you based that decision on the butler's testimony, testimony that changed in the course of two interrogations?" Wescomb asked.

"Yes."

Wescomb shifted to another paper. "Your report indicates that dates were inscribed on the back of these cards. What do you think those were about?"

"The maid said her mistress made note of when a gent came calling," Hulme replied.

"I see. Did some of the cards have more than one date?"

"Yes, some did."

"You state that you found Sergeant Keats' calling card, but not concealed like the others." Hulme nodded. "Were there any notations on his card?" his lordship quizzed.

"No. I don't think she had time to make the note."

"Or is it possible that his visit was of a different nature than her other callers?"

"Might have been," the inspector allowed.

"What steps did you take to verify Sergeant Keats' alibi?"

"I went to Whitechapel and interviewed some of the locals. I found a woman who had seen him earlier in the evening, before the murder. Crickland was her name."

"What else did you do?"

"I went find someone who had seen the prisoner or spoken with him in Ingatestone, where he claimed to be on the seventeenth of this month."

"Did you have any luck?"

"No."

"No one at all?"

"No," Hulme repeated, his eyes downcast.

You're lying.

"What about the sergeant's boots?" his lordship pressed. "According to his statement, he pawned them in Ingatestone to gain money to return to London."

"I talked to the pawnbroker. He said he never saw the prisoner." Hulme was still avoiding Wescomb's gaze.

"Did you talk to any of the other pawnbrokers?"

"I was told there weren't any. Ingatestone isn't a big town, like London."

"Yet, just yesterday Inspector Ramsey did find the sergeant's boots at the exact shop where he said he pawned them."

"Yes," Hulme mumbled.

"While in Ingatestone, did you go into the woods to try to locate the coffin in which Sergeant Keats was spirited away from London?"

"No. It's very dense in that area. It would be a worthless hunt."

"As a man's life is on the line, I would argue it would be a hunt worth pursuing," Wescomb chastised. "Did you at least attempt to verify if any coffins had gone missing the night of Miss Hallcox's murder?"

"None had."

"You spoke with the *all* coffin makers in Whitechapel?"

Hulme's face tightened. "Most of them."

"But not all?"

"No."

"That will be all, Inspector."

Keats let out a measured sigh. That had been brilliant. Wescomb had proved Hulme wasn't as thorough as one would expect. Though in principle he disliked such a tactic, undermining the jury's belief in the competence of the investigating officer was vital in this case.

Arnett rose. "I would like to ask a few follow-up questions, your lordship."

A nod from Hawkins.

"Inspector, why did you not bother to verify all aspects of the prisoner's alibi?"

"I know a good story when I see one," Hulme responded with a smirk. "When the Crickland woman couldn't remember when she saw him in Whitechapel, and no one else had spied him wandering around the streets, I decided it would be wasted effort to go into the middle of the forest hunting some phantom coffin."

"So, in essence, you applied your years of experience as a police officer and decided where best to utilize your energies in this investigation."

Hulme looked relieved at the barrister's explanation. "That's right."

"Is it usual for Scotland Yard to intervene in an active investigation?"

"Doesn't happen too often."

"So perhaps the Yard's involvement in this case had some other motive?"

Wescomb sprung to his feet. "I must protest! The motive is good police work, your lordship."

"Do you have a genuine question, Mr. Arnett?" Hawkins asked.

"No, your lordship. I no longer need to examine this witness."

Hulme dragged himself out of the witness box as if he were wearing Keats' chains. He looked up and their eyes met.

Why are you trying to kill me?

✦

CHAPTER EIGHTEEN

2057 A.D.
TEM Enterprises

The one called Morrisey didn't mind if she sat in the wooden building for hours at a time. In fact, he encouraged it. He'd brought her strange food: raw fish and rice and hot, fragrant teas. Some of it she had to eat with sticks and the cups didn't have handles. She decided she liked that.

Sometimes he would join her, but mostly he left her alone. To her delight, she'd discovered a pond behind the building. Fish lived there, pretty gold and white ones. He'd told her they were called koi. She'd watched them swim in lazy circles, going nowhere. They didn't seem to mind. She tried touching one, but it skidded away, splashing her.

When she grew bored with the fish, she'd watch the flat expanse of white sand in front of the pagoda. It still wasn't right. She'd called out to it a couple of times, asking it what was wrong. It didn't answer. When she'd asked the one called Ralph about that, he said he didn't understand. She decided not to mention it again.

Morrisey talked to her of healing. She listened, but it made little sense. It seemed to help him, though, so she let him talk. His voice was calming, unlike the other one.

Morrisey told her that Ralph was an old friend, though he didn't look very old to her. One time when Ralph was talking to her, she remembered a silver box that moved on wheels. She asked him about it. He said that was Sigmund, his DomoBot. She asked if this Sigmund could visit her instead. That had made the one called Ralph angry.

He was that way today, asking questions, telling her things, getting upset when she didn't remember what he'd just told her. She didn't want to know things until she asked. Then there seemed to be a way of storing the answer so it wouldn't get lost so easily.

"Let's try this again," Ralph began, his voice tight as he wiped his glasses on the end of his tee shirt in frustration. "Do you remember how we met?"

"No."

"Sure you do. We were in preschool together. I hit you and then you hit me back."

"Sounds good," she muttered.

He frowned. "Got us both in a lot of trouble." He replaced his glasses. "What about your parents? Do you remember them?"

The sadness almost choked her. Too much sand had fallen out her mind: she couldn't remember her own family.

"Go away," she ordered.

"What?" Ralph replied, caught off guard.

"Go away!"

"But I thought—"

"Just go away. You're not right for me. I can't think when you're here."

As he rose, she could see the hurt in his eyes.

"I'm not going to give up, Cyn. You can't stay this way forever."

"Why not?" she challenged, confused why he was so angry. Why did he care?

"Because you just can't."

She didn't bother to watch him walk away. It didn't matter. The image of the kitten came again, chasing after the string. She thought maybe that was her, trying to hook her claws into a piece of her old self so it wouldn't slip away.

The one called Morrisey appeared at the edge of the sand. He had someone with him, a man in a black suit. The one called Ralph had called him a spook. She didn't know what that meant, but he still made her nervous, like she'd done something wrong.

After some sharp conversation, the man removed his shoes and socks. His feet were white like the sand. Cynda giggled. Maybe he wasn't so scary after all.

He refused to sit on one of the pillows, so Morrisey settled himself and made the introductions. "Jacynda, this is Agent Klein. He knows you from before."

She angled her eyes upward at the looming figure. He didn't look happy.

"I'm here to find out what happened to you," he announced.

That again. "I'm not right. Someone did this to me."

"Who?"

She shrugged. Every now and then, she had the answer. Then it would disappear, circling away from her like one of the fish in the pond.

"What do you remember?" he asked.

"Nothing," she said. That wasn't quite right, but she wasn't sure she liked this man.

"Do you remember someone putting something against your head?"

"No." Maybe if she kept saying "no," he'd go away.

"Is there anything you do remember?"

"No." Morrisey gave her a curious look, but held his silence.

The one named Klein started peppering Morrisey with questions. All of them were about her.

The noise was getting to be too much. "Go away," Cynda commanded, pointing. "Talk about me over there."

A smirk appeared on Morrisey's face as he rose to his feet. "She has a point. Let's leave her to her thoughts."

"What thoughts? There's hardly anything left."

"What's left is hers, and we need to respect that."

As they walked across the sand, Morrisey turned and gave her a wink.

Hours later, after she had napped, the man named Morrisey returned carrying a tray of hot tea. He wasn't in his suit, but in loose clothes. Maybe he wasn't important here, but one of the inmates, like her.

"I'm sorry about Agent Klein," he told her. "He insisted on talking to you."

She sampled the tea. "I like this."

"It's Russian orange spice. Very pleasant." He took a sip and sighed in appreciation. "What have you been thinking about this afternoon?"

"Kittens."

"And string?"

She nodded and screwed up her face in thought. "Why does everyone want to know who made me like this?"

His face grew solemn. "Because it was a very wrong thing to do."

"Oh." She looked down. "I didn't tell the truth. I remember the fiery tube, the one that made my head hurt."

He looked very puzzled. "Why didn't you tell Klein that?"

"I don't know if he's right or not."

"But I am?"

Cynda thought about it, and then nodded.

He grinned. "I'm very pleased to hear that." Another sip of tea. "You're starting to remember. That's a good sign."

Cynda wasn't sure about that. It was hard to sort through the memories, know where they belonged, know if she could trust them.

"Do the…ah…" She worked on the name, but it wouldn't come. She pointed toward the roof. "Do they ever talk to you?"

"Oh, the dragons? No."

"They won't talk to me, either. I've tried."

"I'm sorry," he said. "Maybe one day." He took a long sip of tea and fell quiet.

"What is your name?"

"Morrisey," he replied.

"No. The other name. Don't you have one?"

He hesitated. "Theo. It means divine gift."

She rolled that around her mind for a while. She liked that. "Can I stay here tonight?"

"If you wish. I'll have more blankets brought to you. It can get quite chilly."

When next she looked over, he was gone.

She struggled and then pulled his name out of the void. "Theee…o."

He felt right, like the nice man in the old place, the one who had cried for her. His name was still missing, but she thought she remembered his face. Her shoulders sagged with the effort. Each day brought a little bit more, but not enough.

—

Over the top of the psychiatrist's bald head, Morrisey caught Fulham's eyes. His assistant shrugged, which told him he just couldn't chuck the fellow out the door. At least Jacynda wasn't around to hear all this, resting after the lengthy psychiatric exam she'd had to endure.

To his annoyance, Dr. Weber was still warming to his subject. "It is important that we treat her Adrenalin Reactive Disorder *now*, rather than letting it continue to worsen," he insisted. "If she recovers, she will be a more balanced individual, a productive member of society."

"She was already a productive member of society."

"No, she was a Time Rover. That profession is just a dumping ground for untreated Adrenalin Reactives because they can't get a job anywhere else."

Morrisey slowly counted to twenty. TPB's shill had been pushing for the treatment the moment he'd first arrived, even before he'd examined Jacynda. That smacked of someone else's agenda.

"She is already showing increasingly violent tendencies," Weber continued. "She threatened me during my interview."

"You were probably annoying her. She has a low threshold for irritating people." *No doubt, you sailed right past it.*

"I was merely asking her questions," he persisted.

Morrisey's eyes narrowed. "What if your ARD treatment makes her worse?"

"It won't. I've studied her case, and she's a good candidate. She should have been treated when it first surfaced at age seventeen."

"Why do you think she lost her memories?" Morrisey probed, wondering how he'd spin it.

"I believe it is a manifestation of accelerated Post Transfer Syndrome, accentuated by the *untreated* Adrenalin Reactive Disorder."

"I disagree. To that end, I refuse to allow the ARD treatment."

The shrink gave him a placid smile. "You have no legal right to withhold that treatment."

"Actually, I do. I've been appointed Miss Lassiter's legal guardian until such time as she returns to a full state of mental capacity and may determine her own medical care."

Weber's expression went dark. "What game are you playing?" he demanded.

"This is no game, Doctor. Unlike you, I know Miss Lassiter would refuse your medicine. She's always done so."

"And done herself irreparable harm in the process."

"That is your opinion," Morrisey countered, gesturing toward the door. "I don't think we need to speak about this any further."

"I'll be filing a challenge. In the meanwhile, I have been asked to follow her case by the Time Protocol Board. That is something your guardianship cannot override."

Morrisey's voice turned cold. "Then issue your reports as you see fit. However, if you attempt to treat her in any fashion without my approval, I'll see your license revoked."

"You are condemning her to a hideous life."

Morrisey drew a deep breath. "I accept that responsibility. Good day, Doctor." *And get the hell off my property.*

THE MOMENT THE door whooshed open, Jacynda peeked out from under the covers. She reminded Morrisey of a small child frightened by a thunderstorm.

"I don't like the bald man," she announced, wiggling around until she sat upright. "Tell him to go away."

"I don't like Dr. Weber either, but he will need to talk to you every now and then."

"Will you be there?" she asked.

Morrisey smiled reassuringly. "If you wish. He will not be allowed to treat you unless I approve."

"Will you?"

"No. You should heal on your own."

"Can I have one of those boxes?"

"What box?" Morrisey asked, puzzled.

"He touched it and it blinked, then it made a funny noise."

"Oh, a computer. Certainly. You can ask it questions, and it will give you answers."

She eyed him dubiously. "How do I know if the answers are right?"

He barely hid the smile. "That's for you to decide."

"Why is…" She worked on the name, her face contorting with the effort. He didn't hurry her. "Why is…" She mimed a long ponytail.

"Mr. Hamilton?" She didn't call him that. "Ralph?"

She nodded. "Why is Ralph mad at me?"

Oh dear. "He's not angry at you."

"Then why does he frown all the time?"

"He remembers the way you used to be, and he wants you to be that way again. He cares very much for you. That's why he's pushing so hard."

"You don't push."

"I know it's better not to."

She hopped out of bed, pulled on her sandals, then stopped at the door.

"Is the bald man gone?"

"For the time being."

"Good." She took a step forward, then turned back toward him. "Who was the man with the flower?"

Morrisey hesitated. It would be best that he not give her a name. She might accidentally tell the wrong person that Defoe had been in residence.

"He is a friend of mine," he replied.

"I don't remember his name." With that, she scooted out the door.

This time, Morrisey allowed the smile free rein.

But you remembered he wore a flower.

—

The following morning, Cynda found a box underneath the pagoda. It was low and black. She sat next to it for a long time, wondering why it wasn't making any noise. Finally, she touched it. There was a beep and an image flashed into the air above it, causing her to rear back in fright. When nothing else happened, she tapped one of the colorful keys projected onto the wooden platform. Another beep.

If all it did was beep, that wasn't going to help her. She grew restless. Perhaps she should go back to her room and stare at the line on the machine. It was all blue now. Morrisey had told her that was a good thing.

Instead, she concentrated on her name.

"Jacynda…Lassiter." She felt proud that she didn't have to look at the tattered piece of paper in her pocket anymore. Maybe if she said it enough times, it'd feel right.

"Query?" a melodic voice asked. It came from the box.

"What is a query?" she asked.

"A question, inquiry, or quiz," the box answered.

"Question." What kind of question should she ask? "Who is Jacynda Lassiter?"

"Jacynda Alice Lassiter, born 9 December 2028, second child and only daughter of Dr. Harvey Lassiter and Alice Lassiter, née Jenkins." The voice droned on, telling her of illnesses and education, of experiences and lovers she could not remember.

While the box spoke of someone named Christopher Stone, an image appeared on the screen. His face made her throat tighten and her chest ache. She had no idea why. By the time the voice ended, Cynda was in tears, floods of them washing down her face and tumbling onto her lap.

"Miss Lassiter?" She blinked to see the somber man standing near the edge of the sand. He looked worried. "What has upset you?"

She didn't respond immediately, wiping away the tears with the back of her fist. He stripped off his shoes with more haste than usual and then hurried across the sand. When he sat on the pillow next to her, he offered a comforting smile.

"If you want to talk about what has distressed you, I'd be happy to listen. If you prefer silence, I will respect that."

She sniffled. "I was asking the…" she pointed at the box, unsure of what to call it, "and it was telling me about Jacynda Lassiter."

"That's what made you sad?" he asked.

"Yes. I don't remember any of it." Another tear tracked down her cheek.

Her companion's stiff posture eased. "Right now, the computer remembers it all for you. In time, you won't need to ask it about Jacynda Lassiter because you'll know who you are."

Maybe he was right. The voice had gone on for a long time, telling of cities she'd visited and people she'd met. People she couldn't remember.

"You've been all over the world in so many centuries. I envy you that."

"What's envy?" she asked.

"It means I wish I could have had a life as rich as yours."

She pointed at the box. "Can I ask it another question?"

"Certainly."

"Who is Theo…" She frowned, the name gone.

"Morrisey," her companion completed with a chuckle.

The box answered instantly, spewing out information like a volcano. The voice kept going on and on.

"Too much," she said. The box kept talking. "Stop!" It didn't.

"End query," Morrisey ordered. The voice halted. He chuckled. "You were testing me, weren't you?"

She nodded. "I don't know who to trust."

"That is wise. Judge for yourself."

She gave him a sidelong glance. She'd expected him to say she should trust him.

As if he knew what she was thinking, he explained, "You are rebuilding your mind. It is up to you to form your own opinions. It would be too easy for me to tell you what to believe, but then you wouldn't be Jacynda Lassiter."

That seemed right. "Can I have some more of the spicy orange tea?"

"That can be arranged." He thought for a moment and then added, "I'll put something on the computer for you. It'll be like a game. You can look at a picture and match it with a word or a name."

"Will it be fun?" she asked, unsure.

"I'll make sure it is."

"No beeping. I don't like that."

"I'll see to it," he confirmed with a grin.

Cynda rose and walked out onto the sand. Dropping onto her knees, she began to trace in it with an index finger.

He knelt beside her. "Do you like drawing in the sand?"

She nodded. "It doesn't move. Maybe I can fix it."

"The sand doesn't move," he murmured to himself, as if that were a revelation. "And it should, at least for you."

"Why?"

"The sand seems to move for you because you're a time sensitive, you feel it passing more acutely than the rest of us. Or at least you did."

"Why?"

Morrisey looked chagrined. "It's very hard to explain, especially with the way you are right now."

He fetched the wooden stick. It was part of a pair he'd given her to eat the strange food that he said would help heal her brain.

"Maybe this will work better."

Holding it in her hand, she began to draw. Nothing special at first, just lines. If something it wasn't right, she smoothed it over with the palm of her hand. Then she jammed the stick into the sand and began to scoop the white particles into big mounds. She could make anything she wanted and if wasn't right, she could do it again.

When she looked up, Morrisey was gone. Sitting on the platform was a teapot and a cup. She would stay and drink the tea until the sun went away. Maybe the dragons would crawl down from their perches and write notes to each other in the glowing letters on the box that beeped.

Ralph Hamilton glared at him from behind those round glasses of his. Morrisey prepared himself for the barrage: Fulham had already warned him that Miss Lassiter's closest friend was not dealing well with her diagnosis.

"She refuses to talk to me. Is that your doing?" Hamilton demanded.

"No. It's her decision."

The man slumped a bit, as if he'd expected another answer. "She will be okay, won't she? Like she used to be?"

"She'll never be the same woman we knew."

"She has to be," Hamilton protested.

Morrisey gave him a sharp look. "Don't assume that different is worse."

"She was different enough to start with," the man shot back.

"Yes, and now she'll be different in a new way. Perhaps it will be to her advantage."

"I hear you're ignoring TPB's psychiatrist and won't let her take the ARD meds."

"He is just following standard procedure, and we both know that Miss Lassiter is anything but off-the-rack. He is discounting the strongest element in our favor."

"Which is?" his employee asked skeptically.

"Her inner fortitude. She's not going to give in. That's not her style."

"What if she doesn't find her way back from whatever happy place her brain went? What then?"

"I will ensure that she is in a safe environment, free of financial concerns for the remainder of her days."

Hamilton shook his head. "Spending the rest of her life building sand castles?" he murmured. "That's just not Cynda."

Morrisey couldn't help but smile. "Which is why, Mr. Hamilton, I still have hope."

CHAPTER NINETEEN

Wednesday, 31 October 1888
Old Bailey (Central Criminal Courts)

The chief inspector was next in the witness box. Keats bit the inside of his lip, drawing blood. This was going to be brutal.

"Chief Inspector Fisher, you are with Special Branch, is that not correct?" Arnett opened.

"Yes, I am."

"And the prisoner is your subordinate?"

"Yes, Detective-Sergeant Keats has been with the Yard since January of last year."

"How has he performed in his duties?"

"With excellence. He is one of my top men."

Which wasn't what you said a few days ago.

"In the early morning of the fourteenth of October you received a summons from Inspector Hulme. What did you do when you arrived at the Hallcox residence?"

"I spoke with Hulme, and at that point I assumed command of the investigation," Fisher replied evenly.

"Is that usual procedure?"

"Not always."

"What led you to that decision?"

"The sensitivity of the situation. If indeed Sergeant Keats were responsible for Miss Hallcox's death, then it was paramount that the investigation be conducted as impartially as possible."

"Why do you think you would be more impartial than Hulme?"

An excellent question. Keats leaned forward, curious to hear the response.

"At the time I felt it was the wisest move," Fisher replied.

"And yet, Chief Inspector, you promptly altered department policy and summoned Dr. Reuben Bishop to the scene. Why?"

"Dr. Bishop has an excellent reputation, and I felt I wanted all avenues pursued in this case."

"You have had difficulties with the Home Office coroners in the past?"

"No. I just felt Dr. Bishop would be a better choice."

"Why?"

"He does not confine himself solely to examining the body. He takes into account the scene of the crime and other minutiae that are often overlooked."

"Did you not summon Dr. Bishop in the matter of a death on the Friday evening before the Hallcox murder?"

"Yes."

"So you were aware that Dr. Montrose had taken up work with Dr. Bishop?"

"I was not aware that Montrose was working with Bishop on a *regular* basis."

"But you were aware that Dr. Montrose and the prisoner were friends?"

"Yes," Fisher conceded.

"How did Dr. Montrose react when he learned his best friend was the prime suspect?"

"With deep shock."

"Was he so shocked that he might have been tempted to alter the evidence in favor of the prisoner?"

Wescomb stood. "I must object, your lordship. The witness could not possibly have known Dr. Montrose's intentions at that time."

"I agree with the defence's objection," Justice Hawkins said.

"As your lord pleases," Arnett said smoothly.

"Chief Inspector," Justice Hawkins inquired, "is it not possible that Dr. Montrose might have overheard the prisoner's name mentioned by one of the constables, or a bystander perhaps?"

"I do not believe so, your lordship. I was very particular as to who knew the truth of the matter."

Hawkins nodded. "What was Montrose's reaction upon learning the news?"

"As would be expected, the doctor was devastated, to say the very least. I sincerely believe that neither Montrose nor Dr. Bishop were aware my sergeant was the suspect until *after* the post-mortem had been completed."

Hawkins nodded again. "You may proceed, Mr. Arnett."

The prosecutor began anew. "In the past, has the prisoner shown a propensity toward women of ill repute?"

"Not to my knowledge," Fisher replied evenly.

"No need to warn him about such behavior?"

"No. By all accounts, he is a sober and well-mannered gentleman."

"Who gives money to prostitutes out of the kindness of his heart?"

"Yes. It is a Christian act, after all."

"I have no other questions."

Wescomb rose. "Chief Inspector Fisher, why did you assign Inspector Ramsey to investigate the sergeant's alibi?"

"I felt the reputation of Scotland Yard was at stake, and I wanted no stone left unturned."

"And it was Ramsey who found the sergeant's boots, proving he was in Ingatestone?"

"Yes."

"Could it be said that the inspector is partial to Sergeant Keats in any manner, perhaps inclined to alter evidence in his favor?"

Fisher shook his head. "No, just the opposite, in fact. The inspector is not fond of the sergeant, and the feeling is quite mutual. That's why I assigned him the task."

Good old Ram. As thickheaded as any you might find.

"At the beginning of this month, Sergeant Keats attempted to arrest Desmond Flaherty and a number of other anarchists. Was he wounded in that action?"

"Yes, quite seriously."

"Did he receive a commendation?"

"Yes, one for bravery."

"That will be all, Chief Inspector."

Fisher looked up at Keats and then returned to his seat.

That went better than I hoped.

There was a brief pause and then Dr. Reuben Bishop took his place in the witness box. Keats leaned forward, keen to hear Bishop's testimony. After a brief explanation of the doctor's credentials, Arnett went to work.

"During the post-mortem, did you note any appearance of violation?" he asked.

"None."

"Was there evidence of sexual congress?"

"Yes."

"The cause of death?"

"Death was caused by asphyxiation secondary to strangulation."

"What was the murder weapon?"

"The sash from her dressing gown being the weapon. The victim was killed a few feet away from the bed. The murderer stood behind her and tightened the sash until life was extinct."

"How did you determine that location?"

"There was urine in the carpet, which is consistent with the bladder sphincter relaxing upon death."

"At approximately what time do you believe she was killed?"

"Somewhere between the hours of nine and quarter past midnight, given the remains of the meal in her stomach and the lack of rigor mortis."

"Were there any other medical findings, Doctor?"

Bishop's moustache twitched. "Miss Hallcox suffered from syphilitic infection."

Arnett nodded. "Was there any external evidence of this infection?"

"No. It was beyond that stage."

"So one of her *admirers* would not know that he was being exposed to the disease?"

"No."

"I would suspect that it would come as a considerable shock to learn the truth."

"Yes," Reuben replied cautiously, "though he would not have learned of it for at least ten days at the earliest, usually three weeks."

"How long would you say that Miss Hallcox had had this disease?"

"It was in the latter stages. We found evidence that the disease had progressed to her brain."

"Then her prognosis was grave?"

"Very likely."

"And anyone who was with her?"

"It would depend on whether or not they contracted the disease."

Keats gut tightened. *Where was this going?*

"That night, were you aware that your assistant, Dr. Montrose, is a close friend of the prisoner?"

"I was aware that he knew Sergeant Keats. That, however, was not germane to my investigation. I am solely interested in physical evidence."

"How admirable. Who summoned you to this investigation?"

"Chief Inspector Fisher."

"Why not the Home Office coroner?"

"I do not know. I was summoned, and I performed my duties as required by law."

"Were either you or Dr. Montrose left alone with the evidence at any time during the investigation?"

Reuben's eyes narrowed. "No. We conducted the post-mortem together. We delivered the findings to Scotland Yard *together*."

"No further questions."

Wescomb rose. "Dr. Bishop, how long have you been a forensic pathologist?"

"Just about seven years."

"How many cases have you handled?"

"I believe it stands at somewhere near sixty."

"Have you ever compromised evidence either in favor of the prosecution or the defence?"

"Certainly not!"

"I didn't think so. When did you learn that Sergeant Keats was a suspect in the Hallcox murder?"

"The following morning, when we delivered the post-mortem findings to Scotland Yard."

"As to those hairs you found in Miss Hallcox's bed, did you compare them to a sample taken from Sergeant Keats?"

"Yes. A sample was obtained from the hairbrush in his rooms."

"Did any of them match as to color?"

"No, none of them matched any of the four types found in the sheets."

"Four? I thought there were only three."

"The fourth sample belonged to Miss Hallcox."

"I see. What of any of the household staff?"

"The hairs match none of Miss Hallcox's domestic staff."

"That will be all, Doctor."

—

"It's your choice, guv," the man offered.

As Clancy Moran saw it, it wasn't really a choice, not with a knife pointing at his belly.

"What's the old fox want with me?" he asked, trying to buy time.

"To talk," was the quick reply. There were four men around him, counting the one with the blade. He could start a brawl, but they'd end it.

"Flaherty never wants to talk to nobody. He just cuts 'em up. Like Johnny Ahearn."

The knife wielder's eyes narrowed. "Well then, looks like you're the next up, don't it?"

Clancy tried to keep his muscles loose as he descended into the cellar beneath a chandlery. There'd be too many of Flaherty's men around to escape, but at least he'd have the chance to snap the bastard's neck before they stopped him. He chuckled at the thought, which earned him a baffled look from his escort. It was probably righteous he'd not received the sergeant's award money. It didn't look like it would have done him much good anyway.

"Knife," the man demanded, putting out his hand. Clancy dug it out and dropped it into the outstretched palm. "Now the one in your boot." Grudgingly, he obeyed.

The door creaked open at the bottom of the stairs and he was pushed through. As his eyes adjusted to the candlelight, his hope surged. There was only one man inside the room—the man he'd vowed to kill.

"Evenin', Moran." Flaherty gestured toward a barrel. "Rest yer feet. We need to talk."

"I don't talk to butchers."

The blade appeared in Flaherty's hand as if by magic. "And I don't talk to fools. So what's it gonna be?"

Clancy squared himself, ready for a fight. "Why'd ya do it? Johnny always watched yer back. Ya had no right to cut him like that."

"I didn't."

"Yer lyin'. I heard—"

"Ya heard wrong," Flaherty insisted.

"Why should I believe ya?"

"Because Johnny was workin' for me. He was tryin' to find my daughter." Clancy rocked back. "So the rozzer had it right."

"The little sergeant?"

"Yeah."

"One of my men saw ya at the Spread Eagle. He said the two of ya were arguin' over somethin.'"

"I was tryin' to stop him from goin' to Whitechapel. Figured he'd get nicked."

"He didn't do it, ya know," Flaherty admitted. "He was in that alley with me."

"Then why's the wind blowin' toward the gallows?"

Flaherty's voice turned bitter. "Why not? They'll hang anyone they please if it serves them."

"Still, he's a rozzer. A fair one, and there ain't too many of those."

"Best we don't argue that one."

"So why am I here?"

"It's plain we don't like each other much. Too many cocks in the barnyard, right?" Flaherty gave a low chuckle. "We got different ideas of how to free Ireland from her shackles. But right now, none of that matters. I have to find Fiona, and I need yer help."

Clancy knew what it took for this man to admit that. They'd been rivals since the moment they'd met, each trying to rally men to the cause in their own way. And now…

He sat on the barrel, letting the tension ebb. "When did she go missin'?"

"Right after I stole those explosives," Flaherty replied, his knife vanishing into a coat pocket. "She was workin' for Effington." He spat on the floor. "Somehow she was found out."

Clancy spat as well. "He's rottin' in hell. I saw what he did to that watchman."

"It wasn't him that took Fee, though. It was one of *the others*."

The skin on the back of Clancy's neck prickled. "Ya mean…"

A single nod. "I know ya cared for Johnny. So did I, and I want the man who killed him. I figure if we find him, we'll find Fee."

"What about the explosives?" Clancy hedged.

"None of yer worry."

"And the rozzer?"

"What about him? We can't do nothin' for him now."

"Maybe not." Clancy rose from the barrel. "I'll do what I can for ya, but after we find yer daughter, I'll not work with ya again."

"Didn't figure ya would."

———

2057 A.D.

TEM Enterprises

As he'd promised, Morrisey made her a game. When she touched the hovering picture above the black box, a question would appear.

Is it a kitten, a shoe, or a horse?

Cynda smiled. This one was easy.

"Kitten," she said. A chime rang. She'd gotten that one right.

Another picture. "Horse." Chime. Another picture. She had no idea. A sad sound came from the machine. That happened two more times and then she stomped off in a huff to play with the fish. When she grew bored, she came back and started over. She got two more of the images right this time.

To her delight, music came out of the box and a tiny dragon sailed across the screen, belching fire as it flew up and perched on top of a golden pagoda. It winked at her, curled up, and took a nap. She started all over again. Each time she got the proper number of words right, the dragon grew a bit bigger.

When she grew tired of the game, she headed for the sand. Dropping to her knees, she started moving it around, trying to decide what she wanted to build.

Then he came, the bald man called Weber. He started asking silly questions. She glared, but he didn't leave. Even the one named Ralph knew better than that.

"Why are you doing that?" Weber asked, typing his notes into his machine again.

"Because it's fun," she replied, pushing sand around.

"Why do you think that?"

She frowned. "Because it is."

Cynda scooped a huge handful and then formed one of the four towers, adding the little impressions at the top with her pinkie. She tried to remember what they were called, but couldn't come up with the word. She just knew they had to be there.

"What are these called?" she asked, pointing at one of them.

"I have no idea."

Then go away. She created the second tower, repeating the little impressions.

"Miss Lassiter?"

"What?" she grumbled.

"You are too ill to be here. You need treatment. You're not going to get better building castles in the sand. "

Castle? She smiled. *So that's what it is.*

She started work on the third tower. There was another series of beeps from the bald man's machine, then he walked off.

Good.

She eyed the thing she'd been building. Castle. "Still not right." She needed one of those water things that went around the outside. She hiked to the black box and asked the question.

"Water thing. Around a … a … castle. What is it?"

"Moat," it replied.

That was it. She needed a moat.

"Miss Lassiter?" Morrisey was on the walkway. She could tell by his face that something wasn't right. He removed his shoes and joined her, kneeling in the sand.

"Very nice," he remarked, his voice even softer than usual.

"I like it." She pointed up at the pagoda's roof. "I built it for them."

"That's kind of you."

She stared at him. "What's wrong?"

"A judge has decided that I do not have the right to keep you from receiving treatment for your Adrenalin Reactive Disorder."

"What's Adren…"

"It means you have a tendency to be more violent than the rest of us."

"I haven't hurt anyone," she told him. At least not that she could remember.

"No, you haven't, but they think you might. The judge is allowing you to stay here, but he did order you to receive the treatment." He looked away. "I'm so very sorry."

Cynda wasn't sure what it all meant, but it seemed to hurt him. The lines on his face were deeper now.

She panicked. "Will it make me worse?"

"I don't know."

That was honest. "If it does, I won't do it anymore." She pointed. "Do you think I should have another...ah....ah...mmm...water thing over here?"

The question pulled him out of his dark thoughts. "Yes, I think you do. The castles I've seen had moats on most of the exposed sides."

Moat. She kept forgetting that word. "You've seen them for real?" she asked in wonder.

"Yes. So have you, or you wouldn't have made this so accurately."

"Maybe I have. I just don't remember." She pointed at the top of the turret. "What are these called?"

"Crenellations. They allow an archer to fire down upon an enemy."

"What's an archer?"

"Someone with a bow and arrow."

"Do you know everything?" she asked, cocking her head.

"No, unfortunately I don't." He sighed and rose. "I will let them know you will accept the treatment."

"Only if I can stay here," she insisted.

A nod. He plodded off, shoulders bent under some invisible weight.

CHAPTER TWENTY

Thursday, 1 November 1888
Scotland Yard

Fisher looked up as the door opened. "Thank you for coming in early, Inspector." Ramsey heaved his bulk into the chair and then yawned.

"What's going on, sir?"

"In a moment. First, what do you think of the trial so far?" Fisher quizzed.

"Well, if I ever need a barrister, Wescomb's the man. He's sharp and he knows how to play to the jury."

"True." Fisher watched his subordinate shift his weight in the chair for the third time. "What's troubling you?"

"To be blunt, sir, Inspector Hulme. He's not doing a proper job of this. He didn't seem to care a lick when I told him about the boots. It's like it didn't matter at all."

"I agree, it's quite odd," Fisher replied.

"It's more than odd, sir. Anderson and I talked to every single bloody coffin maker in Whitechapel. Only one said Hulme had been to see him. From what I hear, he spent his time in the pub in Ingatestone rather than conducting his investigation."

Fisher frowned. "He's had a tolerably good record up to this point. Nothing outstanding, mind you, but solid work."

"I've heard the same," Ramsey concurred. "I keep asking myself why he'd bugger this up so badly. Hulme could look right smart in your eyes, maybe land a job here in the Yard. Instead, he's made a royal cock-up of it."

Fisher opened a desk drawer and extracted a sheet of paper. "I suspect it might have something to do with this." He handed over the sheet. "This is the list of men who frequented Miss Hallcox's bed. They came off the calling cards found in her room."

Ramsey skimmed the names. "Good God, there's enough bluebloods here to start your own country."

"Now you know the sort of pressure that is being applied, not only to Wescomb and Arnett, but perhaps to Hulme."

Ramsey's eyes raised, then he frowned. "Why not us?"

Fisher stroked his moustache. "That's why I called you in. I was summoned to Warren's office last night. A complaint has been lodged at the highest level. He's not happy about it either, truth be told."

"What sort of complaint?"

"About your sterling work on behalf of the sergeant. I have been instructed that there is to be no further effort on any matter related to the Hallcox case. It is Hulme's kettle of fish, so I've been told."

Ramsey glowered. "So let me make sure I've got this." He paused, his face turning ruddy. "You're saying that some posh gent who doesn't know his arse from his ears is telling me not to do my damned job?"

"That's pretty much it."

Ramsey dropped the list on the desk and spread his hands. "Why should I fight them? I've got the best pony in the race, don't I? I play along, Keats'll hang, and I'll be sitting pretty, won't I? He'll be out of the way and someday your desk will be mine, along with the title and the pay packet."

His face went dark as he leaned over and jammed a thick finger at his superior. "No one—not Hulme, Warren or the Queen herself—tells me not to be a copper. If I have to do this under the table, then I will. You understand me?"

Fisher blinked rapidly, unaccustomed to Ramsey's rebellious streak. "As far as I am concerned, Inspector, you are pursuing Desmond Flaherty and the explosives. I will expect your reports to reflect that, no matter your *actual* activities."

Ramsey smiled grimly. "I knew you'd see it my way, sir."

"Please take care, Martin. Your future at the Yard is at stake."

Ramsey's fury dampened. "I know, sir. If Warren's pulling back on your reins, I wonder how high this goes."

Fisher tapped the list where it sat on his desk. "Assume it goes all the way to the top."

—

Keats studied the man who had put him in the dock. There wasn't much to be said about Nicci's butler: middle-aged, eyes glassy, hands with a fine tremor. An alcoholic devoted to his debauched mistress. He might feel sympathy for the fellow if the tables had been turned.

Arnett started right in. "Mr. Landis, how long had you been in the employ of Miss Hallcox?"

"Um, ah, a little over a year, sir," Landis replied, his voice like gravel.

"Enjoyed your service, did you?"

"It had its good points," the butler allowed.

Her liquor cabinet, for one.

"Was she a fair employer?"

"Yes, as they go."

"Paid you well?" Arnett asked.

"Yes."

"As Lord Wescomb has pointed out, apparently she was very *social*."

The butler's face turned crimson. "Yes," he affirmed tersely. Keats leaned forward in the dock, watching the man intently.

"The Friday evening before her murder, Miss Hallcox hosted a party."

The butler shifted his position in the witness box, uncomfortable. "Yes."

"What was the nature of that soiree?"

"Umm ... a costume party, sir."

"Everyone was in costume?"

"Yes."

Costume? Hardly. That's not the way Keats remembered it. Dryads and queens, satyrs and other mythological beasts all cheerfully ravaging each other in a haze of opium and too much alcohol. It was a nightmare he would never forget.

"Was the prisoner in costume as well?"

"Ah, no. Neither he nor his female companion."

"Female companion?" Arnett quizzed, feigning surprise. "What was her name?"

"She didn't give it out."

"Tell us what happened that night when the prisoner arrived."

"He acted in a belligerent fashion, demanding to see my mistress."

"What did you do?"

"I asked her if she was willing to receive him. My mistress agreed. They spoke for a few minutes, and then he left."

"And his companion?"

"She left with him."

"Let's move ahead to the night of the murder. You said the prisoner visited earlier in the evening. How long did he stay?"

"Only a few minutes."

"How many? Two, five, ten?"

"Five, if that. He was out of there like a shot, and very angry."

"Ah, yes, in your statement you indicate he left in a *fine fury*. Did he say anything?"

The butler glowered in Keats' direction. "He said my mistress was an abomination, and that the Devil would claim her soul someday."

Oh, Lord. Trust the fool to remember every word.

"How dramatic," Arnett remarked. "Did that sound like a threat to you, Mr. Landis?"

"It did."

Before Wescomb could object, the Crown Prosecutor continued, "During his second visit that very evening, you stated the prisoner entered the house without your knowledge. Was the front door left unbolted?"

"No."

"Did the sergeant have a key?"

"Not likely."

"Did your mistress let him in?"

"My mistress did not greet guests at the door," the butler replied tartly.

Arnett's eyebrow went up. "Then how did he get inside the house? That is a puzzle, isn't it?"

"Yes, sir."

The lock picks? Surely, Arnett wouldn't dare suggest he'd broken into the house like a common criminal?

The Crown Prosecutor gave pleased nod. "Thank you, sir. That will be all."

Wescomb rose. "Mr. Landis, how long have you been a butler?"

"Five years."

"How many positions have you held during that time?"

Landis instantly went crimson and tugged at his collar. "Six."

"Why so many? Better opportunities?"

"Yes," he responded quickly.

"Your previous positions have been terminated because of your fondness for drink, is that not correct?"

"One or two."

"I have letters from each of your former employers, and they say—"

"All right, all of them."

"Were you drinking before your mistress' body was discovered?"

"I might have had a drop."

"Of course. On the night of the party, you state that Sergeant Keats acted in a belligerent fashion. Could you explain further?"

"He arrived without an invitation and insisted he had to speak to my mistress. When I said she was willing to meet with him, he demanded to know if there was a party in progress."

"Why?"

"Said he didn't want to be there if there was."

"Now that's singular. Most of us like a good knees-up." Chuckles in the room. "Why would Sergeant Keats not want to attend Miss Hallcox's soiree?"

"I don't know," Landis replied, his fingers drumming nervously in his lap.

"What was the nature of this ... *gathering?*"

The butler's eyes widened at the word. It told him Wescomb knew precisely the nature of that evening. "It was ..."

"Go on."

"It was a ..." He coughed, a haunted expression spreading across his face.

"We are waiting, Mr. Landis," Wescomb prodded. No reply. "Perhaps I shall assist. Was this a debauchery, sir?"

Landis nodded stiffly as murmurs spread through the courtroom.

"How many were present?" Wescomb quizzed.

"About thirty or so."

"Is that the usual number for one of Miss Hallcox's *parties?*"

"About. Sometimes it was more, others less."

"Were these participants above the age of consent?" Wescomb asked, his voice suddenly brittle. A collective gasp came from the audience at the implication.

"Of course," the butler replied swiftly.

"Well, at least that's a relief. You said Sergeant Keats emphatically stated he did not want to be at one of these events. Had he been to one before?"

Keats' heart double beat. It was fortunate that Nicci burned through servants as fast as she did lovers, or someone might have remembered him from all those years ago, *en mirage* or not.

"Not that I know of," the butler replied.

Keats exhaled silently.

"Still, it sounds as if Sergeant Keats was aware of your mistress' reputation and had no desire to be tainted by it."

Excellent!

"I object, my lord," Arnett said, rising. "He's leading the witness."

"I agree," the judge ruled.

"I shall take more care in future, my lord," Wescomb replied politely. He turned his attention to the witness once again. "What was the sergeant's reaction when you ushered them into the room where this orgy was unfolding?"

"He was very angry. He began to look for a way out. He seemed very worried about the young lady who was with him."

"I can imagine. Your mistress spoke with them?" A nod. "Did you overhear their conversation?" Another nod. "Please tell us what it entailed."

"My mistress was upset that he wanted to ask her questions instead of participating."

"So he was on official business?"

"I can't say that for sure. I didn't hear much beyond that. I was called away to refresh the drinks."

"Ah yes, I would guess that bacchanals are thirsty work." There were chortles in the courtroom, earning Wescomb a scowl from Justice Hawkins. "How soon did they leave?"

"Almost immediately."

"They did not participate in any manner?"

"No."

"Let's step forward to Saturday, the day of the murder. Please give us an account of who visited your mistress in the last…oh, twelve hours before her death."

The butler paled. "But—"

"No need to reveal his name, Mr. Landis."

"Her first visitor was…a lord at about half past three."

"An elderly lord in his late eighties, was he not?" Wescomb asked.

"Yes."

Turning toward the gallery, Wescomb delivered a knowing smile. "Such stamina at his age. I tip my hat to the man."

Keats joined in the light laughter that rippled through the crowd. It was a masterful moment.

"Who else paid calls on Miss Hallcox that day?" Wescomb asked, not missing a beat.

"A banker at half past five, and then the sergeant."

"Was Sergeant Keats expected that evening?"

"My mistress did send him a note."

"When?"

"At approximately six."

"Filling in her social schedule, was she?"

"I don't think so, sir. She usually didn't send her gents any letters."

"Then how did she arrange these assignations?"

"Spoke with them directly."

"So the note to Sergeant Keats was something unusual?"

"Yes."

"Did you see what it contained?"

"No."

"Come now, we all know that domestic staff peek at their employer's correspondence."

"I didn't. Neither did Tilly."

"That's Miss Ellis, the lady's maid?" A nod. "Was that Saturday a particularly busy day for Miss Hallcox?"

"A bit busier than normal, sir."

"What color is the elderly lord's hair?"

Landis delivered a startled look. "Silver-white."

"What about the banker?"

"Brown."

"And Sergeant Keats?"

Landis stared up at the dock. "Dark brown, I'd say."

"Did any of the men who visited your mistress on that day have black hair? Or, perhaps, any of the servants?"

"No."

"To your knowledge, had Sergeant Keats ever visited Miss Hallcox's bedroom before?"

Landis stiffened. "Not that I am aware."

"Then how did he know where it was?"

"I can't say, my lord. Perhaps the mistress told him."

Wescomb shifted closer to the man. "I visited Miss Hallcox's residence and I inspected that set of stairs that lead to the second floor and your mistress' bedroom. The only vantage point from which you might have seen the killer was from the side hall. Is that where you were?"

"Yes, sir."

"By the time someone is climbing the stairs, only his back is visible. How can you account for your initial testimony to the police that you saw the sergeant's face?"

"Ah, I…"

"Mr. Landis?" Wescomb prodded.

"I thought I saw him."

"Mr. Landis, I remind you that you are under oath."

"Ah…" The butler went pale. He swallowed heavily as his eyes tracked around the room. "I—"

"Mr. Landis, please answer the question," the judge interceded.

"I didn't see his face, only the back of him."

"Was he wearing his hat and coat?" Wescomb asked.

"Yes. I called out to him, but he ignored me."

"So all you saw was the back of a man clad in his outer garments climbing the stairs. Why did you think it was Sergeant Keats?"

"He was short."

"So are a lot of men in London, Mr. Landis. In fact, in this courtroom there are a number of men of *reduced* stature." Wescomb tugged on his waistcoat. "One final question, Mr. Landis. What was it that kept you so *engaged* that you missed the killer's departure?"

The butler's face flushed. "I was…instructing the downstairs maid in domestic matters."

"Domestic matters?" he asked in a jovial tone. "I think not, Mr. Landis." He swung away from the man and addressed the courtroom. "On the contrary, is it not true that while your mistress was suffering her death agonies, you were engaged in sexual liberties with the maid?"

"I didn't know!" the man howled. "God, I didn't know he would kill her!"

"No, you didn't, just as you cannot be sure that it was Sergeant Keats upstairs with your mistress." A palpable pause. "I have no further questions."

Arnett rose. "Has someone put pressure upon you to change your original testimony?"

"No, sir."

"Then why did you say you saw Sergeant Keats' face when you were questioned by the police?"

"It was him. It had to be! No one else would hurt her."

So you'd like to believe.

"No further questions, my lord."

The next witness stood rigidly in the witness box, her eyes darting nervously eyeing the people around the room. When she was handed the Bible, she swore the oath in a quaking voice.

Arnett rose. "Is Annie Crickland your real name?"

"Yes," she replied, "though I'm called Red Annie on account of my cheeks."

"Where in Whitechapel do you live, madam?"

"Oh, here and there, wherever I can find a place to lay my head."

"No fixed abode then?"

"No, sir," she mumbled, looking down.

"Do you frequent the doss houses?"

"If'n I have the money, sir. They're better'n the streets. Rozzers won't let you sleep if you're out there."

How true. As a constable, Keats had been ordered to keep the poor wretches on the move all night. It was no wonder they were exhausted and couldn't work the next day. He'd skirted the rule every chance he got.

"On the evening of the thirteenth of October, did you encounter the prisoner at any time?"

"Yes, sir, near the White Hart."

"That's on Whitechapel High Street, is it not?"

"Yes."

"What were you doing in that area?"

Keats ground his teeth. Arnett was going to make this hard for Annie, and the woman didn't deserve it.

"I was having a wee nip to keep the cold away," she told him, raising her chin in defiance.

"Even though the Whitechapel murderer is still at large?"

She shuddered at the mention of the Ripper. "Yes, sir."

"What did the prisoner say to you?"

"He wanted me to go down an alley with him."

Keats groaned to himself.

"For illicit purposes?" Arnett asked, pouncing on her response.

Wescomb was up again. "Leading the witness, your lordship."

"I agree. Do watch that, will you?" Hawkins requested.

"As your lordship pleases," the prosecutor replied smoothly. "What was the prisoner's purpose with you, Miss Crickland?"

"He wanted to ask me questions."

"Why not do that on the street, in plain view?"

"Not safe that way," Annie replied. "Some folks don't look kindly if you talk to the rozzers."

"What did he ask you?"

"If I knew anything about that Irishman and all that gunpowder he's got."

The spectators started murmuring amongst themselves and it took Hawkins to bring the room to order. Keats chuckled to himself. Someone hadn't bothered to tell Annie that the explosives were not to be mentioned.

"Mr. Arnett, this is your first warning," a glaring Hawkins announced.

"Yes, my lord." Arnett turned his attention to Annie, who seemed confused at all the fuss. "Confining your answers to those regarding the prisoner *only*, has he at any time offered you money in exchange for certain favors?"

Annie frowned. From Keats' experience, she didn't like toffs much, especially ones who talked down to her.

"If you mean did he go for an *upright*, no. He's not that way."

There was tittering in the court. Keats fought to keep the smirk off his face.

"Yet he asked you to go down an alley with him."

"I already told you why he did that."

"Did he give you money?"

"Yes."

"How much?"

"A shillin'. It got me a bed for a few nights."

"He paid you a shilling for information? That's quite generous. Are you sure it was only that?"

"Yes."

"You have been arrested," Arnett said, leafing through his notes, "three times for solicitation and once for stealing a loaf of bread."

"I have, sir."

"So you admit to being a woman on the wrong side of the law?"

Annie's chin raised again, fire in her eyes. "If it comes to starvin' or goin' with a punter, I'll do what I must to eat."

"So offering your *services* to a police officer would allow you a chance to ply your trade unhindered, am I right?"

"No, it's not like that. The rozzers don't do that."

"Why not? Who would you complain to?" Arnett pressed.

"They don't do that," Annie repeated.

"So you are saying that the prisoner has never once offered to pay you for sexual favors or to trade those favors for a blind eye?"

Keats' gut knotted. *He's making me sound like a moral degenerate.*

"He's not like that!" the witness retorted, glaring at the barrister. "Never has been."

That's it Annie! Give him one on the shins.

"Have you heard that he's ever made such an offer to any of the other unfortunates?"

"No," Annie replied. "He's just good with us. He gives us money, tells us to get to a doss house so Old Jack won't find us."

"How eminently philanthropic," Arnett replied sarcastically. "At what time did you speak with the prisoner?"

The high color in Annie's cheeks faded. "I'm not sure. I think it was going on ten."

"Could it have been earlier than ten?" Arnett pushed.

"Maybe. The last time I remember, it was just after eight. I'd had a bit of supper and was walking toward Gunthorpe Street. I went into the pub for a time."

"So you cannot say with any certainty that you saw the prisoner at ten that evening."

"No, sir. But he didn't do it. He's not that kind."

"That will be all, Miss Crickland."

Wescomb rose. "I have no questions of this witness."

The woman slowly made her way back to where she'd been sitting amongst the other witnesses. From the expression on her face, Keats could tell she felt she'd let him down.

Sorry I got you into this, Annie.

CHAPTER TWENTY-ONE

2057 A.D.
TEM Enterprises

Cynda had just added the extra moat when the bald man reappeared, beckoning to her. "Will this hurt?" she asked, edgy.

"No." Dr. Weber pulled a small device out of his pocket. "I will place this on your arm, and you will feel a slight tingle."

"Is that all?" A nod. "Why do I have to have it?"

"It will make you calmer."

Cynda frowned. She felt calm enough, at least when *he* wasn't around.

"Roll up your sleeve and let's get this done."

She did as he asked, and felt the pressure on her arm. As he'd said, there was a slight tingle.

"I will come back tomorrow and administer another dose. In time, we'll switch to a chip that will deliver the medication."

"What's a chip?" she asked.

"Nothing you need to worry about," he responded breezily as he packed away his things.

Cynda never liked it when they told her that. "Can I go now?" she asked, wanting to get back to her castle.

"No, just stand here for a minute or two. I want to make sure there is no reaction."

"How do you know if it's not okay?" she asked.

"Hmm? Oh, it will be," he replied dismissively.

As she waited, she stared at her arm. It didn't look any different.

"Will it turn colors?" she asked.

"No."

She began to feel warm. Too warm, like someone was holding her arm over a fire. "Is it supposed to be hot?"

The bald man ignored her, tapping on that little tablet of his. Click. Click. Click.

Tiny ants began a march up her forearm. They felt like they were on fire. More of them now.

"It's getting very hot," she said.

"It's just your imagination." Click ... click ...

The long trail of ants coursed up her shoulder, encircling her neck. She wiped some sweat off her forehead. Her heart pounded and her stomach turned over. And over.

Click ... click ... click...

The sound grated on her. "Don't do that."

The bald man looked up. "I must make notes about your treatment."

The clicking noise continued, digging into her flesh like glittering knives. She tried to hum to cover the sound, but it didn't work.

Click ... click ... click ...

The ants were in her chest and head now. Whole caravans of them, streaming fiery trails of fury behind them.

She took a step forward. "I said don't do that!"

"Oh, do be quiet!" he snapped. "I can't make notes if you're talking the whole time."

CLICKCLICKCLICKCLICKCLICK

"Stop it!" She pulled the device out of his hands and slung it away. It arced high in the air, then gravity kicked in and it plummeted to the ground. Skidding in a shower of sparks along the walkway, it impacted a wall, disintegrating into dozens of expensive pieces.

"What the hell—" Weber began.

Her clenched fist hit his jaw a second later.

"SHE JUST HIT me," the psychiatrist gurgled around the compress on his bloody mouth. "I gave her the medication and then she hit me."

"I told you she didn't want it," Morrisey grumbled. He gave Fulham a quizzical look.

His assistant leaned close and whispered, "The physician had to give her a sedative. He suspects it was a reaction to the medication, that it put her into a blind rage. He anticipates that she will return to her mellow self in a few days."

"I've never seen one like that," Weber muttered. Dabbing at his jaw, he winced. "Inverse reaction. Very rare." Then he brightened. "This will make a great research paper."

Morrisey's patience fled. "Fulham, get this insufferable bastard out of here, will you?"

"With considerable pleasure," his assistant replied.

Weber puffed up. "I refuse to come back. I don't want to be anywhere near that mad woman again."

Perfect.

Thursday, 1 November 1888
Old Bailey (Central Criminal Courts)

As Alastair waited in the witness box, memories threatened to overwhelm him. The last time he'd been called to testify was at Marda's inquest, to explain why he'd killed a man. This time, the life of his closest friend lay in the balance.

He'd slept little the night before, fretting over what sorts of questions he would face. Arnett had clearly impugned his honor during yesterday's session, and he knew the prosecutor would continue that onslaught today.

After the oath, Arnett opened with the question the doctor had anticipated.

"How long have you been involved in forensics, Dr. Montrose?"

"Only a very short time."

"A month ... a fortnight?"

"I officially began working with Dr. Bishop on the fourteenth of this month *after* the Hallcox post-mortem."

"Ah, so you are a fledgling. Do you enjoy the work?"

Enjoy? Alastair cocked his head. "I find it ... rewarding."

"Why did you decide to take up this profession?"

"It is a fascinating one, and Dr. Bishop is an excellent teacher. I feel it holds great promise."

"I understand that you are a close personal friend of the prisoner."

"Yes."

"Did you not believe it a conflict of interest to assist at the victim's post-mortem, knowing that your close friend was a suspect?"

"On the contrary, I did not know Keats was involved in the case. We were not told that until the following morning."

"Come now, the prisoner is your best friend. Surely you would have known—"

"No, I did not." Alastair fought to keep his anger in check. Wescomb had warned him that if he lost his temper, Keats would suffer.

"You are under oath, Doctor," Arnett replied.

"I swear I did not know until *after* we delivered the post-mortem report."

"Is it not true that *you* were once in court regarding the murder of a man in Wales?"

Here it comes. Alastair forced any reaction from his face, though his gut somersaulted. "I testified at an inquest, yes."

"Why were you in the witness box?" Arnett challenged. "Was it because you were the cause of a man's death?"

"I must object, my lord," Wescomb interjected. "Dr. Montrose's personal history is of no import in this case. He does not sit in the dock for Miss Hallcox's murder."

"No, but he might feel inadvertent sympathy for his friend, having once faced the rope in Wales," Arnett countered.

"I must agree," Hawkins intoned. "Answer the question, Dr. Montrose."

Alastair took a deep breath. "I was summoned to testify regarding the events surrounding the death of the woman I loved, and the man who murdered her."

Gasps came from the courtroom.

"I have no further questions to put to this witness at this time, your lordship," Arnett concluded smugly.

Wescomb rose. "Just to clear the air, what were the findings from that inquest in Wales?"

"That my actions were in self-defence," Alastair replied.

"Thank you. Since Mr. Arnett has brought up the subject, did that experience in Wales give you particular sympathy for Sergeant Keats?"

"Yes. I also know what it is like to be falsely accused."

Murmurs flew through the courtroom. Alastair allowed himself to relax. Arnett's ploy had failed.

Lord Wescomb shifted directions. "Did you treat Sergeant Keats after his injury at the hands of a Fenian anarchist?"

"Yes."

"How serious were those injuries?"

"Quite serious. He had a severe scalp laceration, a concussion, and a broken rib."

"How was his recuperation progressing at the time of the murder?"

"He was improving, though still unsteady on his feet and easily fatigued. I recommended rest."

"In your professional opinion, would Sergeant Keats have the strength to strangle a woman in his debilitated condition?"

"It would be extremely difficult, given the broken rib."

"Even if he employed the sash from her robe?"

"It still would be very difficult."

Wescomb paused to let that settle in the jury's mind. "Is it true that you conducted further forensic studies in an effort to determine the height of the murderer, Doctor?"

"Yes, based on post-mortem evidence." Alastair looked up at the judge, his heart in his throat. "If a demonstration is permitted, my lord?"

Hawkins took his time with the answer. "Providing it is in good taste."

"It shall be, my lord. I would ask that my assistant join me at the front of the room."

"I shall permit it."

A figure rose and made her way forward, accompanied by whispers in the audience. The judge banged the noise back into silence.

"Who is this woman, Dr. Montrose?" he asked.

"This is Mrs. Butler, my housekeeper. She is of similar height to the deceased, my lord, and so will serve in Miss Hallcox's stead during the demonstration."

"I see. Pray, do not be theatrical about this."

"In no way, my lord."

With a nod from Alastair, Mrs. Butler turned her back to him. "Miss Hallcox," he explained in a clear voice, "stood five feet, four and three-quarter inches tall without footwear, as she was at the time she was murdered. As Dr. Bishop has indicated, she was strangled from the rear. At this point, I ask Mr. Kingsbury to join us. Mr. Kingsbury is five feet six and one-half inches, which is very close to the prisoner's height and will serve as a model for this demonstration."

"I thought that Metropolitan police regulations required their policemen be at least five feet nine," Wescomb said, feeding him the objection.

"In that regard, Sergeant Keats is a notable exception. I am quoting his height directly from police records. I also verified it this morning in the presence of the prison warder."

There was murmuring as Wescomb's assistant came forward. Alastair handed him the sash and Kingsbury positioned it on Mrs. Butler's neck.

"You will note," Alastair remarked, pointing to the tableau, "that the angle of the sash is nearly parallel." He gave a nod and Kingsbury lightly tightened the fabric. Through it all, Mrs. Butler maintained a neutral expression as Alastair had instructed her, hands at her sides. He was quite proud of her performance.

The doctor gestured. The assistant removed the sash and handed it to him. "The ligature marks found on Miss Hallcox's neck were not parallel, as would be expected of a man of Sergeant Keats' stature," he explained, stepping up behind Mrs. Butler. Repositioning the sash, he tightened it carefully. "During the post-mortem, we noted that the ligature marks on the back of her neck were not level, but rose, corresponding to someone approximately five feet nine, as I am."

"Could not Sergeant Keats have pulled upward on the sash?"

"Not with his broken rib, my lord."

"What about standing on a chair or a stool? That would change the angle of the ligature mark."

"I doubt the victim would have allowed the murderer time to prepare in such a fashion. Besides, Sergeant Keats' rib injury would have precluded such an athletic feat."

"Indeed. Your conclusion, Doctor?" Wescomb prompted.

"The marks on the deceased were made by an assailant taller than the accused."

"Thank you for this most informative demonstration," Wescomb said.

Realizing he was staring at the sash, Keats forced his eyes away. One thing was clear: no matter what happened to him, Alastair's forensic career was launched as solidly as a new ship puts to sea.

"I wish to cross-examine, my lord," Arnett said, rising to his feet. "Your *demonstration*, as my learned colleague calls it, has been most unusual. From your testimony you would have us believe that the prisoner is incapable of murder."

"I did not say he was incapable of murder, sir. I said that the evidence indicates he did not commit *this* murder," Alastair replied.

Wescomb beamed his approval.

"I see," Arnett replied. "Now if I had a close friend staring at the noose, I wonder if I might be so inclined as to, well, obfuscate the evidence." A dramatic pause. "Do you wish to recant your testimony, Doctor?" he asked silkily.

"No. The physical evidence stands. Sergeant Keats, by virtue of his height, could not have strangled Nicola Hallcox."

"So you say. I have no more questions, my lord."

Wescomb rose. "Dr. Montrose, did you have your findings validated by another impartial professional?"

"Yes. The forensic experts at St. Mary's Hospital reviewed our findings and drew the same conclusion."

"Thank you. That is all."

—

"Damn the man!" Alastair slammed his fist on the table, causing all eyes in the Viaduct Tavern to swing toward him. Reuben retrieved his ale to keep it out of harm's way.

Wescomb shook his head. "I did warn you that Arnett would pull all the tricks out of his bag."

Alastair looked over at his mentor. "In future, Reuben, I think it best I not assist you. My professional opinion will always be in doubt because of that one event in Wales. I shouldn't have wasted your time."

Reuben chuffed. "On the contrary, you've not wasted it. You're the one who found that discrepancy with the ligature mark. I didn't see that."

"Still—"

"Fancy place, isn't it?" Reuben asked, pointedly changing the subject. His eyes roved upward. "I particularly like the painting of the three maidens."

Realizing he would get no further on the topic, Alastair finally took note of their surroundings. The painting Reuben mentioned adorned one whole wall. Above it was a red-tiled ceiling supported by sturdy, cast iron pillars. As he looked around, he noted a man near the bar, watching them. The moment their eyes met, the fellow turned away.

"It's built on top of old Newgate Prison," Wescomb explained. "The cellar still holds some of the cells." He stroked his gray moustache in thought. "On the whole, I think we've done rather well so far. We've shown the inspector has run a slipshod investigation, that there are a number of other gents who might feel the need to put Miss Hallcox in her grave, and proved that the sergeant is just too short to have done the deed." He nodded, pleased. "We have firmly inserted an element of doubt in the minds of the jury."

"Lord Wescomb?" a voice asked.

They looked up at the newcomer. He was dressed like most of the other patrons: suit and bowler. The defining difference was the pen and notebook in his hand. Alastair slipped a quick glance toward the bar. Their watcher was still there.

"Yes, sir?" Wescomb asked.

The man stepped forward to join them. "I'm Robert Anderson, reporter for the Chicago Herald."

"You're far afield, sir," his lordship replied politely.

"So I am reminded each day."

"Ah, that's where I've heard the name. You were with the inspector the night Sergeant Keats was arrested."

"Yes. Quite an adventure. I've been attending the trial and have a few questions to put to you, if you agree."

"Such as?" Wescomb asked, going on guard.

"It appears that certain topics are off limits at the proceedings. Why is that?"

Wescomb's expression grew even more guarded. "That is a question you must put to Home Office. I am not at liberty to answer."

"Home Office," the fellow repeated, making a note. "I have heard that there are still explosives at large in London."

"Rumors come and go like the fog in this city."

"Every now and then, rumors prove true."

Wescomb eyed him. "It depends."

"If you could make a plea to the public on behalf of your client, what would it be?" Anderson asked.

This was a question Wescomb could answer without restraint.

"My fervent request is that if someone saw the sergeant that night in Whitechapel, they must come forward. An innocent man's life hangs in the balance."

The reporter tucked away his notebook and pen. "Thank you, Lord Wescomb. I appreciate your time." He inclined his head and set off for the door.

The peer let out a sigh of relief. "Reporters always make me nervous. You never know what they'll write. Especially one from America." He looked over at his companions. "You're both welcome to come to my home for the evening. We'll take supper and you can help me work on my closing arguments."

"I regret I shall have to pass, Sagamor," Reuben replied. "I am leaving for Dublin on Saturday to consult on a case. There is much that must be done before then."

"How about you, Alastair?"

"Thank you, my lord. I would be happy to accompany you. I'd rather be doing something useful for a change."

"Excellent." Wescomb rose from his chair. "Come on. My carriage should arrive in a few minutes."

CHAPTER TWENTY-TWO

"His lordship is here, Mr. Brown," the maid called out, watching the street from the front window.

"Thank you, Marie," he replied. She hurried past him, her task complete. The butler heard the swish of skirts on the stairs as Lady Sephora descended to meet her husband, as she did most evenings.

"Has Kingsbury arrived yet?"

"No, milady. He sent word that he was delayed and would be here closer to nine."

"A long night indeed," she replied.

Howard Brown adjusted his coat and then opened the front door, stepping outside. He scanned the streets as the coach came to a halt. It was after dark and a silvery mist hung in the air.

Wescomb waved as he exited the carriage. "Good evening, Brown!"

"Good evening, your lordship," the butler called out.

"A bit damp, isn't it?"

"Yes, my lord. It looks like rain."

"He's in high spirits," Lady Sephora observed. "That bodes well. Perhaps I should have attended court today."

Another man stepped out of the carriage. After a word from Wescomb, he headed for the front door.

"Dr. Montrose," Lady Sephora acknowledged with a smile. "Welcome."

"Good evening, your ladyship," he responded, mounting the stairs to the house. He looked drawn, dark circles under his eyes.

"Go on in," her ladyship told him. "Have a seat in his lordship's study. I'll ask Marie to bring you some tea to cut the chill."

"Thank you, my lady."

Wescomb approached, smiling widely. "Good evening, my dear," he called out, doffing his hat in a gallant gesture at the bottom of the stairs. "Today went well. I believe we may just prevail in this—"

There was the hurried sound of footsteps on the sidewalk.

"My lord!" Brown shouted.

The first shot spun Wescomb around like a top. The second missed, shattering a gas lamp farther down the row of houses. His lordship fell to one knee, his face a sketch of pain and surprise. The gunman boldly advanced on him, cocking the pistol, aiming at his forehead for the final coup de grace.

Three shots echoed in the street like cannon blasts. Brown's first bullet missed, the second hit its mark, followed by the third. The assassin staggered toward the center of the street, clutching his chest as blood poured down the front of him. A hansom sped toward him, and for a second Brown thought it would strike him down. Instead, hands pulled the injured man inside. The driver whipped the horse unmercifully, sending sparks from the beast's hooves as it flew away.

Sephora was the first to her husband. "John!"

Lord Wescomb gaped at her. "Hell of a thing, Sephora..."

Then he toppled over.

ALASTAIR HAD JUST settled in a chair when he heard the shots. Bolting down the hallway and onto the street, he found his host cradled in his wife's arms, white shirt thick with blood.

"We need to get him inside as quickly as possible," Alastair insisted.

"Foster!" Brown called, beckoning to a young footman standing at the top of the stairs. "Help me with his lordship."

Once the peer was laid on his own bed, Alastair moved forward.

"Staunch the bleeding as best you can," he ordered as Lady Sephora leaned over her husband, her face alabaster and hands painted in blood. She pressed a cloth into Wescomb's right shoulder, instantly staining it dark crimson.

Alastair stripped off his coat, tossing it aside with no care as to where it landed. "I'll need hot water, bandages, any antiseptic you have," he ordered.

The maid bobbed once and flew out of the room.

Alastair pulled a chair near the bed. "Let me have a look," he said, taking Lady Sephora's place. He pulled back the compress and gently examined the wound, taking care not to touch the injury directly.

Wescomb looked up at him with a sweat-sheened face. "Oh, there you are...young man. How bad is it?"

"Just determining that." Alastair carefully manipulated the peer's arm, eliciting a groan. "Sorry, my lord." His initial examination complete, he gently replaced the compress. "It is as I hoped."

"As you hoped?" Sephora asked, hanging on his every word.

"The bullet has gone completely through the fleshy part of his shoulder. Just continue pressing on the wound while I wash up."

He rolled up his cuffs, poured water into the basin, and scrubbed furiously with a bar of soap that smelled of pine trees. The panicked maid scurried in with a basin of hot water, some of it sloshing over the edge onto the carpet.

"Excellent. Place it near the bed."

The girl wavered on her feet, but did as he asked, full attention on her master. "The bandages are coming, sir."

"Thank you." Alastair dried his hands. "Please bring some hot tea with a tot of brandy in it for your mistress."

"Yes, sir," the maid said, curtseying. The door closed behind her and he heard the sound of running footsteps on the stairs.

Alastair sat next to the wounded man. "Do you feel well enough to assist me, your ladyship?"

Sephora nodded weakly. "I do."

"Your lordship, this is not going to be comfortable," Alastair advised.

"You all say that sort of thing." He eyed his wife, panting and gritting his teeth as Alastair set about cleaning the wound. A deep breath. "How did our…butler," Wescomb asked in between hisses of pain, "come to…have a pistol…in his pocket, my dear?"

There was a noticeable pause before Sephora found her voice. "Brown is a gamekeeper's son. He is familiar with firearms. I thought it prudent that he be armed, given the extraordinary pressure you've faced during Keats' trial."

Wescomb mustered a weak smile. "You're a marvel, my dear."

Sephora's eyes moistened.

His lordship winced again. "Take my advice, Doctor. Marry a smart woman. If I had done otherwise, I would be dead."

"I shall remember that, my lord," Alastair responded with a smile. "There, the bleeding has slowed. A very positive sign."

The maid hurried in with the tea tray. In her wake, the butler appeared at the door with a tray of bandages.

"Perfect," Alastair replied. "Thank you."

"My lord," Brown began, "I have secured the house. I have an armed footman on each entrance and have sent for the police. I fear we'll be thick with Blue Bottles very soon."

"No doubt contributing to the chaos," Wescomb muttered. "Excellent, Brown. When I'm well again, we'll go shooting. I haven't done that in ages.

It appears to be a skill I must endeavor to polish if others intend to make me a target in future."

The man was visibly startled. "I...I would be honored, my lord."

The moment the butler was out of the room, Wescomb added, "Raise his salary, will you Sephora? Can't lose that man to one of our neighbors."

"Most certainly, John."

"If you can hold his lordship's arm steady, I'll apply the antiseptic and then the bandages," Alastair requested.

She clasped hands with her husband and placed a kiss on his damp forehead. Another grunt of pain issued from the injured man, and she winced in sympathy.

"You are going to win this case, John, or they would not have gone to such effort."

Wescomb nodded. "The question is, dare I ask for a continuance? The jury is teetering on the brink. Give them a week and they may swing in favor of the prosecution."

Alastair expertly tied off the bandage. "There, we're done. If you have laudanum in the house, I would recommend a dose to cut the pain."

"Not yet. Not until Kingsbury arrives. We must make war plans."

"You've got a hole in your shoulder," Alastair retorted.

"It's better than a noose around the neck. No arguments; we'll do our work, and then I'll rest."

Sephora abruptly rose and made her way to the chair near the fireplace, her face still ashen. When Alastair next looked at her, large tears glistened on her cheeks. She gave him a wan smile, her hands clutching a teacup.

"Sephora?" Wescomb murmured from deep in the bedcovers.

Suddenly, she was all attention. "Yes, John?"

"Dr. Montrose has not had anything to eat this evening. Can you ensure he receives a good meal?"

"Of course, dear."

"It appears that Kingsbury is about to earn his spurs," Wescomb observed.

"Is he up to the task?" Alastair asked.

The peer caught the doctor's eyes. "He'll just have to be, won't he?"

—

2057 A.D.
TEM Enterprises

Morrisey rubbed his temples to ease the headache. It wasn't working. In front of him, on the vid-monitor, was Dr. Weber waxing verbose about the dangers of untreated ARD. The aggrieved psychiatrist was making the rounds of Vid-Net talk shows. His message was simple: if his patient had been treated when she was younger, the incident would never have happened.

Fulham and Mr. Hamilton were watching over his shoulder. He could feel the mounting tension, at least from Jacynda's oldest friend.

"That bastard," Hamilton muttered his breath. "He should lose his license."

"He hasn't crossed the line yet," Fulham advised. "As long as he only uses her initials and not her name, he's fine."

"Everybody will know it's her," Hamilton protested. "There are only seven or so women currently active in the time stream. You'd have to be stupid not to connect the dots."

Weber's voice rose from the speaker. "Untreated Adrenalin Reactives are a sincere danger to themselves and to society. I have learned this personally and am submitting a request for legislation to make treatment mandatory." He touched his bruised jaw gingerly for emphasis.

Morrisey ground his teeth. The moment the interviewer invited listeners to send in their thoughts, the Vid-Net message boards went ballistic. Hamilton groaned, bringing up a second screen to scan them.

"What are they saying?" Morrisey asked. It would be easier to craft a response if he knew what the public thought of all this.

"Most of them are from the time groupies. Leave it to the Timers to spread a juicy rumor," Hamilton grumbled. "One of them says *Lassiter's too far into Endorphin Rebound and went rogue.* Another writes that *she tried to kill Defoe.*" He chuckled darkly. "This one says she tried to kill you, boss."

"That's ridiculous."

"Not to them. Why else would TPB have issued an Open Force Warrant with her name on it?"

Hamilton was right.

"We need damage control, sir," Fulham counseled. "We need the public to know who's the victim here. It may be very important down the line."

"Exactly what I was thinking." Morrisey swiveled toward Hamilton. "Get the real story out there; just don't mention the Null Mem treatment yet. That's our ace in the hole."

"On the message boards?"

"No. Go where you and Miss Lassiter are known. They'll trust your word better if they hear it in person."

Hamilton thought for a second. "The Time Pod. All the Rovers and groupies go there."

"Then do it. It's time to strike back."

THE FAVORITE BAR of both the Rovers and their groupies, the Time Pod was the marketing ploy of a man who'd made only one trip into the stream and then realized that time travel scared the living hell out of him. Dan Mead promptly resigned his job and opened the bar. It'd been an immediate success, and now the guy was earning way more than he would have as a Senior Rover.

"Hey, Ralph!" the owner called out from behind the cherry wood bar. He was still thin as a pipe stem. Ralph had always joked that Dan and Cynda had been separated at birth.

"Hi Dan, how's it going?"

"Good. Eisler Lager?"

"Yup. Full pint this time."

"So when are you going to come to work for me?"

That was a recurring proposition, one that Ralph had never taken seriously…until now.

"Don't know. Maybe soon," he replied. He'd had about as much of Morrisey as he could handle. It was like working for Albert Einstein and Marie Curie's love child.

"How's it goin' at TEM? Is Morrisey like they say?"

"Worse," Ralph replied, waiting as the amber fluid rolled into the glass.

"What's this I heard about your buddy, Lassiter? Do they really have an OFW out on her?"

"Yup. I don't know why they're bugging her."

Dan placed the pint on the bar with a grin. "On the house." His way of garnering information from those in the know. He lowered his voice. "So what's really goin' on?"

Ralph took a sip of the beer and leaned closer. "You won't believe it."

"Try me."

Later, Ralph settled himself in his favorite corner under the giant movie poster of H.G. Wells' *Time Machine,* the 2029 version. Dan was already moving the tale along, customer by customer. A few were Rovers, and that was the key. Every now and then, someone would shoot Ralph a questioning look and he'd nod. If they wanted more details, they'd come to him.

The bar began to fill up, like someone had fired a starting pistol. It was easy to tell the groupies as they came in two flavors—the geeks and the women. Not that women couldn't be geeks, but it just seemed to fall out that way.

He glanced up at The Wall, as it was called. It was like a scoreboard, but the Rovers were the players and the groupies were the ones who awarded the points. The *Emeritus* Section was for those who'd contributed the most to the profession. Harter Defoe was the only name listed. Time Rover One was the perennial favorite, not subject to the day-to-day rankings. He would always be Rover One, if nothing more than for having the sheer balls to take the first inter-dimensional trip.

The *In the Stream* section changed on a daily, if not hourly, basis. Currently, a Rover named Hubbard sat in First Place. Ralph had never heard of him.

The run report that had moved him so far up the rankings was blinking below his name. On a whim, Ralph tapped on the console embedded in the table to download it.

It was pretty compelling: Hubbard had managed to save a tourist from the jaws of a Bengal Tiger in 1864 India, without harming the animal. Since the tourist in question was the son of a prominent politician and Bengal Tigers were nearly extinct in 2057, he'd received quadruple points.

Cynda was in seventh place and sinking rapidly. That trend had begun even before the bad press. Arguably the best Rover besides Defoe, she rarely broadcast her exploits and resisted having her run reports uploaded to the TimersNet. That had been a longstanding point of contention between them. He'd always ascribed to the "if you've got it, flaunt it" philosophy. If the groupies didn't know what she'd done, she couldn't rise on the list.

There was another entry in the *Memorial* section. Ralph didn't need to download the final run report to know the specifics of Chris Stone's death. Cynda had told him everything. It still hurt. He'd liked Stone a lot. Chris been good for Cynda and for a time Ralph had thought she'd finally found her guy. Then he was gone.

What a lousy way to die. Beaten, overdosed on chloral hydrate, then dumped into the Thames. It was a miracle she'd ever found his body.

His attention moved to the *Deserves to Be Lost in Time* section. That was always good for a laugh. Davies, the head of TPB, was on there, posted anonymously, probably by some furious Rover who'd been fined for violating some mindless regulation. Chris' killer was there too. Dalton Mimes had six times as many votes as the chairman of the Time Protocol Board and was currently in the lead. The time periods suggested for Mimes' trip all had one thing in common: zero survivability.

After another long sip of beer, Ralph eyed the patrons again. As if on cue, a young lady headed toward him. She was petite, cute, and appeared to be in her late twenties. *Just my type.* He smiled in welcome. He had his reputation as a Lothario to consider. Cynda's illness had kept him out of circulation too long.

"Are you a Rover?" she asked breathlessly.

"Chron-op."

"Oh," she said, deflating. "Who do you work for?"

"TEM Enterprises."

"Oh." She perked up. "Have you met Mr. Morrisey?"

"Yes. I work very closely with him." *Far too close.*

Her next question would tell him if she was a geek or Timer.

"Do you know some of the Rovers?" she asked, leaning closer.

A Timer.

"Sure do." He patted the bench seat next to him. "Have a seat. Have I got a story for you."

CHAPTER TWENTY-THREE

"Where's the bald guy?" Cynda demanded, trying to pull on her sandals. When the footwear didn't go on quickly enough she flung them aside, narrowly missing Morrisey.

"Dr. Weber won't be returning," he informed her. "We should talk about what happened."

"Nothing to talk about. I hit him. He deserved it," she replied, glaring, her fists bunched.

"The problem is—" he began.

Cynda left him talking to himself. With an exasperated sigh, he trudged in her wake. His nephew Chris had gone through that stage during adolescence: surly, volatile, and distrustful of any authority figure, even his favorite Uncle Theo. Chris had finally outgrown it. There was no guarantee that Jacynda ever would.

She just has to. He'd made a careful study of potential medical treatments, hoping to find something to ramp down her anger. Nothing had panned out. She was truly on her own.

Though her volatility was definitely going to be an issue, for once she sounded like the old Jacynda. The docile girl was gone, replaced by a high-strung, outspoken hand grenade. It had all begun the moment she'd received the medication.

TPB may have just done us a favor.

He found her at the top portion of the Zen Garden, busily drawing with her chopstick, her face tortured in the effort. "Miss Lassiter?" She ignored him. "I'm sorry for interrupting, but we do need to talk."

The chopstick continued to move with determined precision. "I don't like people who bother me."

Sensing a potential explosion, he opted for a change of subject. "It's coming along nicely." No reply. "Miss Lassiter?"

She dropped the chopstick and began to tug on the band on her arm like a fox caught in a steel trap. "Take this damned thing off."

"As you wish." It'd served its purpose. Tracking her now would be as simple as following the trail of bleeding bodies. He inputted the code, and the band fell away. She resumed the sand drawing.

"We still need to talk," he reminded her gently.

"You didn't keep them from hurting me."

He'd wondered when that would come. "No, I didn't. I tried my best and I failed. I sincerely apologize."

"Means nothing."

"Jacynda, I—"

"Go away! I hate you!" she shouted and pointedly turned her back on him.

Morrisey spun on a heel and left her alone in the middle of the sand. If he remained, he'd say things neither of them were prepared to handle.

THE MOMENT HE'D left, Cynda settled back on her heels, biting her lip. *What did I just do?*

Maybe she shouldn't be mad at him, but she was. He'd failed her. All of them had. None of them had kept her safe.

At least the bracelet was off now. When she spied it, she snatched it up and buried it deep in the sand, pleased to have the wretched thing gone.

The ants sprinted up and down her spine again. Any slight noise made her grit her teeth. She closed her eyes and tried to think of kittens and string. Instead of the vision calming her, the ants captured the kitten, tied it up in the string, and ate it alive.

With a throaty roar, she channeled that fury into action, battering the sand castle into nothingness, methodically destroying the towers, the moat, the great hall and the drawbridge. When she was done, she used her index finger to draw a sandy version of the bald man's face. Then she pummeled it with her fists. Smoothed the sand, redrew the face, obliterated it. Smooth, draw, hit. She repeated that sequence until her knuckles were raw.

"Miss Lassiter?" a mechanical voice asked.

She glared toward the walkway. A tall silver contraption patiently awaited her response.

"Who are you?" she snarled.

"Sigmund. I am Master Ralph's HB Series Domestic Robot."

"So?"

"You requested that I visit. If you prefer not to speak with me, I will visit at another time."

She leaned back on her haunches, thinking things through. A silver robot with a name that started with "S". That did sound familiar. While she debated, he, or it, waited patiently. No annoying beeps or blinking lights. That won him points.

Still, there was one more test. "Do you know what those are?" she asked, pointing at the figures on the pagoda.

His electronic eyes swiveled up to scrutinize the figures. "They are *T'ien Lung*, celestial dragons, who are believed to protect the houses of the gods."

She stood, dislodging the clinging sand from her clothes. "What did you say your name was?"

"Sigmund."

Cynda waved him over. She had questions. Perhaps the silver creature had answers.

—

Morrisey sat in his sanctuary, as he called it, attempting to find some balance. He tried another round of deep breathing to calm himself. Outwardly, it worked, but his mind was still warring with itself. It was all or nothing now. If Jacynda translated her anger into another assault, he would have no leverage to keep her out of an asylum. He was at the end of that rope. TPB and the judicial system had made that crystal clear.

Did I do the right thing? Maybe he should have allowed the psychiatrists free rein. Maybe he'd made a mistake.

"No," he whispered. If he had, the Jacynda Lassiter he so admired would be gone, that exceptional personality subsumed, all in the name of conformity. His nephew had often spoken of her tenacity: once Jacynda made a decision, right or wrong, she'd move heaven and hell to get the job done. It's what had made Morrisey hire her in the first place. She'd proved herself over and over, and if his intuition were right, she'd do the same this time.

Not everything was grim: her adrenalin-fueled temper had worked as a catalyst. In an unguarded moment, she'd admitted to the company physician that memories crowded her like neglected children, all howling for attention. Filing them away was what proved the problem.

"A significant lack of context," was how the doctor had described the situation.

"But how do I help her now?"

He heard the outer door open and the soft pad of footsteps. Fulham and the rest of the staff were gone for the day, expect for a handful of security guards. They never came here unless summoned. He retrieved a second cup from the Chinoiserie cabinet, then set it close to its mate and the iron teapot.

The footsteps would stop every now and then as the visitor moved toward him. He didn't call out. She'd find him eventually. For her, the journey was every bit as important as the destination.

The moment Jacynda stuck her head inside the room, he waved her forward. To his delight, he saw that her hair was combed and she had her sandals on. She was wearing one of the silk kimonos he'd given her. Clearly, she'd thought enough about this visit to tidy up. That meant it was important to her. Her face was scrubbed clean, but that wasn't what caught his notice. It was her expression. Not contrite, nor was it defiant. More troubled than anything.

Let this go well. The last thing either of them needed was more conflict.

"Have a seat," he said as casually as possible, gesturing to the pillow across from him. His heart was beating too fast, and he attempted to calm it.

"I—"

"Tea first," he said. Jacynda settled opposite him, looking around the room in wonder. He gave her the time. She'd never been here before.

As she peered around, he poured a cup and then handed it to her with a bow. She took a sip and then smiled in surprise.

"That's good."

"White tea with pomegranate." Only then did he pour himself a cup. To his annoyance, he noted a faint tremor in his hands.

"What kind of place is this?" she asked, her eyes still taking the tour.

"My sanctuary. You're one of the rare few who've been in here."

She frowned. "Why?"

"I like my privacy."

"Why?" she repeated.

It was clear she would not allow him to evade the question.

"Because I'm not sure if people want to know what I'm really like."

Before she could pursue that personal admission any further, he gently prodded, "Is there something you want to ask me?"

"Ah…yeah." She pursed her lips, deep in thought. He waited her out. "Can you make the ants go away?"

"We have ants in the compound?" he asked, mystified.

She shook her head. "They're inside me," she explained. "Marching up and down, under my skin. I can't get rid of them."

Morrisey shoved aside the image of actual insects.

"The robot…Sig…Sigmund told me that the stuff Weber gave me might have done it. The ants make me angry. I don't want to be this way. It's not right." Her voice quavered. "I need…your help, Theo Morrisey."

He sighed, long and low. She had just turned a corner.

"I think we need to find something to dampen that anger."

"No medicine," she shot back.

"No, that doesn't work for you." He rose. "Come with me. I have an idea."

As Cynda followed him through the rooms, it seemed like she'd stumbled into a private world. She delighted in the waterfalls, the reed matting on the floors and the green carved bird nestled amongst a small bamboo forest. She gently touched the bird's beak. It felt cold.

Noting her interest, he paused. "It's a jade egret," he said proudly. "I found it in China. It's magnificent, don't you think?"

She nodded. "Must be really heavy."

"It is. It cost me a fortune to have it shipped here, but I treasure it."

The practice room, as he called it, had bamboo flooring and one full wall of mirrors. Her eyes were drawn to the swords on the other wall. She wondered what they were for.

"Have a seat and just watch me for a while," he told her.

She found herself a corner and settled into it. He gave a strange look at her choice of location, but didn't comment.

He stood in the middle of the room and then slowly began to move, bending his knees and then moving one foot to the side. Then he began to move his arms around. He turned on a heel, waving his arms around again.

For a while she thought he was playing games with her, but the longer she watched she realized there was a pattern. He'd take a step and do that strange hand waving, then aim in another direction and repeat the gestures. He kept at it, deftly shifting from position to position. It was like a dance for people who couldn't make up their minds which way to go. Sometimes, he would shoot his fist out and make a funny noise.

He did that now. She chuckled. As he turned toward her, a dark eyebrow arched.

"You find me amusing?" he asked, not halting his movements.

"It looks silly," she said.

He curved around into another pose. "It all depends on your point of view."

She'd seen him do this on the sand early in the morning. At least he had until she'd started the drawing.

"What's a...mother ship?" she asked.

His concentration broke for a fraction of a second. "What?"

"Ralph said that when you're doing this, you're signaling the mother ship."

A sour look came her way. "He's being sarcastic. This is Chen Style Tai Chi Chuan. It's a martial art. It teaches you how to defend yourself. And how to calm yourself."

"Would it help me get rid of people who annoy me?"

"Not necessarily."

"Then what's the point?" she asked.

"To help you find balance. That's something we *both* need right now."

Balance? "Will it make the ants go away?"

"Possibly." He dropped into a crouching position and then shifted one foot and then another behind him while he spread his hands in the air.

"What is that?"

"White Crane Spreads Its Wings," he replied.

"All those things have names?"

"Yes."

Now *that* was interesting. Cynda stood near him, watching what he was doing, trying to copy it. She couldn't come close and nearly fell to the matting. She stumbled around and then regained her footing.

He gracefully finished the current movement. "If you're interested in learning a few forms, I'll be happy to teach you."

She thought about that. "Would the shrinks like me doing this?"

His eyes twinkled with mischief. "Probably not, since it's a martial art. I don't think they'd like you to learn any new ways of harming people."

That settled it. "Show me what to do," she said.

CHAPTER TWENTY-FOUR

Friday, 2 November 1888
Old Bailey (Central Criminal Courts)

The courtroom was abuzz when Keats entered and positioned himself in the dock. He'd expected as much. The morning had brought ill news with his breakfast: his staunchest defender, Lord Wescomb, had been shot on the street in full view of his wife.

Although Wescomb would survive, Keats was bitter at the turn of events. Kingsbury had said he would continue in Wescomb's stead, but Keats felt unsure of the young barrister's abilities. To think someone would try to kill a peer of the realm just to smooth his way to the gallows was almost beyond his comprehension.

The trap is closing. Wescomb was going to save me, and now they've ensured he won't.

Staring forward into the courtroom, he immediately noticed a woman. She wasn't young, but possessed a classic beauty.

Lady Sephora Wescomb.

Keats was astounded to see her here, but there she was, dressed impeccably, her head held high. In her own way, she was telling the world that her husband was not gravely injured. If he had been, she would be at his side. It was a powerful statement to whoever had dispatched the assassin.

Seated next to her was Alastair, and next to him the young woman he'd seen at the inquest, Evelyn Hanson. Alastair turned toward her and said something. She nodded solemnly and patted his arm.

Good for you, my friend. You deserve some happiness for a change.

Judge Hawkins entered and the moment after he settled into his chair, he peered down at the junior barrister. "Mr. Kingsbury, I have your note regarding Lord Wescomb's injury. How is he this morning?"

"Improved, my lord."

"That is reassuring news. Please send my regards, will you?"

"Yes, my lord."

"Is it your intention to ask for a continuance?"

"No, my lord."

The judge gave him a perplexed look. "You are certain of that, sir?"

"Yes, your lordship. Lord Wescomb is most keen that our client's case be concluded."

"Well, I see," the judge replied in a tone that indicated he didn't think that was wise. "Then let's carry on."

"Thank you, your lordship. I wish to call forward Mr. Quincy Leonard."

Keats cocked his head. Leonard was the chap who printed his cards. What was Kingsbury up to?

After the oath, Leonard testily explained that the card found in Miss Hallcox's room was not of his manufacture, and did not match the ones in Keats' rooms. Someone, he said, had created a decent imitation, but not the real thing.

"How can you be so sure?" Kingsbury quizzed.

"Not the same quality at all. I use only the best card stock. This," he said, dismissing the evidence with a distasteful flick of his wrist, "is decidedly second-rate. I would not give such a respected customer such shoddy merchandise."

Keats hid the smirk behind his palm.

After a brief recess, the jury returned to hear the final statements in the matter of the Crown vs. Jonathon Davis Keats. It would be up to Kingsbury to speak of what was in Keats' heart, for by law the prisoner was not allowed to testify in his own defence. Uttering a silent prayer, Keats watched the young barrister rise from his seat. Would he be able to rally the jury's sentiments in the prisoner's favor?

"This has been a troubling case from the onset," Kingsbury began, "for not only has a woman lost her life, but Detective-Sergeant Keats has lost what he holds most dear—his career."

The barrister eloquently described Keats' years on the force, his glowing record as he'd served both at Arbour Square, and at the Yard. As he spoke of certain events, Keats' mind relived those moments. Like a young spaniel, he'd been keen to hunt down those who would flaunt the law. Early in his career, he'd caught gangs of robbers, forgers, and even put Desmond Flaherty in jail. This time, the Fenian had outwitted him.

Kingsbury shifted tone. "Esteemed members of the jury, as you weigh the facts, it is vital to remember that there is a dearth of physical evidence that places the sergeant at the scene of the crime. His hair was not found in the victim's bed, though evidence of *three* other paramours were. Who left behind those black strands? It was certainly not my client. You've been shown a riveting demonstration of how the murderer was considerably taller than the detective-sergeant. It is only Mr. Landis' testimony that has placed my client in the dock. I submit that the butler's propensity for drink and stark grief at the terrifying death of his mistress has led him to point the finger of guilt erroneously. He clearly harbors ill will toward the sergeant for reasons unknown. As his attention was elsewhere while his mistress died, is it not possible this false accusation is his way of atonement?"

The jurors were held in rapt attention by the young barrister's oratory. *Wescomb would be proud.*

Keats' eyes wandered. In the spectator's gallery, he caught sight of a familiar figure—Clancy Moran. Their eyes met briefly, then Keats looked away with a twinge of regret. Clancy would never get the reward money now.

"We must admit that the detective-sergeant is guilty on one count," Kingsbury said, addressing the twelve men. "He will admit to the sin of obsession. Fearing for the public safety, he sought to bring Desmond Flaherty and his associates into custody, to prevent *future* attacks upon this city and its populace."

Justice Hawkins leaned forward in his chair, the barest hint of a frown on his face.

The barrister turned introspective. "The very second Keats learnt of Miss Hallcox's death, he should have turned himself in to the constabulary in Ingatestone. He did not. That was a grievous error on his part, and he readily admits it. Yet, when taken in context with this man's brilliant career, it is but a momentary lapse of judgement.

"Jonathon Keats is a copper, through and through. He was willing to risk everything—his life *and* his career—to do his duty. He is only guilty of the sin of obsession, not murder. It is my hope that justice will prevail in your hearts and you will set this man free so that he may continue the fine work at which he excels."

If I am found guilty, it is not because my barristers lacked ardor.

Now it was Arnett's turn. The jurors shuffled in their seats, eager to hear what he had to say. The barrister smiled politely in Kingsbury's direction. "My learned colleague has given us a glimpse of a promising young policeman's career. The prisoner has gone from strength to strength, excelling at each of his tasks. Until that fateful night."

He turned toward the jury. "Admittedly, the victim was hardly a paragon of virtue, but she knew precisely what it would take to bring the prisoner to heel. That was her undoing.

"In the course of the investigation, we learned that the prisoner argued with Miss Hallcox on the night she died and left, as the butler has testified, *in a fine fury*. Later, he returned and spent time in her bedroom. To cover his crime, the prisoner spun a fantastical tale worthy of any Penny Dreadful. He claims he encountered his arch enemy in an alley in Whitechapel."

Arnett took a step forward. "Allow me to paint this picture: five Fenians, all, no doubt, armed, have trapped a single police sergeant, an individual they despise, in a dark alley. An arch criminal finally has the prisoner within his grasp. Why let him live? Instead, the sergeant claims he was accosted, imprisoned in a coffin, and ferried into the country." Arnett shook his head in dismay. "Such a vivid imagination."

He drew himself up. "It is true that Miss Crickland saw the prisoner in Whitechapel, but she was uncertain of the time. We have heard how the prisoner pawned his boots in Ingatestone, but that in itself is not sufficient to acquit him. It only proves that he was in that city *after* the murder. It is the prosecution's belief that the prisoner is guilty of the heinous crime of which he is charged. As our learned colleague observed, the prisoner suffers a deadly obsession—the need to capture the elusive anarchist. That mania clouded the sergeant's mind. I contend that he returned to Nicola Hallcox's house, perhaps used his skills to pick the front door lock, and ascended to her bedroom. It is my belief that Miss Hallcox never possessed any information about the Fenian, but used that ploy to lure the prisoner into her bed. She played him for a fool."

Arnett paused and took a deep breath. "Her deception came at a very high cost. After their illicit sexual congress, I believe she revealed the truth: that she had no information and was suffering from a grave disease. When he grew wroth at the deception, she scorned him."

The prosecutor looked up at him. "Any reasonable man would be angry at having been played for a fool. For the prisoner, it was more than his pride on the line. Not only might he become syphilitic himself, but his golden opportunity had been ruthlessly torn from him."

Arnett swiveled toward the jury. "In a moment of inhuman rage, Detective-Sergeant Jonathon Keats strangled the life out of Nicola Hallcox. He then arranged her body in that grotesque and obscene pose to display his contempt for the woman who had so easily duped him."

No!

"The death of Nicola Hallcox is a travesty that cries out for judgement. I ask you, the members of the jury, to weigh the evidence and find this tormented man guilty of the crime of willful murder."

Some of Justice Hawkins' charge to the jury filtered through the thick fog into which Keats had stumbled. It sounded evenhanded, as the judge weighed the evidence presented from both the defence and the prosecution.

Finally, the justice explained, "A man's life lies in your hands. If you are not so convinced of the prisoner's guilt, then he is entitled to be acquitted. If, however, you are satisfied that he did commit this crime, then it is your duty to say so without reservation. You must determine his fate. That is the wisdom of our law. "

—

It had been the longest hour of Keats' life. He'd spent it in prayer, fingers working the beads of his dead mother's rosary. Now, as the jury filed in, he hoped God had heard his impassioned pleas.

As the Chaplain took his required place, muffled voices came from the gallery. They were taking bets. From what he could hear, they were split as to the outcome. His eyes hopped from juror to juror. None of them looked upward at the dock.

Please, God, you know I didn't do this.

The Clerk of the Court asked, "Gentlemen, have you agreed upon your verdict?"

The Foreman of the Jury rose. "We have."

"Do you find the prisoner guilty or not guilty of the murder of Nicola Therese Hallcox?"

The Foreman paused for a fraction of a second. "We find the prisoner guilty."

Guilty. It hit with all the force of a sledgehammer blow to the gut.

Beneath him, he saw the stricken face of Lady Wescomb, a handkerchief pressed to her lips. Cousin Roddy stared upward at him in horror while Fisher closed his eyes, his lips pressed together in a thin line. Alastair bowed his head in defeat.

How could it have come to this?

The Clerk turned toward Keats. "Prisoner at the bar, you stand convicted of the crime of willful murder. Have you anything to say why the Court should not give you judgment of death according to law?"

His knees like jelly, Keats squared his shoulders and rose with as much dignity as he could muster.

"Yes, I do." He cleared his throat. "I proclaim my innocence in this matter. I did not murder Nicola Hallcox. My only crime was the desperate need to capture Desmond Flaherty."

As he spoke, he felt his fury rising at the injustice. He had dedicated his life to the law, and it had failed him when he needed it the most.

They're going to hang me. What the hell does it matter now?

He steeled himself and raised his voice, pointing his words directly at the jurors.

"By Almighty God, I swear that I did not pursue my *obsession* purely for the chance of a commendation or an advancement in rank. I made the decision to continue my hunt for Desmond Flaherty because he still has at the very least, a wagonload of gunpowder and a substantial amount of dynamite, with which he threatens this city at this very moment!"

As Arnett began to sputter, Kingsbury delivered a subtle nod, along with a hint of an approving smile. Keats was finally saying what he and Wescomb had been denied.

Justice Hawkins called for order as the courtroom swirled into a tempest of voices. Keats took advantage of the mayhem to seek out Fisher in the crowd. His efforts were amply rewarded: his superior's face held an expression of awe.

"Mr. Keats," the justice warned. "You know—"

"With all due respect to your lordship and the Crown, the truth has not been heard in this courtroom. I do not fault you, my lord, but those in the government who hide behind their intrigues and allow the innocent to suffer."

"Is that your statement?" Hawkins demanded.

"Nearly." Keats took a deep breath, his heart pounding so hard it threatened to choke him.

"I have served with pride, alongside men of singularly dedicated purpose. To that end, I ask that my conviction not tarnish the reputation of my fellow officers at Scotland Yard. This stain should fall on my shoulders alone." He gave a nod to indicate he was done.

Justice Hawkins eyed him sternly. "Jonathon Davis Keats, you have been convicted, upon evidence, of the murder of Nicola Hallcox. I find it detestable when a citizen violates the laws. It is *indefensible* when a police officer does the same. No matter your reasons, noble or otherwise, for the crime of which you have been convicted our law knows but one penalty— the penalty of death. I recommend that you make your peace with Almighty God before you stand before His throne. Perhaps He will see it in His heart to pardon you for this hideous crime."

Keats' breath caught in his chest as Justice Hawkins donned the black cap.

"You will be taken hence to the prison in which you were last confined and from there to a place of execution where you will be hanged by the neck until you are dead and thereafter your body buried within the precincts of the prison. May the Lord have mercy upon your soul."

The Chaplain murmured, "Amen."

Keats sank into the chair, proud of his defiance. By evening, his final statement would be in all the papers. There would be hell to pay in Parliament as questions were asked and answers avoided. At long last, this festering sore would be laid open to the world.

He nodded to himself, pleased. He'd done all he could.

That's what being a copper is all about.

CHAPTER TWENTY-FIVE

2058 A.D.
TEM Enterprises

Time passed. A new year began. The shrinks came and went less frequently now. That was a blessing. Cynda had begun a sand drawing, just on a whim, but it had taken hold of her. The sand dragon now had wings and a massive tail. It seemed to her that the more it grew, so did she. Somehow the two were connected.

Like a jagged wound, her mind continued healing in little patches. One moment she wouldn't remember the name of an object or a person, and then it would be there. Sometimes she'd forget it again, but more frequently the words found a suitable niche in her muddled mind.

Hours working the sand and doing Tai Chi with Morrisey had calmed the fire ants under her skin. It hadn't gone smoothly. Some days she would rant at him, furious when she couldn't remember a move he'd patiently taught her over and over. Other days it went better. Memory was still an issue. Always would be.

"Time is a great healer," Morrisey often said whenever things seemed rough for her. Cynda often wondered at his endless patience. She couldn't help but notice there was more gray at his temples now.

At Morrisey's suggestion she'd begun another tradition: every night she asked the computer to pull up a few of her run reports. It seemed to be the best means to fill a few more holes in her past and for her to understand what kind of person she'd been. What it was like to be a Rover. When Ralph had realized what she was doing, he'd taken to joining her. He said it was in case she had any questions. She suspected it had more to do with loneliness than anything.

The reports read like fiction. Could she have rescued a half-dozen tourists from lions in a Roman Coliseum, or spent time in the court of King Henry the Eighth? The *old* Jacynda Lassiter had dined in the same room as Elizabeth the First, watched the defeat of the Spanish Armada. She'd been at the Battle of Trafalgar and witnessed Lord Nelson felled by a sniper's bullet, and later, his corpse being packed into a water cask filled with brandy for the mournful journey to England.

"You're frowning a lot," Ralph observed over the sound of the vintage music coming out of his equally vintage headphones. He'd never taken to the ear implants. "Something bugging you?" She mimed for him to take them off, and he complied.

"Is this all true?" Cynda asked, gesturing toward the screen.

"For the most part. You didn't always put everything in the reports, though. TPB can come down hard on a Rover if they think something was weird about a run." Ralph was rapidly becoming her personal bellwether. He seemed to relish the role. It was a way for them to mend the rift between them.

"It's all weird, as far as I can see."

He chuckled. "I'll give you that." The headphones went back on. His face settled into a smile and he began tapping his fingers in time to the music. He'd said it was a band called Jefferson something or other.

She began reading through the final few reports, which covered her tours of duty in Victorian London and her encounters with two gentlemen: Dr. Alastair Montrose and Detective-Sergeant Jonathon Keats. When she'd finished, she asked Ralph about them.

"Montrose sent you home," he explained, headphones off again. "I'm still amazed a Victorian pulled that off. Of course, the boss didn't breathe a word about that to TPB; they'd have gone nuts."

Montrose. The kind man who'd wept for me. The doctor looked back at her from a scan of a vintage photograph taken when he'd graduated from medical school. Nattily dressed, he radiated confidence, but she thought she saw hidden pain behind the celebratory image.

With a wave of her hand, the screen changed. Now hanging in the air above the keyboard was a photograph of Jonathon Keats. The twinkle in his eye seemed to call to her. "And this sergeant guy?"

"You helped him recover some explosives."

Her gut told her there was more to it than that. Ralph was right: not everything went into the run reports.

"Handsome," Cynda murmured. *Both of them.* Suddenly, she could see herself walking arm and arm along a street with Keats as her exuberant escort. Had he been courting her, then? Possibly. The pleasant memory withered: now she saw herself inside a carriage as he lay dying in her lap after some street battle. She closed her eyes, still feeling the brush of his kiss on her lips. Tears began to form. She fought them back, not wanting her friend to see them.

Just then, a name surfaced out of nowhere. "Who's Fred?"

Ralph grinned. "I wondered when you'd remember him. He's your stuffed ferret. You carried him on your trips, though it was against the regs."

"Then where is he?"

Ralph shrugged. "He went missing in action in '88." For some reason, it seemed important that she know where he was. Something else was absent, something blue with legs, but she had no idea how to ask Ralph that question.

A beep sounded at the door; a moment later, Morrisey entered. He hadn't waited for her to give him permission, which was unusual.

Ralph was instantly on his feet. "Gotta go," he said, clearly uneasy at being in the same room with the man.

The moment the door whooshed closed behind her friend, she spoke up. "Is something wrong?"

Morrisey shook his head. He took a deep breath, letting it out slowly. "I have just received permission for one of your family members to visit you from Off-Grid."

"Off-Grid," she repeated to herself, rummaging through her mental filing cabinets.

"It's a place where people go to live if they don't like the rigid lifestyle required by the Government," Morrisey explained. "Once you're outside society, you stay out."

She tried to remember why her family was out there. When she couldn't retrieve the answer, she put it to Morrisey.

"From what I gather, they went voluntarily," he informed her. "Some people do that for political reasons."

That didn't sound right.

"I have petitioned for this visit since the moment you returned," he continued. "There has been considerable... resistance against this." Morrisey paused for a moment. "It's your brother."

"Brother?" Cynda shivered involuntarily. "I don't want to see him! He tried to kill me. Threw me into the Thames and..." She paused, dismayed. "That wasn't him, was it?"

"No," he said, looking relieved. "Your brother doesn't time travel."

Another stray memory. She blew out a stream of air. "His name is..."

"Blair."

Cynda nodded her thanks. "Why not my mom or dad?" she asked, suddenly skeptical.

"I gather your mother has not been well, and your father didn't want to return without her."

That doesn't sound good.

Morrisey leaned toward the computer. A moment later, a family photograph appeared. Her mother, father, brother and her. All smiling. Before everything had changed.

Blair. As she studied her brother's face, emotions began flooding back with an intensity that nearly overwhelmed her.

Morrisey cleared his throat. "From what Mr. Hamilton says, you dislike your brother intensely, and I gather the feeling is mutual. If you don't want to see him, I'll not finalize the arrangements. I would, however, counsel the opposite course."

"I..."

Just how much effort had it taken for Morrisey to do this? He'd said he'd been working on this since she'd first come back. Months now.

"How much does he know?" she asked.

"That you sustained a head injury. I didn't reveal the exact nature of how that happened, and it's probably best that they not know that."

What would it hurt? She'd endure this for Theo Morrisey, though it wasn't going to be pleasant.

"Okay, I'll do it. I haven't annoyed..." A sigh. She couldn't remember the name, though she'd just heard it. "...in a long time."

"Thank you."

She could have met Blair in the privacy of her rooms. Instead, Cynda chose the pagoda, right out in the open where anyone could see them. Perhaps it was some juvenile payback, though she wasn't particularly sure why she felt the need. Neither of them were kids anymore.

"Cynder?" her brother called from the walkway. She'd forgotten his pet name for her. He was taller than she was, his hair a bit darker. His muscles were corded, like someone accustomed to physical labor.

"Hi...Blair." She waved him over. Mumbling under his breath, he ditched his shoes and crossed the sand. Once on the platform he stared at one of the pillows, then pushed it aside with his foot.

He's going to regret that.

He went somber as he sat down on the hard wood. "Been a while."

"Yeah. What's wrong with Mom?"

"She fell and broke her hip about the same time that you got hurt. It's healing, but very slowly. Right now, she's using a cane to get around."

Cynda didn't know what to say.

Her silence forced her brother to speak. "I know, if she hadn't been Off-Grid, she'd be fine now. You're thinking it, you might as well say it."

From what Morrisey had told her, Off-Grid meant primitive medical facilities, if they existed at all. If her father hadn't been a doctor, her mother might not be alive.

"Why did you go out there?" she asked.

He shook his head. "You mean, why was I *sent* out there?"

"Sent?"

"I told you I went voluntarily. I lied." He looked down. "I nailed one of those little fascist CopBots. I'd been drinking, and when it started harassing some kid flying a kite, I smashed the thing into lots of little pieces. Then another showed up and I nailed that one, too. They really pissed me off."

"You trashed a couple of CopBots?" she asked, amazed. As he nodded, her estimation of him rose by tenfold. She hit shrinks; he smashed CopBots.

Yeah, we're family.

She grinned and gave him a thumbs-up. "Good!"

Blair looked startled. "No, it wasn't good. When Mom and Dad found out I was to be sent Off-Grid, they decided to come with me. They were worried about me making it, you see. They never would have worried about you like that. You were always so confident, so sure of yourself."

"That's bull," she shot back, looking away.

"No, it's not."

There was more there, she could feel it. The shrink hadn't been her first assault. Maybe Blair had a history of this sort of thing too.

"And?" she nudged.

He looked crestfallen. "Okay, I've done this before. I was getting into trouble fairly regularly. When I refused to get counseling to deal with my *issues,* as they called them, the authorities decided I needed to go because I was a *disruptive influence.*"

She was astounded. "They tossed you out for that?"

"It was only supposed to be three years. Then we could come back." He laughed hollowly. "To what? Mom and Dad had to give up everything to go with me. The money they got for the house went to pay off all those fines I'd racked up. Then the new Government took over and made all the sentences permanent."

Endless exile.

Ants began to fire up. She doused them immediately. There was nothing she could do right now, but down the line some changes needed to be made.

"Why are you here, Blair? I understand why the parents couldn't come, but why you? We never liked each other."

He glowered at her. "They wanted me to. They want us to find common ground."

"What's the point?"

"They say it's time we both grew up," he replied.

Ouch.

"You never understood, Cynder. Even though what you do seems crazy, I've always been proud of you."

"What?" she asked, baffled.

"You were so confident. I was just arrogant. There's a difference." He reached over and pulled a pillow under him. "That's better. It was making my butt sore."

Something told her the old Blair wouldn't have admitted that.

"What's up? You aren't like this, or at least I don't think you are. My memories are still jumbled."

"The last year has been a bitch. Mom and Dad never said a word, never blamed me, but every time those tomato seeds appeared, I knew I'd failed. You were thumbing your nose at me, and I couldn't tell you to go to hell."

"Tomato seeds?"

He looked chagrined. "Sorry. I forgot you don't remember a lot of stuff. You bought some of the rare, non-gen modified seeds and smuggled them to us. It's against the law, Cynder. The smuggling, at least. You risked going to jail for us. Mr. Morrisey said it would have been a decade or longer."

"But, I—"

He raised his hand. "Let me finish. If you hadn't taken that risk, we would have starved. That's the cost of my arrogance. Our parents could have died because I thought I had the right to tell Guv to go screw themselves."

"Everyone has that right."

"Not for the price we've paid. I was sure we'd make a living, no hassles. I was wrong, Cynder. It's the Wild West out there. I was so wrong."

She put a hand on his forearm. "You made it, though. You're a tough S.O.B."

"Not tough enough," he said. "My little sis had to bail us out."

"You're here, aren't you?"

"That's Mr. Morrisey's doing. I wasn't even sure if I should come. I wanted to see you, but you might not have recognized me."

True. It was better to fib. "Fat chance," she said. "Let's start over."

"You forgive me?" he asked, incredulous. "For everything?"

"Well…"

"Like painting your new puppy bright pink?" Another sin she didn't remember. "I called him Pinkie Pup," Blair recalled. "Really made you mad."

Her brother broke out laughing louder than was expected. Just releasing tension. Then he grew solemn again. "God, Cynder, it's not gone the way I planned. And when I heard you'd been so badly hurt…"

"Just keeps happening," she said. He gave her a questioning look. *He doesn't know about the chest wound.* Or most of the other things that had happened to her. "At least it seems like it."

"The parents sent you a message." Blair offered her a thick envelope. At her puzzled look, he said, "No hi-tech out there. Dad goes on and on about his new clinic, which is finally up and running. Nothing fancy, just basic medical care. It's given us some extra income because they pay us in food. Oh, and Mom is really pleased with her beets."

"Beets?"

"Off-Grid, it's all about food and security. The gangs are active again. There's talk of more raids on the settlements."

"Geez."

He turned away, caught up in his own thoughts. It was only then that she saw the ring on his left hand. She took a gamble that it was something new, not something she'd forgotten.

Cynda reached over and tapped the silver band. "Ah, bro, something else going on?"

He turned back, sheepish. "I got married a few months ago."

Married? "What's her name?"

"Amanda. Our first child is due in four months."

"Whoa. You move fast."

"Mom predicts it'll be a girl."

"Good. She'll run you ragged."

His face warmed with a smile that seemed to lift the years. "That's why I wanted to see you. Once Mr. Morrisey said you were doing better, I knew I needed to put some things right."

Marriage and a child had put her brother in a whole new category.

"Raise your hand," she said.

"What?"

"Raise your hand." He did as asked, though she could see he felt it was stupid. "Repeat after me."

"Cynder—"

"I—insert your name here—do promise not to be an ass to my sister in the future."

He repeated the sentence back, a grin on his face, purposely leaving his name out.

She matched his grin and raised her own hand. "I, Jacynda Lassiter, promise to treat my older brother, whatever the hell his name is, with the respect he deserves as long as he agrees not to be a complete jerk."

They slapped palms in the air and then hugged, hard.

"God, I've missed you," he whispered. "Amanda and I want to name our daughter after you. Is that okay?"

Cynda pulled back, mouth agape. "I…all right."

They fell back into the embrace, letting their old wounds wash away in mutual tears.

—

Saturday, 3 November 1888
Spitalfields

"Dr. Montrose?"

A young man hesitated in the open doorway as Alastair set aside the instruments he'd been sorting. "I'm sorry, but the clinic won't be open for another week or so."

"I'm not here for that," the fellow replied, already making his way toward the back of the waiting room.

Alastair studied him closely, carefully weighing whether or not he presented a threat. "Then how can I help you, sir?"

"By letting me play postman. I'm Hopkins. I'm an…associate of Jacynda Lassiter."

"Jacynda?" Alastair hurried around the exam table. "How is she? Have her memories returned?"

"She's much better," the man assured him, reaching inside his coat to produce an envelope. "I was asked to deliver this letter to you. She needs some questions answered."

"She is well enough to write me?" the doctor asked, unable to conceal his glee at the news.

"Yes. But if anyone from our time asks you about that, the answer is no," his visitor advised. "I'll come back tomorrow morning to get your reply."

"But—"

The man named Hopkins was already out the door. Alastair eagerly slit open the envelope. A thick sheaf of handwritten paper was inside. He sat in his chair, propped up his feet, and began to read. The first full sentence made him whoop for joy.

Dearest Alastair,

I remember you now. I remember Keats, as well. This isn't the way his life is supposed to be. We need to find a way to make it right again. I may need your help.

"And you shall have it, my dear lady," he murmured, his eyes misting.

CHAPTER TWENTY-SIX

2058 A.D.
TEM Enterprises

At Cynda's request, Morrisey began filling in more of the missing pieces: about the Transitives and how they could look like anyone, how the Virtuals could appear invisible, and why it was the shifters held their secrets so closely. He spoke of what Harter had learned from a Future, someone ahead of them in the time stream. How it all would go to ruin in a few years' time.

With some difficulty, he'd spoken of Chris' death, his eyes filled with barely staunched tears. The longer he talked, the angrier she got. Not at him, but at those who'd played God with her life. Killed Chris. Used that silver tube and put her into the Nothing Time. They'd expected her to become a harmless child, giggling and building sand castles forever.

Not even close.

The bottom line: TPB was her enemy, and that wouldn't change.

"I know you won't remember everything I've told you," Morrisey had said. "I'll put a series of reports on your computer with multi-level encryption as most of this is very sensitive. That way, you can review them when you need."

That was good, but what Cynda really needed was to hit someone. Repeatedly.

Sensing her internal upheaval, from that point on Morrisey gave her a wide berth, as did about everyone else in the complex. To curb the desire to give TPB more ammunition for committal, she worked out at the gym and practiced Tai Chi to calm the ants. She perfected her kicks and punches, but still had trouble with some of the other moves. To break up the long periods of exercise, Sigmund taught her chess and how to strategize. She studied Victorian history. Most important, she worked through things in her head. Day by day the red haze slowly lifted, replaced by icy resolve.

Whoever had made her this way were going to reap what they'd sown.

"Cyn?" Ralph prompted. He was sitting a discreet distance from her, just out of range. She gazed down at the sandwich he'd brought her as a peace offering. This had to be Morrisey's doing. Probably figured she wouldn't hit her best friend. She hoped he was right.

"You always liked Eli's food before," Ralph complained as she picked at the interior of the sandwich critically.

"You sure I like tuna?" she asked.

"You used to. You eat raw fish now; you should be able to eat the cooked stuff, for heaven's sake."

To make him happy, Cynda took a bite. The taste was unbelievable. She moaned. "This…is good," she said through a mouthful of food. "Better than chocolate, even."

"That's more like the old you." He smiled. "Oh, Eli and his wife send their regards."

She raised an eyebrow. He took the cue. "Eli Greenwald the Third. You call him E3. We used to eat there all the time, or go up to the park and have a picnic. You used to smuggle tomato seeds through him to your parents Off-Grid."

E3? She shuffled through the files and then came up with a matching memory. She'd hand him her sandwich tote, the seeds hidden in the bottom, and he'd swap the contraband out for a sandwich and pickles. To the casual observer it didn't appear they'd broken any laws.

Once she finished swallowing, she set the sandwich down reluctantly. "Thanks, Ralph."

"No problem." She noticed his own meal sat still wrapped in front of him.

"Wait a minute, let me work on it…" She screwed up her face in thought, hovering her hand over the wrapper like she could divine what was inside. "Roast beef and…something, right?"

"Roast beef, mayo, and American cheese," he confirmed with an approving nod.

"We'll go to this place together someday."

Ralph's smile faded. "We won't get that chance if you go back to '88, Cyn. They'll kill you this time."

She shrugged. "Maybe, maybe not."

"It's not just about you. Rumors are floating around that TPB has threatened to jail Morrisey if there are any further unauthorized transfers. They'll close the company for good, sell it off to the highest bidder."

"I doubt they'll be able to pull it off," she said, hoping that was the case.

"Is one Victorian's life worth all that?" he argued.

Though the question annoyed her, it was a valid one. "I believe it is, Ralph," she told him. "Keats cannot die that way."

"Was there something going on between you two?"

Cynda looked up, startled. "There might have been, before this." She tapped her temple where the mark still darkened her skin. "I don't know now. I think we took a left turn along the way." She took another bite of her sandwich.

"What about Dr. Montrose?"

"Same story, I think." *Is he jealous, or just curious?* Another thought surfaced. "Were you and I ever...you know?"

Her friend shook his head. "We would just drive each other crazy."

That made sense. She set the sandwich down again. "You're not eating, so what's really going on here, guy?"

Ralph's oval glasses were off in a heartbeat, being polished with the bottom of his shirt. She'd learned that was his way of dealing with stress. "You're my best friend, Cyn. Hell, almost my only friend. We've been like twins since we first met. If you go to '88 and don't come back..."

"We've always been there for each other, right?" she asked.

"Yeah, we have."

"Then we will in the future. I'll know you have my back, Ralph. That's why I'll be the one kicking butt this time, not the other way around."

"You're too damned stubborn," he grumbled. "Morrisey said you'd get better, that you wouldn't give in. I wasn't so sure."

"So the Genius wins this round," she joked.

"Don't remind me."

"You don't like him, do you?"

Ralph's brows furrowed. "Sometimes I do. Mostly I'm not sure. It's funny. I used to think he was a god. Now I can't figure him out."

"Makes two of us." She pointed at his sandwich. "Eat, will you?"

He rolled his eyes. "Yes, Mom."

She rolled her eyes back at him and returned to her own meal, savoring both the sandwich and the unshakeable love of her best friend.

—

The moment Cynda heard the door to the botanical garden whoosh open, she sighed. So much for her quiet meditation. Morrisey stopped a short distance away, not joining her on the bench as was customary.

"I'm sorry for interrupting," he announced. "I've run some computer models. The alternate thread is gaining ground."

"Oh, boy."

"This is something different than a Time Incursion. Usually an alternate thread dies out rather quickly. It's my guess that the instability in 1888 is contributing to the problem."

"Defoe's there. Why hasn't he fixed it? He's Rover One, after all."

Morrisey sat next to her. "I don't think he can. I think it has something to do with you."

Me? "You mean if I do go back, it will resolve?"

"Perhaps, but not necessarily the way we would like."

Which meant Keats might die no matter what. "Damned if you do, damned if you don't," she murmured. "How ugly can it get?"

Morrisey went quiet. *He doesn't know for sure.*

"No clue?"

"If this disconnect becomes firmly embedded in the timeline, it will methodically rumble forward. What sort of changes would occur?" He shrugged at his own question. "Time travel may not exist as we know it. You … me … we may never have been born."

Then I have no choice.

"Jacynda…"

Their eyes met. She saw the desperate plea in them. "I would argue that you're not entirely whole yet."

Cynda agreed. Someone had dropped her box of puzzle pieces and there were a number of them that had vanished under the furniture for eternity. In all likelihood, this was as good as it was going to get.

"The clock is running," she told him. "TPB will eventually realize I'm a lot more with it than they think. I can't go on fooling the shrinks forever."

"I have connections. There are places you can hide where they won't find you."

And have them throw you in jail?

"I've been thinking about this: I'll go back to the night Nicci was killed and intercept Keats *before* he gets to my hotel room. I will insist we go somewhere public, where he's known, so he's seen by a number of people during the time Nicci dies. He won't meet with Flaherty, go on trial, or be up for the noose."

"Sounds too simple." Morrisey rubbed his forehead in thought. "You might meet yourself. That can be very disconcerting."

"You've done it?" Cynda asked. To her knowledge, he'd only made a couple of time trips to deliver information to her in '88.

Morrisey shook his head. "Harter has. Said it was very…" He struggled for a word.

"Creepy?"

"Exactly."

"Does it cause any harm to the timeline?"

"Not that we can tell," Morrisey replied. "You should still avoid it."

Fulham appeared in the doorway to the solarium. "The post has arrived—from Victorian London." He held out a letter. And something else. "Apparently you left this behind, and the doctor felt you would want it."

She'd know that furry face anywhere. "Fred!" She leapt to her feet and snatched him out of Fulham's hands. "Fred," she repeated, squishing the stuffed animal in an enthusiastic embrace.

The assistant bent over and whispered something in Morrisey's ear. He gave a curt nod. "Tell Klein we'll be ready very soon."

Impatiently, Cynda tore open the letter and immersed herself in Alastair's flowing penmanship, Fred in her lap. The first couple of paragraphs were full of the doctor's supreme delight at hearing of her improvement. Then his tone turned dark when he wrote about Keats.

She heard Morrisey's throat clearing, and knew what he wanted.

"He writes, '*All seem to be against him, except for a loyal few. Lord Wescomb's, second, Mr. Kingsbury, performed a masterful job of defending Keats, but the end result is that he has been found guilty of Nicola Hallcox's murder. Wescomb is profoundly upset, dismayed at being unable to navigate the vicious politics that swirl around our friend like a maelstrom. You may well wonder why Kingsbury was in charge of the case: his lordship, Keats' staunchest defender, was nearly assassinated the other night in what can only have been a bid to ensure conviction.'*"

Cynda looked up at Morrisey and saw a troubled expression.

"That's not in Wescomb's timeline," he said. "Things are starting to unravel faster than even I had anticipated."

She returned to the letter. "'*I truly fear the worst. I beg of you, if there is anything you can do to save him please do so, history be damned.*'"

"History be damned?" she repeated. "Sounds like it already is."

Cynda handed over the letter, knowing Morrisey would want to study it further. One of the butterflies swirled around her. She set Fred aside and followed it a few feet until it landed on a nearby flower. It fanned its purple iridescent wings as it drank deeply of the nectar.

You don't care about the future, do you? You just live in the now. Wish we could.

There was a rustle of paper being folded. She found Morrisey studying her intently.

"Klein says if you're going, you need to leave within the next twenty-four hours. TPB is getting edgy. He thinks they know you're better off than we've been letting on."

"You kept them off my tail longer than I expected."

A weary shrug. "He wants you to depart from their facility, not ours."

"Why?"

"Harder to track, for one."

"Where else would I go but '88? Why cloak 'n dagger it?"

"Klein has his reasons. So far, he's played straight with us. I would suggest we do as he asked."

He's hiding the real reason. "Klein's trying to keep TPB from shutting down the company, putting you in jail."

Morrisey looked dismayed. "Yes, that would be one reason."

For a daring moment, she imagined smuggling him to 1888 with her. Just as quickly, she dismissed the idea. Even though Morrisey understood the inner workings of time travel better than any Rover, he was a neophyte when it came to the actual realities of life in another era. He was safer here, no matter what TPB did to him.

"You realize how dangerous this trip will be," he warned. "It is more like a war than anything and we still don't know all the combatants. You may have to kill to stay alive."

"I know." In the past that would have bothered her, but not now. "Have you ever... done that?"

"No," her companion replied.

"Ever wanted to?"

At long last, Morrisey nodded.

"Who?"

"Myself," he replied. "After Mei's death, life no longer seemed important."

"Mei?" Then she remembered the photograph on his credenza of the exotically beautiful Asian woman. She'd seen it every day as she'd headed to the practice room, but never had the nerve to ask who it was.

Morrisey's voice grew distant. "She was my lover. She was pregnant when she went Off-Grid. Mei died in childbirth. So did the baby."

Cynda felt his guilt enveloping her like a brittle Highland mist. To say she was sorry would be meaningless in the face of such a loss. "What kept you from killing yourself?"

"Harter. He made sure I had something to keep me occupied."

"Breaking the fourth dimension?"

"It seemed an impossible task, and it kept me from brooding."

"Not so impossible, apparently." She had to ask. "Did you ever wonder if you could go back and change things?"

"That's why I started working on the project in the first place. It wasn't until after Harter made the first few trips that we began to realize that there might be limitations. Then we lost a Rover..." his voice trailed off.

She'd probably learned all this in the Time Immersion Academy, but right now she couldn't remember the details.

"Harter was devastated. He tried over and over to prevent the death, but nothing worked. Once there's been a mortality within the time stream, something precludes correcting that loss. I have never been able to determine what that is."

Mei and Chris are gone forever.

He looked up at her. "When I finally realized that, it was like losing Mei all over again."

Cynda turned back toward the butterfly where it rested on a leaf. Now she understood his passion for all things Asian—the artwork, the tatami mats, the sushi and Tai Chi. Theo Morrisey was honoring his dead lover every second of his life.

He rose from the bench in a fluid motion. "If you must leave, all I ask is that you make sure you're doing so for the right reasons." His footsteps retreated.

What did that mean? She had no clue. Of all the mysteries she'd worked through, T.E. Morrisey was the most difficult to untangle.

"I've been here too long," she muttered.

"I second that."

The voice was familiar. She glanced around the solarium, trying to find the source.

"Up here," it called. A ball of blue wandered out on a branch, many legs moving in concert. She edged to within a foot of the creature. It was about the size of a shrew, and had eight distinctive appendages.

"Nice color," she observed, thinking hard. "You're not real, are you?"

"I'm real to you," it answered.

She'd seen this thing before. Memories bubbled up unbidden—a monstrous version taunting her and then a smaller one issuing a warning not to go down an alley.

"A warning you ignored," the arachnid observed coolly. "Bought you a knife in the chest."

That memory surfaced as well, evoking a deep shiver. "If my brain's been rebooted, how can you be here?"

"You didn't think that would fix everything, did you?"

"Apparently not." Then she smiled. "It's really you." He was smaller, but just as sarcastic. "You've been gone for a long time."

"So have you," he replied wistfully. "How soon are we leaving?"

"Tomorrow morning should be just about right."

"Good. These hummingbirds are driving me mad."

CHAPTER TWENTY-SEVEN

Just last night, she'd finished her drawing, adding the colored grains of sand that brought the dragon to life. In the sunlight, it almost seemed alive.

Cynda heard the door to Morrisey's private suite open and close, then his tatami sandals on the walkway. How she had grown to love that sound. This hour had become their time to meditate together, or just speak quietly about whatever was on their minds. Some mornings they did not speak at all, the conversation unfolding on a different level.

In deference to the warmer weather, Morrisey was in his green silk robe, the one with the embroidered phoenix on the back. Lithe, he covered the distance with smooth motions and joined her under the pagoda.

She awaited his reaction, anticipation making her fidget with the chopstick in her hands.

Morrisey looked out at the sand and then shot to his feet. "My God, it's magnificent!" He cautiously made his way down the steps to examine her sand sculpture. He paused near a wing. "I have never seen a *T'ien Lung* like this, Jacynda." He beamed at her with a mixture of pride and something indefinable. "It's," he gestured in unusual agitation, "incredible."

Cynda nodded, her heart light. It *was* incredible. And she'd created it.

Morrisey returned to the pagoda, still beaming. "Is it you in dragon form?"

"Yes. The ones on top of the pagoda would never come down to talk to me, so I decided I'd send them a message of my own."

"And so you have. Do you know the significance of the color yellow?" he asked, pointing to the sand dragon.

She shook her head. "I thought it was pretty."

"It is, but it comes with its own lore. *Yellow* signifies a celestial dragon that cannot be captured, tamed, or killed. It is said it will only appear when perfection is found."

Cynda looked back at the dragon and cracked a smile. "Perfection?" Then she laughed, shaking her head. "Hardly. I'm still missing so much."

"Still, you're remembering names more readily now. New memories are being retained." He smiled. "You've moved past building sand castles and throwing tantrums."

"I liked my sand castles," Cynda laughed.

"I knew you could do it," he said, that look of pride returning.

"I wouldn't have if you hadn't run interference for me."

"Then we both deserve the applause."

You more than me.

"There is one more thing before I leave," she said. "It has nothing to do with the Victorians or any of the other stuff. I'd like to see you do Tai Chi with a sword."

His eyes flashed in surprise. "I would be honored," he told her. "You realize I will damage the sand dragon."

"It has served its purpose."

He nodded and then vanished into his rooms. She closed her eyes and waited. Above her, the peg clock marked off the time. It whirled away, seemingly oblivious to the fact that everything was in flux. To it, time was just a certain number of seconds per day.

A few minutes later, Theo Morrisey took his place in the center of the dragon, his dark hair contrasting with the pure white silk of his loose tunic and pants. In his right hand he held a long sword, a red sash tied to the hilt.

He began with a deep bow of respect. As he raised the sword, the morning sun spun a line of gold down the edge. Like a king who has claimed a legendary blade, he flowed across the sand, moving with controlled grace. He was a tiger in the reeds, a heron upon the water, an eagle soaring in the clouds. Human poetry.

Incredible.

When he had finished, he turned and bowed to her again, beads of sweat on his brow. She rose and returned the gesture.

"Thank you, *sensei*," she said. She had never called him *teacher* before.

Visibly startled, the sword quavered in his hand for an instant. Then he rejoined her on the platform, his breathing deep from the exercise.

She waited until he got settled and his breathing returned to normal.

"When I return, will you teach me that?" she asked.

Something flared behind those dark eyes. "When you return, I'll teach you anything you desire," he answered softly.

—

The Government's Complex was as utilitarian as she'd imagined, a fact that only darkened her mood. The knot in her stomach felt like it was studded with a million sharp needles. She was about to do something either incredibly brave, or immensely stupid. Ralph had already weighed in that it was the latter. Their farewell this morning had left both of them in tears.

She'd hoped the farewell with Morrisey would go better, but that looked to be in question. When he didn't jump back into the private grav car after a quick goodbye, her nerves flared up. She couldn't handle another scene like she'd had with Ralph.

Klein was waiting for them, along with a young man. She stared at him, but the name wouldn't fall into place.

"Johns Hopkins," he said. "I delivered your letter to Montrose."

Cynda worked on that for a few seconds. An image appeared: Hopkins lying on a bed, each breath a struggle.

"You owe me a couple beers," he added, smiling. "And Copeland's head."

Copeland. TPB's hired gun. The last time she'd seen him was right after he shot Defoe. *The night my brain was blanked.*

Klein cut in. "Give her the gun." Hopkins produced one from his pocket. "It's a Webley, period authentic. Use it if needed, though I'd prefer that bastard alive."

Considering Copeland's history, it was a sensible precaution. Gingerly, she took the firearm and put it into a pocket. She couldn't miss the frown forming on Morrisey's face.

"She's not your assassin, Klein," he growled.

"Didn't think she was." Klein pointed, "Chronsole room is that way. Before you leave, I need to talk to you, Morrisey."

Her boss nodded, the frown still in place. Cynda stuck out her hand, hoping he'd make this as painless as possible.

"No, I'll see you off," he said firmly.

Her heart sank. *Please don't make this harder than it is.*

As Hopkins escorted them to the chronsole room, Morrisey offered a steady string of advice. That told her how worried he was.

"Find Harter," he said. "He's in London."

"Any idea where?"

"He hasn't communicated with us. You know whom you can trust in that time period. Rely on them. Do *not* do this on your own."

"Yes, boss."

The frown deepened. "Keep in contact on a regular basis," he instructed, handing her something. It was a silver pendant. "If you press your thumb against the photo and your index finger on the back, it will allow you access to the database. I loaded what I thought you might need. It includes an image gallery to help refresh your memory, and you can add new data files."

"It took a lot of time for you to do this for me."

He shrugged, much like a young boy caught giving a girl a lollipop.

The chronsole room and the time pod were as dull as the rest of the building. The chron-op was a woman with pale hair and paler skin. She gave Cynda a bored look and turned back to the chronsole. Ralph wouldn't like this scene. Luckily, she'd talked him into missing this.

Cynda paused before the time pod door. This was harder than she'd expected. She had grown accustomed to Morrisey's stable presence, his wisdom, and his protection. She would truly miss him, as much as she'd miss Ralph. *More.* It felt odd to admit that.

"Miss Lassiter?" Morrisey prompted.

"Sorry. Anything else?"

He looked over at Hopkins. "I would like to do this transfer."

"Why not? You invented the technology," the Guv's Rover replied.

The chron-op didn't look pleased. They were a territorial bunch.

"If you don't mind, I'd prefer to do this alone," Morrisey added.

Hopkins raised an eyebrow at the unusual request. "Okay. Time for coffee," he said. The chron-op gave them all a disgruntled frown, but followed the Guv agent out the door.

Morrisey waited for the door to close. With a trembling hand he gently touched her cheek. A delicate kiss on her lips brushed her lips. It felt warm, inviting. When he drew back, Cynda stared at him, too stunned to reply.

He caressed her cheek again, a sheen in his eyes. "Keep yourself safe, Jacynda. We have unfinished business, you and I."

This was agony. If she failed in 1888, she'd never see this extraordinary man again.

When she didn't speak, he reluctantly drew away. All business now, he took his place behind the chronsole. "I will make this as comfortable as possible, since you're a bit rusty."

She heard a chuckle from her shoulder. "That's an understatement."

Zip it, spider, or you'll have to find your own way there.

Cynda knelt in the time pod, then raised her head, though that wasn't standard protocol. The door closed with a final clunk that made her bones quake.

She saw his lips moving, though she could no longer hear what he was saying. A prayer, perhaps?

On impulse, she blew him a kiss. A tormented smile returned.

He mouthed something, then triggered the technology that would send her back one hundred and seventy years.

The fourth dimension had never felt so lonely.

"NOTHING IS EASIER THAN TO
DENOUNCE THE EVILDOER;
NOTHING IS MORE DIFFICULT THAN
TO UNDERSTAND HIM."
- FYODOR DOSTOEVSKY

PART TWO

✥

CHAPTER ONE

Sunday, 4 November 1888
Hyde Park, London

Satyr exited the hansom at the northeast corner of Hyde Park near Marble Arch, where a crowd encircled someone spouting the wonders of socialism. He straightened his coat and tie, taking time to gather his bearings.

Though his position as Lead Assassin made him answerable only to the Ascendant, Satyr was mindful that the Twenty also wielded considerable power amongst the Transitives. Comprised of various members of the community, apportioned by rank or commercial affiliation, the Twenty were responsible for suggesting policy to their leader. Though the Ascendant was the pinnacle of their kind, it was the Twenty who decided when an Ascendant's time had passed. Then the Lead Assassin came into play, dispatching the old so that they could vote in the new.

An eminently practical system of checks and balances.

The last time an Ascendant had been replaced was at the beginning of the year; Satyr could still hear the pitiful whimpers of his previous master as he prepared to deliver the final blow. Such cowardice made the job distasteful.

Unfortunately, the current Ascendant will not depart so easily.

According to tradition, the Twenty had a representative from each of the major guilds, a few lords, a judge or two, and a single female. Satyr knew the identities of a few of them, though he wasn't supposed to know any of them except for the Intermediary, who acted as a liaison between the Ascendant and the group.

The single female on the Twenty was a holdover from the late 1700s, when someone had installed his mistress in the group as a lark. It was joked that naming a woman to the Twenty was much like Caligula making his horse a Roman senator. That tradition continued to the present day, though the woman was no longer some lowly mistress. She was, in fact, the first female Intermediary and most sought-after courtesan in London.

Before long, Satyr saw her carriage arrive. Her transport wasn't ostentatious, like some. Adelaide Winston alighted with a grace that made the others of her sex appear like draft ponies. With a few adjustments of her burgundy parasol, she set off on the path inside the park. Men made way for her, many touching their caps in respect. Women, however, delivered veiled glares; they understood that her promenade was as much advertisement as exercise.

Satyr eventually overtook her, offering his arm. She took it.

"Good day, Mr. S.," she acknowledged, her voice low and rich. It was plain why men paid a ransom to be with this woman. Even if you did not enjoy the carnal aspects of her nature, listening to her was well worth the price.

"Good day, Madam Winston. I trust you are well?"

"In health, I am very sound. In mind, however, I am troubled. But first, tell me why you wished to meet on such short notice."

He waited until they had passed another couple and had more privacy. "The Ascendant is beginning to cross the line, madam."

"So soon?" she asked. "In what way is he being inappropriate?"

Satyr related the Lassiter incident and the employment of a junior assassin without his knowledge.

Adelaide gave a slight nod to a distinguished gentleman who passed in the other direction. He returned a faint smile of remembrance. "Do I note a fit of pique?" she gently chided.

"Yes," Satyr admitted, knowing she valued honesty. "Nevertheless, he has been acting oddly as of late."

"In what way?"

"He has not been forthcoming about his delays with regard to the plan."

Her brow furrowed. "Has he delivered the…commercial items he has recently obtained?"

The explosives. "No, he has not. When I ask for particulars, I am ignored."

Madam Winston nodded knowingly. "When we press him, he dodges our questions as well. Is it true that the materials are no longer in one location, but scattered about the East End?"

Satyr nodded gravely. "Our leader says it is to avoid any inadvertent accident or discovery by the authorities, now that the Fenians are involved."

Adelaide looked startled. "Why include them? They have no part in this. They only raise the stakes as far as the police are concerned."

"The anarchist in question was not given a choice, madam." As they approached the turn south toward the Serpentine, Satyr told her of Desmond Flaherty and the stranglehold their leader held on the man. His companion's face didn't change, but he could sense tension rising in her body.

"How old is this girl?" she asked.

"Seventeen, I believe."

"Is she unharmed?"

"At present."

They walked on for a time, Satyr scanning the area for potential threats. Though he saw none, he did not relax. Why was he feeling so exposed? Certainly the Ascendant would not attempt to harm him or the Intermediary."

Adelaide Winston's troubled eyes sought his. "I shall present your news to the Twenty. We will demand answers. At no time should he be acting without our approval. Though I have no love of anarchists, this kidnapping is barbarous."

Satyr nodded. "I spoke out against it, but it did no good. I suspect that in the coming days he will order the girl's death, as well as that of her father, to ensure they are no witnesses."

"You are required to follow the Ascendant's orders," she replied softly. "However, I see no benefit to be derived from another murdered girl. Flaherty's demise will bring the wrath of the Irish upon us. Even if they do not avenge him in the short term, they are known to have very long memories."

"I will see what can be done within the confines of my duty."

"That would be best." They angled around the path to return the way they'd come. "This Miss Lassiter, did she truly present a threat?"

An excellent question. "I'm not sure. She was investigating the death of her lover, which as far as I can tell has no bearing on our work. Yet the Ascendant ordered her demise nearly the moment she arrived in London."

The courtesan was quiet for a time. "Have you seen Mr. Livingston recently?" she asked, her voice harboring a different tone.

"No."

"Please locate him if you can. I have not seen him in some time, and that is unusual."

"I may not be the best choice for that, madam. I received an order just this morning to *remove* Mr. Livingston at the soonest opportunity."

Adelaide Winston's eyes widened. "Why would the Ascendant do such a thing? Malachi..." There was a slight tint to her cheeks. "Mr. Livingston is a valued member of our community."

Apparently, there was more between the courtesan and her customer than just commerce. "I am sorry, madam, but no reason was given for the order." A fact that had puzzled him as well. The Ascendant's decision regarding Livingston felt arbitrary.

"This is unacceptable," she said sternly. "We cannot have the Ascendant just dispatching people at whim. Unless... could it be that our leader fears that Mr. Livingston might become his replacement?"

"It is possible," Satyr conceded. "Livingston would be an excellent choice."

"Then I would suggest you take your time carrying out that order, sir."

"I am willing to do that, madam; however, there is no guarantee *he* might not send another in my stead."

She grew pensive. "I wonder how long it will be before the rest of us are considered a threat, Mr. S.?"

—

Ralph might rail against her about taking unnecessary risks, but Cynda knew this was where she belonged. Perhaps it was the hurly-burly of the city that attracted her, the vitality of everyday life. Victorian London was truly a free-for-all. Voices competed with the sound of carriage wheels and the low rumble of wagons moving slowly down the street. A load of hops rolled by as young boys scampered around the street, calling out to each other. A small knot of women traded gossip in a doorway, looking up when someone passed. All of this was muted in 2058, held in check by the rules regarding noise abatement, how long you could loiter on the street, sit on a bench in a park.

Cynda inhaled deeply, which she instantly deemed a mistake. After a prolonged coughing fit, she shook her head at her own stupidity.

Never were that smart, were you Lassiter? The grin came instantly. She had a name, and it had stuck. Though her mind still resembled a moth-eaten sweater, some things were clearer than they'd been before the Nothing Time. She sensed other people's emotions more strongly than before. Danger registered more clearly, almost like a scent in the air. There had been benefits to misplacing her memories. Minimal time lag, for one.

Cynda shifted her Gladstone to the left hand to keep her right free. The pistol was in that pocket, though she didn't expect to use it. Rovers weren't gun sorts of people, though they'd been trained in how to fire some of the older varieties. Most preferred a Neural-blocker. A lot less messy, but frowned upon by TPB.

Her first inkling that she'd lost some of her Victorian savvy was when she went to cross a street and forgot to look in all directions. A hansom rounded the corner at a brisk clip and she had to lurch back onto the kerb to keep from being flattened. Then she felt a tug on her skirt, followed by the rapid patter of retreating feet. One of the toolers had just nailed her. She dug into the pocket and found a few coins missing. Fortunately, the bulk of her money was in the Gladstone. Her interface, buried in the secret pocket, remained safe.

"Money in boots, except for a few coins," Mr. Spider advised from her shoulder. "That's what you used to do."

"That I had forgotten," she grumbled. She'd given a lot of thought and preparation to this journey, but the "taken for granted" parts of her job weren't mentioned in the run reports. Those would give her the most trouble. All the street savvy she'd relied on in the past was either missing or forgotten, making the danger seem much more tangible than before. She would just have to rely on her instincts. She knew who her friends were here. She knew some of her enemies. In the middle was a lot of gray.

Gray could get me dead.

Since she couldn't very well open the case and move the cash about on the street, she tightened her grip on the Gladstone and set off again, leery of what other traps lay in store.

It took a few hotels until she found one that had a room. When the clerk mentioned her accent, as he called it, she claimed to be from New York. That always did the trick.

He consulted his register. "I have only one room available. It has a sitting room with a separate bedchamber. It comes with attendance."

Which meant you had a domestic fuss over you. That sounded good. A maid could bring you hot water for baths. "So why is it so busy?" she asked, signing the register.

"Between Guy Fawkes Day, the opening of Parliament, and the Lord Mayor's Show, rooms are at a premium," the clerk replied.

As he turned to retrieve the room key, his words hit home. "Guy Fawkes Day?"

The clerk turned around. "Oh, of course, you're an American. You may not be aware of our celebrations. It is in honor of Guy Fawkes, who attempted to blow up Parliament as an act of rebellion. It is also called Bonfire Night."

"*Remember, remember, the fifth of November,*" she murmured, her mind awhirl.

The clerk beamed. "I see you've heard the rhyme."

As he selected the key and finished the paperwork, Cynda spied a newspaper lying on the counter. Pulling it toward her, she checked the date.

Sunday, November 4 1888

That wasn't right. She was supposed to have arrived in London on the thirteenth of October, the night Nicci Hallcox met her Maker.

Off-time. It'd only happened to her once before, when she'd come to Victorian London in August to find a missing tourist. She would have blamed this episode on chron operator error, but she knew Morrisey wasn't capable of making such a basic mistake.

Keeping her apprehensions to herself, she allowed the porter to carry her Gladstone to the room. Once she'd tipped him and shooed the dutiful maid out the door, she retreated to the bedroom and reset the interface for the night Keats' life had slid off the rails.

OK, let's try this again.

THE OVERPOWERING SMELL of the river made Cynda's stomach lurch. Why was she here at the edge of the Thames? She was supposed to be a short hike from the Charing Cross Hotel. She glanced down at the interface.

The dial was blank. She gave the stem a twist. Still blank. A sharp shake did nothing to rectify the problem.

Her pulse began to race. *What the hell is this?*

Just then, she heard the creak of carriage wheels and the snort of a horse. Cautiously, she stepped back into the shadows.

The driver was heavily cloaked against the night air and kept looking around, uneasy. The carriage door swung open and a figure climbed out.

"This will do," he said. "It's a short haul to the river, and he doesn't weigh much."

He?

The voice registered. Dalton Mimes, the crazy author in the asylum, the man who'd killed Chris Stone. But what was he doing here? Cynda shrank farther back into a nook near a storage shed, worried he might spot her.

Meanwhile, another man exited the carriage. He was tall and wore a dark coat, his back to her.

Turn around.

With effort, Dalton Mimes and his companion pulled something out of the vehicle. It took her a moment to realize it was a body. As they adjusted the weight between them, she caught sight of the face. Bile rose, scorching her throat.

Chris. She was off-time again. This was the twenty-third of September, the night her lover had been murdered and his body thrown into the Thames. For some reason, she'd been brought here to witness this moment.

As they hefted his lifeless corpse, her eyes filmed with tears. She blinked to clear them.

"Let's get it done," the man ordered. He didn't move like a Victorian. That puzzled her—if he were from '058, her interface should be registering his ESR Chip. *Unless he took it out.* She didn't have one, after all.

Mimes complied, and with much tugging and complaining, Chris' body was carried to the pier and tossed into the Thames like a sack of unwanted puppies.

At the sound of the splash, Cynda's hand dove into her pocket for the firearm, the ants inside her screaming for lethal revenge.

"It won't bring him back," she heard from her shoulder.

"I don't care," she hissed.

"It may make things worse," Mr. Spider said.

"How could it be any worse?"

"Trust me, it can," he nearly shouted.

The voice of her conscience had never steered her wrong. She took three deep breaths, trying to calm herself. There was no way to change the timeline now. Chris was gone. Forever.

He deserved so much better than this.

She forced herself to remove her hand from the pocket, clenching it into a quivering fist.

The cloaked man turned and she finally saw his face in the muted light. Cynda studied him intently, channeling her anger into action. He was tall, with a rigid stance. That seemed an important clue. Frantically, she rummaged in her mental filing cabinets for a name.

"That night in Wapping?" Mr. Spider suggested.

The memory surfaced. She heard the sound of a gunshot echoing off the brick warehouses and Harter Defoe collapsing, blood pouring from his chest.

Copeland. She'd called him Ramrod because of his stiff posture. He was one of the two TPB minions who'd come to collect her when she'd been hauled back to 2057 for trial. The man who'd threatened to shoot her and wounded Defoe instead. Somehow, this jerk was tied to Mimes. But why would TPB want Morrisey's nephew dead?

"Taking the trash out," Copeland joked, gesturing toward where Chris' body had just splashed into the Thames. "Piece of cake."

"You son-of-a-bitch," she spat.

"Did you hear something?" Mimes asked, craning his head around.

Cynda froze. She didn't sense the presence behind her until right before the hand covered her mouth, pulling her further back.

"Quiet. Don't move."

Fear coursed through her as her hand closed on the pistol again. She would have pulled it out if Mimes hadn't moved closer, staring directly into her hiding place. He seemed to be looking right at her. She waited for the shout of discovery. Instead, he blinked a couple of times, then shook his head and backed off.

"Time to go," Copeland called. The men loaded into the carriage and with a clatter of hooves the conveyance rolled away.

"They're gone," her companion said, releasing her. As she turned, a figure appeared out of the air. It was Defoe. Or at least someone who looked like him. With the shape-shifters, you never knew.

"How do I know you're really you?" she asked, still edgy.

"Who else would it be? I'm the one who always saves your skin."

Her eyes lit on the flower in his lapel. "Tell me about the rose."

He smiled. "You said the one I was wearing didn't have the right scent. That was when I knew you still had a working brain. Satisfied?"

She nodded. As she watched, he shifted into a distinguished gentleman, a lion's head cane in hand. He had a white bloom around him, like he was edged in a silvery cloud. She'd seen that once before at the crazy place. The man who'd claimed to be her brother had one of those.

She decided to test a theory. "Change back to the real you."

He looked confused. "What?"

"Just do it."

After a quick look around, he shifted to the form she knew as Harter Defoe. The white outline vanished.

"Okay, now change back."

He easily reverted to the Victorian gent again. As she'd expected, the white edging returned.

"I'll be damned."

"What are you going on about?" Defoe asked.

"Nothing," she said. "Why didn't Mimes see me?"

"I went invisible and took you with me."

"Neat trick."

"It can be useful. So, what brings you here?"

"I didn't intend to be here. Right now, my interface seems to have a mind of its own. I was supposed to go back to the night Keats was framed. I ended up on the fourth of November instead. When I tried it a second time, I was here, in September."

"Playing their games again," he muttered. "I landed in New York City. Couldn't get to London no matter how I tried. Then some messenger boy handed me a ticket for a steamship, so I've spent the last week floating across the pond in First Class, regretting the wasted time."

"So why are you here?" she quizzed.

"Testing a theory." Defoe looked around again, suddenly uncomfortable. "We need to compare notes—something we were going to do the last time, but were interrupted." He straightened his jacket. "Oh, and one other detail—if anyone asks, I'm Malachi Livingston."

"Livingston," she murmured. *Why does that sound familiar?*

"Dr. Montrose has probably mentioned me. I'm on The Conclave."

"You're one of *them*?"

He shrugged. "I got bored. Retirement is fine, but I have to keep my hand in. Let's find a dining room with a quiet corner. I need to rest."

Is this what she had to look forward to? Being bored to tears and having to content herself with meddling in the time stream?

"Pity they don't have sushi here," she lamented.

He shot her a look. "You actually *like* that stuff?"

"I do now. And Tai Chi. Chess, even. I'm getting pretty good at it."

Defoe knit his brows. "I take it Theo oversaw your care?"

"Sure did. He helped me put my mind back together. It took a lot of effort to keep the shrinks out of the way."

"Did he mention the *Duckling Effect*?"

"The what?"

"Oh, Theo," he said, shaking his head.

"Look, I'm tired, so speak English."

"You still have the attitude, I see." He offered his arm and they strolled along the docks. "Just don't shoot the messenger, all right?" She nodded.

"Klein told me that after NMR treatment, the patient often adopts traits of the person most involved in their therapy. It's sort of like a baby duck patterning after its mother. Your sudden love of sushi is a good example."

Morrisey hadn't told her any of that. Part of her was sincerely irritated. Then she shrugged it off. "Beats not knowing who the hell you are."

A chuckle. "You have me there."

"Anyway, there are worse people to pattern myself after."

Defoe's eyebrow quirked upward. "True, but I wonder if the world is ready for a Morrisey-Lassiter hybrid."

"Then they shouldn't have screwed with my brain in the first place."

She paused and turned toward the water, thinking of Chris as he made his solitary journey downriver. She couldn't remember their last time together. It was squirreled away in her memories, just out of reach.

"You'll remember it eventually," her delusion assured.

"He was a great kid," Defoe said softly.

She could only nod, clenching her teeth to hold back a new round of tears.

At least now she knew the truth: Mimes had been involved in Chris' murder, but he'd had help from TPB's minion.

Someone who isn't crazy. Someone who could pay the price for murder.

CHAPTER TWO

The dining room was busy, but with a generous gratuity they were shown into a private area. Cynda sat facing the door.

"Paranoid?" Defoe suggested.

"Hell, yes," she declared, plopping her hat on the table. "Aren't you?"

"Sometimes." He ordered tea and cake, his words brusque. Meanwhile, her delusion shambled across the table and parked himself next to a sugar bowl. He had a fascination with those for some reason.

"So what's going on here?" she asked once the server puttered off.

Defoe held up a hand for silence, then opened his interface and positioned it on the table. "It's set to dampen our conversation. You'd have to be standing on top of us to overhear us." It was a clever trick. To a Victorian, it would look like he was just overly concerned about the time.

"More of Morrisey's fancy software?"

"Exactly." Nevertheless, he lowered his voice. "We are experiencing a power struggle between our time and the future. *Now* is the battleground."

"Morrissey said *now* was very unstable."

"Extremely, or Sergeant Keats wouldn't be facing the noose."

"I thought it was because I sidetracked him a few weeks ago so he didn't catch Flaherty when he was supposed to."

"I doubt it was completely your fault, though you may have contributed to the time aberration," Defoe explained. "I've inadvertently altered timelines before, but nothing came of it. It always went back on track."

"Morrisey thinks someone else had already stirred things up, and I just gave it a bit more oomph."

"Very likely. You play God, and things happen."

She opened her mouth to protest, but bit her tongue as the server approached with a tray. Defoe clicked the interface shut and moved it out of the way.

"There ya are, sir. Nice and hot. The cakes are fresh. I bake them myself," she said.

"Thank you, madam."

Cynda performed the honors, doling out their refreshments as Defoe opened the interface and replaced it on the table.

"Morrisey said things go very badly for the shifters up the time stream," she ventured.

Defoe's smile dimmed. "I'm surprised he told you that. Theo's usually more discreet." He grew pensive. "If he trusts you that much..." He nodded to himself, a decision made.

"I met my first Future in 1979. I gone there to see one of the old moving pictures, *Time After Time*."

"I know that one. H.G. Wells chases Jack the Ripper to 1979 San Francisco to retrieve his time machine. It's one my favorites."

"All utter nonsense, of course," Defoe replied. "Still, it was great fun listening to the audience discuss the possibility of time travel, little knowing that someone from nearly eight decades into the future was sitting among them."

"I wish I'd done that," Cynda said wistfully.

"I didn't pay much attention to the man sitting to my right until we'd left the theater. As we reached the street, he said, "Not quite accurate, is it, Mr. Defoe?"

"That had to spook you," Cynda said, grinning.

"It did. He said his name was Robert Anderson, and the news he brought was anything but good. He told me what happens to the Transitives once their secret is made public knowledge." Defoe took a long sip of tea. "Needs brandy," he grumbled.

"What year was he from?"

"2075. Apparently he and some of the other Futures felt it was time we knew what was coming."

"Does Guv know this?"

He shook his head. "Anderson said laws are enacted to prevent shifters from passing the ability when they die, keeping them out of sensitive Government jobs." He frowned. "In the future, Rovers can't be shifters."

She dropped her spoon on the table. "Why not?"

"It's a safety issue, they say. If you can look like anyone, you could mess with history and no one will know."

"But *you're* a shifter," she said, trying to get a handle on this. "You *and* Morrisey. You guys invented this technology, and then you're not safe enough to be part of it?"

He shook his head. "According to Anderson, the Transitives begin to fight back in 2065, going underground. By 2083, another group takes advantage of our distraction and it all goes to hell. Our petty war makes us lose the most important battle: our future."

"What happens?" she asks.

"He wouldn't tell me."

"But you said he was '075. How would he know—"

"I think he got the word from a Future further up the time stream."

Cynda huffed. "Great. Like a little bucket brigade of warnings trickling down to us."

Defoe delivered a disgruntled look at her analogy. Fortunately, the server returned, checking on them. Once the woman was gone, beaming at another one of his compliments, Defoe opened his interface again.

Leaning back in the chair, he said, "Those ahead of us are becoming actively involved in whatever is going on here. I think this time period is critical for them in some way. We were both off-timed for a reason."

"Why not just tell us Copeland was involved in Chris' death?" she said, adding more sugar to her tea. "Why not just help us outright? It's not like it's going to get any more screwed up."

Defoe arched an eyebrow as if she were being naïve. "There's far more at stake than just Chris' murder. Some of the Futures want the Transitives' secret to be revealed much earlier. They feel that if the world knew of them in the late nineteenth century, then the sanctions wouldn't be put in place or, if they were, they'd be removed by the twenty-first century."

"That's overly optimistic."

He issued a weary sigh. "Well, that's not our problem. We need to find out what's happening *here*, and what it has to do with the explosives. Did Morrisey tell you how the Transitives are organized?"

"Yes," she said, cutting a piece of cake.

"What do you know, so I don't have to repeat myself?"

Cynda set the knife aside, sad the food had to wait. It looked yummy. She closed her eyes and visualized the shifters' organizational tree. It seemed to help if she saw something in her mind before trying to verbalize it.

"The Ascendant is the top dog," she began. "He has eight killers at his command: the Lead Assassin and the Seven, who follow the Lead's orders. The Lead is always a Virtual. There are the Twenty who report to the head guy and determine when it is time to replace him. Then there's The Conclave, which is more for show than anything."

Only after the fact did she realize why she'd earned herself a frown. His alter ego, Livingston, was a member of The Conclave.

"Did Theo discover who was the Ascendant at this point in history?" he inquired.

She shook her head. "He's working on it. He said something about going to some special archive collection."

"That sounds right. A lot of the Transitives' history is not in electronic form. How about the membership of the Twenty?"

Cynda dug the pendant out from under her bodice, pulling it over her head. Clicking it open, she pressed her thumb against the picture of her parents. Nothing happened.

"Index finger on the back," her delusion called out from near the cake. He was holding a small piece between two legs.

Thanks.

Once the device had acknowledged that she had legitimate access, the photo vanished and the dial lit up.

"Morrisey's doing," she explained in response to Defoe's mystified expression. "He gave me a database of images so I can look through them every night and refresh my mind."

"He's known for those sorts of gadgets," her companion observed with a smirk. "Sort of like Q in the old James Bond movies."

"Who?"

He grimaced. "Never mind. It was before your time."

She put the pendant near her mouth. "List Twenty," she murmured.

Names began marching across the tiny screen. "Let's see. We've got a Jackson, Marshall, Hyde-Smith, McClelland, Winston, Rivers, and Baron-Reid. That's all he could—"

"Do you have a full name for Winston?" he asked, his voice suddenly brittle.

"Sure." She addressed the device. "List particulars for Winston." The screen lit up, filling with information. "Adelaide Winston, age twenty-eight. Born—"

Defoe's cup slammed down onto the saucer, his eyes distant. He wiped his mouth with a napkin.

Whoa. I hit a nerve.

"You know something about her?" Cynda ventured.

"It appears she's one of the Twenty," he replied brusquely, as if that were the only answer. His eyes snapped back to hers. "What do you intend to do next?"

"Try to get back to the middle of October, I guess."

"Don't bother. I suspect you won't be allowed."

Her mouth dropped open. "But that screws up everything I planned!"

"So?" he chided. "You're a Rover. Think on your feet for a change."

Jerk. He'd been cranky ever since she mentioned the Winston woman.

"Well, maybe I can call in a few favors. Flaherty has to come forward and save Keats."

Defoe snorted. "You're a fool if you think he'll do that."

That did it. No one called her a fool, even the Father of Time Travel.

"So what are *you* going to do, then?"

He closed his interface and tossed money on the table, not bothering to answer. "Let's get out of here."

Right before they made their transfers, Cynda dug out the business card from the hotel. "I'm at the Arundel at Victoria Embankment." He didn't write any of it down. That she envied. As she started to say goodbye, he triggered his interface and was gone.

"He's a piece of work," her delusion said.

"Yeah, he is."

The moment the transfer stabilized, she checked the interface. November fourth, the day she'd checked into the hotel. She made a beeline toward the closest newspaper boy, exasperated she had to use newsprint as a means to verify the date. Both the paper and the technology agreed. At least that was a start.

"Time for Plan B," she muttered. *Whatever the hell that is.*

—

So many times he'd been in this room awaiting Adelaide's arrival, always with a mixture of elation and heady desire. Tonight was different. She had never mentioned she was a member of the Twenty, never indicated she had a loyalty to anyone but herself. Likewise, he'd only shown her Malachi Livingston's form, not his real one. More than once he'd wanted to bare his soul, tell her he was really Harter Defoe, a man from the future. He'd never been able to take that leap of faith.

Neither of them had been totally honest, and that made it worse.

The door opened and she hurried into the room. Adelaide never hurried in any fashion.

"Malachi?" When he did not offer his hand in their special greeting, she halted abruptly. "Is it truly you?"

Only then did he take her hand and make the sign in her palm. She returned it.

"Thank heavens," Adelaide said. "No one has heard from you in over a week. I was so worried."

"I was indisposed," he responded coolly, stepping back.

"Even your assistant, William, was concerned about you, as well. He came calling the other day to ask after you. Where have you been?"

"Recuperating—someone tried to kill me."

Horror filled her face. "He said he'd—"

Defoe held his tongue, forcing her to speak.

Adelaide regained her composure. "Only this morning, I learned that the Ascendant has ordered your death, for no apparent reason. I urged the Lead Assassin to slow the process so I might have time to warn you."

"I was injured almost a week ago," Defoe informed her with a frown.

Confusion clouded her face. "That does not follow with what he told me."

Defoe didn't bother to explain that he had enemies in two different centuries. "Since when does the Lead Assassin speak so openly about murder?"

Adelaide sank into a nearby chair with an agitated rustle of silk. "I pray that you will forgive me for what I am about to tell you."

She was afraid. *Of me, or her master?*

"I am a member of the Twenty, Malachi. I am the Intermediary between that body and the Ascendant. I do not readily reveal that fact to anyone. The longer I have known you, the more I've come to realize you're an honorable man, and now I regret not having shared that confidence earlier."

She sounds so sincere.

"Once this crisis is over, I intend to resign from the Twenty and go to Paris. I have already found someone to purchase the house and the furniture." She looked directly at him, pleading in her voice. "I intend to start over, Malachi. I sincerely pray you will join me."

He pushed aside her offer. "What crisis?"

She paused for a moment, struggling with the change that had come over him. "The Ascendant is playing us, one and all," she explained. "If we do not have a satisfactory answer out of him by mid-week, he will be replaced. The Lead Assassin is in agreement with me on this point. We cannot risk exposure."

"Who is he?"

He expected her to refuse him that information, but she did not hesitate. "His name is Hezekiah Grant. He is, by most points, a somber and pious man. However, as of recent he has begun to act quite oddly."

"What is behind all this?"

"The Ascendant said that we had the opportunity to obtain some explosives that we might pass onto certain sympathetic Transitives in Russia."

"Why stir up trouble with them?" he asked.

"We believe the rise of the Bolsheviks will not prove advantageous for Britain. Our loyalty is not only to our kind, Malachi, but also to our nation.

The Twenty discussed it and decided the plan had value. Then he enlisted that anarchist, Flaherty, to steal the explosives, even going so far as to kidnap the man's daughter to hold him in check."

"That was not part of your plan?"

"Heavens no," she said. "I can only imagine the terror in that child's heart. We are very upset at this news. It is clear now that he does not intend to convey this merchandise to the appropriate people but has his own scheme for its use."

"How many of the Twenty do you know by name?"

"Only a few. We hold privacy as our greatest shield. I suspect the Lead Assassin knows some of the others as well."

"What of him?"

"I must admit I first thought him an abomination. My opinion has changed as of recent. His true name is hidden from us."

Defoe had one last question. If he did not ask it, he would implode. "Do you truly love me, Adelaide, or was it all a ruse to make me trust you?"

Her eyes misted over as she nodded. "Yes, I do love you. I realized very early on that our trysts were more than just the pleasure between a man and a woman."

In the beginning, he'd not come to this house for anything but time spent with a beautiful courtesan, one of the perquisites of the job. The nights he spent with Adelaide had changed his mind. A few hours in her arms were not enough. He wanted more.

"Does the Lead Assassin know of your feelings?" he quizzed, still unsure of her loyalty.

"I suspect he does."

"Was he one of your gentlemen?" Defoe asked peevishly.

"Not that I am aware."

"Will the Lead Assassin try to fulfill his contract against me?"

"He will have to, eventually, or face being killed himself. If he delays, there is no guarantee the Ascendant will not dispatch another. Apparently, he has already done so in another matter."

"I see."

Adelaide rose. "I will press for the Ascendant's removal. I will not risk your life, Malachi."

He drew her close to him, wincing when she put her hand on his healing wound. She laid her head on his chest. This was not a courtesan with a customer, but a trembling lover, fearing rejection. He had encountered many lying women over the centuries.

His heart told him that Adelaide Winston was not one of them.

Monday, 5 November 1888
Newgate Prison

Keats stared at the ceiling, waiting. His pocket watch rested on his chest, the cover open so he could consult the dial. In a few short minutes it would be his birthday, but there was little cause for celebration. Last year he'd been a blissfully happy man, having just successfully completed a complicated case involving international forgers. Now he was thirty-three years old, and had fallen further than even his father could imagine.

The cell door opened and Alastair entered. Keats swung his feet over the edge of the bed, surprised to see his friend so early in the morning.

"I know you're probably not in the mood," Alastair said with a muted smile, "but I did want to visit you on your birthday."

He remembered. "Not much to celebrate, is there?"

"That remains to be seen," was the reply. The doctor turned to the two guards. "May we have some privacy? I need to examine the prisoner's wounds."

Once the door closed behind the pair of them, Alastair took a seat on the bench, placing his Gladstone and a newspaper next to him. He gestured for Keats to remove his coat and shirt.

"There's no point," Keats protested, working on the shirt buttons. "Tomorrow morning, it will no longer matter."

Alastair didn't reply as he continued his examination, carefully palpating along the broken rib. "Healing very nicely," he remarked. "Your head wound is much improved. There's still a scar, but your hair hides most of it."

"Stop being so damned positive, will you?" Keats barked. "We both know—"

"Until that final moment, I will keep hope," Alastair thundered back. "You can be all gloomy if you want, and Lord knows you have the right, but nevertheless I feel this will be resolved."

"How can you be so sure?" Keats asked.

"Jacynda has returned. I received a note from her late last night."

He started in surprise. "Is she herself now?"

"It would appear so. The letter was most coherent. If she can be restored to us, so can you. She'll *not* let you hang, Keats."

For an instant, he felt hope. "So you say," he conceded, pulling on his coat. "How is Lord Wescomb?"

"Improving. He has been writing letters to everyone who carries any weight. And lest you think you're forgotten..." Alastair handed off the morning paper.

Keats scanned the newsprint, then blurted, "They're bringing the matter up in Parliament tomorrow morning?"

"Indeed. Questions are being asked in the newspapers as to why the explosives were not allowed into testimony. Why your execution is being rushed. Why the government is not providing any answers. The city is in an uproar."

Keats tossed the paper aside. "It won't matter. Parliament won't convene until after I'm dead."

"Perhaps enough pressure will be applied to stay the execution until we get this sorted."

Keats scoffed. "You honestly believe that?"

"I refuse to give up on you," Alastair said firmly. He packed his stethoscope into the Gladstone and snapped it shut. "I'll be back this afternoon to see you." He dug in his pocket and placed a pouch of tobacco on the bed. "Happy Birthday, my friend. May it be one of many more."

"Thank you," Keats answered softly, picking up the gift. "For everything."

⊹

CHAPTER THREE

A comfortable bed didn't prevent Cynda from tossing and turning the entire night. After spending so much time formulating her plan, it was getting trashed by people she'd never met. It was bad enough TPB and Guv were messing with her life. Now there were the Futures, some vague group of people with their own devious agenda.

"Too bad, guys," she murmured. "Mine takes precedence. Keats is not going to hang."

To perk herself up, she ordered a big pot of coffee and some breakfast. After that, she'd start with the big dog. You should always have one of those in your corner.

The letter she penned to the Prince of Wales requested his assistance in a matter of extreme urgency. Since he believed she'd saved his life a few weeks earlier at Effington's dinner party, the least he could do under the circumstances was send her a polite reply. If he ignored her, she'd have to track him down on her own. Finding the Royal would be easy compared to locating the anarchist.

Cynda began pursuing that thread. "Who wants Flaherty in prison?"

"The police," Mr. Spider replied. He was nestling down on top of the linen napkin, as usual.

"The coppers for sure," she agreed. "Who else?" Then she smiled. There was one person who'd want to see him swing: Johnny Ahearn's widow. Nothing brought out the desire for vengeance more than having your husband's throat cut, especially when you were left to raise a child alone.

She synced up with TEMnet and posed the question to Ralph. He came through with the address where the Widow Ahearn lived in Stepney.

Thanks. How's it going there?

Not good. TPB knows you're gone and has begun formal proceedings against the boss.

Oh, boy. Send him my best.

Will do. Pull this out of your hat, Cyn. We're all counting on you.

No pressure there.

Will do. Later, guy. Log Off.

Logged off.

—

Cynda had always been in awe of women who were pregnant. They held mysteries inside of them she could not fathom. Would never fathom. That was one of the reasons why there were so few women Rovers: childbearing ceased to be an option once you began traveling through time. Something about hopping through the fourth dimension altered the ovaries, and not in a good way. The guys weren't affected. Another inequity.

Cynda hadn't expected a warm reception, but Johnny Ahearn's widow didn't even bother to invite her into the small hovel. Instead, Mrs. Ahearn leaned in the doorway, a protective hand on her vast belly. Given the girth, noticeable even under the full skirts, her time was near.

"I am a friend of Sergeant Keats," Cynda began.

"The rozzer they're gonna hang tomorrow?"

Ouch. "Not if we can stop it."

"What's that got to do with me?" the woman asked, now frowning.

"I need to find Desmond Flaherty."

The widow grew wary. "Why?"

"Because he can save my friend. Flaherty and a few of his men were with Keats the night of the murder. They can testify that he didn't commit the crime."

The widow rubbed her belly in thought.

"I only need one of them to come forward and tell the cops what happened," Cynda pleaded. "Sergeant Keats is innocent. He can't die, Mrs. Ahearn."

"Why not?" the woman retorted. "My Johnny did. Someone cut his throat, did ya know that? Cut off his—"

"Someone? I thought Flaherty did it."

The woman shook her head. "Not him."

Now that's interesting. "I'm sorry for your loss, but—"

"Loss? Ya know nothin' of that," the woman spat. "I'll not save a rozzer. If ya want help, go to the priest."

"What priest?"

"Nowlan." With that, the door banged shut in her face. As Cynda turned away, she thought she heard the sound of weeping.

After ensuring the shawl covered her head, Cynda padded into the church. It wasn't as grand as some of Europe's mighty cathedrals, but she could still feel the divine power here. As she moved forward, she counted five heads bowed in prayer.

She stopped in front of the altar. Around her came the sputter of candles and the slight click of rosary beads, overlaid with hushed murmurs. Her eyes rose to the crucifix, to the face of the man from Nazareth.

Cynda slid into a pew and knelt in prayer. She'd never been very religious. She'd traversed time, witnessed religions at their best and their most cruel. Still, there was something out there she couldn't quite fathom. Some called him God. Some said it was a Goddess. Others said it was multitudes of the same. Cynda had no idea what was the truth. She only knew that when things were very bad, *someone* was always there to comfort her.

When she finished her prayer for Keats, she looked up. The priest was older, his collar not as white as some she'd seen. Was it Nowlan? She doubted a church this small could afford two clerics.

"Are you all right, miss?"

"No, I'm not, Father," she replied quietly. "A dear friend of mine is going to die tomorrow. They're going to hang him for a crime he didn't commit."

The priest's face went expressionless.

"Flaherty knows he's innocent. So does anyone else who was with him that night. Any of them could come forward and save him. I think you know at least one of them."

Nowlan looked around and lowered his voice. "Ya should put yer faith in God, miss."

"I do, Father, but I know God expects us to do the right thing. If not, what's the point of all this?" she said, gesturing toward the altar.

No reply.

"You can help me make this right."

Still no reply.

The priest was her only conduit to the anarchist. It was now or never. "Tell Flaherty I want to talk to him. I promise I'll not sell him out to the police. He needs to hear what I have to say."

The priest eyed her skeptically. "Why should I?"

"Because he has no one else who can help him now."

A moment passed. Then Nowlan motioned for her to follow him. They left the church out a side door and into the night toward the graveyard in the back. He stopped in front of a mound of dirt. The crude headstone proclaimed it the final resting place of Johnny Ahearn. The father-to-be had been thirty-seven years old. His missus was much younger, maybe nineteen, if a day. Cynda couldn't fault the widow for her bitterness.

"Did ya know him?" the priest asked quietly.

"No, I didn't."

In the far distance she heard a train's whistle, low and mournful.

"Here's the deal. I'll help Flaherty find his daughter if he testifies about what happened that night in Whitechapel."

Nowlan stared at her. "How can ya find his daughter when he can't?"

"Because I know that there are *others* at work here."

Their eyes locked in mutual understanding. Then the priest murmured under his breath and crossed himself. "Be back tonight, at six," he told her. "If he wants to see ya, he'll tell me. If not, we'll pray together for yer friend's life."

"Fair enough." She handed the priest a five-pound note. "Give it to the widow, will you? I think she'll take it from you better than from me."

As Cynda turned to go, the cleric touched her arm. "That sergeant did the same. Why?"

"Because he's a good man. There aren't many of them left."

As she reached the gate that led to the street, she looked back toward the grave. The priest was on his knees in the dirt, head bowed, evidently seeking divine guidance.

Whatever it takes.

—

Cynda returned to the church at the appointed hour, her stomach balled into a tight knot. Since she'd not received a reply from the prince, that left her trying to convince the Fenian to save a policeman's neck. To prepare for the meeting, she'd spent the afternoon researching Flaherty, looking for any weaknesses. His daughter was the only one. Defoe was probably right: she was being foolish, but sometimes you just had to gamble.

The church was deserted, the parishioners celebrating Guy Fawkes' thwarted attempt to reform British government. She adjusted her shawl and hurried down the center aisle toward the altar. Two rows from the front, she slid into the pew and waited. And waited. No sign of the priest or the Fenian.

Come on.

There was a creak of wood as someone slipped into the pew behind her. Fighting the urge to turn around or fidget, she waited. After a few seconds, the man moved and took a place next to her.

She looked over. Desmond Flaherty was scruffy, but there was intelligence in his tired eyes. He seemed different than that night in Green Dragon Place when he'd nearly killed Keats.

"Why're ya here?" Flaherty asked gruffly.

"To save an innocent man."

"There's nothin' that can be done now."

"You were there that night," she insisted. "You can tell them."

"They'll not listen to an Irishman. They want the little sergeant dead, that's plain enough." He dug in a pocket and retrieved a small canvas bag. "These are his. Show 'em to the coppers and tell where ya got 'em. Maybe they'll see he wasn't lyin.'"

She shook her head. "They can ignore the evidence. They can't ignore a person. You have to come and testify."

Flaherty snorted and dropped the bag back into his coat. "Ya got no sense, girl. Why would I spend years in prison for a damned rozzer?"

"Because it's the decent thing to do. It's what you would've done in the past."

His eyes flared with sudden anger. "What do ya know of it?"

"I know your wife died because some damned fool decided to shoot into a crowd of unarmed citizens. You couldn't kill the idiot with the gun, but you could harm the people who sent him. I understand revenge." *Better than you know.*

Flaherty shook his head. "I can't. If I turn myself in, they'll kill my daughter."

"The ones who can look like anyone they want?"

The man's breath caught.

"I know about them," she said.

He looked around them, wary, and lowered his voice. "How?"

"One of them tried to kill me."

"Was he was tall, black-haired, dark eyes like the Devil himself?"

"Sounds familiar."

A snort. "Ya could be him, for all I know."

"But I'm not. How's this for a bargain? You give *written* testimony that Keats was in Whitechapel at the time of the murder, and I'll help you find your daughter."

The Fenian stared at her as if she'd just proclaimed herself Empress of India. She stuck out her hand. He didn't take it. She left it outstretched.

"You'll not get a better offer," she pledged, refusing to give an inch.

"*Written*, ya say?"

"Yes. We'll go to Lord Wescomb and—"

"No toffs."

"Wescomb is Keats' barrister. He's fighting to save the sergeant's life."

The Irishman shook his head. "Don't matter. I've been all over Whitechapel and couldn't find Fee."

Her arm was beginning to cramp. "It's simple: you want your daughter safe, and I want Keats alive."

"Why?" He cocked his head. "Are ya lovers?"

"No. It's deeper than that."

Flaherty glowered at her, then took another quick look around the empty church. Satisfied, he called out, "Ya hearin' this, priest? What do ya say?"

Father Nowlan stepped out from behind a cloth screen and crossed the sanctuary like a silent breath of wind. He sat in the pew in front of them.

"It's not what I say." The cleric looked upward into his Savior's mournful eyes. "It's what He says. 'Blessed are they which are persecuted for righteousness' sake: for theirs is the kingdom of Heaven.'"

"Ah, by all the saints," the Fenian muttered. "Paddy's been ridin' me, as well."

Cynda quirked an eyebrow. "Paddy?"

"He was the one who took the copper into the woods. I've had to stop him from goin' to the rozzers a couple of times. His heart's too big."

She extended her hand further. "I'll do everything I can to find your daughter. If Keats is free, he'll do the same."

It was her last card. If the anarchist didn't take it, she was out of the game.

He studied her face and then gave the faintest of nods. His rough hand shook hers.

My God.

"I'll get ya what ya need," he said. "Be at the Aldgate Pump in an hour. But know this—if ya cross me, I'll have no choice but to kill ya."

"Fair enough." *You'll have to stand in line.*

—

"Mr. Keats? There is a gent to see you, sir."

A dark-suited man entered the condemned cell. He had prominent ears, closely cropped beard and a solemn demeanor.

The executioner.

"Good evening, Mr. Keats. I am Mr. Berry."

Keats stuck out his hand. "I would say it is a pleasure to meet you, but that would be lying, sir."

A slight smile stole across the hangman's face. "I wished to speak to you of the morning."

"I understand." Keats sat on his bed, composing himself.

Berry cleared his throat. "Shortly before eight, I will come to you and pinion your arms. Once we are at the scaffold, I'll place the white cap on your head and pull it down to cover your eyes. I will position the rope, and then shortly thereafter you will be at peace."

"I hope so," Keats said. "I am a slight man, and that does give me concern as to your calculation of the drop."

"Approximately ten stone?" Keats nodded. "Then I shall employ a drop of six feet. That should be sufficient."

Keats felt his blood chill. This was an unholy science.

"If this must happen, I am pleased you are to do it, sir," he remarked. "You have an excellent reputation."

"Thank you. For my part, I urge you to make your confession so that you may find peace within yourself and with God."

"I have confessed, sir, but not to the crime for which I am being executed. I will not lie to satisfy the newspapers."

Berry paused. "You claim to be innocent?"

"Yes. God knows my soul and when I stand before Him, I will repent for many things, but not the death of Nicola Hallcox. Her blood is not on my hands."

Berry shuffled his feet uncomfortably. "You will give me no trouble in the morning?"

"None. You are only performing your duty."

A sigh of relief. "Then I shall take my leave. Rest easy. I shall make it painless."

And for that, I will be eternally grateful.

—

It felt like a wake.

Alastair took a sip of the fine whiskey in his hand. Across Lord Wescomb's study, Chief Inspector Fisher also had a whiskey, but he'd not touched it. Lady Sephora sat near the fire, an embroidered shawl around her shoulders, as if the room would never be warm enough. Her husband was at his desk, pouring through a stack of law books and muttering to himself. Every now and then, he'd slap a book shut and select another.

"John," the lady called out. He looked up instantly. "Come sit with us. You have done what you could."

His lordship closed his eyes for a moment, then rose from his desk with a sigh. He sat near his wife, taking hold of her hand.

"There has to be a way to stop this madness," he murmured.

"I don't think there is," Fisher replied, his voice flat. "It is much like a runaway train. You can apply the brakes, tear up the track, and nothing happens. It only goes faster."

Alastair took a sip of his whiskey, letting it burn down his throat.

Jacynda cannot let Keats die. But where was she? What was she doing?

His thoughts drifted to the prisoner. Keats had been very quiet that afternoon, and that had made their last meeting particularly poignant. To keep himself from breaking down, the sergeant had spoken of his nephew, of his grandparents. At the end, he mentioned he'd brought his will up to date. In all ways, Keats was disengaging himself from this world. Preparing himself for the end.

As we all must.

—

It was an odd procession. Cynda held the lead, followed by Flaherty and the hulking presence of Paddy. For a big man, he moved fairly quietly. Flaherty, to Cynda's surprise, was damn near silent.

No wonder Keats had trouble finding this guy.

She'd not expected Paddy to come with them, but he'd insisted. When that decision had been made, Flaherty swore under his breath.

"They'll put ya in jail, ya know that."

Paddy nodded. "I did wrong. It's not as bad as some say."

"He probably won't mind prison. He's too big for anyone to bully," Mr. Spider observed.

As they'd made their way across London to Marylebone, first by omnibus and then on foot, they'd worked through the stages of this unlikely marriage of convenience. The first part had been devoted to threats. Flaherty had let her know if this was a trap, she was the first to die. She'd retaliated by telling him that if anything happened to Lord Wescomb, nobody would take the time to find his daughter. She'd expected him to react in anger. Instead, he'd given her a grave nod and set his jaw.

They'd walked the last mile, nerves on edge, none of them knowing when they'd encounter a constable on his beat. Cynda kept moving ahead at a pace steady enough to make progress without triggering anyone's interest, the pair following her lead. Their dress was too shabby for this part of town, but that couldn't be helped. Flaherty in full evening dress wasn't going to make this meeting any more acceptable.

Cynda paused at Wescombs' front door, doubt forming a lump in her throat. This could go wrong in so many ways. Squaring her shoulders, she knocked. Behind her the two men waited, knives concealed from view.

The moment after the door opened, she began working on the face. *Howard Brown.* According to the notes on the pendant, she'd gotten the butler his job with the Wescombs. The smile on Brown's face was genuine. That made it worse. It felt like she was betraying a friend. No matter what happened, he was going to detest her before the evening was over.

"Miss Lassiter," he exclaimed with a smile. "How unexpected." The smile vanished when he noticed the pair behind her.

"Mr. Brown," she greeted awkwardly. "I'm sorry, but this has to happen. These two gents need to be inside…now."

"Miss, I can't allow that. They don't look—"

Flaherty pushed forward, pressing his knife against the butler's fine coat just at heart level. "Best not to think, my friend. Just let us in, nice and gentle, and this'll go right fine."

The butler's eyes widened as his hand headed for his pocket. Cynda grabbed it, then removed the pistol lodged inside.

Too close.

The knife pressed harder, to the point where Brown winced.

"What is this?" he demanded.

"I'll tell you more once we're inside," Cynda said. She started to put the gun in an empty pocket, but Paddy took possession of it.

That was fine. *As long as they don't know about the other one.*

Brown's face grew grave. "If any harm comes to the Wescombs, I'll see *all* of you hang for this."

"Fair enough," Cynda conceded. "Inside, now. The longer we're on the street, the more danger there is."

The moment the door closed, Brown's quick breaths rose in intensity. His eyes moved to the coat rack and back to her in a silent plea. Two bowlers.

Ah, crap. "Who else is here?" she demanded.

"People you don't want to annoy," Brown replied. "I suggest you be on your way."

"Who is it?" she pressed.

Brown glowered. "Besides my employers, a chief inspector of Scotland Yard and Dr. Montrose."

"Chief Inspector *Fisher?*"

The butler gave a terse nod.

Oh, stellar.

Flaherty chuckled. "We're playin' to a full house. Take us in quiet as ya can. Yer gonna announce the woman, and then she'll tell 'em who we are. Course, two of the gents'll know me right personal."

Every step down the hallway drew them closer to the moment when it could all fall apart. If Flaherty didn't keep his word, he could kill the lot of them. When they stopped at the door, the anarchist flicked his knife closed. He casually lit a cigar and took a long puff. Smoke clouded around them.

"Put that out!" Brown grumbled.

Flaherty ignored him. "Don't raise a fuss. I don't want to hurt anyone, and that's God's truth."

Brown shifted his eyes toward her, making one last silent appeal.

"We're here about Sergeant Keats, nothing more," she said.

A low sigh came from the man. He tapped on the door, awaited the response and then entered.

"My lord, my lady. I...apologize, but a situation has arisen over which I have no control."

Wescomb leaned forward. "What sort of situation, Brown?"

Cynda stepped around the butler.

"Jacynda?" Alastair called out, rising with a smile. "Were you able to—"

"I'm sorry about this, but there is no other way."

She stepped aside to allow the most dangerous man in Britain into the room.

CHAPTER FOUR

"Good God!" Fisher shouted, leaping to his feet. "Flaherty!"

The cop's wide-eyed stare brought her attention back to the Fenian. Flaherty brandished a tight bundle of dynamite, three sticks bound with cord. One short central fuse rose from the creation.

Oh God, what have I done?

With a grin, he puffed on his cigar, causing the end to grow brilliant red. Then he brought it uncomfortably close to the end of the fuse.

"Good evenin', all," Flaherty greeted jovially. "I hope ya don't mind me smokin' here."

Alastair rose, his hands balled into fists. Next to him, Sephora's pale fingers clutched the arms of her chair, her eyes riveted on the dynamite.

"What is this?" Wescomb demanded, rising from his chair as well. "Why are you here with…that?"

Cynda cut in before things got any worse. "As the chief inspector noted, this is Desmond Flaherty," she glared at him, "who failed to mention he was bringing *dynamite* to this meeting." She shifted her eyes back to the others in the room. "And this is Paddy O'Donnell," she told them, indicating the man to her left. "They're here about Keats."

Despite his wary expression, realization dawned on the peer. "I see. Brown, come over here and sit next to the chief inspector so as not to alarm our…guests."

"But my lord—"

"Not to worry, Brown. Just have a seat." The butler did as he was told, glaring at Cynda the entire time. "The rest of you, please settle in so Mr. Flaherty does not feel inclined to use his cigar in an explosive fashion."

Cynda didn't sit, but purposely positioned herself behind the anarchists. Tempted as she was to jam her hand into her pocket to feel the comfort of the pistol hidden there, she didn't dare. That was her edge. Could she shoot Flaherty faster than he could light a fuse? And what about Paddy?

"Holding us hostage—"

"Not doin' that," Flaherty replied to Fisher's accusation. At his nod, his companion produced a couple sheets of dog-eared paper from inside his coat and handed them to Alastair. "Yer little sergeant's due to hang in the mornin'," the anarchist explained. "I'm here to see that doesn't happen."

"Good heavens!" Alastair exclaimed, shifting through the papers. "These are witness statements regarding the night of the Hallcox murder."

Flaherty nodded. "Keats was in Whitechapel with us when that posh lady was killed. He could'na strangled her. Ya see, I was one step away from cutting out his liver, when the mercy of God stayed my hand." His laugh was low and harsh. "Nah, that's not right. It was that damned priest's fault. Instead of cuttin' him up, I had Paddy hit the rozzer on the jaw and take him into the country to get him out of the way for a time."

The chief inspector's face displayed a volatile mixture of indignation and sudden hope. "How did you get him out of London?"

"In a coffin," Paddy replied. "I makes them. It's steady work."

No kidding.

Fisher pressed on. "Where did you leave Sergeant Keats?"

"Near Stock, in the woods."

"Keats said he walked for a very long time before he reached the train tracks," Alastair recalled.

Paddy shrugged his huge shoulders. "If'n he'd gone south, he'd a been right in Stock quick as ya please. Musta got lost."

"Did you tie him up?" Fisher asked.

A nod. "With some strips of red cloth."

Cynda moved her attention away from Flaherty for a moment. Alastair was studying the papers, hands trembling. When his eyes rose to meet hers, she winked. That earned her a nervous smile.

"Tell me precisely what happened that night," Fisher ordered.

Flaherty frowned. "It's on the papers."

"Tell me anyway." A pause. "Please."

"One of my men said he saw the sergeant talkin' to that whore...Red Annie," Flaherty explained. "We found him near Old Montague Street about quarter till eleven."

"You sure about the time?" Wescomb quizzed.

"I am."

"Then what happened?"

"He tried to arrest the lot of us, can you believe it?" Flaherty shook his head. "That rozzer's got some brass."

With another nod from his boss, Paddy unceremoniously dropped a canvas bag on the polished walnut table next to Alastair. Passing the papers to Sephora, the doctor opened the sack. The first item to hand: a pocket watch. A flick of the cover and a sigh of relief. "It's Keats'. It's inscribed to him."

"Right sorry about breakin' it," Paddy offered sheepishly. "It happened when I hit him."

Alastair's face lit up. "It's stopped at 10:57."

Wescomb's moustache twitched upward in a smile. "Are you two willing to swear in court that Sergeant Keats was in your presence on that night at that exact time?"

"I won't," Flaherty stated flatly. "That paper'll speak for me."

"I'm not sure they'll believe a piece of paper."

The Irishman looked over at his companion.

Paddy nodded. "I'll tell 'em. It ain't right, him hangin' for somethin' he didn't do, even if he is a filthy rozzer."

Fisher whistled under his breath. "Why are you doing this?"

"Because this young lady made a deal with me," Flaherty replied.

"What deal? If you think—"

"Mr. Flaherty needs our help, Chief Inspector, and even though I know that goes against your grain, that's the deal," Jacynda replied.

"What sort of help?" Fisher demanded.

"It's my daughter, Fiona. She was workin' in Effington's household and went missin' right after I stole the explosives. Someone took her. I can't find her now. None of us can. Ahearn got close, and they cut his throat."

"Ahearn," Fisher said. "We thought—"

Flaherty shook his head. "I didn't kill him. He was like family to me. And God help the bastard who did if I ever find him."

"Where are the explosives?" Fisher asked.

Flaherty's face clouded over. "If ya find my daughter, I'll give ya the lot of them with no trouble."

The chief inspector leaned back into his chair with a whoosh of air. "I'll be deuced."

"With these statements and the new evidence," Alastair said, gesturing toward the watch, "will that be enough to halt the execution?"

Wescomb's lips thinned. "Perhaps. It depends on who is willing to listen to us."

"Would Justice Hawkins help us?" Alastair asked.

"We may need to go to the Lord Chief Justice himself."

Fisher looked intently at the Fenian. "Who are these people who took your daughter?"

"I don't know their names," Flaherty replied. "They look like anyone they want."

Silent words were traded around the room.

"I see," Wescomb replied. "I have heard of such people."

"They are usin' my daughter to make sure I do what they want. If I don't, they said they'd gut her like one of the Ripper's..." His voice caught, and he lowered the dynamite. The cigar was going out, but he made no attempt to prevent it.

"Good Lord!" Sephora exclaimed. "How old is she?"

"Just sixteen, ma'am, though she claims to older. She'd said she'd got herself a position. I didn't know it was at that bastard's house, or I'd've never let her go near him."

The chief inspector cocked his head. "Did you kill Hugo Effington?"

"No, I didn't get the chance. I woulda, though, and been quite proud of the job."

Wescomb thumbed through the papers. "Very complete." He looked up, scanning the faces around the room. "It might be enough, along with Mr... O'Donnell's testimony."

"God, I hope so," Alastair murmured.

Makes two of us.

The clock began to chime. When it reached nine, Flaherty straightened up. "Is it a deal?"

"I do not like this precedent," Fisher complained, shaking his head. "Nevertheless, it's the best we have. If it saves Keats' life, I will live with it." He looked over at Flaherty. "Your man must remain here. I will personally see to his safety."

"It wouldn't be right to punish him for my sins," Flaherty protested. "It was me who told him to take the rozzer out of Whitechapel. I thought if I bought myself some time, I'd find Fiona, set it all right."

"I will do what I can when it comes to Mr. O'Donnell's defence," Wescomb pledged.

Cynda kept her smile to herself. The big Irishman had just scored a peer of the realm as his barrister. The gesture wasn't lost on Flaherty. He gave Cynda a pleased look and then an approving nod.

"That's all right, then."

Wescomb rose, the papers in his hand. "As far as I am concerned, you brought these papers to us to right a wrong, not because of your daughter. It will not play well with the jury if they feel you are to receive some reward for your testimony."

Both Fenians nodded. "I didn't take no brass for this," Paddy added, "and I won't have no one say I did."

Wescomb smiled. "Over here, gents; let's get these signed."

As Flaherty approached the peer's desk, he tossed the dynamite to a startled Brown. "Hold this. I'll want it back, ya understand?"

Cynda rolled her eyes.

"Sign or make your mark, sir," Wescomb said, handing Flaherty a pen.

The Fenian bent over and scrawled his name at the bottom of the document.

While Paddy placed an "X" on his statement, Sephora made her way toward Cynda. Her face was pale, her eyes sharp. Cynda braced herself.

"I see Alastair's report of your recovery has not been exaggerated," Sephora whispered. "While I am pleased by that, what in heaven's name kept this man from killing all of us if this had gone ill?"

Cynda tapped her pocket. "This pistol. I was behind him the entire time."

"You would have shot him in the back?" her ladyship asked, incredulous.

"Yes, if it came to that."

Sephora's sharp gaze softened. "It was an incredible gamble."

"No, it was insanity. Gambling is less risky."

With a nod, the woman swept away. Cynda suspected it would be awhile before she was welcomed here again.

Alastair joined her a moment later. "You are…" he shook his head in dismay.

"I thought it'd only be Wescomb tonight. I had hoped Sephora would be upstairs or at one of her meetings. I had no idea the rest of you were here."

"It still might not work."

"It has to."

After a moment's reflection, he asked, "Would you do such an outrageous thing for me?"

"Hell, yes."

He gently touched her cheek. "That pleases me to hear it."

She leaned closer to ask a question. His eyes widened, and then he shook his head.

"Good," she replied. "That might make it easier."

"There is no guarantee that he wasn't one of Nicci's paramours. He might not have left his card behind."

"It's just a chance I'm going to have to take."

"Miss Lassiter?" It was the chief inspector. Alastair stepped aside.

"You are extremely fit for someone who was unable to testify only a few days ago," the policeman observed. "Another remarkable recovery on your part."

"I assure you, Chief Inspector, I was truly incapacitated."

"Perhaps." He half turned to watch his lordship talking to the two Fenians. When he looked back, he barely succeeded in keeping his composure. "I don't know how you did that, but I owe you for it."

"Don't let them hang Keats. That's all I ask."

"That might be more difficult than you think."

DESMOND FLAHERTY EXITED the house via the servant's entrance and melted into the darkness, Cynda at his side. "Glad I didn't have to use the dynamite. Woulda made a helluva mess."

"You wouldn't have had the chance."

"The pistol in yer pocket?" he asked, a sly grin spreading across his face.

"You knew?"

"Of course. Ya let go of the other one too easy-like."

She chuckled. "You're an old fox."

"I'll hold ya to that bargain, missy," he declared, his voice suddenly taut. "I want my daughter back, one way or another. Ya hear?"

Cynda nodded.

The anarchist had crossed sides tonight, putting both his life and his daughter's on the line. No matter what happened, they owed him, even if Keats didn't survive.

—

The change into the posh clothes was the easy part. She made a point of wearing the necklace the prince had sent her in gratitude for supposedly saving his life. That event seemed so long ago now, though it had only been a few weeks by the 1888 calendar.

Now came the hard part—taking on Victorian society at one of its most stalwart locations—the gentlemen's club. It took a great deal of negotiating skill to even get her inside the door and parked in a sequestered room away from the main part of the establishment. Theo Morrisey-level skill, to be honest. She'd kept calm, explained her purpose, and then refuted every one of the objections, including the one concerning her sex.

"If this is some ploy to garner the prince's interest—" the club steward warned, brows furrowed.

"I am involved in an investigation." She produced the Pinkerton card with her name on it, the one Ralph had created.

The steward stared at it, dumbfounded.

"The case involves stolen explosives. A large amount of which could be used against *the Royal family*."

The man kept staring at the card. She opened her mouth to give him hell, but then closed it. He was working through the options, and none of them looked attractive from his point of view. If he chucked her out the door and she was legit, he was in for it. If he annoyed the future king with a crazy woman, he might well lose his cushy job.

She greased the wheels. "I consulted on this very issue earlier this evening with Chief Inspector Fisher of Special Branch and Lord Wescomb, a member of Parliament." Fisher's and Wescomb's cards traded hands.

Those cards tipped the scales in her favor. "I shall speak with the prince's equerry," the steward announced before heading into the den of nineteenth-century testosterone. She settled on the couch, a heavily brocaded thing with lilies carved into the walnut back. She'd half expected it to have nude nymphs instead.

"Amazing," her delusion announced, sidling along the piece of furniture. "I figured you'd be out of here in a flash."

Second miracle of the night.

"This one's a long shot," the spider added. "He didn't answer your note."

Doesn't matter. I have to pull out all the stops.

Seven minutes later, the steward returned with another man. She guessed him to be the prince's equerry and in his hand were the calling cards.

Fortunately, he recognized her from Effington's party, which was good. She didn't remember him.

"Miss Lassiter," he acknowledged with a slight bow. "It is a pleasure to see you again."

"Thank you," she said, itching to get on with this. "I need to speak to the prince, or at least pass a message to him."

He gave the steward a look and the man took the hint, leaving them alone.

"His Highness received your message this morning."

"And did not answer me," she said directly. "With all due respect, sir, this is far beyond polite correspondence."

As succinctly as possible, Cynda presented the equerry with an overview of why Keats must live to see another day, including Flaherty's testimony.

Meanwhile, the man fingered the three calling cards. "What is Lord Wescomb doing about this new evidence?"

"He and Fisher are speaking with anyone who will listen to them. They want a stay of execution so the new evidence can be presented. It should lead to Keats' exoneration."

"Why would this anarchist come forward?" the man asked bluntly.

"To save his daughter's life," she responded.

By the time she'd finished telling him about Fiona, she realized they were not alone. Someone stood at the doorway. How long he'd been there, she was uncertain. Cynda remembered the face from the photos she'd studied in the carriage on the way over. She rose and curtsied deeply. "Your Royal Highness. I apologize for interrupting your evening."

"Miss Lassiter," the Prince of Wales acknowledged, his heavy-lidded eyes traveling the length of her in frank appraisal. "You are a very persistent woman." He indicated the cards in his equerry's hand. "I was not aware you are with Pinkerton's."

"We have kept it rather quiet."

"So it would appear." When he moved into the room, the equerry shut the door behind him. "You must know that it would not be proper for me to interfere with the courts."

"I know, Your Highness; however, if it were known that you are watching this case with considerable interest, there might be a better chance that Sergeant Keats would receive justice."

His eyes narrowed. "You make it sound as if he has enemies besides the anarchists."

This is where it got dicey. Bertie had a reputation as a consummate womanizer and he might well have been one of Nicci's paramours, though according to Alastair, the prince's calling card was not one of those found in her possession.

"There were a number of..." *Oh hell.* She discarded formality. "I'll be blunt. There were a lot of bluebloods who were bedding Nicci Hallcox," she explained, "and they don't want their names made public. Especially since she had syphilis. Pressure is being brought to bear to ensure Keats dies quickly so that the whole thing can be swept under the rug."

The future King of England blinked at her extreme candor. "What of the people who actually have the explosives?"

"We're not sure who they are," she replied. That really wasn't a lie. They could look like anyone. *Even you.*

The prince moved closer. "You are convinced of this man's innocence?"

"I am. He's a good cop, through and through."

The trace of a smile. "I see you are wearing the necklace I sent you."

"Yes. It is very pretty."

"So are you."

She blinked in surprise. "Thank you, Your Highness."

He looked over at his equerry and then back. "I think a note will not carry the same weight as a visit from one of my emissaries," the prince surmised. "I shall have that person discuss the matter with both the Home Office and the PM and ask how they intend to proceed in light of this new evidence."

Relief washed over her. "Thank you, Your Royal Highness."

"There is a quid pro quo, however," he said, his eyes sparkling.

"Dinner?" she asked, hoping that was all he was expecting. It was all he was going to get.

He nodded. "It will not be onerous. In fact, it could be quite pleasant."

"A meal only, Your Royal Highness."

He blinked again and then smiled widely. "Exactly. I think it will be more exciting to talk to you about your profession rather than participate in other... pursuits. I can do that with any woman."

By the time she'd risen from the second curtsy, he was gone, his equerry in tow.

"You're on a roll," Mr. Spider said, landing with a plop on her shoulder. "I am impressed."

Don't be. Unless Keats is alive at 8:01 in the morning, this is all theatrics.

CHAPTER FIVE

Tuesday, 6 November 1888
Near Stock

"I hope you're enjoying yourself, Mr. Posh Detective," Ramsey said, detangling a thorn bush from his suit. It was one of his better ones. *By the time we get done here, it'll be the worst.*

"I think I miss Chicago more than I realized," Anderson replied, removing thorns of his own.

Ramsey had to agree. Summoned out of his bed by the chief inspector, he'd been stunned to hear Flaherty had confirmed the sergeant's alibi. Based on the two Fenians' statements, Ramsey had been charged with finding the coffin in the woods near Stock.

In the middle of the bloody night.

Knowing how difficult it would be, he'd brought Anderson with him, figuring the Pinkerton fellow might as well get some exercise. After all, if he was going to be miserable, he'd make sure others were as well. Inspectors were very good at that sort of thing.

Around them, a group of ten men from the local pub were working through the underbrush, fueled by alcohol and the promise of a sizeable breakfast come morning. The pair who found the coffin would get five quid each and their names in the *Chicago Herald*. That would bring any man out into the forest.

Between scrabbling over wooden fences and tangling with the various nasty bushes, it'd been hours of frustration for all. Four of the searchers had given up and headed back to town. Ramsey couldn't blame them. As for himself, he'd stay until daylight, when it would be too late.

When he next looked around, Anderson was gone. Ramsey groaned. *Just my luck; he's going to get lost, and I'll get the blame.*

"Where the hell are you, Anderson?"

"Where you should be—standing by the coffin," the man called back.

"What? Keep calling out," Ramsey bellowed. Anderson continued to chide him as the inspector charged through the bushes like an enraged bear. Branches slapped at his face and pulled at his clothes. He made it to the clearing at the same time as the other men. The American was kneeling next to an overturned coffin, a smug grin on his face.

"Good thing I came along," he joked. "You Limeys couldn't find your behinds with both hands."

"Oh, sod off," Ramsey laughed, still catching his breath. "Are you any good at sketching scenes, Anderson?"

"I'll do my best."

Positioning the men and their lanterns to best effect, Ramsey examined the area around their find. He spied two strips of red cloth. *One for the hands, one for the mouth.* Just like one of the Fenians had said in his statement. Ramsey pocketed them. Setting his own lantern aside, he knelt and slowly righted the toppled coffin. Anderson leaned closer, pencil scratching rapidly in his notebook.

"You, bring that lantern closer," Ramsey ordered. One of the locals complied, illuminating a dark stain on the coffin's interior. "I think that might be blood," he proposed.

"Probably from the blow to his face," Anderson agreed.

Ramsey nodded. "Can you imagine waking up in this thing? I'd have pissed myself."

"There, on the inside of the lid," Anderson pointed, "it looks like a boot imprint."

Keats, you lucky little bastard. Ramsey would bet a month's pay the marks would match one of the boots from the pawnbroker's.

The inspector looked up into a row of anxious eyes. The men were shuffling from one foot to another to deal with the cold. "This is it, gents. You've done it. Let's get it on the wagon and back to town. I'll pay you all fiver and treat everyone to breakfast."

A throaty cheer erupted from the group. A couple of men hoisted the coffin while another picked up the damaged lid.

Ramsey rose. "We've got everything we need." Anderson's troubled expression reined in his triumph. "We've got time, don't we?"

"It's just after five in the morning," the reporter observed. "It will be a near thing for the telegram to arrive in time to halt the execution."

Ramsey's roar of frustration rent the forest, scattering birds from the treetops.

—

In the distance, Alastair could see the faint stirrings of dawn. If there had ever been a day that he wished he would never see, it was this one. Despite their very best efforts, his best friend would die this morning.

He'd come to know Keats quite by accident. He had appeared at the door of Alastair's free clinic one evening, helping a limping constable. The man had broken his ankle and was in considerable pain. While Alastair treated him, Keats had asked all sorts of questions, all with a purpose, now that he thought about it. The sergeant had been testing him, finding out what sort of person he was. All through that first meeting, he'd acted the part of a fop out for a night's jolly in Whitechapel. It wasn't until Jacynda arrived earlier this fall that he'd learned Keats' true vocation. Once they'd crossed that hurdle, their friendship had deepened.

Which only makes it harder now.

Behind him, he heard the endless pacing of Lord Wescomb. It was amazing the man was still on the move, given his recent wounding. The three of them—the peer, the doctor, and Kingsbury—had made the rounds until half past three in the morning. They had cajoled and argued with Home Office, met with the Prime Minister, even sent an urgent appeal to the Archbishop of Canterbury and to the Queen.

Nothing had come of it.

Nothing.

The pacing stopped.

"We should leave now," the peer advised in a voice made hoarse by a night's worth of pleading. "There will be a scrum outside of the prison. We do not want to be caught in that."

"I would advise you not to attend, my lord. Your health is still at risk," Alastair said.

Wescomb waved him off. "I must do this. It is my failure, and I must face it head on."

Alastair nodded somberly, though he disagreed that it had anything to do with Wescomb's abilities. After one last whispered prayer, he followed the lord down the darkened hallway.

Lady Sephora waited at the foot of the stairs.

"John…"

The peer embraced her with his uninjured arm. "We have done all we can, Sephora. It is truly in God's hands now."

A single tear wound its way down her pale cheek. She made no effort to brush it away, allowing it to be joined in a moment by another. And then another.

A most elegant elegy for our dear friend.

—

As the time drew near, the crowd milled outside the prison like cattle in a tight corral. Cynda guessed there must be at least five hundred Londoners awaiting the death of one man. Some were selling hot potatoes and others broadsheets that supposedly contained Keats' last words. Still, there was a solemnity here that had been missing at past executions.

To her annoyance, one of her memories returned in full force, reinforced by a particularly vivid run report. The year was 1760, the execution of an earl at Tyburn Hill, west of London. A tourist had insisted he wanted to see a "genuine hanging" and had paid her employers extra for the privilege. Worried what might happen if a junior Rover took the assignment, she'd reluctantly taken the trip.

They'd waited for nearly three hours for the prisoner's arrival from Newgate as his escort fought their way through the thousands packing the route and the area around the scaffold. During that time, she protected her charge from the dregs of London's underclass: pickpockets, belligerent drunks, blousy prostitutes hunting customers, robbers, and unscrupulous vendors of all sorts.

At that time, the long drop wasn't in use. No quick or painless death; just slow strangling at the end of a rope. The locals called it "dancing the Tyburn jig." She'd kept her eyes averted during that horror, but the tourist had watched every agonizing minute with morbid fascination. Despite the garish spectacle, he'd been elated. He'd witnessed a bit of history, he said, and then promptly purchased one of the broadsheets as a souvenir for his wife. When Cynda returned home, she informed TIC that she would never go near another hanging.

And yet here she was.

At least the ritual had changed. Now the executions took place inside Newgate Prison, away from the crowds, every attempt made to preserve the condemned's dignity.

Except this time it was Jonathon Keats.

"What if 'e's not good for it?" someone called out behind her, jarring her out of her sickening recollection. "If they can 'ang 'im, they can 'ang any of us."

"He's the one," another protested. "They nicked him right proper."

"Not sure 'bout that."

Cynda felt hope stir. If they weren't sure, maybe history wasn't either.

"I've got all my legs crossed," her delusion announced. "Hard to hold on that way, though." That made her smile, despite the situation.

Thanks.

She returned her gaze to the flagpole. The bell would toll when the drop was opened, and then they'd run up the black flag. If she could sense the seconds passing from out here, what was it like for Keats?

Just then, she caught sight of a man working his way through the crowd. He passed a chimney sweep, then paused and shook hands with the fellow. Her mouth fell open. T.E. Morrisey was clad in period garb, looking more like a clerk than a toff with that bowler. He was carrying a pasteboard suitcase. He approached her with a casual nod, as if this rendezvous had been planned.

"What are you—?"

"It's supposed to bring good luck," he explained, offering his soot-stained hand.

She continued to stare. He had no business here. It was too dangerous for him. And yet... Cynda bit her lip in frustration. It was good to see him again.

Morrisey moved closer, lowering his voice. "Things are melting down at home. I'll tell you more later."

Oh, what the hell. They shook hands, her frown deepening. He might have invented this technology, but as a Rover he was a babe in the woods.

One more person to worry about.

"All... right. Stick close and ensure nothing you value is in a pocket." *Like your interface.*

He nodded ruefully. "Already learned that lesson. Luckily, the urchin only got a shilling."

"That's nearly a fortune around here." She leaned closer and whispered to him of the previous night's events.

He smiled in approval. "Excellent. I wondered how you were going to handle the situation since your original plan went awry."

"It's time!" someone called out. A shout went up around them.

Cynda jammed her eyes shut and prayed harder than she ever had in her life. *Come on! You know it's not supposed to be this way.*

She felt a reassuring hand on her elbow. "Keep faith," he said. "History often has a mind of its own."

Cynda had nurtured similar hopes last night, riding high on the adrenalin rush. Now, as she stood outside this stone prison, one of hundreds awaiting the flag to rise, she knew only one thing for certain.

Time had become her enemy.

—

Keats heard the sound of the key in the lock: he was as ready as any man could be. He'd arisen at dawn, shaved and taken only a cup of strong tea, refusing the brandy and food they'd offered.

But it was not the executioner who stepped into his cell.

"Chief Inspector," he said, his heart swelling in gratitude.

How could I ever think you would forget me?

Fisher's demeanor had changed. He didn't carry himself with as much authority, and though immaculately dressed, it was easy to discern the emotional and physical toll these few weeks had exacted.

At least I shall be at peace when this is over.

The two guards departed without saying a word. His superior waited until the door shut behind them and then he spoke. "Sergeant, I thought..." He shook his head. "It is absurd to be so formal at this moment."

Knowing he needed time to compose himself, Keats kept silent, hearing the seconds tick off. When his mentor finally did speak, his voice almost broke. "I have come to offer my apology, Jonathon. I have failed you. We should have been able to prove your innocence, just as we should have found the true killer."

"We were all fighting a losing battle," Keats replied. "I do not hold you or Ramsey accountable in any way."

"That is very gracious. Still, I came to make peace with you." He halted for some time. Keats began to worry that he wouldn't finish what he wanted to say before the executioner arrived.

"I must admit, Jonathon, I am rarely in awe of other men, yet your final statement in the courtroom was one of the finest I have ever heard." His eyes moved away and he blinked rapidly. "They have reprinted it in the newspapers. It is what is fueling the fury around this debacle."

"Sir, I—"

There was the turn of a key in the lock. The cleric stepped inside the cell.

"It is time," he said solemnly.

Keats delivered a short nod. He didn't know what to say. How should he thank Fisher for being the father he'd always wanted?

They began to shake hands, but that wasn't enough. His mentor embraced him. Keats could feel him trembling with emotion. He was doing the same. When they broke apart, Fisher murmured, "The truth will out in time. Rest easy, Jonathon. Your job is done."

"Thank you … J.R. I could not have asked for a better man to guide me."

"That remains to be seen." His voice broke again. "I'm sorry, I cannot be present when … I cannot watch this travesty unfold."

"I do not want you there," Keats said, feeling tears in his eyes. "It would only make it worse." He wiped them away as a figure appeared in the doorway. It was Berry, the executioner.

He cleared his throat. "I must pinion you, sir."

The chief inspector paused at the cell door, gave Keats a final nod and then went his way with unsteady steps.

The hangman positioned Keats' hands and made final adjustments to the straps. "I understand you have not confessed to this crime."

"No, sir, I have not. I swear before God that I did not kill her."

The hangman paused in his preparations, his face troubled. "I have no desire to execute an innocent man, but I must perform my duty."

"Yes, you must. Just as I did mine."

The procession moved down the corridor toward the execution shed, a lengthy troop of officials, and the condemned. The Chief Warder headed up the procession, followed by other warders, the chaplain, then Keats and Berry. Behind them were more officials. Though the hangings were no longer public, there still needed to be witnesses.

Keats heard the many footfalls. To his ears, his were steady and did not falter. He took comfort in that. Sweat streamed down his back, though the air was chilly. As they entered Bird Cage Walk, he looked upward through the grills to the open air, the last time he would ever see the sky.

"One moment, please," he said, halting. There was a brief murmur of protest from one of the men, but it was silenced by Berry.

Tipping his face upward, Keats drank in the morning light. Soon, he would be part of that light, free of the burdens of this life. He would repent to his God in person, and perhaps be able to see his beloved mother again. How he longed to feel her arms around him once more.

"Thank you." With that, he resumed his progress across the uneven flooring. They would leave him on the rope for an hour, then conduct the post-mortem. Once all the proper paperwork was in order, they would bury him here with the other criminals, covered in quicklime. There would be no final resting place where his family could visit and lay flowers. Instead, his body would become part of the foundation that other condemned men would pass over in years to come.

As he walked, the cleric intoned prayers. Keats was only faintly aware of the words. Soon, they would hoist the black flag and post a public notice that Jonathon Davis Keats had been executed for Murder on this Sixth day of November, One Thousand Eight Hundred and Eighty-Eight. Someone would probably keep it as a memento.

As they entered the open area inside the prison walls that housed the execution shed, Mr. Barry placed the white cap on Keats' head.

This is it.

Keats' eyes darted toward the witnesses. There were about a dozen reporters and officials. To his relief, Alastair was not present. He had not wanted his best friend to watch him die. He had said that repeatedly. Perhaps Alastair had finally acquiesced to his most fervent wish.

As he entered the door to the execution shed, he began trembling. This was truly the end. When they had him stop on top of the trap doors, the cap was pulled down, obscuring his vision of the mechanism that would kill him.

Raw panic seized him. Why was he going to his death like a passive lamb? Why didn't he fight them, shout out his innocence, bellow curses at their heinous deed?

Keats took a deep breath and mastered his fear, though it still choked him as tightly as any rope. He would die with as much dignity as he could muster, if nothing more than as a final tribute to his family and to the man who had been his mentor.

He held his breath, waiting for the feel of the hemp, its weight around his neck, the positioning under his left chin. All the while, muffled words were being exchanged.

Get on with it. His courage was not endless. He could only hold the panic in check for so long.

More murmuring. Then raised voices.

"What is the matter?" he demanded.

"One moment. We're sorting this out," someone said.

His anger exploded. "Sort it out on your own time, will you? If you mean to execute me, do it, by God! If not—"

The cap was abruptly removed. He blinked in the muted light of the execution shed. Near the door was a knot of men, talking animatedly. Involuntarily, his eyes drifted upward to the scaffold. To the rope.

"Best not to look that way, Mr. Keats," Berry advised, giving him a slight turn.

"What is going on?" he asked again, his throat suddenly arid.

"Some matter about your execution, sir," Berry replied. His tone was clipped, evidence the hangman was displeased with the interruption.

To his surprise, Keats now saw Alastair in the group. Wescomb's voice rose above the others. Then the group parted. The Chief Warder moved forward.

"Mr. Keats, I am to inform you that there has been a stay of execution."

"What?" He struggled to understand. "What do you mean? I am pardoned?"

"No, sir. It is a stay only."

Wescomb hustled forward, his face florid with exertion. "We have witnesses who place you in Whitechapel during the time of the murder. They can prove you are innocent of this crime."

Keats' mouth dropped open. Despite the executioner's warning, he turned to stare up at the rope. His mind recalled the walk from the cell, the feel of the cap, the hollow sound of the trap doors beneath his boots.

What if they don't exonerate me? What if I have to face this again?

"I cannot," Keats cried, pulling back. "Dear God, not again!" Then he lost the will to stand.

—

In the distance, Cynda heard St. Sepulchre's bell tolling the hour. Six... seven... eight. Then its mournful sound ceased.

"Come on," she whispered.

The crowd shuffled restlessly as voices relayed a message.

"No hangin' today!" someone shouted.

"What?" another called back. "Why not?"

"Stay of hex-e-cution," the first voice shouted back.

There were hoots of displeasure. And a few cheers.

"I knew they'd not 'ang 'im," a man said. "They'd never 'ang a copper."

Oh, God, it actually worked.

"Very well done," Morrisey murmured, his voice full of pride.

"It's not over yet."

They still have time to kill him.

CHAPTER SIX

Keats regained his senses, shivering intensely. He felt someone pull a blanket up on his chest. Was this what it was like to be dead?

His hand fumbled for his neck, but only found his collar open. There was no soreness or abrasion. No rope.

I'm dreaming.

"Keats?"

Blinking open his eyes, he found himself in the cell, Alastair watching him intently. "Ah, that's better," his friend remarked, his face filling with relief. "I have sent for some tea."

"I have been asleep, haven't I? They will come for me soon." *Come to take to me to my death.*

"Only when they have everything resolved."

I dreamt it all. It hasn't happened yet. Keats' shivering returned.

"Easy there. You're fine, just a nasty shock."

"What?"

"The new evidence has thrown the city into turmoil. So many questions are being asked," Alastair explained.

"What?" Then he remembered Wescomb saying something about witnesses. "What has happened?"

The doctor placed a hand on Keats' shoulder, smiling broadly. "Flaherty came forward on your behalf."

"Flaherty?" he exclaimed, struggling to a sitting position over Alastair's protests. "Why?"

"It is a very strange tale," the doctor replied. "Lie back and I'll tell you all of it."

Keats complied, allowing his friend to reposition the blanket. He stared at the ceiling as Alastair's voice filled the cell, recounting the remarkable events of the previous evening. It was a fight not to interrupt.

In the middle of the tale, a cup of tea was delivered. After Alastair added a dose of something from a flask he had in his jacket pocket, Keats pulled himself into a sitting position and took the proffered cup. The liquid shook along with his hands.

"Sip it slowly. It has a fair amount of brandy in it," the doctor advised.

"Go on. I must hear the rest of it." He worked on the strong brew as Alastair finished the story.

"Then you have all of my possessions from that night," he surmised.

"Everything but your notebook. That is still missing."

Keats could only shake his head. "I still don't believe it."

"Frankly, they had little choice. Somehow, Jacynda succeeded in speaking with the Prince of Wales and made an impassioned plea on your behalf."

Keats' mouth dropped open. "How did she do that?"

"I did not ask. His Royal Highness sent his *own* man to Home Office and to the Prime Minister early this morning to express his gravest concern that justice be served. It was only then that things came to fruition."

"Then why did they take me to the scaffold?" Keats asked, baffled.

"We did not receive notice until the very last moment, my friend," Alastair explained, his eyes radiating sympathy. "Lord Wescomb and I were detained by the crowd and had just arrived at the prison when the word came." He sighed deeply. "It was a near thing."

Keats forced a wan smile. "I was as prepared as a man can be for the end. Now, if they uphold the verdict, I don't know how I will cope."

"You must trust that they will not. There is much debate on this issue. I gather the matter will be heard by the Lord Chief Justice himself, so there will be no question of partiality."

Keats snorted. "Partiality? My trial was rammed ahead, as was my appointment with Mr. Berry. I would hate to think what would have happened if I'd received special treatment."

He knew he sounded bitter. *What man wouldn't be?*

Alastair rose. "You're regaining your temper. That is a good sign. I apologize, but I must go. I'm to testify at Effington's inquest this afternoon."

"Full day you have there, my friend," Keats remarked sourly. "Hanging in the morning, inquest in the afternoon."

"I shall return this evening," Alastair continued, apparently knowing it was best not to argue. "Please rest. You've had a tremendous shock. It would be very unfortunate if your health collapsed because of this."

Keats clutched the cup in his hands, knuckles whitening.

As the cell door opened, he called out, "Alastair?" His friend turned. "Thank you for all you've done."

A heartfelt smile was the reply.

—

The argument began the moment they left the prison and headed toward Victoria Embankment.

"I'm not a complete neophyte," Morrisey insisted. "I conducted considerable research before I left."

"As far as I'm concerned, you know nothing," Cynda replied.

"That's a bit arrogant, don't you think? You were in the same boat a few months ago and I gave you the benefit of the doubt."

"That's not the point," she retorted. "It's an entirely different ball game here, and you need to remember that."

"Really," he said dryly. He gestured toward an omnibus as it crawled past them. "I never would have guessed."

Tired of his attitude, she started planning ahead. "Since you're here, we need to get you a room at the hotel."

"That shouldn't be too difficult."

"Harder than you think. It's tourist season. If they don't have a spare, then we'll have to room together. If anyone asks, you're my brother. I'm registered as a *Miss*, so they'll find it odd if I suddenly conjure up a husband," she said, mentally checking off obstacles. The hotel would have to come up with a cot. No way would they share a bed.

"Then what?" he asked.

"Then you get some sleep." *While I figure out what to do with you.*

THE FRONT DESK clerk rewarded them with a dubious expression. No doubt enterprising unmarried couples had tried this tactic before.

"We do not have a spare room and to allow…your sibling…into yours is not our usual arrangement," the clerk commented. He wasn't the nice one she'd met when she'd checked in.

"I am aware of the issues of propriety, sir, and what effect it might have upon the other patrons of your fine establishment," Morrisey spoke up. "However, it is an unusual situation. I need a place to stay."

"It is very important, sir. I had no notion he was coming to London. There is a sudden illness in the family," Cynda said, playing the sympathy card. "If you could provide a cot for him in the sitting room, that would be an immense help to us."

"An illness?"

"We have a member of the family who has taken a turn for the worse," Morrisey explained. It wasn't quite correct, but taken to the extreme, it could easily mean Keats.

"Oh, I understand," the clerk said, suddenly becoming more solicitous. "I do hope all resolves for the best."

"So do we," Cynda responded demurely. "Thank you."

"A cot is easily arranged. I shall fetch a second key for you, Mr. Lassiter."

"I appreciate your assistance, sir," Morrisey replied.

Cynda mentally let loose a sigh of relief. Whether he liked being called by her last name or not, at least that problem was solved.

For the moment, anyway.

HER NEW ROOMMATE had barely enough time to put down his suitcase when she demanded, "So why are you here?"

The look she received was pure disappointment. "You're not happy to see me?"

Cynda settled on the couch, unsure of what to say. He sat as well, stretching his arms overhead. There was a faint pop of vertebrae. The disappointed expression didn't change.

"Look, I'd be happy to show you around if this wasn't a giant mess," she explained.

"That's the only reason you don't want me here?" he asked tersely.

"No." She met his gaze straight on. "I owe you. You kept me safe while I healed. That means everything to me. I don't want to let you down. I couldn't handle losing another…"

He held his breath and then slowly let it out. "This wasn't done on a lark. I had no choice. TPB came calling with a warrant for my arrest. Fortunately, Klein knew about it ahead of time, so we laid plans right after you left. Looks like I'm here for the duration."

For the duration? She shook her head. "That's not an option. You don't know anything about—"

"If I go back, I'm in a cell, and I won't be able to help you at all."

"What keeps them from shutting down the company?"

"I temporarily transferred control to Alegria."

"Who?" Then it clicked. "Chris' mom?"

"Yes. My sister is enough removed from all the politics that they don't dare do anything to her. So at present, the company has gained a respite of sorts."

Got to give the guy one thing: he's a brilliant strategist.

"I let Klein know about your off-time excursion the night Chris died."

Cynda looked down at her hands. Her mind replayed the sound of the body splashing into the river. She forced herself not to shudder.

"That had to be very hard for you," Morrisey said softly.

When she looked up, she saw that expression in his eyes again. Like he was lost. He always had it when he talked about Chris. "At least we know Copeland was involved, and that leads right back to TPB."

A nod. "How did Harter look that night?"

"Tired. He was way bitchy."

"He can get that way."

"Did he ever say anything to you about…" Her mind blanked. She fished for the pendant and looked at the last few files she'd accessed. "Adelaide Winston. I told him she was one of the Twenty, and he got all weird on me."

"He mentioned a Winston in this time period but gave no details."

"Well, she's one of the top courtesans in this city."

"Not surprising he'd know her. Though against the rules, Harter has enjoyed a number of women over the centuries."

She smirked. "I never crossed that line. TPB would have caught me for sure. Rover One can get away with murder."

"Not quite. However, I'm pleased to see you're using the pendant," Morrisey observed.

"My spare brain," she quipped. "It never fails."

His boots came off and he assumed a Lotus pose on the couch. "I'm glad I'm here. Between us, we can sort this out."

He sounded so positive. "You should take a nap," she counseled. "You need to mitigate your time lag."

"I'm perfectly fine."

"I'm serious."

"So am I," came the curt reply.

This one's going to be a challenge.

———

Ramsey heaved his tired bulk into a chair. If he hadn't been in Fisher's office, he would have let loose a sizeable yawn.

"You look knackered, Martin," the chief inspector observed.

"We're a pair," Ramsey replied.

His superior smiled faintly. "Sleep has come at a premium recently."

"I heard they almost hanged him."

A nod. "Very close. If the Prince of Wales had not intervened, our sergeant would be in the ground by now."

"The prince?"

"Yes. I'm not sure how His Royal Highness became involved in all this. I think it had something to do with the Lassiter woman."

Ramsey snorted and then dropped a sheaf of papers on the desk. "My report," he announced. "I found everything right where the Fenian said it would be. The coffin is downstairs with the boots, locked up in a storage room with a constable at the door. He knows that if he budges, I will tear him apart. I have arranged for another constable to relieve him at two-hour intervals. They know how important the job is."

"Good. I've done roughly the same with the Fenian. I feared someone would knife him."

For a time, the room went quiet.

"Go on, say it," Fisher prompted.

"Hulme botched this investigation from the start," Ramsey blurted out. "First, he didn't find those calling cards at the scene. Every fellow's allowed a mistake every now and then. But then he didn't bother to follow up with Keats' alibi like he should have. He even misplaced the pawn ticket for the boots. He was sitting in the pub in Ingatestone rather than doing his job. What is wrong with him?"

"Perhaps you should ask him."

"Well, I intend to."

"Don't stray too far, Inspector. We may be summoned in front of the Lord Chief Justice this very afternoon."

Ramsey rallied. "So it's going that high, is it?"

"Yes. There's been hell to pay in the papers, questions flying right and left. Even Mr. Stead of the *Pall Mall* has weighed in, and his verdict is that something is definitely amiss with Keats' conviction. His readers are writing letters to the paper, asking why the sergeant is paying the price for others' sordid behavior."

"About damned time," Ramsey muttered.

"Amen to that." Fisher leaned back in his chair. "I trust Mr. Anderson has enjoyed his time with the Yard?"

"He has, especially the part in the woods last night." They shared a laugh. "He's the one who found the coffin. You know he's with Pinkerton's, don't you?"

"Yes. I found that out just after I'd assigned him to you."

"Good," Ramsey said, rising from his chair. "Will the new evidence do the trick?"

"I pray so. Lord Wescomb will do his very best, of that I'm sure."

Ramsey nodded and headed downstairs to double-check the secured storage room one more time. He'd be damned if any of the evidence went missing on *his* watch.

—

Rather than arguing with someone more stubborn than she, Cynda bundled her charge off to the East End. As they trudged along Aldgate High Street, she desperately tried to work out a strategy.

"You need to wear him down," Mr. Spider advised. "He's no different than any other new Rover. He needs the full orientation routine."

Her delusion had a point. New Rovers were always so enthusiastic, so wired they just couldn't relax and do their job. Depending on the time period, that distraction could be fatal.

She smiled when the answer came to her. It would be the perfect solution. *One tour coming up.*

The 'orientation tour' involved hauling the new Rover's butt all over creation until he or she got too sleepy to move. After a good snooze to mitigate the lag and ramp down the high adrenalin, the brain would work much quicker. The upshot was that you lost fewer new Rovers that way.

Usually they caved in after about an hour. After two hours of trudging Morrisey all over Whitechapel and Spitalfields, showing him the most infamous pubs, most of the Ripper murder sites, Alastair's former clinic, and Annabelle's Boarding House, he was just beginning to flag.

What is it with this guy?

By the third hour of hoofing it around, she was about to call it off, fearing she'd met her match. Finally he caught her arm, pulled her out of the flow of pedestrian traffic and said in an exhausted voice, "I know what you're doing. I've read all your run reports. This is the 'orientation tour' gambit, isn't it?"

Oops.

"Okay, you got me, boss. Why didn't you say something earlier?"

"I wanted to see all these places. That's why I asked you to show them to me."

"You just wanted to make sure *my* brain was working right."

He nodded contritely. "Well, at least now I know the East End fairly well." He yawned, trying to hide it with his palm.

She put his hand on his shoulder, leaning closer. "Here's the deal: I work alone. I don't need a babysitter." *Especially someone who's not a Rover.*

"I know your history, Miss Lassiter, but right now you have a choice of me riding shotgun or wandering around on my own. I ask you, would you turn an apprentice traveler loose on these streets?"

Bull's-eye. He knew her too well—she would do anything to keep a new Rover safe, even one who wasn't supposed to be here.

"Throw him a bone and maybe he'll back off," Mr. Spider suggested.

Good idea.

"You need sleep, and I need to do some work without you around. Let's split the difference. I'll take you to the hotel. We'll go out *together* this evening."

"What are you going to be doing in the meantime?" Morrisey asked, his suspicions clearly aroused.

"Going to an inquest," she said.

"Oh, that sounds rather benign," he replied, chagrined. "In that case, I suppose I could use a bit of a rest."

"Good. Tonight, we go hunting for Fiona. We owe an anarchist his daughter."

Morrisey nodded, barely stifling another yawn. "Fine. Now get me to a bed before I collapse."

Works every time.

CHAPTER SEVEN

Ramsey hammered on the door to Hulme's rooms in Cheapside. He got a gruff reply granting him entrance. To his surprise, the door was unlocked. That was sloppy. Good coppers made enemies.

Inspector Hulme sat at a small desk in a dark, unventilated room. A half empty bottle of scotch sat in front of him, and a revolver next to that. Perhaps he had more enemies than even Ramsey could imagine.

"What do you want, Inspector?" Hulme asked. He wasn't slurring his speech, so maybe he'd not been at the liquor that long.

"I want to know why you buggered the Keats investigation."

Hulme didn't look up as he topped off the glass. "So what did I do wrong?"

Ramsey listed off the mistakes, raising one thick finger at a time. By the time he hit ten, he quit. "I asked around about you. You're a good copper. What happened?"

"I did my best," the man replied in a gruff growl.

"The hell you did," Ramsey barked. "You ignored evidence a green constable would have found. Why?"

"Makes no difference," Hulme said, not meeting his eyes.

"It's a man's life at stake!"

"Yeah, it is," Hulme grumbled. "Mine. I had no choice. They told me if I did my job proper, I was in for it."

"Who?" Ramsey demanded.

"Our *betters*," Hulme replied caustically.

"Who?"

"I can't tell you. That'd only make it worse."

"Were their names on those cards?"

A nod. "They said they knew everything about me. *Everything.* So I didn't do my job, figuring it'd never get to trial. I thought someone would pull strings and get the sergeant off. I never thought—"

"That they'd hang him? Where were you this morning when they were putting the noose around his neck? Tucked in your bed, all safe and sound as a—"

"Goddammit, you don't understand!" Hulme roared, surging to his feet. "They'll destroy my career!"

"They don't have to." Ramsey snorted. "You did it yourself."

He saw the truth hit home. Hulme sank down into the chair. Woodenly, he pulled open a drawer in the desk. A black notebook dropped just in front of the revolver.

"It's Keats," Hulme said in a thick voice. "I found it in the alley in Whitechapel."

"When?"

"The day after Fisher received the sergeant's alibi. Tell Keats I'm sorry."

Ramsey collected the item and rifled through it. Inside was the pawn ticket for the sergeant's boots, the one that had gone "missing."

"You intentionally hid evidence that might have cleared a fellow officer," Ramsey seethed. "How can you live with yourself?"

Hulme drifted toward the small window, pushing back the heavy curtain, his braces hanging free. "I can't. Not anymore. They'll keep pushing me, using me. I'm done for."

Ramsey's eyes lowered to the gun. Perhaps it wasn't just for protection.

Sensing a fleeting opportunity, he dropped the notebook into a pocket and then quietly lifted the revolver. Slipping the thumb catch back, he broke open the gun and deftly dropped the cartridges into his hand. He barely got it back in place on the desk when Hulme turned toward him.

"Why are you still here?" he asked. "I've told you my tale."

"I'm still here because we coppers have to stick together. Come forward, Hulme. Give us names. We'll kick those toffs in the nads, teach them some manners."

Hulme shook his head.

"For God's sake, don't let them win."

Hulme scoffed. "They always win. You know that. Now get the hell out of here!"

Ramsey did as the man asked, dropping the cartridges into his pocket the moment he was out the door. Unless the inspector had more tucked somewhere in his rooms, the future might not be as bleak as Hulme imagined.

—

Inquests were boring, at least from Satyr's point of view. You listened to dull testimony about how the deceased had shuffled off this mortal coil, and then the jurors affixed blame... or not. In this case, none of them had any idea who had slipped that knife into Hugo Effington's heart.

Tempting as it was to proclaim to the packed room, *I did it and I'm extremely happy that cruel tyrant is dead*, Satyr held himself in check. *En mirage* as a humble clerk, he stood at the rear of the room, an excellent vantage point from which to observe the proceedings. His disguise was perfect. Clerks were ubiquitous: no one paid them any attention.

At the very front, in the first row, was the veiled widow, recently returned from New York. Inky black was not Deidre's best color. He wasn't surprised that there were no sobs from behind that dense shroud. She was well rid of the man, and only the rules of etiquette kept her from dancing a jig.

Pity I shall never share your bed again. Too many questions might be asked, though he'd certainly enjoyed his time *en mirage* as her lover. The real Reginald Fine was in India, with no notion that someone was having a great deal of fun at his expense.

At least he won't be charged for a murder he didn't commit.

According to the newspapers, the police were stymied. No jealous lover to blame and the widow was on a ship to America when her husband died.

Dr. Montrose testified next. His firm voice and commanding presence was impressive for someone so new to his job. Satyr listened with interest as the doctor spoke of that night: the horrific discovery of Effington's still-warm body, the mysterious disappearance of Miss Jacynda Lassiter, and the hellacious warehouse fire.

Satyr smiled to himself. The fire *had* been hellacious. He'd always had a certain talent with combustibles.

"At that time, did you have any notion of where Miss Lassiter had gone?" the coroner inquired.

"No, I did not," Montrose replied.

"And yet, I understand she reappeared a few days later."

Satyr straightened up, on the alert. *Twig was alive?* Now that was news he'd not heard.

"Yes," Montrose replied. "In the meantime, she had suffered a mental collapse, no doubt from the horrific nature of the event. She remembered no details of that evening."

If she's still among the living, would she be here? His eyes scrutinized the females in the audience. *Too old, too dowdy, too heavy...*

A woman sitting three rows behind Deidre caught his notice. She was clad in a steel-gray dress and fully veiled. *Could it be?* He would have dismissed her outright as some aggrieved relative, except she had a particular way of holding herself not usually seen in women of this century. A gifted assassin could always suss out his prey.

His smile widened. Tobin had made a very grave error. He should have left her in the asylum.

Fool.

The coroner began to question a member of the Fire Brigade. Now truly bored, Satyr left the inquest. Twig would be out soon. He couldn't wait for a personal chat with one of Bedlam's former inmates. Somehow, she'd put her mind back together. He wanted to know how she'd achieved that miracle.

Then he'd let her know the game was not over yet.

DEATH BY PERSON or persons unknown. Alastair hadn't expected anything else for the verdict. Still, he would need to send Reuben a letter in Dublin, reporting the outcome. He waited until the majority of the room had cleared and then exited the building, holding the door open for a lady clad in dark gray.

"Thank you, Dr. Montrose," she replied.

"My pleasure, madam," he said.

"Want to share a cab?" the figure asked.

He started at the blatant invitation. The woman carefully raised a portion of her veil. A wink came in his direction.

Jacynda. "I should have known." The veil dropped. "Where are you headed?" he asked.

He offered his arm and she took it. "The Arundel Hotel. The sooner I'm out from under this damned veil, the better. It's driving me nuts."

"Very effective, though."

"I thought so."

"I will join you and then take the cab on to Lord Wescomb's. I wish to ensure he is resting. He was at the prison this morning and it was very hard on him."

As he waved down a hansom, a prickling sensation began, then increased. He hunted for the source.

Jacynda turned toward him. "What's wrong?"

"Someone *en mirage*," he whispered. "Very near."

Casually, she surveyed the scene. "Near the lamp post. The one who looks like a clerk."

"How do you know he's—?"

"Later," she whispered back.

"He was at the inquest, in the back of the room," Alastair observed. "I thought I felt something, but I wasn't sure."

"I knew I should have sat further back," she said.

"I would not advise a confrontation on a city street."

He heard her sigh. "All right, I'll behave myself."

He helped her aboard the cab. She supplied the address and the jarvey urged the horse forward. Once they were rolling through the streets, she lifted the veil.

"That's better," she said, scratching her nose.

Alastair took hold of her free hand and squeezed it affectionately.

"It is so good to see you again. I did not have the opportunity to tell you last night."

"How's Keats?"

"Bitter. The stay of execution came at the very last moment. At least they hadn't put the rope on his neck yet." He felt his companion wince. "I'm sorry, that was crude of me."

She squeezed his hand. "I can't imagine what it would be like to have been there."

"He was quite brave." *Better than I would have been.*

"I was outside the prison, waiting to see if they raised the flag. Morrisey kept telling me to have hope, but—"

"Morrisey?" he asked, puzzled.

"Theo Morrisey, my boss. He showed up this morning. He has this silly notion of keeping me safe."

Alastair couldn't keep the frown away. "Is he someone you can trust?"

"What? Oh, yes. He's fine."

"I see," Alastair murmured. He leaned closer. "You said you could tell that fellow on the street was not as he appeared," he said, keeping the conversation cryptic, though he doubted the hansom driver could hear them. "How?"

"It's been that way ever since this," she replied, tapping her temple.

Alastair blinked in surprise. "I'd keep that secret. Perceivers are not well regarded, and you're not even one of us."

She gave him a strange look, but held her silence. That wasn't like Jacynda. She still tended toward profanity, but something was different about her. Why did that surprise him? She had undergone such a profound mental disruption. Certainly she would be altered, wouldn't she?

"What did they do to you, exactly?" he asked.

"They used a device that disrupted my memories, sort of…erased my brain," she said.

"How long did it take for you to heal?" he asked.

"Nearly four months."

"That long?" he exclaimed, astonished. "I had thought that with your advanced medicine, it would have gone more quickly."

"I started with almost nothing, only my name. It just took time." She let out a small chuckle. "Plus a medication error."

When she didn't offer any further information, he decided not to press further. The uncertainty in her voice told him she wasn't completely healed, no matter how she tried to cover it.

He would have placed a kiss on her cheek when he bid her farewell at the hotel, but the veil was in the way again. A squeeze of her shoulder sufficed. As he climbed back into the hansom, calling out his address, he felt that odd sensation.

Their watcher had followed them.

———

The Lord Chief Justice's chambers were more crowded than was comfortable. Extra chairs had been brought in, but still it was chock-a-block.

Fisher chose a seat away from the fire, knowing the room would get toasty soon enough. Ramsey sat next to him, the heavy bags under his eyes bearing witness to his lost sleep. Next to the inspector sat Kingsbury, appearing equally worn.

Fisher willed himself to relax. It failed. His nerves had been in a tangle since the moment a reporter had barreled out of the prison shouting the news.

A stay of execution. He had almost wept on the spot.

Ramsey lightly touched his sleeve. "It's truly a second chance, sir," the inspector murmured. "We can set this right."

"That is my prayer."

On the other side of the room, Justice Hawkins was settling in, as was Arnett and two men he did not know.

"Who are they?" he asked Kingsbury.

"The one on the right is from Home Office, the other no less than an emissary from His Royal Highness, the Prince of Wales."

"There does not seem to be goodwill between them," Fisher observed.

"No, there isn't," Kingsbury replied. "Home Office is taking a hiding in the papers. I gather the Queen is quite distressed by this whole disaster. Home Office has tried to shift the blame to Warren, but it's not working as well as they'd hoped." Kingsbury looked up. "Ah, here he is."

They all rose in respect as Baron Coleridge, the Lord Chief Justice, entered his chambers.

"Do be seated," he said, looking around the room as he sat behind his desk. He glanced down at a list of names his clerk had given him upon his entry.

"Which of you is the representative from Home Office?"

A thin man with a bristly moustache rose and gave a slight bow. "I am, your lordship."

"I note His Royal Highness has an emissary here, as well. That is most unusual."

Another man rose. "It is His Royal Highness' opinion that this is a most unusual case, your lordship."

"So it appears." Coleridge studied the list for a bit longer. "Chief Inspector Fisher and Inspector Ramsey?"

"Just here, your lordship," Fisher replied.

"Mr. Kingsbury?"

The junior barrister stood. "Chief Justice. Lord Wescomb asked me to send his regrets. The events at Newgate this morning have compromised his recovery and he has returned to his bed."

"I'm truly sorry to hear that," the man replied, setting the list aside. "I see the Crown Prosecutor is here, as well. Excellent. We shall proceed."

There was a tap at the door and a clerk hurried in. He bent close to Fisher and handed him an envelope. The chief inspector ripped it open.

Is there no bottom to this dark pit?

He handed it to his subordinate.

As Ramsey read the contents, his hands began a fine tremor. "My God…" he whispered.

Before Fisher could reply, Coleridge began. "Mr. Kingsbury, state your position as clearly and succinctly as possible."

The junior barrister rose. "Thank you, Chief Justice. We have secured a stay of execution based on compelling new evidence that proves Sergeant Keats is innocent of the murder of Nicola Hallcox."

"What is the nature of this evidence?"

"Two Fenians have come forward, my lord, and have sworn that they were present with Sergeant Keats in Whitechapel during the time that Miss Hallcox met her end. Mr. Paddy O'Donnell is willing to testify that he struck the sergeant, placed him inside a coffin, and transported him out of the city. The other witness, Mr. Desmond Flaherty, has signed a statement indicating his presence with the sergeant that very evening."

The Lord Chief Justice leaned forward in his chair. "Fenians? Consider me stunned, sir."

"As was I, your lordship," Kingsbury said. "It was most unexpected."

Justice Hawkins sighed. "I should be surprised at nothing when it comes to this case."

"In addition, my Lord Chief Justice, we have a witness who has testified that she saw the sergeant in Whitechapel at forty past ten that evening. She stated he was walking on the very street that would lead to his confrontation with the Fenians."

"Why did this witness not come forward earlier?" Coleridge asked, frowning.

"She was concerned about her safety, my lord. She is Irish, you see, and did not wish to incur the wrath of the anarchists." Kingsbury shuffled the papers in his hand. "As for physical evidence, Inspector Ramsey has located the coffin. There are marks on the lid that match perfectly the sole of one of the sergeant's boots. In addition, Inspector Ramsey has obtained the sergeant's notebook, which was found in the alley where Keats said he was set upon by the Fenians."

"Who found the notebook in the first place?" Coleridge asked.

Kingsbury looked toward Ramsey, who rose.

"Inspector Hulme passed it onto me, my lord," Ramsey said.

"When?"

"Just this morning."

Coleridge sported a frown. "How long has it been in his possession?"

"Since the twenty-sixth of October."

"Good heavens. Why did he not enter it into evidence at the trial?" Coleridge's frown deepened. "We must have this man explain why he did not do his duty."

Fisher rose. "That will not be possible, my lord." He indicated the message he'd received. "I have been informed that Inspector Hulme was found dead of a gunshot wound about an hour ago, in his rooms. It is surmised that he took his own life."

Coleridge sank back in his chair. "This has to be the most remarkable case I have seen in all my years in Her Majesty's service." He eyed Arnett. "What has the Crown to say of this new evidence?"

"I am taken aback at the news of the inspector's death, my lord. I was not aware that he held the prisoner's notebook in his possession, and can give no possible reason why he would have done so." He turned toward Fisher. "As to the Fenians and this new witness, what manner of compensation have these people been promised for their testimony?"

"None," the chief inspector replied.

Arnett huffed. "I find that unlikely given Flaherty's animosity for the constabulary."

Before Fisher could reply, Kingsbury interjected, "Well, there was one offer, if you may call it that."

Arnett pounced. "What was it?"

"Lord Wescomb has offered to represent Mr. O'Donnell when he comes to trial," Kingsbury replied innocently.

Arnett scowled.

"With no disrespect meant to his lordship, that is hardly an incentive to offer testimony in this case," Coleridge replied.

The Chief Justice swiveled toward the Home Office representative. "I must put a question for you, sir. Where I understand the need not to ruin the reputations of the men who unwisely availed themselves of the victim's services, I do not comprehend the other interdiction. Why did you enjoin both the defence *and* prosecution from speaking of the stolen explosives?"

The Home Office mouthpiece spoke up. "It was to prevent panic, my lord. The citizenry would be overly frightened. They are not equipped to handle such disturbing news."

To Fisher's astonishment, Ramsey rose again. "I disagree. The public is a lot smarter than you give them credit for. Besides, it's already common knowledge in the East End."

"You misunderstand me, Inspector," the Home Office representative replied smoothly. "Our concern was for the people *who matter.*"

Before Ramsey could burst out in fury, Fisher gave a quick tug on his sleeve. The inspector grudgingly returned to his seat.

"Self-righteous bastard," he muttered under his breath.

"Careful, Martin. They will be your masters soon enough."

"That may be true, but I'll be biting them in the ankles as often as I can, that I promise."

No doubt you will.

The prince's spokesman cleared his throat. "Contrary to what my colleague in Home Office says, both His Royal Highness and Her Majesty hold deep regard for all our citizens, be they lesser or greater. The prince, in particular, has been dismayed at how this trial has brought turmoil to Scotland Yard, especially at a time when they have a myriad of other more important matters to attend to, including the safety of Her Majesty."

It was a strong rebuke delivered in velvet tones. The Home Office man fell silent, his arms crossed in sullen displeasure.

Coleridge nodded his approval. "Very well, Mr. Kingsbury, bring me your new evidence. The Crown Prosecutor may file objections as he chooses, then I shall weigh as to whether the convicted man deserves to be set free or make a second and final journey to the hangman."

"My lord, we hope that you might make that decision as promptly as possible. This whole ordeal has been incredibly difficult for the sergeant."

"No doubt. Just send me your evidence, sir. I will give it due consideration as my schedule permits."

"As your lordship pleases," Kingsbury said.

IN THE HALLWAY outside the chambers, Ramsey whispered, "Surely they can't have the fix in all the way to—" he gestured with his head toward the closed door.

"Let's pray the rot hasn't risen that high," Fisher replied. "If so, this mighty empire is foundering on the rocks."

CHAPTER EIGHT

Upon her return, Cynda found Morrisey awake, reading a newspaper. At his elbow was a cup of tea. The furniture had been moved to create an open space, suggesting he'd practiced his Tai Chi during her absence. Much like a chameleon, he was rapidly adapting to his surroundings. She wasn't sure if that was good or bad.

He studied her clothes with a critical eye. "Is that what is required for an inquest?"

"No. Just trying to be invisible. Not everyone knows my brain is back from vacation, and I'd like to leave it that way." The hat and veil came off immediately, followed by the mantelet. "That's better. I can actually see."

She stepped inside her bedroom and closed the door. A rummage in the wardrobe produced her old costume, all patched and faded. Waltzing through the front lobby looking like a beggar would invite problems. She'd have to slip out some side door. The spare room at Pratchett's Book Shop would have been an ideal solution, but she had to admit she liked a hot bath every now and then.

"How's your time lag?" she called out, pulling on the worn skirt.

"Better. I had a long nap and some tea."

"Excellent." *Not as good as sex, but it works.*

"I gather you're changing clothes," he called back. "Do I need to do the same?"

"Yes. We're headed for the East End. Dress down-market. We got away with what we were wearing this morning, but at night it's best to blend in."

She heard noises from the sitting room. "Luckily, I brought something appropriate," she heard him say. "I gather the garments can have lice or fleas in them if you buy them secondhand here."

"He did read the run reports," Mr. Spider announced. "Sobering thought."

Morrisey would remember *all* those details. She just remembered most of them.

Cynda heard him open his pasteboard suitcase. His boots hit the floor with two pronounced thumps.

"I met up with Alastair Montrose at the inquest," she reported.

"Oh." Then silence.

"Morrisey?"

More silence.

"Hello, boss?"

"One moment. I'm still dressing." Now that was *so* Victorian.

"The first time you were here, you saw me in a bathtub. Why can't I see you in your underwear?" Oh, she was enjoying this. How many Rovers got to mess with the Genius?

"Because this Victorian underwear is embarrassing," he groused. "All right, I'm decent."

She rolled her eyes and stepped out, still buttoning her bodice. He was tugging on his boots. Other than his clean-shaven face, he could easily be mistaken for some loser in the East End. The clothes were perfect.

Then she remembered his special ability. "Why don't you go *en mirage*? It'd be easier."

"This takes less concentration."

"Which means you don't shift often," she replied.

He seemed surprised at her knowledge. "No, I don't," he said. "No real point." He mussed up his hair and stuck on the slouch cap. He looked disreputable. "Stop fretting. I promise I won't do anything stupid."

"Well, that's at least one of you," Mr. Spider said, peering into her boss' luggage. He jumped out of the way as Morrisey snapped it shut and stashed it by the couch. "Tidy, isn't he?"

Overly.

THEY RETRACED SOME of their route through Whitechapel and Spitalfields. While Morrisey was methodically cataloguing streets and sights, she was listening to the ebb and flow of conversations.

"The smell is so strong here," he remarked, his nose wrinkling in spite of himself. "I knew it would be bad, but..." Just then, his attention was drawn to a constable standing on the other side of the street.

"They're all over the place. Still hunting the Ripper," she explained. *Pity they never catch him.*

"I've read about all this and seen some of the photographs, but nothing prepares you for the reality," he mused, turning in a full circle to get a panorama.

"No. Nothing can."

"How do you cope?" he asked suddenly. "One moment you're *there,* and then you're here. There is such a difference between the two worlds."

She wondered if he'd understand. "That's part of the thrill. Here you have to live by your wits. At home..." She shrugged. "I just run afoul of the rules all the time."

He turned cocky. "So do I. I'm a wanted man now," he said in a low voice. "I find that amusing."

Until they throw your butt in jail.

A voice called out to them. Cynda turned, knowing it sounded familiar. A bootblack. A young one.

"Miss Jacynda!" the boy cried. He grinned widely as she worked on his name. His face was grubby, like most of them, but there was a brightness to his eyes that she recognized.

"Hello there, how have you been?" she said, buying time. *A young kid about twelve.* As he moved forward toward her, she noted the limp. That helped.

"I'm right fine." He peered up at her quizzically. "How 'bout you?"

"I'm much better." He opened his mouth to help her out, but she held up a hand. "Let me do it." *Yes, that's it.* "David Edward Butler."

He cheered and broke out in a smile. "You remember me! You didn't the last time." Then he gave Morrisey a curious look. "Who's this gent?"

"Davy, this is Mr. Morrisey."

"Ah, yes." Morrisey offered a hand, and the two of them shook. "You are the son of Dr. Montrose's housekeeper."

"Right you are! Pleased to meet you, sir." Then David peered down at her companion's boots and shook his head in mock despair. Cynda winked at her boss and he took the hint. As Davy applied his talents, she used the opportunity to solicit the kid's street knowledge

"We're looking for a missing Irish girl. About sixteen or so. Her name's Fiona. We think she's somewhere in Whitechapel."

"What does she look like?" Davy asked, applying the polish.

Cynda did as best she could with what Flaherty had told her.

Davy's eyes rose from his work. "Lots of Irish girls in Whitechapel."

"I know. I just thought I'd tell you in case you hear something."

"I'll see what I can find out."

"Do it carefully," Morrisey warned. "There are people who won't want her found. It might be dangerous."

"I'll be careful." Davy signaled for him to switch feet. Then he looked up again, frowning. "You sound posh, but your clothes aren't. You slummin'?"

It was Morrisey's turn to wink. "Something like that."

"Ah, well, that's all right then." The kid went back to work with a vengeance.

A block after they left Davy behind, Cynda pointed toward a puddle of muddy water. Before she could explain, Morrisey walked through it to obscure some of the bootblack's handiwork, which clearly out of place with his garb.

"Quick study," the spider observed from her shoulder.

Too quick. Those kind usually get in trouble.

It took her some time to relax. It was bad enough she was reacquainting herself with 1888, but having a beginner in tow just made it harder. She fretted about every seedy character who eyed them, the thick traffic, the pick pockets.

"I'm fine," her companion said. "Stop worrying."

"I'll try."

With each pub, dining hall, and street market they visited, she felt herself slipping back into the rhythm of Victorian London. It felt right. Every now and then she'd whisper some bit of advice to Morrisey and he'd nod in response. He rarely asked questions, but his attention remained sharply focused. They'd chatted with newspaper boys, costermongers, a couple of whores, a butcher, and a girl selling milk. Morrisey hadn't complained once, not about the throng of people or their lack of bathing habits. By now he should be begging for fresh air.

Points for style, boss.

The strangest thing was the contented look on his face. She hadn't expected that. "You act as if you're enjoying yourself," she observed.

He offered his arm and she took it, as would be expected. "I am, in many ways."

"Why?"

"At home, I'm too well known. I'm stared at all the time if I go out in public. It's one of the reasons I keep out of view." His expression transformed into a genuine smile. "Here, I'm no one. It's refreshing."

She hadn't ever thought of that. "It must be weird to be so famous."

"It's a double-edged sword. I see why Harter hides himself away like this. It has a certain appeal."

Along with some downsides.

Not wanting to ruin his good mood, she said, "Come on, I'll buy you a pint. Watch what you say. The pub will be crowded."

The Ten Bells was packed, as usual. After muscling their way to the bar and claiming their drinks, they found a spot in the back of the room.

"Right friendly place, ain't it?" Morrisey remarked. His thick working-class accent sounded natural. He had the advantage on her: he was a native.

"Not hearin' much that helps us, though," she replied, trying to match him.

"Well, at least the ale's worth the time," he said, taking another sip and smacking his lips.

She nearly burst out laughing. If the Vid-News reporters ever caught wind of T.E. Morrisey slumming in 1888 London, their readership would double.

"Is it always like this?" he asked quietly.

She nodded. "Friday's a holiday. They want to get a head start on the drinkin'."

"No, no, he's good for it!" someone shouted above the din. "They're all crooked, those rozzers. Don't want to pay for a leg-over like the rest of us."

That generated raucous laughter. To her astonishment, Morrisey called out, "Why pay for what ya get for free?"

Before she could issue a warning, a man answered, "Right ya are, sor. That's what I'm sayin'."

"I'm sure I saw him with old Polly," another said. "He's got to be the Ripper. How else could he get away with it?"

"I bet he was goin' to do that posh bint like the others, but he heard 'em comin' and ran away," a woman said.

"Not that rozzer," a young woman piped up. "He's a good sort. He'd slip me tuppence every now and then, tell me to get home safe."

"Oh, I'd slip ya brass too, but you'd have to earn it," a man said, elbowing her.

"I know yer kind, Tom. Yer all talk." More rude laughter.

"I heard someone spoke up for him. Some Irish girl," another man added. "She's lucky Flaherty gave the word or she'd be payin' for that dearly."

"Yes, she was lucky," the woman said pensively. "But it was the right thing to do."

"I wouldn't do that for no rozzer," the one called Tom shot back. "Ya heart's too big, Mary. Ya can't see the truth for what it is."

Mary?

Cynda thought she'd seen her before. Young woman. Red shawl, no hat. Some night in… She couldn't quite remember. It had been in front of the Ten Bells. Then it fell into place.

"What's wrong?" Morrisey asked.

"Nothin'. Done with yer pint?" she asked, working hard to keep in character.

He took a final sip. "Ready."

Once they were back on the street, she leaned close and delivered him the stock lecture about blending in.

"I think I did rather well," he said peevishly.

"You did, but you're always supposed to be part of the scenery."

"If I remember, you're not very good at that, either. Is that why you dragged me out of there?"

"Part of it." Cynda took his arm. "The other part's the downside of being a Rover."

"Which is?"

"Seeing people who are going to die."

"They're all dead, Jacynda," he replied gently.

"Yes, but I know *how* she dies, when…where." *Every damned detail.*

Morrisey looked puzzled. "Who are you talking about?"

"Mary Jane Kelly. She was the woman in the pub talking about how good Keats was to her." Cynda watched as the name hit home.

"The Ripper's next victim," he murmured.

"This Friday, early in the morning, in Dorset Street." She'd not taken him there during their tour. That would have been ghoulish.

He looked away, his mind somewhere else. If he'd seen the crime scene photos…

You shouldn't have to face this.

It was one of the hardest things that a Rover had to handle: everyone you met was dead. Some of them would haunt you forever. For her, it was Kate Eddowes: laughing, playfully putting her hand on the shoulder of the man who'd mutilate her in Mitre Square a few minutes later.

"Look, you can't stay here," she pleaded. "We'll find somewhere else for you to go—"

"No," he retorted, "I *need* to be here." His voice went rough. "This…" he said, gesturing around him at the teeming streets, "is real. I made this possible. Why shouldn't I see the human consequences of my so-called genius?"

"Only if you can handle it. Not everyone can."

Silence. He took her arm again. "Where to now?" he asked, his tone flat. That told her the subject was closed.

"I want to check in a few more places and see if we can pick up any word of Fiona."

He fell in step next to her, face somber. "I don't understand. You haven't asked anyone about the missing girl. How can you find her that way?"

"Sometimes, all you have to do is listen."

Wednesday, 7 November 1888
Rose Dining Room

To Satyr's relief, Tobin was not present at the breakfast meeting. That would have generated a major incident, and he wasn't ready to eliminate his rival. The Ascendant was just sitting down when he arrived.

"Good morning, sir," Satyr greeted pleasantly, laying his hat and coat aside. He put on his best manners, hoping to keep his superior open and sociable. Perhaps then he could begin to figure out what was going on.

"Mr. S.," was the cool reply. The Ascendant opened up his newspaper. "What is this? A stay of execution? What in heaven for?"

"New evidence, I gather," Satyr said. The news had pleased him immensely. It had never been his intention to ensnare a Scotland Yard detective in Nicci's murder. He'd just employed Keats' form because it seemed the best way to obtain the information he wanted.

Satyr sat with a flourish and then rang the bell. Two waiters came through the door immediately, hands cradling plates and bowls filled with hot food.

His superior waited until the servers were done and the door closed behind them before he replied. He dropped the paper on the table. "Well, won't matter anyway."

"Why not?" Satyr asked, picking up the lid to the sausages. The scent was erotic.

"Soon a man's guilt or innocence will be weighed by a higher authority than the courts."

"How soon?"

"Lord Mayor's Day."

From Satyr's perspective, it was a day best kept to one's rooms, as getting around the streets of London was penance. Give the citizenry a day off, and they exploited it shamelessly.

"Is that when you're delivering the explosives?" he asked pointedly.

The Ascendant gave him a sidelong glance. "I have a couple of tasks for you and I want them performed promptly, without error, unlike some of your previous efforts."

Satyr halted mid-chew and then washed the bite of egg down with a sip of tea. "Such as?" he asked.

"Kill the Fenian."

"You should note that Flaherty's death will risk fanning Irish anger."

"Then make it look like a Jew did it. That way the Irish will take their anger out on the Hebrews, not us. And remove his daughter, as well," the Ascendant added, daintily buttering a piece of toast. "She is superfluous at this point."

Professionals do not kill innocents.

The Ascendant noted his silence. "If you do not wish to follow my orders, I will give Tobin the job, at which time you will no longer be considered Lead Assassin. Do you understand?"

Satyr had seen this one coming. "Tobin is not a Virtual. Tradition requires that he be one to replace me."

"If I say that Tobin will become Lead Assassin, then he will."

So that's the way you're playing it. He debated whether he should tell his superior about Miss Lassiter, then thought better of it. The Ascendant would just dispatch Tobin again and perhaps the fellow might get lucky the second time around.

If anyone is to kill her, it will be me.

"You should be aware that The Twenty's patience grows thin. You have not treated them as tradition requires, and that makes them inclined to *rethink* your status."

To his astonishment, the Ascendant shrugged. "I am not worried about them or any others of this world, Mr. S."

"You owe them an explanation, sir," Satyr pushed.

"I owe them nothing! I have my marching orders, and they do not come from the Twenty."

Who is dictating his decisions? There was no one higher than the Ascendant.

Satyr leaned closer. The man's eyes were glassy. The pupils didn't seem the right shape. *Opium?* He had none of the telltale signs of abuse. Besides, he was religious man who didn't take strong drink, except the wine during Communion.

"Who has issued those marching orders?" Satyr quizzed.

"No one you would know," was the smug reply.

Satyr pushed back from his breakfast, sincerely disappointed at leaving the fine food behind. "I shall be seeing to my work," he said, gathering his outer garments.

"I expect a full report tomorrow morning."

"As you wish, sir."

"Lest you do not understand, Mr. S., this is your last chance."

Satyr gave his chief a knowing nod.

So you think.

CHAPTER NINE

When Inspector Ramsey appeared at his cell door, Keats groaned. He'd been dreading this moment.

"Sir," he said, not bothering to stand. It no longer mattered if the man hated him or not. His career was gone.

"How are you doing?" The inspector's concern sounded genuine. There was no hint of the arrogance that had fanned Keats' dislike of the man since the day they'd first met.

"It's been rocky, sir. One minute I hold great hope, and then the next I know I am a dead man."

Ramsey drew out the bench with a noisy scrape and lowered himself onto it. "Got to be hell," he said, shaking his head.

What is this? He'd expected the Ram to lord it over him.

Perhaps it was time to repay the man. "You did ... a remarkable job, sir."

Ramsey's eyes caught his. "I shouldn't have had to. That was Hulme's job."

Keats' temper flared at the name. "Damn the man's incompetence. If I am found innocent, I'll tell him that personally."

"Don't bother. He died this morning, one shot in the temple. It looks like suicide."

"Good Lord!" Keats exclaimed. "What would drive a man to that?"

"He admitted he was being ridden hard by some of the higher-ups to make sure your alibi didn't stick. He said they were holding something over him."

Keats' mouth dropped open in astonishment. "Then there *was* a grand conspiracy to see me hang."

Ramsey ran his thick fingers through his hair, then let his shoulders drop. "I may have pushed him to it, I don't know. He was on the edge, that was clear. He was brooding over a revolver and a bottle of scotch. It's when he gave me your notebook."

"He had it all along?" Keats said, scratching his chin in thought.

"Yes. Found it in the alley."

"My God," Keats murmured.

"I took the bullets out of his gun when he wasn't looking," Ramsey replied.

"That was decent of you," Keats said, surprised. "But maybe he had more."

"I don't know," Ramsey said. "I was hard on him. Maybe too hard."

"He knew what he was doing was wrong." Keats swore under his breath. "They've tampered with the investigating officer, lost or withheld evidence, tried to murder my barrister. They'll do something this time around. I'll still hang."

"Maybe not. The Prince of Wales is involved now. The Royals know a bit about riding people hard. It's what they do best."

Keats was caught by the man's honesty. "Why did you do all this? You hate me."

The inspector frowned at him. "Fisher asked me to."

"Ordered you to, more likely."

A nod. "He didn't have to, though. I would have taken it on anyway."

"Why?" Keats challenged.

"Because the other men would always think I'd let you go to the noose just to be rid of you. Then they'd wonder if I'd do the same to them."

Keats didn't know what to say. He'd so misjudged this man. Misjudged so many things in his life.

Ramsey retrieved something from under his coat and dropped it on the table with a thump. "Your diary."

"Why do you have it?" Keats asked, furious someone may have read his personal thoughts.

"It was evidence. Don't worry, I only read your last entry. It's what made me realize I might have been wrong about you."

Before Keats could reply, the cell door creaked open. Kingsbury entered. Behind him was Alastair. He could read nothing on their faces. Nevertheless, his heart began to pound.

"Sergeant?" Kingsbury began. "The Lord Chief Justice has issued his ruling, in record time, I might add." In the hall, Keats heard someone complaining about a lost bet. His heart sank.

"Am I still for the rope, sir?"

The barrister's face formed into a triumphant smile. "No, Mr. Berry's next appointment will not be you."

"What?"

Alastair shot both fists into the air like a prizefighter at the end of a match. "You're a free man, Keats! Do you understand? Free!"

Before he could react, Ramsey slapped him hard on the back, nearly knocking him over. "Bloody hell, you did it, gnome."

"I'm free?"

"Absolutely," Kingsbury replied. "Arnett grilled Mr. O'Donnell, but nothing he could do would shake that man's basic honesty. He couldn't shift the other witness' testimony either. Miss Kelly put you in Whitechapel at just the right time. The Crown Prosecutor finally gave in. The Lord Chief Justice accepted the new evidence, in total, and your conviction has been overturned."

"Dear God..." he whispered, collapsing onto his cot. Then a moment later, he shot to his feet. "How soon can I leave?"

"At this very moment."

EUPHORIA FLOATED HIM out of Newgate Prison as guards called out their best wishes, including the two who'd watched over him.

"Cost me five shillings, you did," one said. "I'da thought they'd hang you for sure."

Keats smiled wanly. "I won't say I'm upset you lost the bet."

The guard laughed. "Stay outside these walls, will ya?"

"I'll do my best."

The moment he stepped outside the prison walls, he looked up, just as he had in Birdcage Walk.

Thank you, God. I shall never forget this.

He followed Alastair to a waiting carriage. Once inside, the elation began to wane, like air from a leaking balloon.

"Are we going to my rooms?" Keats asked, realizing they were in motion.

"No, we're going to my home," Alastair replied. "It'll be quieter there. I have a spare room, and you are welcome to it as long as you wish. I think it might not be prudent for you to return to your rooms for a few days. Not everyone is pleased that you have been found innocent."

"Have they arrested the man who tried to kill Lord Wescomb?"

"No. We had hoped he would appear at one of the hospitals or clinics for treatment, but it hasn't happened."

"Which meant he had a private patron to care for him."

"Or he's already dead and in some obscure grave," Alastair concluded. "I believe I might have seen the man. Someone was watching us at the Viaduct Tavern. I've given the description to the police. From what I hear, it is a match to the one Wescomb's butler supplied."

Keats went quiet. He had nothing else he wanted to ask. He half-expected someone to stop the carriage and haul him back to the scaffold.

He was only vaguely aware when their journey ended. Once inside the house, he hung his coat and hat on a peg near the front door in a mechanical fashion, not registering any of the details around him. He heard the sound of hurried footsteps coming down the hall toward them. It was a woman in a white apron. She looked about thirty or so, with brown hair and a welcoming smile.

"Mrs. Butler, this is Sergeant Keats. He'll be staying with us for a time," his host explained. "His conviction has been overturned."

Her face broke out in a huge smile. "I'm so happy to hear that, sir." The woman looked Keats straight in the eye. "I'm pleased you proved 'em wrong," she said.

Alastair handed over a parcel. "These are his old clothes. If you could tidy them up, that would be ideal. We may have need of them soon."

"Certainly." She scurried off before Keats could thank her.

The parlor was small, but not empty. A figure rose from a chair. "Jonathon?"

Part of his oblivion lifted. "Jacynda…" He felt her arms around him, embracing. He was on the verge of tears, though it he knew it was undignified.

Cynda felt Keats shiver. His face was sallow, pinched. He had aged in a few short weeks. Behind them, Alastair murmured something and left them alone.

"Sit down, you look awful." In the end, she had to guide him to the couch and then he still would not loosen his grip on her hand.

"I am found innocent. I won't have to go back to the prison," he said, hoarsely. It sounded like he was trying to reassure himself.

"What's going on with him?" Mr. Spider asked, studying him from her shoulder.

Nothing good.

"Jonathon?" It took a moment for him to realize she was talking to him. He looked over with bloodshot eyes. "When was the last time you slept?"

He didn't reply.

Alastair came out of the kitchen, a tray in hand. He quickly assessed the situation. "If he needs to rest, there's a spare room upstairs. It's his for the duration."

Keats didn't stir. He reminded her of a child's toy whose spring had run down.

She took his hand. "Come with me. You can have tea later."

"If he needs something to help him sleep, let me know," the doctor said softly.

She nodded and led the former prisoner to the bedroom. Without a word, Keats removed his jacket and boots and then swung his feet into the bed. She'd expected some comment about propriety. Nothing.

"It's like someone forgot to turn off the light when he left," Mr. Spider said, perching on the headboard.

Like me, after the reboot.

She tucked the blanket around him and sat on the bed. He snaked a hand out from under the covers and grasped hers. "Alastair told me what you did, with Flaherty and the prince."

"It was the Fenian's decision in the end. I couldn't have forced him. It was because of his daughter."

Keats frowned. "Is he willing to give us the explosives if we find her?"

Cynda nodded, though her gut told her it wasn't that simple.

"Let me rest and then I'll go out tonight."

"Promise me you won't go on your own."

There was no reply as his eyes drifted shut. Cynda placed a kiss on his forehead. "I've missed you," she said.

She sat next to him until his breathing grew deep and regular. Carefully rising from the bed, she tucked his hand back under the covers.

"I'll keep an eye on him," her delusion offered.

"Thanks," she said quietly.

Even in sleep, Keats did not look at peace.

SHE FOUND ALASTAIR in the parlour, sitting on the couch. He looked older as well, evidence this ordeal had affected all of them in some way.

"He was in good spirits when he left Newgate," he said. "Now, he is so distant."

"Not surprising, though," she replied. "After a huge shock, the mind has to regroup." She huffed. "I've done that a couple of times myself."

"I am still concerned about him. He is very bitter, and though I understand that emotion, I fear what it might do to him in time."

"What about his position at the Yard?" she asked.

Alastair shook his head. "I doubt he'll be welcomed back. Fisher would want him, Ramsey as well, but his affiliation with Miss Hallcox has tainted him in some eyes."

"Then what will he do if he isn't a cop?"

"Private consulting, perhaps. He has the skills. It just depends on whether he is willing to give up his dream and move in a new direction."

The irony wasn't lost on her. "You know that well, don't you?" she asked.

"Yes," he said, meeting her eyes. "I would have had a fine house, a wife, a growing practice if I'd remained with Dr. Hanson. Now I have a nice house, a nascent practice and I am my own man, free to come and go as I choose."

"Any regrets?"

"Certainly. I regret losing Evelyn. However, recently she and I have been meeting again. We've never gotten to the heart of the matter between us, but I suspect that will come eventually."

"Is there any chance…?"

"I'm not sure," he said. "We must clear the air between us first."

"That is encouraging news, Alastair," she said, though part of her felt a pang of loss. If he and his former fiancée could find their way forward, it was for the best, wasn't it?

Yes and no. In stray moments she'd thought of what it would be like to stay in London with him or Keats. It would stomp on all the rules, but would that matter if she was happy?

"Jacynda?" he asked gently.

"Hmm?" She looked up at him. "I was thinking what it might have been like."

"With me… or with Keats?"

Cynda spread her hands. "That was the problem. I care for you both. I choose one, I hurt the other."

The doctor nodded and rose. "I'll go check on him. No doubt he's asleep, but I still worry. He's had a tremendous shock."

"He's talking about going out to try to find Fiona. Please, don't let him go alone."

"I won't."

"Thanks. I'd better get back to the hotel. Morrisey promised he'd stay put, but he can be willful."

She heard a chuckle as Alastair ascended the stairs. "Pot calling the kettle black, I'd say."

—

In some ways it was very devious, but it paid to be cautious. Just because someone named Morrisey was at Adelaide's doorstep asking to see Mr. Livingston, didn't mean the visitor was the real item. The Theo *he* knew avoided time travel at all costs.

"Are you ready?" Adelaide asked. Defoe tapped a kiss on her cheek, inhaling the soft scent of her perfume.

"I am," he said, fading from view.

He watched as his lover opened the door to the drawing room, taking his place next to her, unseen. If this were an enemy, he would be in for one hell of a surprise.

"Mr. Morrisey?" she asked politely.

The man bowed effortlessly. No one from 2058 would be able to do that…except Theo. Years of dojo training made the gesture as automatic for him as breathing.

"Good evening, madam," the man replied. "I apologize for my abrupt arrival."

Adelaide maintained a discreet distance. "My butler said you are trying to locate Mr. Livingston. Is that correct?"

"Yes, madam. He is a business associate of mine, and I have some information I need to impart to him of a most urgent nature."

Complex speech. Theo always used more words than were needed, but so did the Victorians. Defoe moved closer.

"I am sorry, Mr. Morrisey. I have not seen him for over a week."

"Oh." The man said, looking genuinely taken disappointed. "Do you have any notion of where he is staying?"

Adelaide delivered a demure shake of the head.

"Then I apologize for impinging on your time, madam." Another bow and the fellow left the house as quickly as possible.

Defoe shifted into view right before he exited the front door. Once on the street, he watched how the man moved. It was Theo: he had a certain rhythm to his step. Defoe hurried to catch up with him.

"Damn," his friend muttered. "Where are you, Harter?"

"Here," he said, *en mirage* as Livingston.

Morrisey was in a defensive posture in a heartbeat. Once he realized how that appeared, he straightened himself, glancing around the street, chagrined. Beneath the calm exterior, Defoe knew his friend was steaming.

"No wonder people shoot you," Theo remarked.

Defoe laughed. "It's good to see you again. Come along, let's go back inside."

"If you haven't heard, Keats is free."

Defoe halted mid-step and swiveled toward him. "I'll be damned. She actually pulled it off."

"Of course she did," Morrisey replied, sounding annoyed.

"So what in the hell are you doing here?" Defoe asked.

"TPB has issued a Restricted Force Warrant for me."

Defoe laughed. "Welcome to the criminal classes, Theo. I knew I'd corrupt you eventually." He waved him forward. "Come on, I'll re-introduce you to Adelaide. You need to know what's going on here."

—

You didn't get to be Lead Assassin by waiting for your superior to die in his bed. Unless, of course, you were busily suffocating him with a plump pillow. Satyr couldn't tell which of the Seven was tailing him. That ability eluded him. Still, he knew it was one of them. *Tobin?* Most likely.

Just to make it sporting, Satyr had not varied his form, but kept to his most favorite, the one the Seven knew so well. He continued his way down the lane and then turned into the first passageway, one of the narrow ones that the East End seemed to favor. As he walked, he studied the walls around him. What few windows he spied were hidden behind shutters.

Excellent.

He shifted into nothing and then waited by a drainpipe. That was his edge. Only one of the Seven was a Virtual, and Archer's loyalty was solid. Satyr had made sure of that.

His hunter warily entered the narrow passage. If he'd been smart, he would have paused to listen for Satyr's footsteps. But this one wasn't smart. That meant he was one of the newer ones, still too unseasoned to take on someone of the Lead Assassin's cunning.

Satyr waited a millisecond after the man passed him, then whispered, "Boo!" He caught the junior assassin, mashing his face into the brickwork. A knife skittered into the debris at their feet.

"So which one of my little birds are you?" he hissed.

The man shifted out of pure fright. It wasn't Tobin, but Dailey, the most junior of the Seven.

Why send the most inexperienced? *Because he's so expendable.*

Satyr immediately flipped Dailey around, so his body was in the line of fire should there be a second menace in his wake.

"What are you doing, you fool? You're not good enough to kill me."

"He s-s-said I had to."

"Tobin?"

A frantic shake of the head. "The As-s-scendant," Dailey stammered.

Satyr loosened his grip on the man's neck.

"I didn't want to. He s-s-said he'd have Tobin cut me up if I didn't. I figured I might get lucky."

"Why kill me?"

"He s-s-said it was because S-s-saint Michael told him to."

What's this nonsense?

Satyr shoved the fellow away in disgust. Tradition allowed the Lead Assassin the choice of whether he killed the challenger or not. It was usually more instructive to leave a bloody corpse so the others would take the hint.

Not in this case. He scooped up the knife and tossed it to Dailey, who barely caught it in his shock.

"Leave London," Satyr ordered. "If I see you again, I will cut you into thin ribbons and relish every moment of it, do you understand?"

Dailey nodded furiously. "Thank you, sir. I don't want to be in the middle of this." He took off at a dead run, his boots slipping on the stones.

Satyr listened to the fleeing footsteps while straightening his gloves. The Ascendant had declared war against his own Lead Assassin. This was unprecedented.

Dailey was right. No one wanted to be in the middle of this.

—

One of the guards sat on the stairs outside the building. It was the newer one, the replacement for the man who'd tried to assault the Fenian's daughter during her captivity. Satyr had particularly enjoyed that kill. In his mind, nothing was as evil as taking advantage of a helpless prisoner, especially a woman.

The guard was smoking a pipe, looking like he belonged there, though still on the alert. This one had some talent. Satyr quickly dismissed him, slipping him sufficient coins to ensure he'd not be easily found. The man hurried away into the darkness.

As Satyr pushed open the door to the abandoned saddler's shop, the aroma of well-oiled leather greeted him. He'd always liked that smell. Continuing toward the back room on silent feet, he listened intently. Beyond the door he heard muted voices. He eavesdropped for a time and then smiled. It was not the conversation you'd expect between a guard and a captive.

How romantic. Fiona Flaherty had found herself a beau, someone who would try to protect her. That complicated matters.

He returned to the front door and closed it heavily. Shifting out of his favored form, he headed toward the back room. The voices fell silent. There was the sound of boots moving across the room and the creak of a chair, the guard resuming his place.

With a tortured sigh, Satyr felt in his pocket for the knife and went to do his duty.

CHAPTER TEN

"Jacynda will be upset we didn't include her on this jaunt," Alastair said, reining in his long strides so Keats could keep up with him.

"She's always angry about something," was the mumbled response.

"Not recently. She's changed."

The sergeant gave his friend a long look. "We all have. You in particular. Lost your high ideals, haven't you?" he chided.

The words stung. Though some of the initial shock had worn off, he knew his friend was still inside that prison, looking up at the rope. It would be some time before Keats recovered fully. In the meantime, he'd have to make do with the sergeant's sharp tongue and abrupt changes in mood.

Near dusk, Keats had arisen from his bed and announced he was off to Rotherhithe to find the anarchist. It had been impossible to dissuade him. He'd quickly donned his older set of clothes, mussed up his hair, and been ready to set out. Alastair hadn't had the time to find suitable clothes, so he'd opted to go *en mirage* as a dockworker. It was an unpleasant compromise, but better than allowing the distracted sergeant to wander around on his own.

"I never thought I would do this so willingly," Alastair grumbled.

"At least you have the option."

"You still can't shift?" he quizzed.

"I haven't tried for a very long time," Keats replied. "It just doesn't matter anymore." His tone of voice said otherwise.

"I don't see why you need to speak to Flaherty," Alastair said.

"I must know where he's been looking for his daughter. That way I won't waste time."

"He may well cut your throat just for something to do."

"That might be a blessing," Keats replied.

Alastair fell quiet. There was no point in arguing.

Flaherty's situation wasn't much better. The Irishman had made the ultimate sacrifice for his daughter. The Fenians would never trust him again, not with him coming forward to help a copper.

When they reached the church, Alastair suggested, "I'll go in and find the priest. You wait here."

"He won't know who you are."

The doctor had forgotten he was *en mirage*. That was unnerving. It was becoming too easy. As they entered, Keats genuflected and headed for the front pew. Alastair joined him.

Keats peered up at the crucifix. "I feel a bit like Job," he said, "as if God and Satan had made a bet between them to see how strong I was."

"The Devil lost," Alastair said.

A faint smile returned. "Maybe."

The priest appeared. Then he recognized Keats. "Sergeant?"

"We're here about a missing lamb," Keats said.

Nowlan frowned. He beckoned and they followed him outside the church, into the graveyard.

"Wait here." Then he left them alone.

Keats pulled his coat tighter. "Is Johnny Ahearn buried here?"

"This way," Alastair said, leading him through the gravestones.

The sergeant studied the grave. "Has his wife had the child yet?"

"No." It was the Fenian, the priest at his side. "What ya doin' back here, little sergeant?"

"I owe you my life," Keats began. "And though I should arrest you on sight, I've come to pay my debt. I need to know where you've been looking for your daughter and—"

"What's this game?" Flaherty asked, frowning.

"No game. I'll help you find her, but I have to know—"

"Ya brought her here a couple hours ago."

"What? I didn't—"

"Yer off in the head," Flaherty said.

"No, I'm not!"

"Ya brought her here, to Father Nowlan. She said ya promised ya'd keep her safe, and ya did."

"It wasn't me, Flaherty," Keats admitted. "I had no idea where she was; that's why I came to talk to you."

"Then who…" Flaherty asked.

A slight wind blew through the graveyard, ruffling leaves near the old stone fence.

"It had to be one of the strange ones," the priest said, crossing himself.

"Apparently her captors decided she was of no more value," Alastair offered. "I am relieved they didn't harm her."

Flaherty had his knife out in an instant. "Yer one of them. I know yer voice, and it don't go with that face."

Alastair groaned, then shot Keats a desperate look.

"Go on, you've already stepped in it," his friend advised wearily. "He might as well know it all."

The transformation went smoothly, but still left the doctor queasy.

"What the hell is goin' on here?" Flaherty demanded.

"We're both what you call strange ones," Keats explained. "Alastair can look like anyone he chooses, but he's not practiced enough to do it properly."

"Ya can change as well?" Flaherty asked, the knife still out.

"Not anymore. You took that from me when you hit me on the head in Green Dragon Place."

Flaherty's eyes narrowed. "Ya was with him that night?" Keats nodded. "Looked like a woman, didn't ya?" It was Alastair's turn to nod. "If yer one of them, ya know who took my daughter," Flaherty growled.

"No, we don't," Keats replied.

"I don't believe ya."

"Do you know every Irishman in London?" Alastair challenged. "Of course you don't. Same with our kind."

Flaherty spat on the ground in disgust, then reluctantly tucked the knife away. "No wonder ya always seemed to know what I was about." He spat again. "Don't matter. Fee's safe now, and that's what counts. I sent her with her man to Dorset Street. I've got friends there. They'll look after her."

Keats felt their advantage waning. They'd not found the girl, so Flaherty had no obligation to help them. He could arrest the Fenian—he was still a sergeant—but that wouldn't yield the explosives. And it would tear his soul apart in the process. Still, he had to make the effort.

"We need to know where you've stashed the dynamite and the gunpowder," he said. A stronger gust of wind blew Keats' coat open, making him shiver.

"Come into the church. It's raw out here," the priest suggested.

Keats didn't move. This had to be decided now.

"Yer a stubborn little fella, aren't ya?" Flaherty grumbled.

"I don't want those explosives used by you or anyone else."

"I wouldn't kill anyone," the man replied. "I was after somethin' bigger than a few dead coppers."

"What?"

A look of pride stole across Flaherty's face. "That bit of fancy glass. You know, the one the old cow's stud built."

It took Keats a moment to translate. "The Crystal Palace? You'd destroy Prince Albert's masterpiece?" he asked, astounded and repulsed at the same time. Keats' grandparents had taken him there when he was eight, and he fondly recalled the massive glass structure and the astounding dinosaur sculptures. He remembered standing inside the glass building, gazing upward into the sky, sure he'd been transported to another world.

"You are a barbarian, sir," he shouted, his fists bunched.

Flaherty laughed. "Why not? It'd upset folks right proper. Get their notice. Maybe they'd finally let Ireland go free."

"No, it'd just bring more laws down on our heads. They don't think like we do."

Keats realized what he'd said the moment after the words tumbled out of his mouth. *We.* Somehow he'd crossed over to Flaherty's side without realizing it.

"Whoever made you steal those explosives won't use them on that *fancy bit of glass*, as you call it," Alastair argued. "They'll kill people. Lots of people."

"I know." Flaherty's good humor faded as he swore under his breath. He waved them forward. "Come on, I'll show ya where the first batch is stored."

"First batch?" Keats blurted.

"The explosives are spread all over creation, best as I can tell."

Then it's worse than we thought.

———

The hotel room was immaculate. Fresh flowers rested in a vase on the table near the window. The bed was made, and clean towels sat near the washstand. It was missing one thing: Theo Morrisey.

Cynda held her temper until the maid had departed and then let loose a stream of abuse under her breath.

"You did the same thing on your first trip," Mr. Spider reminded her. "You left your handler and went off on your own. Got into trouble almost immediately."

"But I'd been through the Rover Academy," she argued. "I had a clue what I was facing. If he ends up hurt or dead..." She blew out a puff of air. "Where are you, you idiot?"

"Hunting Defoe?" the spider suggested.

Cynda gave her delusion a nod. "Exactly."

She extracted the pendant and went to work. Defoe's extreme reaction to Adelaide Winston was the best clue she had. A few minutes later, she was in a hansom cab heading toward the woman's upmarket address. She'd made sure to take the necessary precautions: proper manners, nicest dress, pistol tucked in pocket.

Who says I don't know how to act like a lady?

THE COURTESAN'S BUTLER was a solemn sort. Most of them were, but he probably had to be even more circumspect. This was a house in which the obscenely well-off got their requisite tumble with what was reported to be one of the most beautiful women in London. They paid handsomely for her time. And for her discretion.

Expertise always costs more.

He disappeared into another room. When he returned, Morrisey was right behind him.

"Ah, Miss Lassiter, good of you to join us," he said, all formality.

She issued a tight smile in response. "I was concerned when you weren't at the hotel," she said sweetly, mindful of the butler. *I'll give you an earful later.*

"Such things happen," he tossed off lightly. "Mr. Livingston is in the drawing room." He offered his arm and she followed his lead.

The other founder of the time immersion industry was in a room defying description. Everything was flawless: the carpet, the draperies, the furniture, and even the paintings. A Victorian scholar would have sold his children into white slavery to have a photo of this perfection.

Defoe was *en mirage* as that Victorian gentleman again. He gave a nod and then turned his attention to the other woman in the room. The moment his eyes lit on her, his expression changed to one of frank adoration.

It was easy to see why: Adelaide Winston possessed flawless skin, hair, the works. The gown was apricot silk and flowed around her like a cloud. Though she had to be Transitive to be one of the Twenty, there was no white outline. What you saw was the real Adelaide in all her glory.

Wow.

To her surprise, Cynda didn't feel inferior. It was what the woman did best: she made you feel comfortable within your own skin.

"Which is why Defoe is in love with her," Mr. Spider observed.

Love?

"Definitely. Look at his face."

Her delusion was right. *I'll be damned.*

The moment Adelaide rose from her chair, Defoe was at her side. Cynda stifled the snicker. Rover One was acting like a love struck teenager

"Adelaide, this is Jacynda Lassiter," Defoe introduced.

"Good evening, Miss Lassiter," Adelaide said. "Welcome to my home." The timbre of her voice was pitched to command your attention without the need to shout.

"I apologize for arriving without an invitation," Cynda replied.

"I am honored you did."

As Cynda settled into a chair near Morrisey, she felt the woman's eyes on her, assessing her. Adelaide resumed her own chair, perched like royalty, but behind the pretty face was a brain as sharp as a stiletto. Their eyes met and a simple gesture of respect was traded.

"Miss Lassiter has been in on this from the start, Adelaide, so we can be completely candid." One of Adelaide's eyebrows rose ever so slightly in what might have been protest. "She is the one who saved my life."

Cynda kept her surprise hidden. Defoe wasn't usually that open with compliments.

"I see. I thank you for that, Miss Lassiter. I am very pleased to see you survived your own ordeal."

Cynda inclined her head. No need to tell the woman she was only paying Defoe back for all the times he'd saved her.

"I was explaining the Ascendant's mission, at least what it was in the beginning." She adjusted a stray fold in her skirt. "The Ascendant was charged with obtaining a wagonload of explosives with an eye toward providing them to certain parties in Russia. We felt that causing turmoil amongst the Marxists would be of benefit. Russia is growing more unstable, and some of us fear they will replace the Czar at some point."

They got that one right. Though it would take another three decades before the Bolsheviks ushered in the future Communist state.

"Your Ascendant stole *three* loads of explosives," Cynda pointed out. "That's a lot of turmoil."

"That is where he began to disobey us," Adelaide conceded. "He was only supposed to acquire one load of dynamite. Involving the Fenians was his next error. He has been making too many as of late." She paused, then lowered her voice conspiratorially, even though only the four of them were in the room.

"A vote will be taken tomorrow, once all of the Twenty have returned to London. He will be dispatched by the Lead Assassin, and a new Ascendant will take his place."

A palace coup.

"Just as long as the next one leaves me alone," Cynda muttered.

"Before the Lead Assassin completes his task, I will request that he learn the location of the explosives for us. I'm hopeful the Ascendant can be convinced it would be an honorable gesture to reveal that information before he *retires*."

Now that's a sales spiel: you're going to die anyway, but here's your chance to do the right thing.

A tap on the door. The butler appeared and whispered something in his mistress' ear.

"Already?" she asked in surprise. "He wasn't supposed to arrive until later. I shall come to him." Adelaide turned toward her guests apologetically. "I have a visitor and must see him alone for a few minutes."

Defoe's brow wrinkled.

"It is the Lead Assassin," she explained, as if divining his thoughts. "I must ensure he will not harm you, Malachi. If he agrees to that restriction, I feel we should include him in our discussions."

"You trust him that much?" Defoe asked.

"For the moment."

The moment she was out the door, Cynda posed the question. With the Victorians out of the room, she went informal. "Why would this guy want to hurt you?"

"It's Malachi Livingston that's on the Ascendant's hit list. I have no idea why."

"Why not? He's trying to kill everyone else," Cynda muttered.

The door opened.

"Yes, Mr. Livingston is present," Adelaide answered cautiously. "There is to be no attempt under this roof, do you understand?" The newcomer nodded. "Good. Then we shall discuss the situation at length."

Their hostess entered, then turned to make the introductions.

"This is Satyr, the Lead Assassin," she began.

Cynda examined the newcomer. A solid white bloom encased his form. That wasn't a surprise. The chief assassin would be *en mirage*.

Which means he could anyone.

She took inventory. Dark hair. Dark eyes. That matched her patchy memory. *No macassar oil.* That didn't seem right.

He started in surprise the moment he saw her.

"You gave your word, Satyr," Adelaide warned, taking her place next to Defoe. "None of my guests are to be harmed."

The visitor didn't answer, but let his gaze skip over the others, one by one. He frowned at Morrisey, whom he wouldn't know. Then a predatory smile appeared. It didn't match the face.

"How fortunate," he said.

The voice sounded wrong.

"We've met before," Cynda said, testing him. "At Effington's party. Surely you remember."

In lieu of a reply, he slid a hand into his coat pocket.

Before she could call out a warning, a sharp crack split the air. Adelaide staggered a few paces, bewilderment on her face. A vast crimson stain was forming on the front of her apricot dress.

Defoe was on the move before the rest of them. He caught his lover as she tumbled toward the floor, cradling her in his arms. Another gunshot, this one aimed at him. There was a bright burst of shattering glass, followed by a cry from Theo. A third slug tugged at Cynda's hat as it flew by.

Her hands shook so badly that her first shot missed. The second clipped the assassin's arm. He swore at the sudden pain, his form changing as he took off at a run, colliding with the butler in the long passageway.

The man who threw her in the Thames. She'd always remember that face.

CYNDA FOUND MORRISEY kneeling at the woman's side, carefully pressing a Dinky Doc into Adelaide's neck. He stiffened when the readings appeared. He reset the device, fumbling with the settings, then touched it against her neck again. Adelaide's pain eased. Behind them, Cynda heard the butler shouting for someone to send for a doctor.

"How bad?" Defoe demanded, frantic.

Morrisey shook his head. "It hit her heart."

It took Cynda a few seconds to process what he'd said: Adelaide was bleeding out with every beat. She knelt next to their hostess, taking her hand.

Rover One fumbled for his interface. "I'll take her home. We can heal her."

Cynda took his arm, though he fought her. "No. Don't waste the time you have left."

"Listen to her," Morrisey said, his voice breaking. "She'll die before you get there. Be with her at the last. I never had that chance with Mei."

"Damn you," Defoe shouted. "Leave us be!"

Cynda didn't move, but continued to hold the woman's hand. It grasped hers reflexively. Morrisey tried to pull her away, but she shook him off.

"If you are touching her when she dies," he warned, "you will become one of us. Is that what you want?"

No.

Cynda retreated, shaking from the adrenalin churning inside of her. "What about him?" she asked, indicating Defoe.

"He's already a Virtual."

"But it has to do something."

"It will, but I doubt you'll get him away from her," Morrisey whispered. He sank onto a chair, his face ashen. It was only then she noted the thick line of blood running down his scalp and onto his face.

She grabbed a linen napkin from a small serving table and pressed it onto the wound.

"Hold this," she said. A trembling hand rose and did as she asked. A quick treatment with the Dinky Doc reduced the bleeding. His color improved.

Their eyes met. His were glistening. She knew it had nothing to do with the injury. She wet her handkerchief and gently began to remove the blood from his face.

Though she tried not to listen, she heard Defoe's loving whispers and Adelaide's faint responses.

"We shall go to Paris, my love," he said, his voice thick and quavering with emotion. "We will buy a small home and you shall grow beautiful flowers. We will travel, you and I—"

"Malachi…"

"You are the only one I have loved, Adelaide. All the centuries, you're the only one. You cannot leave me."

A thick cough. "I know…love you."

Defoe kissed her. There was a faint murmur from her lips and then she fell silent, draped over his arms like a sleeping angel. A shudder ran through him as Adelaide Winston no longer drew breath.

Cynda's head bowed in grief. Morrisey pulled her close, their tears intermingling.

Suddenly, Defoe was on his feet. The bloom around him vanished, along with the image of Malachi Livingston. Now it was his features.

"I will find him!" he shouted, breaking the unearthly silence. "I will stop him!"

"You can't," Cynda said. "Her death is embedded in the timeline now."

He wasn't hearing her. "I know what he looks like!" he crowed. "I can do it."

"But he's not—"

"Harter, no!" Morrisey called, but his friend was gone, the characteristic transfer halo hovering in the air near Adelaide's body. It wavered for a second, then vanished.

The butler gaped, dumbfounded. "I've never seen a shifter like that."

There was a hammering on the front door, then the sound of running footsteps. The butler crossed the room, opening the door a slit. He shut it instantly.

"It's a constable," he said. "The maid must have sent for him." He gestured to the far door. "I'll tell him you'd already left before this happened. That's all he needs to know. Go on!"

It took Morrisey to pull her out of the room. Cynda could only stare at their hostess. Even in death, Adelaide Winston was beautiful.

THEY HALTED A few streets away to examine his wound.

"It's stopped bleeding," she told him. She sounded calm, but inwardly she was a mess. The bullet might have killed him. Only a few inches and…

"It makes no sense…she let him in the house…clearly trusted him." Morrisey's words were coming out in a rush now. "Why would the Lead Assassin kill her?"

"It wasn't Satyr. His name's Tobin. He shifted right after I nicked him. He was the guy who claimed to be my brother and took me out of Bedlam."

Cynda hailed a cab. The jarvey gave them a concerned look, what with the fresh blood on Theo's collar, but wisely didn't comment.

Once they were on the way to the hotel, she squeezed Theo's hand reassuringly. He stared ahead, like a blind man. He was letting the loss overwhelm him, burrowing headlong into the memories of his own lover's death.

She had to get him talking. "What will happen to Defoe? He was touching her when she died."

Morrisey blinked a couple times, but didn't answer.

"What will happen to him?" she repeated.

He turned toward her with grateful eyes. "Since he's already a Virtual, it's said that if you keep taking from the dead, insanity is the final gift."

"Then it was him," she said softly. "Defoe wasn't after the prince at Effington's party. He came back to kill Satyr. He blames him for Adelaide's death."

And I told Rover One right where to find him.

CHAPTER ELEVEN

It took Keats some time to pick the lock on the warehouse door. He didn't have his tools and it fell to using a couple pieces of wire. As he worked, Flaherty and the doctor stood watch.

To relieve his nerves, Alastair joked, "To hear the Crown Prosecutor tell it, you're a master criminal who can open a lock in a fraction of a second. Lose your touch in the nick, my friend?"

"It would help if I had my lock picks," Keats fumed.

"I'm sure the rozzers will give 'em back," Flaherty assured him. "Ya just gotta ask nice and polite-like."

"We could just break it open," Alastair suggested.

"Don't want to leave any trace that we've been here." Keats tugged on the lock. It popped free. "There."

After a quick look around, Flaherty opened the warehouse door.

"Come on, I'll show ya where they are." His voice echoed more than Alastair had expected. As they walked further inside, the reason was made clear: the warehouse was empty.

Flaherty rotated in a slow circle, his mouth open. "I swear, the gunpowder was here!"

"If you're lying to me," Keats hissed, jabbing a finger in the anarchist's direction for emphasis, "I will personally introduce you to the hangman. Mr. Berry and I are *very* well acquainted."

"I ain't lyin'. No need."

Keats slowly deflated, wiping a hand across his chin. "How many casks of gunpowder did you have left?"

"Twenty-four. But they had me repack it into half barrels."

"Four dozen." Keats shook his head at the thought.

Alastair watched as his friend made as thorough a search as he could with the light of a candle he'd brought from the church. He appeared about to give up, when he spied something. He waved his companions over.

"Hold this," he said, shoving the candle into Alastair's hand. He ran his fingers through the black material. "Gunpowder." Something shiny caught his interest and he extracted it from the black grains.

"It's a coin," Alastair said, holding the candle closer. "Sixpence." He frowned as he examined it closer. "Shouldn't it be silver?"

Keats glared at Flaherty. "Shall I add forgery to your list of offenses?"

"That's not my doin'."

Keats swore under his breath, then dumped the coin into his pocket. Dusting off his hands, he stood. "Let's get out of here before a watchman sees us. I have no desire to spend another night in jail."

After they secured the door, Keats sat on a thick coil of rope by the water's edge, filling his pipe as if this were just another evening's jaunt. After striking a match, the tobacco came to life. He tossed the match into the water.

"How many other sites are there?" he asked.

"Seven," Flaherty answered, kneeling next to him. "I'll take ya to them."

Keats nodded, his eyes fixed on a point across the water. "We'll make the rounds, but I'm willing to bet they'll be empty."

His pipe went out. Swearing, he lit it again and took a few deep puffs. Aromatic smoke rose in a thin column.

"We'll check the other sites, then I'll let the Chief Inspector know that you're no longer the primary threat."

Flaherty shot him a skeptical look. "Will he believe ya?"

"He has no other choice."

—

Thursday, 8 November 1888
Rose Dining Room

The moment Satyr entered, the Ascendant looked up from his newspaper. Faint surprise flickered across his face. Then his expression reverted to neutral.

"Mr. S.," he acknowledged cautiously.

"Sir," Satyr replied, skipping the courtesies. He sat in his appointed chair, amazed that Tobin wasn't already in his place.

He could read the headlines from here. The report was in all of the newspapers. It wasn't often that a courtesan was gunned down in her own home. To his distaste, the killer's description sounded eerily familiar.

Only amateurs use firearms. Only dead men use my likeness when killing another.

Satyr had arrived at Madam Winston's shortly after the crime, as per their arrangement. Taken aback at the unthinkable news, he'd wandered throughout the house, unseen, listening in on conversations with the butler, the police, and the hysterical maid. Whoever had co-opted his form knew it was the best means to gain entrance to the house. Since only Satyr and the now dead courtesan were aware of their appointment, the other assassin had just gotten lucky.

Acting on a hunch that this wasn't an isolated event, Satyr had contacted those few members of the Twenty that he knew and they spread the word amongst their compatriots. Not quickly enough. By morning there was more grim news: three others had met Adelaide's fate.

Sixteen members did not constitute a quorum, so no vote could be taken on the Ascendant's future. Through targeted assassination, his superior had bought himself another day or two of life, until the Twenty reorganized. Pity it had come at such a high cost.

"We appear to have lost our Intermediary," Satyr said, pointing toward the lead article.

The Ascendant's expression grew wary. "No doubt a dissatisfied customer," he said, derision icing the words. "I never liked meeting with her. The whore of Babylon, if there ever was one."

Satyr wisely did not voice what was on his mind.

"You should be aware that I have disbanded The Conclave," the Ascendant remarked. "They are of no further use."

Satyr arched an eyebrow. "Why? They're harmless enough."

"It was time. Hastings is not pleased, but that is of no concern."

He's methodically removing any potential rivals.

"The Intermediary was not the only casualty last evening," Satyr informed him coolly. "I understand three other members of the Twenty are now dead."

The Ascendant responded with a noncommittal shrug. "Crime abounds in this country. Is the Flaherty girl no more?"

"She has been dealt with." *In a truly creative way.* He smiled at the thought of how he'd paid off his debt to the unlucky sergeant.

"Excellent. For a time, I thought you were losing your edge, Mr. S."

Satyr inclined his head at the comment, all the while pondering the best way to slay the viper in their midst. Still, he would not touch the Ascendant until the Twenty gave their blessing, though he had adequate reason to do so. His instincts told him to let this game play out.

"What about Flaherty?" the Ascendant inquired. "Is he dead?"

"I will deal with him today," Satyr lied.

"Good."

"Have the explosives been delivered?"

"They will be. Tomorrow morning," the Ascendant replied.

"What's this about an angel?"

His superior's face went blank. "I do not know what you're talking about." He gestured toward Satyr's empty plate. "Aren't you eating breakfast? Surely you will want some of these fine sausages."

Satyr was up in a flash. "No, sir, I am not dining this morning. Tobin can join you. I'm sure he's excellent company." He halted near the door, then turned. "In future, do not send one of *my* Seven against me."

Their gazes locked in mutual distrust.

"I will send anyone I choose," the Ascendant responded evenly.

"You may," Satyr said, "but next time, I shall return the favor."

—

Cynda stared at the note. It held both good and bad news.

"Alastair says they found Fiona Flaherty. Somebody looking like Keats rescued her, though the doc has no idea who that might have been." Cynda sighed. At least their bargain with the anarchist had been fulfilled.

"Hmm? Oh, that's good," Morrisey said, his back to her. He'd logged onto TEMnet and was tapping out instructions for Fulham in an attempt to locate Defoe.

"Flaherty took them to the explosives, but they're gone."

No reply.

"You want to go down for breakfast?"

"No."

"Any sign of Defoe?" she quizzed.

"No. He's not home."

"Side-hop?"

"No. He's vanished," was the curt reply.

Since Morrisey wasn't budging and she was hungry, she treated herself to breakfast in the hotel dining room. Her appetite was back, and other than a certain blue spider, she still had no time lag effects to speak of. The reboot had done her some good, though she doubted most Rovers would be willing to undergo that hell just to gain a few more months of employment.

As she finished her breakfast, she cast another quick look at the couple sitting near the dining room's entrance. They'd been watching her, trying desperately to appear nonchalant.

Dabbing her mouth delicately with the napkin, she thanked her server and rose from the table. Sure enough, the couple was up and out of the room in a flash, headed for the front door. That cinched it. She had to find out who they were.

When she caught up with them, they appeared extremely interested in a poster advertising a girl's school in Paddington.

"Excuse me," Cynda said. "Can I help you? You've been following me, so I figured you wanted something."

"I told you we were too close," the woman grumbled.

"She's never seen us before," the man argued.

"Let's go down that way for a chat, okay?" Cynda said, gesturing toward a side street.

"Ah, we can't possibly—" the man began.

"Do it. Now!" The menace in her voice did the trick. They halted in a side street, clearly flustered by her presence.

"Who are you?" she asked.

"Ah, we can't tell you that," the man replied nervously.

"Yes, you can," Cynda countered. "That way, I don't get nasty about you following my ass all over London."

She waited for the startled expression at her raw language. Instead, the woman fished a tattered notebook and a short pencil out of a pocket, eyes aglow. "Good heavens, she's just like they said."

"Prudence!" the man hissed.

"Oh, this is perfect. I never thought we'd have a chance to talk to a *Past*."

"Prudence!" the man hissed again, louder.

Past? The ha'penny dropped. "You're Futures, aren't you?" Cynda asked. The woman nodded before caution ruled.

"Why are you following me?"

"You're Jacynda Lassiter! I mean, what an opportunity. You're a legend," the woman gushed.

Her companion shook his head in dismay. "Before my colleague goes any further, you must forget you saw us."

"Not likely. So why come from…" Cynda waved her hand to indicate sometime in the future, "to watch me work? I'm good, but not legendary."

"Well, according to DeMoss, your techniques were responsible for—"

"Pru!" This time the man's warning worked, and the woman's lips snapped shut.

Drat. I was so close. "Were you following me the night I stopped the assassin at the party? My interface registered someone, but the readings were inconclusive."

A cautious nod.

"So why aren't you registering now?"

"We blocked it."

"Why didn't you block it that night?"

The man looked chagrined. "We forgot," he admitted.

"So where else have you been?" The two traded looks. "Come on!" Cynda cajoled.

The fellow cleared his throat. "In Rotherhithe, near the Spread Eagle and Crown when you attempted to cross the water to Whitechapel; the night you were tossed under the beer wagon, and—"

"Never mind." Why hadn't she seen them before? What else was she missing?

After a quick look around, he offered his hand. "I'm Thomas, by the way."

"Glad to meet you, Thomas." They shook. "Is your last name Anderson?"

"Ah...no," he said.

It was worth a try.

"Prudence," the woman said and giggled.

This was embarrassing. "I've never had my very own entourage before," Cynda remarked. "I really must screw things up."

Pru became engrossed in the tip of her pencil.

Oh great. "Any tips so I don't get myself shot, stabbed, or my brain remapped again?"

Silence. At least from the two in the alley. Out on the street, a baked potato vendor called out his wares in a sing-song voice.

"That bad, huh?" she said, growing nervous.

"Not really good," the man admitted.

"Fate-of-the-whole-world stuff?" Cynda joked.

The man looked at her sharply. She'd hit home without meaning to.

"You're remarkably calm about all this," he said.

"Mostly because I don't have a clue what's going on. Something's up. Something bad, but I don't know what. It would be a great help if you guys could fill me in."

"You don't know?" he asked incredulously.

"That's what I just said," Cynda shot back.

"That's not right. By now you should—" He stopped abruptly. "Why is it going wrong?"

"Just a hint would help," Cynda urged. *Please.*

Prudence shook her head. "Tampering with history. Can't do it. Cost us our grant."

"You have a *grant* to follow me around? I really must screw things up if you got funding."

The two Futures traded looks, and then Thomas moved closer. "I would suggest that you take a visit to..." He looked around. "Tomorrow, Lord Mayor's Day. Anywhere in the East End. Just be careful when you do."

"Well, I could do with a bit of a holiday," Cynda mused.

"It won't be any holiday, that I can tell you." Thomas pulled out what appeared to be a pocket watch, but it was fatter and a bit more rectangular, like a vintage cigarette case. "It's clear, Pru. You ready?"

"Wait, you're leaving?" Cynda said.

"Our time is up for this session."

"But—"

There was no light, no sound. And no people. Time travel technology had clearly made some awesome improvements.

—

Theo was pacing. She'd never seen him do that before. "Fulham is trying to track down Harter," he blurted before she could say a word. "He's having no luck. Klein doesn't have him, either. No one knows where he is." He shook his head. "This is so off the rails."

"Why not go back to the party and catch him?"

"We don't dare, not in front of that many people," Morrisey replied. "Too dangerous."

"How about when they take him to jail?"

"That's a possibility."

"Well, if you wait long enough he'll surface eventually," she replied.

He gave a grunt of displeasure. "I want him somewhere safe."

She draped her mantelet over a chair. "There were a couple of people downstairs. They kept staring at me, so I asked a few questions. They say they're Futures, and from the technology I saw, I don't think they're lying."

"Why are they so interested in you?" Morrisey asked, all attention now.

Because I'm a legend.

"They've got a grant to follow me around." She snorted. "Can you believe that? They said I should know what's going on by now, and since I don't, they suggested a trip to *tomorrow*."

Morrisey frowned. "Why tomorrow?"

She threw up her hands and headed for the bedroom. If she was off to the East End, she wasn't wearing her nice dress. As she changed, she realized that she'd have to buy mourning clothes for Adelaide. The steel-gray gown wouldn't be dark enough for Defoe's loss.

Cynda returned to the sitting room to find Theo staring into the fire.

She flipped open her interface. "Along for the ride, boss?"

A distracted nod. He pulled out his own interface and began copying her settings.

"It's a major holiday. The streets will be packed, so make it four in the afternoon," she said. "Might be less crowded."

"Really?" he said crossly. "I've actually been to a Lord Mayor's Show. How about you?"

"Yup. In 1789." She'd lost her interface in the midst of the crowd and when she'd caught up with the thief, he'd already handed it off to an accomplice. She'd gone ugly on him and gotten arrested for assault. Once in jail, an inmate had tried to steal her boots. Nasty memory.

Like most of them.

CHAPTER TWELVE

Friday, 9 November 1888
Whitechapel

They'd arrived in Hell.

Cynda's first gasp was filled with acrid smoke, causing her lungs to spasm. Coughing hard, she flipped the interface closed and buried it inside a deep pocket. Then she crouched low, positioning a handkerchief over her nose and mouth. Around them, flames leapt upward in seething columns and slithered across the ground like hungry lizards.

Someone cried out her name.

A few feet away, Morrisey was on his knees, hand grasping his chest. She hoisted her companion to his feet and they staggered forward, only to be confronted by a flaming barrier. They went left. Another wall of flame.

"This way!" Cynda managed to gasp.

They fled down a narrow passage. When they reached the next street she expected some respite, but around them buildings burnt cherry red. A crush of people pushed their way along. Some carried children or the elderly. Many had meager possessions on their backs. Around them, Cynda could hear the cries of those trapped by the flames.

Above his handkerchief, Morrisey's face was soot-streaked, his eyes wide with fear. "Are we off-time?" he asked in a raspy voice.

She pulled out her pocket watch and flipped open the dial.

9 November 1888. Twelve minutes after four.

"My God," he said when she showed him the reading. "What has happened?"

A constable stumbled by them, then plunged to the ground, his wool coat smoldering. Cynda helped him up. "What's going on?" she demanded.

"Fire all along…the East End," he wheezed. "Wind…pushing it."

"How'd it start?"

"Fenians…" The man drifted away into the tumult of bodies.

"We must keep moving," Morrisey urged. They pulled each other along, stumbling half blind through the forest of fire. Embers danced ahead of them like merry sprites on a summer's eve, alighting on roofs, igniting anything flammable. A few of them landed on Cynda's skin, causing her to slap at them like they were fiery bees. The air thinned, making each breath tenuous. When the roar increased behind them, they turned as one to watch the firestorm surge upward, seeking heaven.

As thick smoke obscured them, Cynda shouted, "Forward hop!" Wiping away the tears so she could see the dial, she set her interface as he copied her settings. Kneeling, they vanished into the future, not caring who saw them.

Friday, 16 November 1888

Hell had followed them.

One week later London was still burning. In shock, they merged into the multitude of the dazed and injured. Hungry children howled in their mothers' arms while gloomy men herded their families west.

How far did this reach into the East End? What was happening to Alastair, to Davy and his mom? Where they still alive?

"Come on," she urged. "We have to find out exactly what's happened."

Numbly, Morrisey followed in her wake. She shot him a worried look. *I never should have brought you with me.*

Eventually, they found themselves near Trafalgar Square. A line of wagons stood in front of the National Gallery as men scurried out with hastily snatched artwork, trying to save them from the conflagration.

Across the street, St. Martin-in-the-Fields was ablaze, flames shooting out its roof. The ancient church had survived the Great Fire of 1666, even when the mighty St. Paul's Cathedral had succumbed. St. Martin's luck, and that of the rest of the city, had finally run out.

They stopped to catch their breath at the base of Nelson's Column. A crowd had gathered there, their eyes on the fire line as it marched toward them like a vast red army. To the east was a solid sheet of flame, five stories high. It roared in a way that defied description, as it greedily fed on whatever crossed its path, be it stone, wood or human.

"Look!" Morrisey exclaimed, pointing.

The south bank of the Thames was aglow, fire advancing along the docks toward Southwark.

"Both sides? That's not possible!" *Unless Flaherty double-crossed us.*

"They're coming!" someone shouted.

With a clatter of hooves, a line of mounted men advanced from the west. Cavalry. Orders were shouted for the crowd to disperse. When no one complied, the soldiers drew their swords and pistols. Frightened screams erupted, followed by the bellows of outrage.

"The 'ell with you lot. We're not leavin'," one man called, brandishing a club.

"You started this! We'll finish it, you bastards!" another shouted.

Cynda grabbed Morrisey's arm, dragging him away from their exposed position. She knew what a mob felt like right before it took on a will of its own. This one was teetering on the edge.

"What are you doing?" he demanded.

"Saving our butts," she said.

When the volley of gunfire erupted a heartbeat later, they threw themselves to the ground. Morrisey wrapped his arms around her, pulling her tight against him. A crisp order echoed in the air, followed by another volley.

Cynda pulled herself away from her companion and stole a look back toward the square. A pile of writhing bodies lay at Lord Nelson's feet. The wave of survivors surged back against itself, trampling the weaker ones in an effort to escape. There was a tangle of legs and arms, squeals of agony.

Cynda pulled Morrisey to his feet. "Run!"

Ducking between charging horses, they finally fled the open ground and down a side street.

"Let's get out of here," she ordered.

He acted as he hadn't heard her. "This can't be happening," he said, and then began to cough from the smoke.

"Interface!" she shouted. He pulled it in slow motion, his eyes never leaving the melee in the square. She snatched the watch, set it, then jammed it into his hand. He vanished.

A blaze of sparks flew down on her, stinging her face and arms, burning into her dress. Hands quaking, she set her own interface. The last thing she heard was the shrill keening of a woman mourning her dead husband.

Thursday, 8 November 1888
Arundel Hotel

Someone was stamping on her skirts, calling out her name. Cynda curled up tighter, the sorrow so strong she thought it might crush her.

"Jacynda?" a voice called near an ear, followed by a deep, racking cough.

"Theo?"

She found herself on the floor of the hotel room, in his arms, his smoky face inches from hers. His scalp wound had opened up again, bright blood trickling against blackened skin. He looked as destroyed as she felt.

They embraced, hard. When they broke apart, he studied her anxiously.

"Are you injured?" he rasped.

Cynda responded by trying to cough out a lung. She felt something cold against her neck. *Dinky Doc.* Her breathing eased.

"You, too," she advised.

He reset the device and then treated himself. A few breaths later his wheezing diminished.

"We have to stop this," she said, trying to rise.

Theo caught her arm, helping her up. "I'll let Klein know what's happening," he said. "You get some rest. We'll figure out what to do." When she opened her mouth to argue, he put a single soot-covered finger on her lips. "Please, just do what I ask."

She didn't protest as he led her to the bedroom. When he offered her a wet cloth, she cautiously washed her face, wincing at the petite burns. He was doing the same in the basin, stripped down to his trousers, braces hanging free. As he cleaned himself, she kept removing smoky clothes until she reached a final petticoat and her onsie. Then she leaned back in the chair, eyes still stinging. They kept opening and closing of their own free will.

There was at least four or five miles between Whitechapel and Trafalgar Square. In one week, it'd turned to ruin. Her mind began to shut down, overwhelmed at the enormity of what they faced. "I have to stay awake," she murmured.

"You won't be able to. I gave you something to help you sleep. Just don't fight it."

"You what?" she asked groggily.

"Nevermind." With Theo's urging, she crawled into the bed. He jammed her interface under the pillow.

"Theo…"

"We'll stop this, I promise."

She felt a lingering kiss on her forehead.

"Don't go anywhere without me," she murmured. "It's too dangerous."

Then there was oblivion.

—

"I refuse to accept this. Until those explosives are found, you are still with Scotland Yard, do you understand?" Chief Inspector Fisher insisted, his back to Keats. They were alone in his office and though the initial reunion had been poignant, his superior's attitude had changed the moment the sergeant had handed in his resignation.

"The men don't want me here," Keats replied, expecting this argument. That was plain enough. Only a few had come up to him and shook his hand, signaling their pleasure at his acquittal. The rest had pointedly kept their distance, as if his misfortune might somehow be communicable.

"Their attitudes will change," Fisher replied. "Give it time."

Keats shook his head. "Theirs might. Mine will not, at least in the short term. It's all wrong now. In truth, I have little faith in what we do anymore."

His superior turned toward him. "I must admit I feel the same, but we have a duty to perform. Until those explosives are secured, this city is at risk."

"Sir, I—"

"I need your expertise, Keats. Do this for me, if not for the Yard."

Keats looked away, thinking it through. There was more here than just the explosives. Fisher would be vindicated if they brought this case to a successful conclusion. He acquiesced. "As you wish, sir."

The chief inspector openly sighed in relief. "You believe Flaherty's claim he has no knowledge of where the explosives are hidden?"

"Yes, I do."

"Blast," Fisher muttered. "Who do you think has them now?"

That was the question Keats and Alastair had argued most of the previous night. All indications pointed toward the Transitives. Now he had no choice but to stoke Fisher's suspicions regarding his kind.

"Sir, I think it's best we discuss that *outside* of this building."

Fisher eyed him. "I see." He stuck Keats' resignation letter into a drawer, then collected his hat and coat. "Let's take a stroll along the Thames."

—

Friday, 9 November 1888
St. Paul's Cathedral

Theo's second visit to Lord Mayor's Day was less fiery than his first. He arrived at half past nine in the morning, dressed in his best clothes and promptly bribed himself into the choicest vantage point in London: the dome of St. Paul's Cathedral. He'd hoped to be alone, but that wasn't the case. There were a few others up there, including a family. The eldest daughter kept shooting him coy glances when she thought he wasn't looking.

He turned his attention to the view. It was breathtaking, though wet. Still, the rain didn't seem to dampen the festive mood on the streets. People were milling about, setting up in their favored locations to watch the Lord Mayor's Show. He remembered seeing it as a child, fascinated by the golden coach that carried the Lord Mayor to the Royal Courts, and the wicker figures of the two giants, Gog and Magog, the guardians of the City of London.

In any other circumstance, he would have felt on top of the world. He was experiencing life as it really was in the late nineteenth century. Now he understood why Harter lived for this sort of adventure. It had been so many years since he'd felt this alive. What was technology compared to this?

Theo peered down at the street. He knew what was about to happen, but if he tried warning people, who would believe him? He could go to the government, but that risked exposing the Transitives or getting him locked up as a loony.

"Damned if you do, damned if you don't," he muttered.

Now I sound like Jacynda.

Hours passed until the need to find a gent's toilet became increasingly important. Just as he was about to head down the stairs, the first explosion lit up the sky. It was to the northeast of the church, near Bethnal Green.

Below him, people on the street grew uneasy, talking amongst themselves. He made note of the time on his interface: half past eleven, just about when the Lord Mayor reached the Royal Courts of Justice. Precisely five minutes later, another detonation.

The family hurried down the stairs, along with the other onlookers. At street level, people began to disperse, moving toward their homes. Theo took a deep breath and waited. Two blasts were not enough to create the destruction he'd witnessed.

With clockwork precision, ten more explosives followed at exactly five minutes apart, spreading in a line from north to south, the final one near Limehouse.

Theo frowned. That didn't explain the Rotherhithe fires. Gritting his teeth, he waited. Ten minutes after the last blast in the East End, they began again on the south side of the river. There were seven of them and they were exactly twenty minutes apart.

After making the requisite trip to empty his bladder, it'd taken two transfers to zero in on the location of the first explosion. The trips took their toll, rewarding him with a buzzing head and a churning stomach. Still, he was where he needed to be. Jacynda could not handle this sort of travel now. Though her Endorphin Rebound was in remission, it could easily return. They couldn't chance that.

He was the best choice for this—the freshest of the Rovers.

A Rover? Not really. He didn't have what it took to do this day to day. What he did possess was an analytical mind, and that might tip the balance.

Once he'd found the location of the first explosion, he cautiously moved into a dismal rear yard behind an equally dismal tenement. Mud puddles dotted the ground. The yard was a jumble of abandoned items, all of it useless. Victorians wasted little. From recycled dog muck to ashes from the fireplace, they found a use for everything. If anything was left out where it could be stolen, it was truly junk.

Something caught his notice—a half-sized barrel jammed up against the gas pipe, partially covered with a ratty tarp. It would have been easy to miss it in the scattered debris. Theo knelt and gently pulled back the covering. Something was scrawled in red paint on the side of the barrel.

"R12:7." He frowned. Twelve explosions in the East End, seven in the Docklands. What did the "R" stand for?

Three sticks of dynamite were attached to the back of the cask, one with a detonation cord. There didn't appear to be any other mechanism to trigger the explosion, which meant the bomber would have to go from barrel to barrel to start the process.

"Too crude," he said, frowning. Yet the detonations had been precisely five minutes apart. How did they accomplish that?

Now what? If he moved the device, someone would know he'd been here.

Theo returned the tarp to its original position and stepped back. A moment later he was on the move, in search of the next site.

—

Thursday, 8 November 1888
Arundel Hotel

Six p.m. on the dot. Cynda snapped her interface shut with more force than necessary, swearing under her breath. She'd been put to sleep about eleven in the morning and now it was seven hours later. No Theo.

"You're a dead man, I swear it," she groused.

"You can't murder your boss," Mr. Spider advised, scooping up a scone morsel from a plate on the writing desk.

"Why not? He drugged me."

"He knew you needed rest."

"Okay, so I'm rested. Where is he?"

"Playing Rover. Why don't you just admit it? You're worried."

"Hell yes, I'm worried. Do you have any idea of what will happen if he gets hurt while I'm supposed to be watching him?"

The arachnid gave her a stern look. "It's more than the paperwork and you know it."

She opened her mouth to toast the little nuisance, and then groaned. "Yeah, I know. I've grown rather fond of him." More fond than was probably sensible. "He might be smart, but he's not a Rover. He doesn't have our instincts. Those only come with experience."

"Neither did you in the beginning." The creature scoured the plate in search of crumbs. "Are there any more scones?"

"No. You've had enough."

The spider's response was uncivil.

Until now, she'd held off contacting Ralph to see if the boss was in 2058. If Theo wasn't there, that'd just raise alarms and possibly put TPB on his tail.

Ten more minutes then I rat him out.

Three minutes later Cynda stood in front of the kneeling figure, tapping her foot, hands on her hips. The moment her boss looked up, she planned to nail him. Then he looked up. He was pasty gray, his eyes unfocused. His fingers clutched the interface, turning white at the knuckles. Classic time lag.

She dropped to her knees. "Theo?"

He gaped at her in wonder. Carefully prying the interface out of his hand, she wound it to recover its past history.

"Eight trips? You idiot!"

"Had to," he said, weaving like a cobra captivated by its handler. "Know what happens." A pause, and then he stared at her as if she'd just appeared in front of him. "Hellooo?"

Not good.

"Come on, boss, let's get you to bed."

"I'm Theo," he corrected, trying to frown, but failing.

"Okay, Theo. Time for you to get some rest." *So you'll have some brains left when this is all over.*

He squinted at her. "You're pretty. Have I ever told you that?"

Oh geez. Time lag came in a couple versions. Lag usually made Jacynda bitchy. Rumor said Defoe was the same way. Other Rovers acted drunk, like they'd had one too many casks of rum. Evidently, her boss was one of those.

"Great," she muttered, hauling him to his feet.

"The room is spinning," he announced. "Counterclockwise."

You sure I can't kill him?

"It's looking better every minute," the spider replied.

"The bed's yours," she announced, hauling Theo in that direction.

"Alone?" he said, quirking an eyebrow.

That's payback. She'd once said the same thing to him during one of her bouts of severe lag.

"Yes, on your own."

"Pity, you'd be fun," he said, nearly mirroring what she'd said to him.

Maybe he's not as lagged as I think.

She sat him in bed, pulled off his shoes and coat. All the while, he gazed at her, enraptured. He needed an endorphin rise to counter the lag and the quickest way to achieve that was chocolate. She handed him a piece from the stash in her Gladstone.

Theo acted like he had no idea what to do with it.

"Ralph always opened them for you," her delusion suggested.

Thanks. She peeled open the Victorian-style wrapper. "Here you are."

"Don't like it," he said, pushing it away.

"Eat it anyway." He shook his head. She counted to ten. "Eat. The. Chocolate." *Or I will stuff it up your nose.*

"Does it work that way?" Mr. Spider asked, dubiously.

We'll find out.

Four pieces of chocolate later, Theo's eyes appeared less glazed—a sign his brain was coming back online. That eased some of Cynda's anxiety. If he could recover this fast, he'd probably not done any permanent damage.

"Read notes. On interface," he muttered. "Fulham sending maps."

"Was it the Fenians?"

A light snore was his reply.

CHAPTER THIRTEEN

"Okay, I won't kill him," Cynda announced. Luckily Theo was asleep so he couldn't hear her. "Actually, I've very proud of him."

As he'd painstakingly hopped all over Lord Mayor's Day, then at set intervals into the future to judge the fire's progress, Theo had dictated comments into his interface.

"I didn't know you could do that. I really should read the holo-manual some day."

The interface beeped. Text appeared in the air above it, an incoming message. It wasn't from TEM Enterprises.

Cyn?

Hi Ralph. Why you at Guv?

Until the boss returns, company's locked down.

"Locked down?" *What about his sister?* she typed.

TPB's not touched her. We just can't do business as usual. Fulham and I are at Guv now. How's the boss?

Sleeping. Tried to fry his brain with all the transfers.

He learnt from the best. Sending you maps and newspapers.

Thanks.

There was a long pause. *Be careful. This looks way bad.* Another pause. *Love ya, Cyn.*

She whistled under her breath. He'd never said that in all the years they'd known each other. It felt final.

Love you too, guy. Keep the lamp lit, will you?

You got it. Log off.

Logged off.

THE MAPS APPEARED shortly thereafter, a stark blueprint of London's devastation. The explosives ignited fires along the south side of the river in Rotherhithe, and in the East End. Driven by a strong wind, the flames moved resolutely westward. By the end of the first day, they'd reached the Aldgate Pump near Leadenhall Street. By the third, they were consuming St. Paul's, and by the seventh they were turning Britain's beloved national art treasures to so much powdery ash. The firestorm finally died out almost ten days later, coming perilously close to the Houses of Parliament and

Westminster Abbey. By Fulham's estimates, nearly seventy-five percent of the city would be destroyed.

Three-quarters of London gone. It was unfathomable, even though she could trace the fire's path on the map, street by street. Cynda heaved a sigh of relief when she realized that Alastair's house was still there, miraculously untouched. Annabelle's Boarding House was gone; so was St. Botolph's Church, Spitalfields Market and most of the pubs she'd frequented.

"Pratchett's is gone," her delusion observed, poised on the side of the map. "This hotel, too."

"Scotland Yard and most of Whitehall," Cynda added. "At least it didn't reach the Wescombs' house."

A familiar sound made her turn. Three newspapers sat in a pile on the floor, the whirling colors of the transfer fading as she watched. She scooped them up. The newspapers were from Scotland and Ireland. Not a surprise: the presses in London wouldn't be functional for quite awhile.

The first one was dated November 16, a week after the fire began, and it detailed the locations of each ignition point in the East End.

Words leapt out at her:

Horrific loss of life

Riots widespread–Army called out

Jews, foreigners and Irish face street justice

Mobs roam West End on pillaging rampage–hundreds dead

By the time she reached the final newspaper, published on the last day of the year, she could hardly breathe. The articles spoke of armed mobs, mostly in the posh West End. They'd stormed houses, robbing, raping and murdering with little police interference. Mayfair, Kensington and Marylebone were the hardest hit.

"The Wescombs live in Marylebone," her delusions said.

"I know."

By the time London finally regained control of its streets, nearly ten thousand souls had died by fire, disease or anarchy.

The heart of the British Empire was about to sustain a massive coronary.

We have to find a way to stop this.

—

"This is unbelievable," Keats exclaimed, bending over the map he'd spread out on the writing table in Cynda's hotel room. Alastair peered over his shoulder. "I realize you know things we don't, but this is so outlandish, Jacynda. This must be a mistake."

She glowered, not in the mood for this battle.

"Remember, this is their home," Mr. Spider whispered from her shoulder. "Imagine what you'd say if someone told you everything you care for was about to be destroyed."

Her delusion was right. She softened her tone. "I saw it for myself. London will burn if we don't stop this."

Keats was unconvinced. "Are you sure you're well? You were hallucinating for a time and—"

Alastair gently touched his sleeve. "If you look closely, you'll see small burns on her cheeks and hands. This is real, Keats."

The sergeant loosened his collar. "How far does the fire extend?"

After directing a nod of gratitude to Alastair, she pulled out the second map, laying it over the first.

"It burns for *ten days?*" Incredulously, Keats traced his finger west until it halted near the Westminster Bridge. "That far."

Alastair raised his eyes from the documents. "How bad does it get?"

She placed the newspapers in front of them and then retreated to the window as they sifted through the articles. Below her, people bustled along the street. Some carried baskets, no doubt with food purchased for the holiday. *Food that might never be eaten.*

She heard Alastair murmur, "My God. So many dead."

"I see Newgate Prison survives," Keats observed sardonically. "How fitting." Pages rustled as he began to count the circles on the map. "Nineteen explosions?"

Theo's groggy voice came from the bedroom doorway, "They use a half-barrel of gunpowder, three sticks of dynamite." He was haphazardly tucking in his shirt, oblivious to the startled expressions from their visitors.

"Go back to bed," Cynda ordered. "You need your rest."

"Just make the introductions," he retorted, running a hand through his hair in an effort to tidy himself.

She opened her mouth to argue, but decided against it. "This is Dr. Alastair Montrose," she announced, "and Detective-Sergeant Jonathon Keats." She angled a thumb in Theo's direction. "Gentlemen, this is T.E. Morrisey, my boss, and the man who made time travel possible."

"I am honored, sir," Alastair said, stepping forward. "I must admit to being in awe of your accomplishments."

"Thank you."

"Mr. Morrisey," Keats replied tersely, keen to get past the pleasantries. "What else can you tell us about these devices?"

"I did not find a triggering mechanism, so they must light them by hand," Theo replied. "Nevertheless, all of the explosions are at precisely-timed intervals."

"How do they accomplish that?" Keats asked.

"I am not sure."

And that's driving you nuts.

"The newspapers say that the dockland bombs were all in warehouses owned by Hugo Effington," Cynda reported. "That should narrow it down a bit."

"Still, we'll have to go through them all one by one," Keats muttered. "It will take considerable time." He scrutinized Theo. "Who do you believe is behind this plot, sir?"

"The Ascendant," Morrisey said. "It's why he had Adelaide Winston murdered, to buy himself time. As Intermediary, she was pushing for his replacement."

"How in heaven's name do you know—" Keats began.

"I'm one of you."

The two Victorians traded looks.

"Hezekiah Grant is your leader at present. Do either of you know him?" The two men shook their heads. "I'm not surprised. He seems to have led a nondescript life," Theo said.

Cynda scowled. "Not very nondescript when he orders people killed right and left."

"That wasn't in his original timeline," Theo explained. "Something has happened to him."

"Or someone," she mused. "I keep wondering where Copeland is in all this. It's not like the old military jock to be out of the picture for very long."

"Who?" Alastair asked.

"Someone from our time," Theo answered. His tone said he wasn't willing to say more.

"He's not one of the good guys," Cynda explained.

Keats shifted the top map aside, staring hard at the one indicating the primary detonation sites. "Destruction of this magnitude will disrupt Parliament, even the Royals. In catastrophe, there is always an opportunity for assassination." He looked up. "We have to inform the chief inspector. He must take precautions to secure the city and protect the Royal Family."

"He's not going to believe Jacynda is from the future," Alastair protested.

"Just tell him I have inside information," Cynda advised. "He might think Pinkerton's has better sources than the Yard."

"Then let's hope he's in a receptive frame of mind. He was very dismayed this morning when I suggested *we* might be involved. Now I have to tell him just how bad it can get."

"Take the first map, not the second," Theo said. "Hint at the level of destruction. That's all he can know."

Keats nodded, rolling up the appropriate document and tucking it under his arm.

"We'll handle the bombs in the East End," Morrisey insisted. "You just concentrate on those in Rotherhithe.

Keats shook his head. "Fisher will *not* approve of your involvement."

"He does not have a choice."

The sergeant's eyebrow rose. "You are the visitor here, sir. Just because you're Jacynda's superior does not mean I trust you."

Before this degenerated any further, Cynda jumped in, "He's one of the reasons you're alive, Keats. If he hadn't helped me rebuild my brain, you'd be six feet under right now."

Keats tugged on his collar without realizing it. "You vouch for him, then?"

"Without reservation."

"I see." He thought for a moment, then dug in his trouser pocket, sorting through a handful of coins. He selected one in particular.

"Flaherty divided up the explosives between different warehouses in Wapping and Rotherhithe," Keats explained. "After he was done, someone else moved them, without his knowledge." The sergeant held a coin. "I found this in one of those empty warehouses, under some gunpowder. Perhaps you can tell me what this is."

The coin spiraled into the air, and Cynda caught it. "Looks like sixpence."

Theo took it from her. "No. In this time period, England's sixpence coins are silver. This is..."

"What?" Keats asked eagerly.

"Not silver," Theo replied. He shifted the coin around with a finger. "I'll run some tests. It may just be a crude forgery attempt."

Alastair cut in. "I understand some of what you do, sir, but why involve yourself so deeply in our time? Why take the risk?"

"Because we *all* have something to lose," Theo replied. "If history changes, it ripples forward. The world we know will be altered forever."

Cynda watched the two Victorians come to grips with that.

"At least you've given us a chance," Alastair said.

"Only one," Theo replied. He gestured toward the second map. "If we fail, that's our legacy."

Behind them, a clock struck eight in Fisher's private study. The chief inspector drummed his fingers on the desktop. In Keats' experience, that was an indication of considerable mental turmoil. He gave Alastair a worried look.

Fisher leaned toward them. "How could Miss Lassiter possess this amount of detail unless she is involved in the plot?"

"She is not an anarchist, sir," Keats insisted. "She just has contacts that are very free with their knowledge."

Fisher's brows furrowed. The finger drumming continued, increasing in tempo. "You wish me to go to the police commissioner and inform him that we have uncovered a conspiracy to incinerate most of London, and that all the evidence we have is based solely upon a woman who has recently had a mental collapse?"

"Yes," Alastair replied without hesitation.

Fisher's frown deepened. "Yet you say Flaherty has no part in this, which leaves *your* people as the prime suspects."

"Yes, sir," Keats admitted.

The chief inspector tapped the map that lay in front of him. "Why so many explosions?"

"With a firestorm at their backs, the displaced will have few places to head but west, toward their richer neighbors. Anarchy will be the result."

Fisher began to tap his tented fingers together. A decision was imminent.

"I am of two minds on this, but I dare not risk the city. I shall present this to Sir Charles. I question whether he will believe me, especially if he finds *you're* involved, Sergeant."

Which is why I have no future at the Yard.

"While you are doing that, sir, I would like to go to Rotherhithe, see what I can learn there. Jacynda's source was very vague about the placement of the explosives in that area. I will need help to find them."

"How many constables will you require?"

"To tell you the truth, I believe Fenians would be better."

"Fenians?" Fisher exclaimed.

"I know it sounds outrageous, but they have as much to lose as anyone. They will be blamed for this, even if the plot proves to be of a different nature."

"It would be better if you use constables," Fisher advised.

"On the contrary," Keats countered, "the dockworkers will be able to move through the warehouses more quickly, as well as spot anything that looks out of place."

"Well then, I shall trust your judgement, but keep some constables at the ready in case of trouble, do you understand?"

"Yes, sir."

"I will make arrangements to handle the bombs in the East End. If Miss Lassiter and her companions wish to assist, then fine, but *we* are in charge of this operation."

"Yes, sir," Keats confirmed with a nod.

Fisher turned to the doctor. "I'd like you to come with me. Your sincerity may tilt the police commissioner into believing this incredible tale. After all, you know Miss Lassiter's reputation better than I."

Alastair barely hid his surprise. "As you wish, Chief Inspector."

"Speaking of which, where is she?" Fisher asked. "Why did she not come with you?"

"Marshalling aid of her own, I believe," Alastair replied.

The chief inspector snorted. "At least it won't be just us in the soup if this goes wrong."

—

Retrieving his belongings from Mrs. O'Neill's boarding house had fallen out like Keats had anticipated. The Rotherhithe landlady swore at him for being a rozzer, then handed over his personal effects. He'd left her the extra tobacco in gratitude for not making the ordeal any harder than it was.

As he walked away, Keats stuck his spare pipe and the list of warehouses in a pocket and discarded the rest. He had no need for the theatrical makeup Jacynda had given him. No need to run from the law any longer.

Nevertheless, there were times when he could still feel the chains on his wrists, hear them dragging across the ground as he moved. Still feel the cap being pulled down over his face. Someone had willing tossed him to the executioner. Someone who had much to hide. When this was over, he would begin his own hunt.

He wandered around Rotherhithe until he found an unoccupied set of stairs leading to the Thames. There, he sat and studied Jacynda's list. Effington had owned a number of warehouses. Fifteen, to be exact.

He heard the sound of boots behind him. "Good evening, Clancy."

The Irishman hesitated. "How'd ya know it was me?"

"You've been following me ever since the boarding house."

Clancy laughed. "Yer smarter than ya look."

"Some days."

The large man descended the stairs and sat next to him. "Good to see yer alive. Close one, that."

"Very." Keats tugged on his collar again to loosen it. He could no longer stand anything tight around his neck.

"Ya owe me that reward," Clancy said.

"You didn't turn me in," Keats replied, sensing no anger in the other man's words.

"I kept ya alive while ya were free."

"I need you to keep me that way a little longer. If you do, I'll be happy to pay that debt." Keats gestured toward the paper. "This is a list of Effington's warehouses in Rotherhithe. I suspect we will find the explosives in some of them,

"Why ya think that?"

"I just do. I need your help, Clancy. Someone is planning a very unpleasant surprise for our fellow citizens come tomorrow." He tucked away the paper and told Clancy what they'd learned, without mentioning Jacynda's involvement or that of the shifters.

His companion whistled softly. "Sweet Jesus, it'll be a massacre. We Irish'll be blamed."

"Very likely. I need your help, and that of some of the dockworkers. We have to go through all those warehouses, find the bombs, and then I'll disarm them."

"Why can't the rozzers do that?" Clancy asked, looking skeptical.

"If I bring a swarm of Blue Bottles in here, the plotters may move the bombs somewhere else. We need to have them think everything is going as planned."

Clancy shook his head. "Not sure if the others will want to be part of this."

"If all this burns, they'll be no work for months. Nothing like the threat of starvation to motivate a man."

The Irishman nodded grimly. "Ya have a point. Come on, I'll take ya to 'em."

CHAPTER FOURTEEN

Friday, 9 November 1888
Arundel Hotel

Cynda stared into the darkness for a couple of hours, unable to settle down. Too much was parading through her mind. A quick check of her watch showed it was nearly four in the morning. Over in Dorset Street, Jack the Ripper was making short work of Mary Kelly.

Shivering at the thought, Cynda rolled out of bed. She wedged herself in the bedroom door, bone tired. Theo looked up from his maps, dark half-moons under his eyes.

"Can't sleep?" he asked in a voice that grated like sandpaper. She shook her head. "Neither can I."

She drifted to the couch and flopped down. "What's worrying you?"

Theo made a frustrated jab at the maps. "The precision of the explosions. That's not feasible using Victorian technology."

Which left only one option. "Someone from our time is helping them," she ventured. Theo nodded wearily. "Copeland?"

"He's my odds-on favorite right now." He joined her on the couch. "I forwarded the coin to Fulham. I'm hoping to have a report soon."

"Then you're doing all you can."

"I'm not convinced of that." He leaned back and closed his eyes. "I've been naïve."

"How so?"

"I thought that once we sorted Keats' timeline, everything would be fine. I thought—" Theo halted abruptly.

"Go on," she prompted.

He looked over at her. "I thought how wonderful it would be here with you. I imagined us going to the theater together, maybe to the zoo. We would hire one of those colorful boats and float up and down the Regent's Canal."

Theo was a daydreamer? She never would have imagined that.

"We would sip wine as we floated along," he suggested. He wore a lazy expression, like they were already on the water. "I see white swans gliding by us in the brilliant sunshine, the trees in full leaf, and…" His enthusiasm dimmed. "That's not going to happen, is it?"

His unusual pessimism was jarring. "Not right now," Cynda responded gently. "But someday."

He leaned in closer to her. "Someday." He gently ran a finger along her cheek. She held her breath, anticipating what might follow.

Just then his interface lit up, vibrating across the top of the desk.

"Fulham has the worst sense of timing," he grumbled. He returned to his work, but not before giving her a fond smile.

Cynda returned to bed and was finally trudging down that muzzy tunnel of sleep when she heard Theo saying something to her. Something about the coin and going to 2058. When she forced open her eyes open, he was already gone.

—

In the presence of mine enemies. They were all around Keats, some thirty dockworkers, trying to keep out of the rain. Keats thought he recognized some of their faces from his time at the call-on shelter, back when he'd still been on the run. They'd all rubbed elbows together, trying to find a job when there were too few to go around. From what he could tell the majority of them were Irish, with a few Germans and Russians thrown in for good measure.

Rousting most of them out of their beds, Clancy had gathered the ones he trusted most. That still hadn't made it easy. The argument had flowed back and forth between them ever since they'd gathered. Most of them would be happy to cut Keats' throat and call it a day. It was only the big Irishman's presence that held them in check.

Keats' patience vanished. "Look lads, it's this way—we find for those explosives, or the docklands are going to burn. You know what's in these warehouses. Tinder. One good flame, and it's all a blast furnace."

"Why should we help ya?" one of them called out. "Yer a bleedin' rozzer!"

"Because you're going to be the ones to suffer. There will be no work for *months.*" He let them cipher out the consequences on their own.

One of the men spat at his feet. "Don't want nothin' to do with this. Flaherty—"

"Didn't set the bombs," Keats retorted. "He knows better than to hurt his own."

That registered. There was more mumbling.

Clancy chimed in, "Gents, this rozzer's on the level. We all know there's others out there that'll do us harm. It's plain and simple. We need yer help."

More murmuring. "Ya pay us for our time?"

"Yes," Keats replied. "More than going wages." He'd sort that out with Fisher later.

"How da we get inside?" someone else called out. "They're all locked. Ya could nick us for breakin' in."

"If we can't find a someone with a key, I'll bust them open," Keats assured them. "I'm a copper. I can do that sort of thing." He sent a silent thank you to the chief inspector for insisting that he stay with the Yard.

An old man came forward. He had only one eye, the other hidden behind a dingy patch. "Yer not lyin', are ya?"

Keats shook his head. "I wish to God I was."

The old man crossed himself. "I were afraid of that, lad."

As rain poured off his bowler, Keats waved the wary watchman forward and presented his card.

"I'm Detective-Sergeant Keats with Scotland Yard, *Special Branch*. I need you to open all of Hugo Effington's warehouses. You do have the keys, don't you?"

"You were in prison."

"I was. Now I'm here. Do you have the keys?"

"I do, but I can't—"

"My responsibility. There are explosives in those buildings. You wouldn't want all of the docklands to become a fireball, would you?" Keats added, just to up the ante.

"Explosives?" The watchman's eyes skimmed over the group standing behind Keats. "What about this lot?"

"They're here to do their civic duty. Are you prepared to do yours?"

The man caved. "As you like, sir. I don't need no trouble."

With the swift application of a set of keys, the doors to the first warehouse opened.

"All right gents, listen up. We are looking for half-barrels with dynamite attached to the side of them. Call out if you find one. Just to be clear, if you think this a chance to nick a few goods for yourself, I'd not recommend it."

"There's only one of ya. Toss us in jail, will ya?" someone chided.

"No, I'll not waste my time. I'll strap you to one of those barrels and light the dynamite myself."

"Ya can't do that!" the man protested.

"And I'll help him," another voice called out as its owner bulldozed his way through the crowd.

Keats looked up at Inspector Ramsey's broad face. "Good morning, sir."

"Detective-Sergeant. Carry on."

"Ten of you come with me," Keats called out. "The others go with Clancy and the watchman. Start working through the other warehouses." No one moved. "Hop to it lads, so you'll all have a job come evening."

—

"Ah, excellent," Fulham announced after Theo staggered out of the time pod. Then he took a good look at his boss. "Sir? Are you all right?"

"Not really," Theo replied, leaning heavily against the chronsole, his mind drenched in thick fog. His respect for the Rovers rose even further.

Ralph Hamilton quirked an eyebrow as he shoved a candy bar across the counter. Theo shook his head.

"They're your brains," the chron-op replied.

"I doubt I have that many left, anyway." He gave his assistant a sidelong look. "What keeps TPB from knowing I'm here?"

"As far they're concerned, you're Mr. Hopkins. At least, that's what your interface is telling them."

"Well done."

Theo took a couple of steps, managed to find his balance, and then followed his assistant out of the chronsole room.

"Any sign of Harter?" Fulham shook head. "How about Alegria? How's she holding up?"

"Your sister is doing just fine. Anytime TPB pulls another legal stunt, she just bats it back in their court."

"Never play poker with her, Fulham. She'll clean you out every time."

"Thank you for the warning, sir. Might I suggest you visit Guv's physician? You look awful."

Theo rubbed his temples, trying to ease the constant headache. "It's just lag. It'll resolve."

His assistant fixed him with a frown. "Oddly enough, I have heard that same comment from Miss Lassiter. You do remember what happened to her?"

Yes, I do.

Three serious Guv agents, all in their wormhole-black suits took over escort duties. He was herded to a small meeting room. Sitting in one of the ergo chairs, hands folded over her ample chest, was M. A. Fletcher, formerly a member of the Time Protocol Board. Her fiery red hair was highlighted by the glow of the recessed lights.

An acknowledged genius at miniaturization, it was joked that if you gave Fletcher a two hundred-story skyscraper, in an hour you'd have something that would fit in your pocket. In reality, her talents lay in nano technology, but it made a good story nonetheless.

Fletcher greeted him with a nod, which he returned. "Been a while, Morrisey. You look like death warmed over."

"Been traveling." Gingerly, he settled into a chair. For some reason all his bones ached.

"So Klein said. What's it like?"

"Tiring, exhilarating. Frightening."

Fletcher gave a knowing nod. "Frankly, I'm surprised they got you out from behind your computer."

"Blame it on the Restricted Force Warrant. I stay here, I'm in jail, so I figured it was time to experience the monster I created."

A wry chuckle. "Well, I'm sure as hell not going to get myself shrunk to a nanobit just out curiosity, that's for sure."

Klein arrived at that moment. "Fletcher. Morrisey." The agent tapped his foot twice on the floor plate, and a table slowly rose into position between them. He took a seat. "How's Lassiter?"

Theo shot Klein a questioning look.

"You can speak freely," the agent assured him. "Fletcher's in the loop."

"Miss Lassiter is holding it together," Theo replied. "I've not seen any signs that she's out of control. If anything, she's more subdued than usual."

"Did she really bust TPB's shrink in the jaw?" Fletcher asked.

Theo nodded. "Quite a scene," he commented with a smirk.

"Wish I'd been there."

The senior agent cocked his head. "I forwarded that coin to Fletcher. Figured she might be able to help us."

"Cue miniaturization expert." She tossed the disk on the table. "As you guessed, it's not of 1888 origin. This critter contains a miniature amplifier. It receives a signal, pumps it up and passes it on."

"What sort of signal?" Theo asked.

"We're not sure. It's not electromagnetic or a vid-rad frequency. Common waveforms do nothing to excite it; neither do temperature changes, humidity or atmospheric pressure." Fletcher leaned forward. "Why is this thing so important?"

Theo frowned. "How open are we being here?"

"Her security clearance is equal to yours," Klein replied.

Theo tapped on the table and a small keyboard projected itself onto the top. Another tap, and a port appeared into which he synced up his interface. A holographic display shimmered into being in the air above the keyboard, the electronic version of the maps he'd created while in the East End.

"9 November 1888. Lord Mayor's Day. 19 explosions ranging from Bethnal Green to Rotherhithe across the Thames." He pressed a key. "On 12 November…"

By the time Theo finished his holographic destruction of London, Klein's eyes were closed in thought. A vein throbbed near his temple.

"Damn, that's ugly," Fletcher said. "Will it ripple forward?"

"Very likely." Theo gestured at the disk. "One of the Victorians found this near where they were storing the explosives. I began to wonder if it had something to do with the accuracy of the detonations."

She grinned. "I think it does. What if a time pulse initiates a chain reaction, moving forward coin by coin?"

"How does that trigger the explosion?" Klein asked.

"If the coin heats up during the process, they just need to have in contact with the gunpowder," Theo explained.

Fletcher picked up the coin, studying it under the lights. "Which means your Victorians had a technological power assist."

"TPB?" Klein pounced.

"Not their style," Fletcher replied.

"Don't be so sure. They kicked you off the Board right before this whole thing fell out," Klein countered. "Seems like a move to keep you out of whatever they're up to."

"Davies isn't that smart," Fletcher maintained. "Trust me on this."

Klein leaned back. "Who, then? Do you know anyone doing this sort of work?"

"We haven't gone this far yet," Fletcher replied, shaking her head. "Just basic products like the chrono-tint wall color that changes every couple of hours. Making a damned fortune off that stuff." She picked up the coin. "I estimate this is at least ten years down the line. Actually, less now."

She grinned, deftly rolling the disk over the knuckles of her right hand and then back again. "We'll reverse engineer it. I love it when someone else does the R&D."

Theo's headache edged up another notch.

"Oh, come on, gentlemen," Fletcher chided. "We all know this came from the future. Just admit it."

"That's the last damned thing I want to admit," Klein said.

Fletcher spread her hands. "No other conclusion." She looked over at Theo for support.

"Agreed," he said reluctantly. "At present, we use pulses to determine the location of a Rover during Inbound and Outbound travel. There's also some pulsing during side-hops." He frowned. "Any Rover with an interface could trigger this sequence. They might not even know they're doing it."

"But you didn't set them off," Klein argued.

"Just luck, I guess."

"What happens if you don't stop this? How big of a ripple will there be?" the agent demanded.

Theo keyed the question into the computer, without bothering to input a security screening code. Guv's computer system would be airtight.

Unlike his computer, this one didn't generate a Renaissance or Baroque painting in the air above the keyboard while it cogitated. Instead it painstakingly constructed an image of a beehive. All the bees were drones. *Guv's view of an ideal society.*

"Task complete." Even the computer voice was bland.

"Run task report," he ordered. The hive melted away. "The truncated version," he added.

"Destruction of 1888 London will substantially affect the power of the British Empire for a period of nine point three years. Other opportunistic governments will take advantage and capture British colonial outposts, including India, Burma, Singapore and Egypt. This disruption will significantly impact British capabilities in the First World War and delay Allied entry into the Second World War. With the rise of Russia in—"

"Cut to the chase," Klein demanded. "What about 2058?"

"Unknown," the computer replied. "Unable to determine extent of changes beyond the end of the twentieth century due to unspecified parameters."

"What parameters are those?" Theo asked the computer.

"Indefinable."

Fletcher scoffed. "God, that's helpful."

"What are the chances of a total disconnect between 1888 and 2058?" Theo quizzed.

"Ninety-six point two percent."

Fletcher whistled.

"End query," Theo murmured. "With so much change, time travel may not be discovered the second time around, or be significantly delayed. My guess is that we have one shot at this."

"You going back?" Fletcher asked.

"Of course," Theo replied. "That's where it's all happening."

Klein shook his head. "My bosses will have a fit."

"Don't tell them."

"Yeah, right. I'm the one stuck here taking the heat, Morrisey."

"From whom?" Theo scolded. "If this plot plays out, neither Guv nor you may exist."

"Don't remind me."

"There's one another matter," Theo began. "Both Miss Lassiter and Harter have been off-timed. Did Guv have anything to do with that?"

Klein shook his head. "Too hard to pull off."

Which means you've tried it.

"What's off-timed?" Fletcher asked.

"A Rover sets their interface for a specific location and time, and are diverted to another by a secondary source," Theo explained. "Miss Lassiter found herself at the exact moment my nephew's body was discarded in the Thames." He paused, about to hand Guv the ammunition they needed to bring down their hated rival. "Dalton Mimes was there… and so was Copeland. He was involved in Chris' murder."

The senior Guv agent's face actually cracked a smile, the muscles twitching slightly as if unaccustomed to the task. "You know, my gut told me he was good for it."

"Copeland?" Fletcher asked.

Klein ignored her, his smile widening. "If we can get him to roll over on Davies and the rest of the Board…"

Theo slowly rose from the chair, unsteady on his feet. He didn't care about this petty war anymore. No matter how Guv played it, Chris was still dead. "I really need to get back."

"TPB is in the process of shutting down all travel to 1888, saying it's too unstable," Klein advised. "They're pulling out all the tourists and the Rovers. Sending in a big team isn't going to be an option."

"I agree," Theo said. "How many can I have?"

"Whoever I commit to this mission may not return. That means they have to be unmarried." The agent frowned, thinking it through. "Three agents plus Hopkins. He's already in '88. I'll tell him you're in charge of the operation."

"Thank you."

"If you find Copeland," Klein began, the smile appearing again, "send him our way."

"Of course." *Providing he's still breathing when I finish with him.*

✢

CHAPTER FIFTEEN

Friday, 9 November 1888
Arundel Hotel

When Cynda kept ignoring his attempts to rouse her, Mr. Spider threatened to build a web in her left ear. That pulled her out of bed faster than any alarm.

"Other Rovers get nice delusions," she groused, rubbing the sleep from her eyes.

"You get what you deserve," was the swift reply. "Besides, the boss is back. He's all fired up."

The instant she exited the bedroom, Theo popped up out of the chair and started talking nonstop. She only caught some of the words: *sixpence, time pulse, gunpowder.*

Then it hit her. "Time pulse? That's from *our* time."

He nodded energetically. "It's my guess there's one of those coins in each barrel. When a time pulse reaches it, it heats up and sets off the gunpowder, which ignites the dynamite, all at strict intervals. Before it does that, however, the pulse is passed on to the next coin, and so on."

Cynda lowered herself onto the couch. "You suspected something like this, didn't you?"

"Not exactly, but I've always felt there was something bigger at work than a few disgruntled shifters. Until I saw that coin, I'd thought I was just being paranoid."

"Can we stop them?" she asked.

His energy began to fade. "I'm not sure."

"If we don't, we're marooned."

"That's a distinct possibility." His tone was gentler than usual, more introspective.

"Well, there are worse places to be exiled," she remarked. "I've been to some of them."

What would it be like to live here? She could easily pawn the Prince's necklace for money and live comfortably by Victorian standards. Her knowledge of the future would work in her favor. There'd be Sunday carriages rides in Hyde Park with Sephora. She could visit the Crystal Palace with Keats, have lunch with H.G. Wells, watch Davy Butler grow up.

It sounded great, but she knew it would get old very quickly. Society's complex rules would chafe her just as much as in 2058. Once the disease shield wore off and the Dinky Docs were exhausted, she would be at the mercy of nineteenth century medicine.

Then there was the matter of Theo. She'd already noted Keats' disapproval. How well would Alastair and the sergeant take to his presence on a permanent basis?

"You're forgetting something," Mr. Spider nudged.

The bombs.

Her eyes met Theo's. He'd been thinking along the same lines. If they didn't get this fixed, London would be a pile of ash.

"I think it's best we *don't* get marooned," he said.

"I heartily agree."

They all stood under a rotting overhang, out of sight of the locals and constables as the rain pelted down unmercifully. Cynda's boots were leaking and she was wet to her ankles. Her male disguise was a disadvantage: she was used to having more layers to keep her warm.

"You understand what you have to do?" Theo asked, brusque even for him.

"Yes, I understand." Hopkins said. He was being polite. Theo had repeatedly explained the plan until Cynda thought their heads would explode.

"What about you?" Theo asked, eyeing her.

"I got it." *The first time you told me. And the fifth.*

His uncharacteristic case of nerves was fueling hers. If he was that worried, what chance did they have of stopping this?

Theo turned his intense gaze to the three Guv agents behind her. "What about you guys?"

Three nods, all in unison. They never spoke. *Maybe they're all mutes.*

"Your first priority is to neutralize the explosives. If you can capture the delivery man, that's great, but it's not paramount."

None of this was new. He could have summed it up easily: find bombs, disarm them, head to the nearest pub to celebrate.

"One last thing." He lowered his voice dramatically, so they had to crowd close to hear him. "Do not use your interfaces to communicate, to execute a transfer or even a side-hop. If you create a time pulse within fifty yards of any of the barrels, you may trigger an explosion and start the chain reaction prematurely. We go about this low tech. Understand?"

That was new. *Nothing like saving the best for last.*

"Expect some pushback," he warned. "If you have any trouble with a local, turn them over to the constables. You'll find one patrolling the street near your location. If they give you any problems, let them know that Sir Charles Warren, the police commissioner, has approved our efforts. If anyone asks, you're with Pinkerton's. Once you've finished, go back to the rendezvous point."

"How did you get Warren to sign off on that?" Cynda asked, perplexed.

"I didn't. Someone else pressured him." The look he gave her told her not to pursue the issue.

"Got it," she said. "Can we go now?"

"Yes."

There were grunts of acknowledgement as the pack scattered. Hopkins took off at a brisk pace, heading north with the other agents. Then it was just the two of them. Cynda was only a few blocks away from her first location, so she waited for Theo to leave. He didn't. Instead, he stepped closer.

"I know what I'm supposed to do," she said, her patience gone.

He put his hand on her cheek. It felt warm to the touch despite the weather. He'd forgotten she was dressed as a man. Luckily, no one was nearby.

"I wanted you to know…" He hesitated. "I…" Clearly unable to put his feelings into words, he bent closer and kissed her lips. The kiss was feather light. When she didn't pull away, the second was stronger, more insistent.

This feels right.

She wrapped her arms around him, pulling him closer. The last kiss warmed her all the way to her cold toes.

Theo drew back. He smiled, as if he'd won a major victory. "That's all I needed to know. Keep yourself safe, for me."

"Don't do anything stupid," she cautioned, her eyes threatening to fill with tears and embarrass her. "The paperwork would be a bitch."

He laughed and strode away, opening his black umbrella. Right before he turned the corner, he blew her a kiss. Cynda watched until he was no longer in sight. A shard of foreboding sliced through her. She shook herself, trying to ignore it. Theo Morrisey would take care of himself. They'd sort things out later. She had bombs to disarm.

She heard a slight pop and found Mr Spider had just opened his own umbrella. That was just too weird for words.

If this went wrong, there would be no TEM Enterprises, no job or family. Theo would be just some guy walking around London in the rain, trying to find a way to get them home. Whatever home might be like at that point.

"Let's get this fixed," the spider urged.

Johns Hopkins leaned against a mailbox. It was garish red, with that stylized VR on it to let you know the Queen owned the thing. Why bother to put the initials on it? She owned almost everything as far as he could see. He cut into the nearest backyard through a wicker gate and surveyed the terrain. Privy, outdoor water pump, a patch of mud that might have been a garden in the summer. Consulting Morrisey's map, he skirted along the side of the house to where the barrel should be.

Nothing.

For a second, he thought he'd entered the wrong yard. He searched the area again. No barrel. A thick knot began forming in his stomach as he headed for his next location.

"Where the hell are you?" Cynda muttered. Mr. Spider bounded off her shoulder, floating downward with his wee umbrella. "You see anything?"

"No."

She studied her paper again, trying to keep stray drops of rain from falling on it. At least the deluge had let up. Jamming the paper into a pocket, she did one more circuit. No barrel. Her interface said it was half past ten. They were cutting it too close.

HOPKINS WAS LOSING time. The woman in front of him was huge, with fists any boxer would envy. He'd hoped the constable loitering in the street would hear the commotion and deal with her, but so far that hadn't happened.

"I don't like no strangers waltzin' around my house," she exclaimed, glowering at him.

"Yes, ma'am."

"You a rozzer?"

From her tone, it sounded like a good idea *not* to be a police officer. "No, ma'am. I'm with…" The Pinkerton cover wouldn't work with this sort. "I'm with the gas people. We were concerned about a leak."

"Oh…" she said, her arms uncrossing. "Why you workin' on a holiday?"

"Just my lot in life," he said, spreading his hands.

That seemed to mollify her. "Well then, have a look round. I don't want to pay for no gas that I don't use, you understand?"

"Yes, ma'am," he said, touching his hat in respect. She retreated into the house to screech at an indeterminate number of grubby urchins.

He let loose a puff of air and then spent time examining the gas pipe as expected. When she didn't return, he headed toward where the barrel would be. It wasn't there.

"Now come on," he said, swiveling in the mud. A few minutes later, he was back on the march toward site number one, the knot in his stomach now the size of a baseball.

CHAPTER SIXTEEN

Theo knew precisely where the barrel should be without consulting his map. It was conspicuously absent. He circled the yard, twice. No bomb.

A prickle of warning swarmed up his back. He turned to find a man watching him from beside the gate that led to the alley.

"Copeland," he said, tensing.

His nemesis greeted him with a sadistic smile. "The geek freak himself. I couldn't believe when they said you were here."

"What do you have to do with this?"

"Almost everything." Copeland pulled something out of his pocket. It looked like a Vespa box. Before he could react, Theo was on his knees, fighting for breath.

"Neuro-blocker," Copeland informed him. "The great equalizer." He dialed the thing down a couple notches and administered another dose.

As Theo folded over, nose nearly touching the mud in an effort to pull enough air into his lungs, he heard Copeland call out. A short time later, three sets of worn boots lined up in front of him.

"Warm him up a bit, lads. He needs to get into the proper frame of mind."

—

"Lassiter?" Hopkins trudged into view.

"Did you find them?" Cynda asked.

"No. You?" She shook her head. He issued a choice expletive. "I talked to the others. They're having the same problem. I don't understand," he complained. "Morrisey said the bombs were there."

"Now they aren't," she replied, staring at her pocket watch. Just past eleven. She began to wind the interface.

"You're not supposed to sync up," he warned.

Cynda ignored him. Hopkins sucked in a deep breath, waiting for the first concussion. All they heard was a dog barking in the distance.

"You got lucky," he said.

"Luck has nothing to do with it. That means the barrels are not within fifty yards of here."

"So sayeth the Morrisey," Hopkins muttered.

The second hand marched forward, but there was no indication that she'd synced up with 2058. Cynda gave it another wind. Nothing. "What's yours doing?"

Reluctantly, Hopkins performed the same movements. His head slowly rose, eyes wide. "I'm not syncing at all. Not even with Guv. It's like they're not there."

Cynda waited as he came to grips with what that meant.

"The time distortion has moved passed us," he said in a barely audible voice. "We're stuck here, aren't we?"

"You got it."

As Hopkins paced and stewed, Cynda sat on a well curb, trying to parse out the future without a roadmap. Every now and then she'd look down at her interface. There were thirteen minutes left before the first explosion. Providing their foes would keep to the same schedule as before.

"Why not? They have the upper hand," Mr. Spider commented. He was watching one of his real cousins rebuild its web on the pump spout after the rainstorm.

Despite the desperate situation, she found herself fascinated by the small creature. It was weaving anchor threads from the spout to the water pipe. When one of the threads didn't attach, the spider tried it in another location. When that didn't work, it moved to different place on the spout. That thread caught.

"It's adapting to the pump spout's curve," she murmured. "Changing the design as it goes."

"I told you we were smart," Mr. Spider remarked. "So are you."

She didn't feel that way right now. Theo would have worked this out in a flash, with time to spare.

Cynda looked back at her fellow Rover. "Why are they using advanced technology to trigger the explosions, but letting some local tote the barrels around?" she asked, skeptically. "Doesn't make sense. It's too dangerous: the cops are everywhere."

"They did it the first time." He was still on the move, churning up the mud, burning off energy. She'd been like that once, before the NMR.

Before Theo.

She was about to tell him to knock it off when it hit her.

"No footprints," she exclaimed.

Her tone of voice made him stop. "What?"

"Theo said there were no footprints around the barrels. It was bothering him. He finally chalked it up to the heavy rain."

"Makes sense."

"Unless they were never there in the first place." She thumped her forehead with a palm, like it would jolt something loose. "Come on. How are they doing this?" Another thump. "How can they deliver the bombs on short notice without using a local?"

A second later, her mouth dropped open. "Oh geez. That's it!" she announced.

"What?"

"They use a time jump. No hassles with the cops, no chance of being delayed. Damn, that's brilliant."

"You've lost it, Lassiter." Hopkins shook his interface at her. "No time travel, remember? We're orphaned, and so are they."

"Just because *we* can't access the time stream doesn't mean the people *ahead* of us have the same problem," she argued. "The disconnect may not have reached them yet. Their interfaces may still work, at least in the short term."

"Even if that's true, no one would transfer explosives through the time stream," he protested. "That's insane."

"Not *through* time. A side-hop, here in '88. You can set those so fine there's virtually no time differential. You do it right, you don't access the stream."

"But they'll set off their own bombs."

"Not if they configured their time pulses correctly."

Slowly the light dawned in Hopkins' eyes. Then he sagged in defeat. "We tipped our hand too soon. They can deliver the barrels seconds before they detonate. We won't be able to stay ahead of them unless we can jump ourselves."

He sat next to her on the well curb. "We're done for. We'll never get back. My future is gone."

"Mine too," she said. "I was supposed to become a legend and—" She leapt to her feet. "Of course! They're here somewhere. I know it."

"The bombs?" he asked, completely confused.

"No, my entourage. They've followed me since I first arrived in '88. Why miss the final curtain?"

To HER RELIEF, Cynda found them almost immediately. Thomas was leaning up against a lamppost arguing with Prudence. They jolted to attention when she skidded to a halt in front of them.

"Hi guys," she said. "Life's sucking here, if you haven't noticed."

"We were debating that very point," Thomas replied.

The younger Rover arrived at that moment. "Hopkins, meet Thomas and Prudence. They're academics from *upstream*."

"Hello," Pru said gamely.

Hopkins only nodded, his frown deeper now.

"Are your interfaces still working?" Cynda asked.

"Yes," Thomas confirmed warily. "Why?"

She grinned. "Good, we need to borrow them."

"That's not possible," Prudence told her. "It will cost us our grant."

"It will cost you more than that if this plot goes all the way," Cynda shot back. "Your future's just as much at risk as ours."

Pru shook her head, but with a definite lack of conviction.

Cynda got the sense they were waiting for something. *But what?*

"How about..." Mr. Spider whispered in her ear. Then she grinned.

Cynda produced the pistol with a decided flourish. "Consider this the first inter-century timepiece robbery." She gestured toward her companion. "Give the nice Rover your pretty pocket watches and we'll be on our way."

Thomas beamed his approval. "We have no choice. Right, Pru?"

"That's how I see it," she agreed.

The interfaces changed hands.

"Do they work the same?" Hopkins asked, the frown still in place.

"Roughly," Thomas replied. "Just be careful with the settings. They're precise to the millisecond."

Whoa.

"What about the time pulse problem?" Hopkins asked, still dubious.

"You won't have any difficulties," Pru said with a wink. "They're configured differently."

For the first time that day, Cynda felt a surge of hope. "You do the first six, Hopkins, I'll get the last six."

"But what about Morrisey?"

What about Theo? The shard of worry buried itself deeper into her chest.

"Assume he's not in the picture," she said, trying to ignore what that meant. "Catch up with me when you can."

Dropping the gun into her pocket, Cynda saluted the pair. "We'll be back." *Hopefully.*

Hopkins tossed an interface in her direction, and then vanished.

"Show off," Cynda muttered. She followed a few seconds later.

THOMAS HEAVED A heavy sigh of relief the instant they were gone.

"*The first inter-century timepiece robbery,* and we were here," Pru crowed. "It'll be a great anecdote for the book."

Thomas tugged on her sleeve, angling his head toward the newcomer who had just joined them.

Pru reined in her enthusiasm. "Good morning, Mr. Anderson. I trust that's how you wanted that to go?"

Robert Anderson nodded. "Exactly. Thank you. I always appreciate the help of upstream academics."

"We didn't anticipate it getting this chaotic, to be honest," Pru confided. "Her timeline is way off."

"It's all off-kilter right now."

"We will get our interfaces back, won't we?" Pru asked nervously. "We're not allowed to stay a full day."

Anderson stared into the distance, thoughtful. "If this doesn't succeed, it won't matter anyway."

11:27:55. NO SIGN of a bomb at the first location. Advanced technology wasn't always your ally. She wouldn't necessarily hear or see the barrel arrive, not with how silent her two observers' transfers had been. Cynda ground her teeth and forced herself to wait.

"Come on, you jerks." The worry registered more sharply now. What was Theo doing? No doubt he'd realized the situation, but why hadn't he checked in with her or Hopkins?

"Eleven twenty-eight," the spider announced.

"I know, I know."

Cynda began to hum to relieve her accelerating nerves. To her surprise, what came to mind was an old Rover ditty that became progressively bawdier as the song progressed. It was Chris' favorite. Somehow, it seemed to help.

She kept her voice low. "If I were a Rover I'd do London town. I'd do the town from bottom to Crown. There'd be no man that I'd turn down, if I were a Rover in London town. I'd start with a boot jack, he'd have the knack, then find me a copper who'd do me right proper…"

She continued to hum the naughtier bits and then suddenly broke off. Near the privy was a barrel. It hadn't been there a few seconds before.

There was no time for finesse. She sprinted across the open stretch and launched herself at the container, ripping the three sticks of dynamite off the side and flinging them all directions. Flipping open the knife Theo had provided, she pierced the cork bung and pulled. It popped out, and she drove a hand inside the barrel.

"Where are you?" The interface began to vibrate—the one-minute warning. "Don't be shy. Come to mama…"

If Theo was wrong about this… Her fingers touched something metal nestled on top of a paper liner.

Up came the coin. "Yes!" She slung it in the nearest mud puddle, triggered her interface and hurled herself to the next location.

HOPKINS PACED BACK and forth between a pub and the fence near the street. He'd become a Rover because it'd sounded so amazing. Now he could be stuck here for life, however short that would be. Or get blown to bits. That'd really piss off his mom. She'd wanted him to be a dentist.

He slowly completed another circuit, conjugating one of his favorite swear words under his breath. Then again. A cask appeared out of nowhere.

"Oh God, Lassiter was right."

—

Cynda propped herself up against a fence, exhausted. She'd hopped back five minutes to rest because her heart wouldn't stop pounding. Once she caught her breath, she'd go after the remaining casks.

"Good job," her delusion said.

"Thanks," she wheezed. "I never would have seen that last one if you hadn't pointed it out."

The spider acknowledged the compliment. "We make a good team."

"Got that right. Let's just not do the umbrella trick for a while, okay?"

"Lassiter?" It was Hopkins. She'd never get used to those silent transfers.

He was staring at her, his face smudged with what appeared to be gunpowder. "Who are you talking to?"

No reason to hide the truth any longer. "I was talking with my hallucination. Don't worry, you keep traveling and you'll earn one of your own." *Or more than one.*

"You actually talk to it?" he asked, incredulous.

"Sure. He's been a great deal of help."

The expression on Hopkins' face said he thought she was over the edge. *Your turn's coming, kid.*

"Did you get them?" she asked.

"Yes. The interface seemed to be able to sense where they were. Made it a lot easier."

She straightened up. "I'm going to disarm Theo's two, then try to find him. You go to Rotherhithe and help Keats. We have no idea if the bombs are already in place over there, or they'll ferry them in at the last minute. I'll join you as soon as I know the boss is okay." Then it dawned on her Hopkins probably didn't have a clue what the sergeant looked like. She fumbled for her pendant.

"No need. I studied the files before I came. Thought it best I know which Victorians you'd been interacting with."

Smart guy. "See you sooner..."

"Or later," he shot back with a grin, trading the old Rover joke between them.

They coordinated their interfaces and went their separate ways.

CHAPTER SEVENTEEN

Cynda would have gotten them all if it hadn't been for the bowler. When she couldn't find Theo at the first location, she disarmed his bomb, her nerves taut. She'd been about to move onto number two when she spied the bowler lying in the mud. Its brim was ripped and battered. A broken umbrella lay nearby.

Heart sinking, she dropped to her knees to study the footprints around the hat. This was more than push back. This felt like an ambush.

In the distance she heard a hollow thump, the last bomb detonating right on schedule. "Oh, God." Cynda flipped open the interface, intending to jump back and warn Theo of the ambush.

"I wouldn't do that."

She whirled to find a man watching her. He was of medium build, dressed like a Victorian. He'd arrived without her hearing him.

A Future. "Why not?"

His expression went flat, like someone trying to project an image of impartiality. "Because you just can't. There's a reason this has happened."

She glowered at him, gripping the interface so tightly the stem dug into her palm. "Who are you to tell me what to do?"

"I'm Robert Anderson. I'm from your future."

The man Rover One had spoken of. "You have anything to do with this?" she asked, gesturing toward the hat.

"No."

"Then who has him? Copeland?"

Anderson held out his hand. "I'm sorry, but I have to have the interface first. Then I'll tell you."

"That's blackmail!"

"I need to get this back to the academics or there will be consequences upstream. We've bent the rules as far as we dare at this point."

"How do I know you're not lying?" she demanded, livid at being cornered like this.

Anderson frowned. "Nothing but my word."

"Which means nothing to me. You might be the guy who talked to Defoe, you might not."

"I am. I'm also the one who off-timed him to New York and sent you to the Thames the night your lover died."

She reeled back. "Why are you guys doing this?"

"Because we have to. Things are so off track we have no choice." He gestured toward the watch. "Please, just give me the interface."

"Damn you!" With a cry of anguish, she tossed it at him. Anderson caught it on the fly.

"Thank you." He tucked it in a pocket. "Copeland has your boss."

"Where?" she snapped.

"Defoe is the key to all this," he replied, avoiding her question. "Copeland's masters want him. We've hidden Rover One in the time stream while we figure out why he's so important to them."

"Why take Theo?"

"Your boss is leverage. All that matters to Copeland is that he remain on the good side of his employers. He'll do anything to stay alive."

Anything.

"Is Theo dead?"

"Not yet."

She shivered. "How do I find them?"

"Copeland has a cat's-paw here in '88 named Hezekiah Grant. He's the weakest link in the chain."

"The Ascendant," she whispered. Theo had spoken of him. She fumbled with the silver pendant, pulling it out. If this had Grant's address in the files…

"Don't bother," Anderson advised. "He's in hiding. Within a few hours, Grant will be contacting you. You should be preparing yourself for that moment. It's your best chance to get Morrisey back alive."

A second later, Cynda was staring at empty air.

Too slow. Five stories in each warehouse. Thousands of barrels to search. Most of them were the huge ones, but a smaller one could be tucked in amongst them. Keats heard muttering amongst the men. They realized the futility of this gesture as much as he did.

He moved to the next barrel. "Mind you, be careful!" he warned.

"If'n I was bein' careful, guv, I'd be in a pub right now 'steada in here with you," someone called back.

"He has a point."

Keats turned toward the familiar voice. "Hello, my friend. How is life in the East End these days?"

"Quiet so far," Alastair replied, shifting a barrel to examine it. "Fisher was given orders to pull the constables back and let Jacynda and her people handle the problem."

"Who issued that order?" Keats asked, taken by surprise.

"Warren."

Keats snorted. "I had hoped she'd be out of this."

"You're mad if you think that. According to Mr. Morrisey, you should find one of those coins in each of these barrels. He said you should remove it first thing. It's how the detonations are triggered."

"Of course," Keats muttered under his breath.

Ramsey thumped down the row. "Doctor, we have need of you. One of the lads tangled with a hogshead and got his foot mashed."

Alastair threw Keats a resigned look. "I'll be happy to help."

They'd taken only a few steps when there was a muted explosion. Shouts erupted outside.

"Where did that come from?" Keats called to a man near the door. "Was the blast on this side of the river?"

The man shook his head. "North, I think."

The East End.

KEATS WAITED FOR the watchman to return so they could lock up. Of all the warehouses, this was the least full, the easiest to check. They had to have missed something. He ducked inside for one last look.

He walked down the closest row again. This was futile. No wonder the newspaper accounts had reported no one knew exactly where the bombs had been placed.

As he returned to the double doors, he noted a piece of tarp in a corner. Had they looked under it? Keats knelt and flung the cover aside. He was rewarded with a barrel decorated with strange red writing on the side. A quick shift of the cask brought the dynamite into sight.

"How did we miss you?" he muttered. As his fingers deftly worked the rope holding the dynamite in place, a glancing blow struck him hard on the back of the head. He slumped against the barrel, struggling to remain conscious.

"Bloody rozzer!" A swift kick hit his thigh, then there was the sound of running footsteps.

Besides the pounding of his head, there was some sort of queer buzzing sound. A moment later, he was grabbed by the collar and hauled him to his feet. "Too close," a voice said. "We're out of here."

Then everything went frigid black.

KEATS CAME TO his senses, his head on fire, mind tumbling like an acrobat in a stage show. He wanted nothing better than to vomit.

"You okay?" a voice asked.

He made it to his knees, bending over in an effort to reduce the throbbing headache. Slowly lifting his head, he studied the man. Young. Worried, if the expression in his eyes counted for anything. Then he saw the pocket watch in the fellow's hand.

"You're one of them?" he managed to croak.

The man nodded. "I'm Hopkins. I work with Lassiter. I'm sorry I did that, but the bomb was due to go off right after I found you. I jumped us back a couple minutes to be safe, then disarmed it."

"Thank you," he said, still stunned. "You saved my life."

"Part of the job. Lassiter would never forgive me if anything happened to you."

"I heard an explosion. Is Jacynda unharmed?"

"Last time I saw her."

Keats rubbed the back of his neck. *Blast, that hurts.* "Did you see who hit me?"

"No, sorry."

"Not surprising, really. Nobody likes a copper."

The newcomer offered his hand, and Keats used to it to rise.

"We'll work as a team. There are six more. Either they're already in place or will arrive shortly before they detonate," he said. Hopkins tapped his interface. "I can find them for you," he added, a smug grin on his face.

"Arrive from where?"

"Best you not know."

"Do I have to go into that blackness again?" Keats asked. "I didn't like that a bit."

"No. That was so against the rules I don't want to even think about it."

Keats winced, his head spinning again. He tried to steady himself and nearly fell.

"Hold still." Something cold pressed against Keats neck. He remembered that sensation. It'd been that night in the carriage, after Flaherty had struck him on the head. Jacynda had put something against his neck and he'd felt so much better. The same was happening now. His headache eased immediately and with it, the dizziness.

"What did you do to me?"

"I played doctor, but don't tell anyone." The man rolled his eyes. "Lassiter is *so* not a good influence." He stuck something in his pocket, then held his pocket watch in front of him like a compass. Revived, Keats followed him, rolling his neck from side to side to diminish a slight cramp.

"You know about the coins?" Keats nodded. "Just keep them as far away from anything flammable," Hopkins explained. "And don't put them in your pocket," he said, gesturing toward one of his own. It sported a sizeable scorch mark.

As they walked the row of warehouses, Hopkins studied the watch dial and then smiled broadly. "It's already in place. That'll make it easier."

"I don't understand," Keats replied.

"They changed the bomb delivery schedule in the East End. Made it lot harder. They didn't over here. Probably figured we wouldn't find them in time." Hopkins gestured. "In this one," he advised, "ground floor, near the north end."

"How long do we have?" Keats asked.

"Five and a half minutes, as long as they don't change the timing."

Keats didn't want to think about that.

"All right lads. It's in here," Keats called out. The dockworkers swept in, racing down the row of casks while calling out encouragement to each other, betting who would be able to find the bomb before the other.

Inspector Ramsey stomped over. "Any luck?"

"Found one in the first warehouse. It's taken care of." Keats did the introductions. "Hopkins works with Miss Lassiter."

"Pinkerton's?" Ramsey asked. The young man nodded. "Are there any of you left in America?"

"Probably not," Hopkins replied, smiling.

A dockworker skittered out the door of the nearest building.

"Oy, rozzer. It's here!" he shouted, jumping up and down like he'd found the Crown Jewels.

Keats took off at a run. The barrel was in an empty space near the back of the building, a knot of men ringed around it.

"The rest of you lads clear off. Go help the others, and I'll work on this one."

There was the sound of rapidly retreating footsteps.

Keats dropped to his knees and carefully removed the dynamite, setting it on the floor near him. Then he dug out the cork and went hunting inside for that strange coin. He couldn't find it. Swearing under his breath, he kept digging. He found the paper liner that kept the gunpowder dry. Something cool brushed his fingers. He pulled out the coin and sighed with relief. He jammed the cork back into the cask and waved forward one of the constables who was nervously hovering nearby. "Roll this out of here," he ordered.

He was surprised to find Ramsey standing just behind him. "What was the thing you took out of the barrel?"

Keats displayed it on his palm. "A very strange coin. According to Hopkins, it detonates the gunpowder."

He watched as the color drained out of Ramsey's face. "There's more here than you're telling me."

"There's more here than I know."

The moment they cleared the door, two dockworkers sung out, beckoning them forward. Keats split off toward one warehouse and Ramsey toward another. In the distance they could see Hopkins and Alastair entering a third.

By God, we're going to do it.

———

The question was always the same, but it didn't really matter. He didn't have the answer. Theo spit a gob of blood from his mouth, narrowing missing Copeland's boot. It earned him another backhand across the face. The pain was everywhere now, every nerve competing to shout its own private agony.

He'd been beaten by Copeland's men, then taken to a huge building. When he'd first arrived, it had smelled of wool. Now he could only smell his own blood.

Copeland's face came into view. "It's an easy question—where's Defoe?"

"Don't know," Theo said in the barest of whispers.

"Where'd you see him last?"

"Here, in London. He transferred, and I haven't seen him since."

"That's bullshit."

Morrisey stared at him through swelling eyes. "I don't know where he is."

"Why did you go back home?"

"Looking for Defoe," Theo lied.

"Not buying that. You could just send a message. What were you up to?"

When Theo didn't reply, another fist landed in his stomach. As he fought not to vomit, Copeland started to circle him, like a lion.

There was a commotion. Through the painful haze, Morrisey tried to focus on what was happening. Voices. One was panicky. Copeland's was harsh.

"What do you mean the all bombs didn't go off?" his captor demanded.

"Only one, in the East End. They found the rest of them," the man answered breathlessly.

"How in the hell did they do that?"

"I don't know."

There was a grunt of pain as someone paid the price for delivering the bad news, then the sound of a body being dragged away.

Somehow Jacynda had stopped them.

"Not going well?" Theo asked, wishing he had the strength to laugh in Copeland's face. "She outwitted you, didn't she?" he said.

Another tremendous blow—this one to the head. Theo's ears rang like church bells on Easter morning.

Copeland stepped closer. "Seems all I got left is you, geek freak. Where's Defoe?"

"I don't—"

The chair went out from under him, and Theo landed hard on the wooden floor. A second later a boot catapulted into his ribs. Bones snapped. He tried to cry out, but he couldn't get enough air.

"Give him another round, lads."

Blows rained down on him from all sides, so many he could hardly feel them anymore.

Jacynda. It was her face that comforted him as he slipped into the darkness.

"AH, CHRIST," COPELAND swore. He rubbed a hand across his chin, trying to figure out how to work this to his best advantage. The failure of the plot was going to cost him everything if he didn't find Rover One.

"This one's a waste of time. Load him up, drop him in the Thames," he ordered to the trio standing over the body. "If he's still alive, cut his throat before you do. Cut anything you want."

"What about his boots?" one of the toughs asked.

Copeland smirked. "Strip him bare, I don't give a goddamn. Just get him out of my sight." He tossed each of them a sovereign and then scooped up the prizes he'd taken from his victim.

One last chance. This time he had to come out on top.

✠

CHAPTER EIGHTEEN

It was near dark when Cynda finally staggered back to the hotel room, drained. Despite Anderson's assurance that the Ascendant would contact her, she'd spent the afternoon hunting for Theo, increasingly desperate as the hours passed. When there'd been no explosions or raging fires in Southwark, she knew they'd triumphed. Without Theo, it felt like a hollow victory.

She'd no sooner changed into a dress when Hopkins arrived at the door.

"We didn't lose one warehouse," he reported. "Keats is the hero of the hour."

She smiled. "He deserves it. Morrisey's still missing. Copeland has him. He's trying to use him as leverage for us to turn over Defoe."

Hopkins didn't seem surprised. "That Future, Anderson, caught up with me in Rotherhithe after I'd found all the bombs. He told me what was up and then insisted I give him the interface. I'd hoped I could keep it until we could use our own."

When she didn't reply, Hopkins began to open and close his own pocket watch over and over in nervous agitation.

"I hope you don't mind me taking over like this," he said. "You're the Senior Rover here and..."

"No, you're best for this," she told him, staring at nothing. "I'm too close to this."

"Is there something between you and Morrisey?"

She looked over at him. "Not sure yet. We spent so much time together while I was healing that we're like an old pair of shoes. Except he'd like to take that friendship a lot farther."

"Well, from what I've seen he's a little odd," Hopkins replied, "but he seems like a good guy."

She smiled. "I don't date higher up the company food chain."

"No one will raise an eyebrow about that."

Cynda shrugged. There was more to it than just the boss issue. More than she wanted to confront right now.

"You could always quit TEM Enterprises," Hopkins suggested.

"And go where?" Cynda asked. "Time In Motion won't hire me. TPB will see to that, especially after my brain reboot."

"You could work for Guv. You're used to odd people, so Klein won't bother you."

"Maybe. I just don't know right now." Cynda looked over at him with curiosity. "What about you, Hopkins? You got a special someone?"

"Had one. She bailed after I was shot. Couldn't handle it."

Cynda nodded. "It takes a Rover to understand this crazy job."

"Or Morrisey. He's one of us now."

Which is why we can't lose him. "Here," she said, offering Hopkins the pistol. "In case you run into Copeland. This time, you'll have the upper hand."

"Thanks." He paused as he opened the door. "I'll let you know when we find Morrisey. I'm sure he'll be okay."

Cynda threw him a thumbs-up. The moment he was gone, her control began to unravel. She teetered between tears and the urge to tear the room apart.

"You need to be out there," Mr. Spider urged.

"I can't walk all over the East End forever."

"I don't think you'll have to."

She eyed her delusion. He had an uncanny way of seeing the future.

"Okay, we go out again."

Cynda had just reached the lobby when one of the hotel's staff handed her a message. After mumbling a thanks and pressing a coin into his hand, she ripped open the envelope, praying it was good news.

The Ascendant summons you. Your carriage awaits.

"Trap?" Mr. Spider asked, peering down at the note.

"Sure. But if there's any chance this guy knows where Theo is, it's worth the risk."

Sitting at the kerb was an unmarked carriage. It looked exactly like the one that had claimed her at Bedlam. Steeling herself, she climbed in, shoving the bustle behind her. As her eyes adjusted to the darkness, she saw a silvery bloom of light directly across from her.

It might have been a mistake to give Hopkins the gun.

A figure slowly faded into view like the Cheshire cat, no weapon in sight. The face was familiar. Black hair, dark eyes. That arrogant smirk.

Too much macassar oil.

This was the real deal.

"It is a pleasure to see you again, Twig." He gave a sharp rap on the roof with his cane, and the carriage pulled away from the hotel.

"You're Satyr, the Lead Assassin. You were at Effington's party," she recalled.

"Yes, you saved my life and you did it with such grace."

Cynda snorted, knowing b.s. when she heard it. Memories flipped over like a row of dominos. She saw the silver tube, felt his hand placing it against the side of her head. "Why did you do this to me?" she said, tapping her temple.

His expression didn't alter. "I had my reasons. I admit it was cruel, but you *are* still alive, and clearly in possession of all your faculties. That, in itself, is quite remarkable."

"That's not an answer."

"It's the best you're going to get at the moment," he replied.

"Why do you keep trying to kill me?"

"We do have a history, don't we, Twig? That evening I threw you under the beer wagon," he said, smiling at the memory. "Oh, and at the docks. You survived the warehouse fire. Then this," he said, tapping his own temple. "I've never met someone with such tenacity for life."

He didn't sound proud of his attempts to kill her, like Mimes had after he'd rammed the knife into her chest. If anything, she heard a hint of remorse. That was the difference between them. Satyr's eyes always looked pensive as he tried to end her life. Mimes' glowed with sexual ecstasy.

"Why does the Ascendant want to see me?"

"He said he wanted to meet the woman who had *discomfited the angels.*" Satyr leaned forward, causing her to tense once more. "You knew I was here before I went visible. How?"

"I'm just good."

"It's more than that. Come on, tell me."

Why not? It would let him know she wasn't completely unarmed.

"I see a fuzzy outline around someone if they're *en mirage.* I never could until you blanked my brain," she said.

Satyr chuckled. "An unintended consequence. I'm very fond of those." He leaned even further forward, a curious fire in his eyes. "How *did* you reclaim your mind?"

"I had a friend who wouldn't give up on me."

A knowing nod. "You were fortunate." He relaxed against the seat, apparently satisfied.

Cynda ran a bluff. "You told me a lot of things that night you toasted my mind. I don't remember all of them. Like where you got that device."

"I never told you that."

"Then what did you tell me?"

"That I was responsible for the deaths of Johnny Ahearn, Nicci Hallcox and that insufferable Effington."

"Why frame Keats for Nicci's murder?"

"Purely an accident," Satyr replied. "I saw him enter her house and thought it would be fun to use his form. To be honest, there were others I would have rather let fall into the noose than the sergeant."

"Why'd you kill Nicci?"

"She thought I was Keats, and in repayment for rutting with her, she was willing to reveal where the explosives were stored. She'd scored that bit of knowledge from Effington, which meant both of them were liabilities."

Would he know who Morrisey was? She sanitized the question. "A companion of mine is missing. He was helping diffuse the bombs. Do you know where he is?"

Satyr frowned. "No, but I suspect the Ascendant might. He was crowing about something when I was ordered to collect you." He shifted position against the cushions. "You've annoyed a very powerful man, and I'd like to thank you for that."

"Does your gratitude involve a knife in the chest or hands around my throat?"

"Neither. At least not yet."

It was a bizarre truce of sorts. She got the sense he wanted to be here, not just because his master had sent him.

"What's this angel thing about?"

Satyr let out an annoyed sigh. "From what I can tell, the Ascendant claims he's been talking to a messenger from Heaven."

"Did you ever see him, the angel I mean?"

A shake of the head. "I tried, but if he actually exists, he was very stealthy." Satyr carefully adjusted a glove. "Was it really Defoe who tried to kill me?" he asked.

That was the clincher. The only people who knew of Rover One's real name were her contemporaries, or those ahead in the time stream. "Yes, it was Defoe. He and Adelaide Winston were lovers. He blames you for her death."

Satyr shook his head. "It was Tobin, not me. He used my likeness. He's the Ascendant's favored man at present. Until I cut his throat, that is."

"No little silver tube for him?"

"He doesn't deserve that honor," her escort snapped.

"How much did you know about the Lord Mayor's Day plot?"

"Very little. I still don't know all the details."

She gave him the shortened version of how things had fallen out without mentioning the Futures.

"Good heavens," Satyr said, shaking his head. "I have been blind. I should have confronted the Ascendant sooner."

Cynda had to ask. "You're obviously from…" she gave a vague wave. "Who are you?"

As he weighed the question, Satyr pushed aside the curtain and stared out into the darkness. With a nod, he turned back to her. "We have enough time. You've certainly earned that, Twig." He drew in a deep breath and then let it out slowly. "My name is Michael Gordon."

"Sorry, never heard of you."

He gave a bemused smile. "I'm surprised given my history. When I was five, my parents were told that I had a monster buried in my mind, and if I didn't receive psychiatric treatment, that creature would break loose and kill people."

Cynda blinked. "It did."

"It needn't have been that way. I was not a wicked child. If anything, I was rather benign, fond of reading books and grav-boarding." There were the makings of a grin, but it didn't quite come to life.

"I had one of those," she said, dredging up a memory. "I modified it so it would go higher and faster. When I busted my arm, Dad took it away from me."

"I never tampered with mine. I never tortured animals, or daydreamed how someone's blood would feel on my hands."

"So how did you—"

He frowned her into silence. "I had none of the usual markers of a serial killer. Still, I was snared by some innocuous test I took when I was in first grade.

I was diagnosed with Pre-Emergent Sociopathic Disorder. That brought me to the attention of the Interventionalists. Are you aware of them?"

She would have spat on the ground in disgust if they hadn't been in a carriage. "Yeah, I remember those creeps." Shrinks who thought they could prune a kid and take them in a more "socially acceptable direction."

"I failed the same test. They tried to pull that crap with my parents. They ignored them."

Satyr's face saddened. "My parents did not. To save their beloved son, they gave the psychiatrists *carte blanche*. By the time I was fifteen, I'd undergone medication regimes, behavioral modification, long stints in rehabilitation camps, even Electrical Stimulus Avoidance Therapy."

Cynda shuddered. She'd heard about that. Attach a series of electrodes to a child, and if they thought or acted wrong, *zap!* The voltage went up each time. It was legalized torture masquerading as legitimate therapy.

"So let me guess—you killed them all, didn't you?"

"My parents? Oh, no. I don't hate them. They did what they felt was best. Instead, I killed the one man who went out of his way to persecute me—the psychiatrist in charge of my case. I took a great deal of time with him, no quick death for that fiend. Of course, then I'd validated all his work." His expression darkened. "At least he didn't live to collect the applause."

"So how'd you get here?"

He waggled a finger. "Patience, Twig. This is my story, after all. After I canceled my psychiatrist, I turned myself in. There was the trial, conviction, then more tests, more medication, all of it. When none of it worked, they gave me the advanced treatment," he said, pointing to his temple.

"They Null Mem'd you? Why? You'd only killed one person, not a city."

"To reverse my psychopathic idiom, was the official explanation. In truth, they were furious I'd terminated my doctor, as if he were somehow inviolate. After they flushed my brain, I became part of a government study. The goal was to rehabilitate predators into polite members of society. I was put with another psychiatrist who patiently reconstructed me to ensure I wouldn't feel the need to kill ever again."

"Didn't work," she observed.

He grinned. "No, it didn't. I rebuilt myself one memory at a time, and I learned from my mistakes. If I was supposed to be a monster, I would become the best there was."

Cynda glowered at him. "With all you'd been through, how could you do that to me? You know what kind of hell that is!"

The grin faded. "It seemed right at the time. It still does."

She slumped back in the seat, arms crossed over her chest. The ants were waking up. "Then just get on with it, will you?"

His expression hardened. "Once they realized the treatment only made me worse, my ESR Chip was removed, I was dressed in rags and put in a time pod."

"They orphaned you on purpose?" She shivered involuntarily. "I figured maybe you'd stolen an interface or something."

"It was deliberate. When I finally came to my senses, I was in 1768, in Bedlam."

Cynda winced. In that time period, asylum inmates were shackled, beaten, starved, and taunted by gentry who came to see the mad people like caged animals in a zoo.

Satyr's voice dropped. "I nearly did go insane in that place. I finally escaped—without killing anyone, I might add. I lived on the streets, stealing to survive. Because I showed promise, I was taken under the wing of a professional assassin, who became my patron. He taught me a code of honor. He was my guide to a new world."

"You imprinted on him." *Like I did Theo.*

Satyr looked puzzled. "I'm not sure what you mean."

"Nevermind…go on."

"I honed my skills during that time, but I longed to be anywhere but the eighteenth century. It was unbelievably filthy," he said, shaking his head. "I'd about given up hope, when I stumbled across a Time Rover who wasn't paying attention. I bade my patron farewell and hitched a ride to 1887."

"You can't hitch with a Rover," she argued.

"You can if you've got a knife at his throat." As she opened her mouth to ask the question, he shook his head. "He did as I asked, and so I set him free. I doubt he reported the incident."

"Got that right," she agreed. Allowing a crazy to get from one century to another was a career-ending move, especially when the crazy wasn't supposed to be in the time stream in the first place. "So who was he?"

"I didn't bother to ask. We weren't going to exchange letters down the line."

He had a point. "Were you a shifter, then?"

"Yes, purely by accident. A lucky one, as it turned out. That's how I found my patron, who was also Transitive. He taught me what I needed to know."

"You're a Virtual. You did it twice. I've heard that's suicidal."

Satyr shook his head. "Only once. I'm not stupid. I was very stunned to realize I could vanish. I think it had something to do with the NMR."

He took a deep breath and added, "Once here, I applied myself, rose through the ranks of the Seven until I became Lead Assassin. Quite a astounding resume, don't you think?"

"Almost unbelievable," she said, cautiously. "This whole spiel could be a lie."

"It could, but it isn't."

For some reason she believed him. "Why did you revert after the NMR? Didn't you imprint on your shrink?" She had with Theo.

"Walter wasn't the warmest of people, though he did try to ensure I didn't come in contact with anything violent in nature. In his self-absorption, he forgot his bookshelves."

"Walter Samuelson?" she blurted.

"Yes. I would guess you know his brother, the author, intimately."

"Oh yeah, I know him." Dalton Mimes, the man who'd put a knife in her chest.

"Samuelson had a selection of his brother's books. I took to reading them when he wasn't around. Graphic and extremely violent, every one of them. Mimes is a very sick man, you know?"

She wasn't going to argue that one. "How many people have you blanked?"

"No one but you."

The carriage ground to a halt.

"Why only me?" she demanded. "Why was I so special?"

An eyebrow rose. She was baiting the bear.

"I used the device because we need someone on our side," he said.

"We?"

When those dark eyes met hers, she saw unimaginable sadness.

"I was not the only one they orphaned. When the study was decommissioned, they jettisoned us like some foul cargo into the time stream. Psychopaths, serial killers, the lot. All that mattered was that their failures disappear."

Cynda's mind reeled. The questions poured out. "Who did this? TPB? How many?"

"The Time Protocol Board was involved. At least a dozen of us, if not more, were turned loose to ravage our way through time."

Over a dozen Satyrs. *No, not like him.* He'd adopted a code of honor, of sorts. There was no guarantee the others had.

"Are any of them here in '88?"

"You're thinking of the Ripper, aren't you?" he asked.

"Yes. He'd fit the bill."

"I don't think he's one of ours."

Cynda sorted through memories. A name surfaced. "You're Drogo."

"Yes. We all had our code names. I was named after the patron saint of coffeehouses. Rather ironic—I've always disliked the stuff."

"I found the word on a sheet of paper in Chris Stone's pocket after they pulled out him of the Thames. Do you know how it got there?"

"No, I'm sorry." A second later, Satyr's voice grew rough. "I've long had nightmares of what it was like for the others, and what terrors they'd visited on the innocent in whatever time periods they've been abandoned. You're one of us now. You can help right this wrong. Someone must pay for this atrocity."

Before she could reply, Satyr opened the door and stepped out, surveying their surroundings. As he helped her down the stairs, he leaned close and whispered, "Think like an assassin. It might keep you alive."

CHAPTER NINETEEN

The warehouse was large and, for the most part, empty. The gas lamps hanging from the ceiling sent flickers of light in all directions. It smelled like dirty lanolin; stray bits of wool clinging to the floorboards hinted at its original purpose.

"He's summoned the Twenty," Satyr remarked. "What's he up to?"

She followed his gaze to a knot of men at the far side of the room. All of them were *en mirage*, huddling together like sheep threatened by a pack of wild dogs. There were solitary figures scattered around them, like sentinels.

Probably the other assassins.

Two men stood apart from the others. One was Tobin. The other looked like a clerk.

Cynda frowned. "That's the Ascendant?" she asked under her breath. She'd been expecting someone grander, more flamboyant. Someone worthy of the destruction he'd sought to create.

"Unremarkable, isn't he?" Satyr replied with an edge of sarcasm.

"About time!" the man snapped like a petulant schoolboy. "What took you so long?"

Satyr took her elbow, marching her forward. She couldn't help but notice a large, rust-brown stain in the middle of the floor. It looked like dried blood.

Her heart executed a somersault. "Miss Lassiter," Satyr began, "this is the Ascendant. And Tobin, a *junior* assassin."

When Tobin glared at her, Cynda dismissed him with a brief glance, directing her attention to his superior.

"I would not have you in my presence if he had not commanded me to do so," the Ascendant grumbled. He gestured. "Give her the box."

Rather than coming near her, Tobin tossed her a small parcel, a pasteboard box with twine around it.

"The archangel said that I should give it to you at the last," the Ascendant said.

Archangel?

Stripping off the twine, she carefully opened the parcel, wondering if scorpions were native to England. A bloody handkerchief lay inside. She pulled it back to reveal a pocket watch. Opening it, she found the dial smeared with dried blood. A couple quick winds made it light up. Rovers always carried gold ones, in honor of Harter Defoe. She knew of only one man who carried a silver interface.

Her head swimming, Cynda clicked the watch shut, dropping it into her pocket. *Maybe someone stole it from him. Maybe it's someone else's blood.* As she shifted the piece of cloth, she saw the ring. His ring.

She slipped it on her finger. It was only then she noticed the message scrawled inside the box lid.

Give us Defoe. You get what's left of the genius

Cynda stuffed the box and the handkerchief into a pocket. Once her hands were free, she clenched them into fists so no one would see them shaking.

"Where is he?" she hissed.

"The archangel smote him," the Ascendant replied, as if that explained everything.

"What archangel?"

Grant drew himself up. *"And at that time shall Michael stand up, the great prince..."*

"Daniel 12:1, if my memory is correct," Satyr said dryly.

The Ascendant delivered a scathing look toward his Lead Assassin. *"And there was war in heaven: Michael and his angels fought against the dragon."*

Something clicked. *"Revelations,"* Cynda said.

"12:7," the Ascendant clarified.

R12:7. The lettering on the outside of the gunpowder barrels.

Murmuring broke out amongst the Twenty. Apparently they weren't aware that their leader had been taking orders from Heaven.

The Ascendant took a step closer. "The archangel warned me of you, woman. He warned me how the denizens of Hell would try to stop our work. You and your master, he said, were particularly cunning."

Theo was the Devil? That was ridiculous. It was hard not to laugh in the man's face, but too much was at stake.

Cynda turned to the group of onlookers. She needed allies. "So what do the Twenty think of all this?" There was shuffling of feet, but no one spoke up.

Great. No balls in that bunch.

"I must admit that I did not think the Devil's minion wielded that much power," the Ascendant observed, hands clasped behind his back as he paced back and forth like a headmaster confronted with an unruly student.

Minion? She'd been called a lot of things, but that sucked. Well, if she was the Devil's gofer, she'd be his advocate.

"The Archangel Michael told you this?" she asked, making sure she sounded incredulous. "How do you know he wasn't lying to you?"

The Ascendant fumed. "He cannot lie. He is the sword of the Almighty!"

"Really? So how did you meet this Michael person?"

"How dare you mock God's Highest Messenger?"

"When and how?" she pushed.

"The Archangel Michael appeared in pinwheels of glorious light, kneeling in front of me, seeking my aid. He anointed my forehead and I saw Heaven in all its glory."

She caught Satyr's eyes. They'd gone flinty. He'd traveled through time. He knew what those pinwheels meant.

It was so clear now. Take one deeply religious man, add a bit of time travel, stir in a whiff of instability and... *Drugs?* He'd said he'd been anointed, seen Heaven. Someone had dazzled him with an Outbound arrival, fed him a line and made sure his mind was dazed enough to take it, courtesy of some twenty-first century hallucinogens.

And it worked.

"When did this visitation arrive, sir?" Satyr asked, voice ripsaw sharp.

"It was two nights before the holy feast of St. Michael, in late September. I remember it clearly. I was in my study, praying. I summoned you the next day and put the plan in motion."

"We ordered you to acquire a *single* load of explosives," one of the Twenty protested. "You acted without our approval."

Aha. The sheep are getting cranky.

"At St. Michael's behest, I altered the plan. Neither you nor the Lead Assassin were to be made aware that you were doing God's holy work." The Ascendant chuckled dryly. "I found that quite entertaining."

Clearly, Satyr did not. He tightened his grip on the head of his cane, the only outward sign of his increasing anger. "What did this messenger look like?" he queried.

"Dressed much as you are. Black suit and such. He stood erect with the authority of God, and had a voice that reached to the ends of the earth."

Copeland? Was it possible?

"It fits," she heard from her shoulder. Cynda gave a minute nod.

"Did the archangel order my murder?" she asked.

"Yes, which Satyr badly bungled."

The Lead Assassin's knuckles went white on the cane.

"It was revealed to me that a holy battle would be enjoined and all must be purified by fire. The heathens, Gog and Magog, would be destroyed on the ninth day of the eleventh month."

"Neither I nor the Twenty were informed of this *holy* crusade of yours," Satyr said. He moved slowly into a new position, closer to the pack. Tobin stiffened, sensing the threat.

"No. It was my task alone," the Ascendant replied, waving a dismissive hand toward the group. "You would not have understood."

"That was unwise, Ascendant," one of them said, stepping forward.

Tobin was on the move in an instant, but Satyr was faster. He put himself between the assassin and the man who had dared to speak up.

"No, Tobin," Satyr said. "That's not the way it works."

"I can kill you," the junior assassin replied, his voice wavering.

"No you can't," Cynda sneered. "You couldn't even kill me."

Tobin made the mistake of looking toward her. The knife was at his throat before he could react.

"Think carefully about your future," Satyr advised. "You've had your warning." He gave him a shove toward their superior.

"Why did you order the murder of Adelaide Winston?" Cynda asked. The murmuring in the Twenty grew.

Those Revelations just keep coming.

The Ascendant didn't answer. The bold man stepped forward one more pace. "Why did you have the Intermediary killed?" he demanded.

"She was going to have me replaced," their leader replied. "I think you should take a lesson from that."

"You've lost, don't you see it?" Cynda chided.

"No! You have hampered our work, but this was just the opening trumpet blast. We will still succeed!"

"With what?"

"The explosives, of course. We still have thirty-seven half barrels and plenty of dynamite. We shall begin anew tomorrow morning. Tomorrow London will burn!"

"You can't do that," someone protested from the back of the group.

"I can. I shall," the Ascendant replied. "If you oppose me, you are my enemy." She gave that time to sink in.

"Just how many of the Twenty are required to vote the Ascendant out of office?" Cynda inquired.

"Seventeen," Satyr replied instantly.

Cynda did a quick head count. They only had sixteen.

There's got to be a way. "What does it take to become a member of the Twenty?"

"Nomination by another member," Satyr replied, "but you must be Transitive."

Damn. That was her final card in the game.

"Miss Lassiter?" Satyr asked. "A test, if you will permit me."

Another one? She could only nod, unsure of where he was headed.

"One of my assassins is in this room, and he is currently invisible. Point him out to me."

"This is nonsense!" the Ascendant protested. "No one can see a Virtual when they are hiding their form."

Cynda swiveled, looking for the characteristic bloom. There it was, standing near one of the wooden posts that supported the massive roof.

She pointed. "There."

"Archer. Reveal yourself."

The one named Archer materialized into view as gasps and frenzied whispering broke out amongst the Twenty.

"This has no bearing," the Ascendant insisted. "She is not one of us."

"If she can truly see us, she is as much Transitive as we are. A Perceiver ranks even higher than a Virtual, because they are so rare," Satyr countered smoothly.

Cynda could have kissed him for that, though that would have put her within knife range. There was no guarantee how long their truce might last.

"She is deceiving all of you. She is the Devil's whore, can you not see it?"

He'd gone too far. "Now wait a minute—" Cynda began.

The brave man took another step forward. "By tradition there must be a woman on the Twenty. I nominate this person," he called out, pointing toward her. "Do I hear a second?"

"You can't do that," the Ascendant growled. "She's not—"

"Second!" another voice called, suddenly full of confidence.

"Third!"

"We are now seventeen strong," the first man announced. "How do we vote on the future of the Ascendant? Yea for life, or nay for death."

There was a long pause. Cynda's heart thudded. If they backed down now, she was dead. They all were, if they took the time to think about it.

From near the front of the pack, a tremulous voice called out, "Nay!"

"Who was that? Was that Cartwright?" the Ascendant bellowed.

"Nay!" another shouted, while staring at the one named Cartwright like he'd just witnessed something extraordinary.

"Hastings? What is this treachery?" their leader demanded.

"I'm no traitor!" Hastings shouted back. "I did your bidding, and you repaid me by disbanding The Conclave. How dare you treat us so shabbily?"

"Your opinion does not matter. None of you. I will not stand for this."

Cynda bit her lip to stay silent. The Ascendant was digging his own grave. Another voice. "Nay!"

Emboldened, thirteen more nays erupted like gunshots, echoing off the warehouse ceiling in rapid succession. Then they all looked toward her.

Their superior waved Tobin forward and the assassin took a step closer in her direction. There was no other woman present. If he cut her down, the Twenty was out of options.

She hazarded a quick look at Satyr. The Lead Assassin didn't twitch a muscle. This was her battle.

"Will the *real* Archangel Michael put things right?" she asked.

Satyr's eyes widened at the use of his first name. "Yes," he replied.

"Then I shall do the same for him and his kind."

He nodded in respect, a pact made.

"Nay!" she shouted.

Cynda heard the shriek the moment she exited the double doors. Tobin or the Ascendant? If the young assassin had been stupid enough to get between Satyr and his boss, that was his decision.

"The King is Dead! Love live the King!" she called out.

Hopefully the new Ascendant would be less gullible.

—

What's left of the genius…

Cynda lit a single gas lamp in the hotel room, but she knew that all the light in England would not push back the darkness. Chris' death had wounded her in ways she'd not thought possible. It had only been a harbinger of Theo's loss. Emptiness enfolded her like a tomb, choking the air out of her lungs, pressing down on her like a mountain range.

Cynda laid his interface in her palm. This was guilt that would never fade—the kind that had haunted Theo about his beloved Mei. It would become part of Cynda now, like her skin. Any reminder of him would call up that failure. His dark eyes, the silken whoosh of the sword moving though the air, the tang of the spicy tea, the soft brush of his voice. She remembered the anticipation she'd felt each morning when he emerged from his rooms. The genuine friendship they'd forged.

She could see her path leading to this moment so clearly now. Chris had gently pried open her heart so she knew love when she saw it. Alastair and Jonathon had nurtured that hope, each in their own way. It had been Theo who'd showed her love could truly be hers, if she were willing to take the risk. She hadn't, at least not in time.

Unconsciously, she tightened her grip on the pocket watch. There was a noticeable click. Puzzled, she found it had opened, but not to reveal the dial. She pried open the new compartment. Inside was photograph of her, clad in period garb. He'd apparently taken it from one of the monitors in the chronsole room. Theo been carrying her with him all the time, and she'd never known.

Cynda dug for her own interface and hunted for that tiny catch. It was there, hidden unless you were looking for it. The compartment sprung open. Instead of her face, it was Theo's. He was clad in a suit, his handsome features reminding her of the last time she'd seen him. She lingered over the image. His athletic build, strong jaw, bright eyes and dark hair. Then she saw the inscription.

To my beloved Jacynda
There is no other in my heart,
Yours through time,
Theo

Her breath caught in her throat. She didn't fight the chest-wrenching sobs or the tears, but let them flow, wetting her hands, her chest, the interface.

She'd put history back on track, and it had destroyed them in the process.

"Why?" she cried. "I did what I was supposed to do. Why him?"

Silence. Time was known for that. It picked at your bones like a scavenger, yet demanded you worship it like an omnipotent god.

Her interface vibrated, and she jumped. It was a message from Hopkins, which meant GuvNet was finally online.

Get to the corner of Commercial and Whitechapel Street fastest way possible.

She wanted to ask if they'd found Theo, but it would take too long to open up a link and type out of the question. Instead, she wiped the tears out of her eyes, knelt, and made the hop.

Hopkins was pacing again, back and forth like a windup toy. "What took you so long?"

She wasn't going there. "You found him?"

He swiped a hand across his mouth in frustration. "Not yet. Copeland sent a ransom demand to TEM Enterprises—we give him Defoe or..." He didn't have to finish the sentence. "Everyone's going ballistic back home. That's why I need you."

"For what?"

"I've set the others out in a grid pattern around the borders of the East End. I need you to help. Maybe we can triangulate Morrisey's position using the interfaces."

"Theo doesn't have an active ESR Chip," she said, crestfallen.

"I know. They're too easy to find and remove. We've learned that the hard way." The Rover's interface buzzed. He flipped open the dial. "All right!" he crowed. "Now we get to work."

None of this made sense. "What's going on?"

"Morrisey's chip is passive. Klein wouldn't let him come here without one. It won't register unless it's activated by a specific code. Guv can do that once we're in position. As soon as the chip's active, we just need to zero in on it to locate your boss."

Her fragile hope collapsed. "Our interfaces are too short range for this, Hopkins. We only get about twenty feet in any direction."

"Guv will use our combined interfaces to form a low power transmission grid and they'll give us a boost from home. It'll take longer this way, bouncing the signals back and forth, but it'll work," he reassured. "Don't worry, Lassiter, we'll find him."

Hope struggled to its feet again, brushing off its bruised knees.

"Tell me what you want me to do."

CHAPTER TWENTY

Cynda studied the grid pattern on her watch dial, fidgeting while the painstaking process unfolded. Once the passive ESR Chip had been triggered, the five interfaces worked in unison to triangulate its position.

"This is taking forever," Mr. Spider groused.

He was right. Something told her that if Theo was still alive, he didn't have that much time. According to her interface, he was in a particular section of Whitechapel—an area she knew intimately. The dial changed again—down to a few streets.

"Screw this," she said, and performed a side-hop into a nearby alley.

The Angel Pub on Whitechapel High Street was packed, a raucous din cascading out the front door. Watching the dial's reaction, Cynda edged past the watering hole and farther down the street.

Then she stopped and waited until the dial updated. The location was behind her. She hurried back and then continued down the street. Again, the location was behind her. This time she turned left into Angel Alley, the noisome passage at the side of the pub. Like most of the alleys in Whitechapel, this one doubled as a latrine for those who wanted to make room for one more pint.

"This is really bad," the spider lamented, ducking under her shawl. His voice muffled, he added, "Makes all my eyes water."

Cynda covered her nose with a handkerchief, moving resolutely forward. The passage was narrow, bordered on both sides by brick buildings. *A perfect place for an ambush.* Only the thought of Theo kept her going.

Partway along, she passed a pile of refuse, a tattered tarp piled up against the wall. The dial was still catching up, recalibrating her position in relation to the other interfaces, bouncing signals between each of them and 2058's advanced technology. It was like trying to make a phone call to Mars using a piece of string and two coconuts.

"Come on!" she snarled. He was here somewhere. The grid pattern refreshed itself. She spun around and hurried back, only to stop at the trash pile. On impulse, she illuminated it with the glow from her watch. Three fingers were barely visible protruding from the edge of the canvas. Frantic, Cynda yanked back the tarp.

"Theo!" He was curled in the fetal position, his clothes shredded. She knelt and touched his hand. Cold.

One finger slowly uncurled in response.

"Yes!" She yanked the Dinky Doc out of her pocket and placed it against his neck. *Hypothermia. Profound shock. Multiple internal injuries.* Any other man would be dead, it was just his superior physical condition that had kept him alive this long.

"And you," the spider remarked, crawling out from under the shawl. "Love is a powerful reason to hang around."

Still, that edge was quickly fading. To her horror, Theo's body began to shift form, becoming what he might have looked liked as a boy. Then he changed to a face she knew well: *Chris.* Her heart nearly stopped.

"Not good," Mr. Spider said.

"No kidding." Transitives shifted like that when they were losing control, like Keats that night in the carriage. *When they're dying.*

She let the Dinky Doc do what it thought best.

"Come on, Theo." He shifted again, to her form, and then back to himself. "Come on, guy. You can make it."

Boot steps crunched in the passageway. She tensed.

"Lassiter?"

She signed in relief: it was Hopkins. "Here!" she called out. "I found him!"

The junior Rover skidded to a halt at her side, dropping to his knees. Between the two of them, they hauled Theo to a seated position. She winced at the sight. His left arm dangled uselessly. Blood had clotted on one side of his face from a jagged cut, and it appeared his nose was broken. Blood stained his shirt, his trousers, even his boots.

"Oh my God." Hopkins swallowed hard. "We need to get him home."

"No," she replied. "He's too cold for the transfer. We'll take him to Alastair. Once he's stabilized, then we can move him."

A low moan issued from the torn man's mouth. "Ja…cynda?"

She moved in close. "You got it in one."

"Cope…land," he murmured. "Neuro…"

"Neuro-blocker?"

A faint nod.

"That's how he got me," Hopkins explained. "I was trying to get my breath one minute, and the next I had a bullet in the heart. I can still hear him laughing."

Fury spiraled with her, coiling like a venomous snake. Copeland didn't have the guts to fight man to man, so he'd downed his victims with technology.

"He'll do the same to you if you're not careful," Mr. Spider advised, looking down from her shoulder at the wounded man.

We'll see.

"Why didn't Copeland just kill him?" Hopkins whispered.

To their chagrin, Theo overheard the question. "Don't know," he gasped. "Gave them money. Told them to…" He coughed hard. "throw me in Thames."

Like Chris.

"Put me in wagon. They got drunk. I escaped." He turned slowly toward her, trying to peer at her through his swollen eyelids. "Knew you'd…find me."

Her heart trembled. "Damned right. Stay alive, okay? You die on me, and I'll be really pissed."

The swollen eyelids blinked slowly, painfully. "Too much…paperwork." Her laughter was a trade-off for tears. Cynda pressed the Dinky Doc to his neck once more. The readings had marginally improved. At least he wasn't shifting in front of Hopkins.

More boots in the passageway as the other Guv agents arrived. Cynda was grateful when Hopkins took charge, ordering them to find some way to get the wounded man to Alastair's house.

"We'll get things squared away," the junior Rover assured her.

"Thanks."

He marched off, barking orders just like Klein.

As they waited, Cynda wrapped her shawl around Theo and cradled him her arms, trying to instill warmth. She cautiously brushed a kiss against his cheek, tears springing into her eyes. If things had played out differently, she would be holding his corpse right now.

"In case you've forgotten, we have unfinished business you and I," she whispered into his ear. That no longer seemed enough. After a thick gulp of air, she tried again. "I love you, Theo."

His bloodshot eyes opened, trying to focus on her face. He attempted a smile, cracking the dried blood on his cheeks. "Then it was…worth it."

"Only if you live." He nodded and closed his eyes again.

She gave him a hefty dose of painkiller, whispering encouraging words until he fell asleep. All the while, the ants raged inside her, demanding retribution.

Finding a coach this late at night hadn't been an option, so the Guv agents had commandeered a wagon. The driver didn't seem to mind, not with a shiny sovereign in his hand. Thanks to the medication, Theo was blissfully unaware of his surroundings. As they prepared to lift him, Cynda tugged on Hopkins' sleeve.

"Treat him like a corpse. We don't know who's watching. I want Copeland to think he's dead. And don't contact 2058 yet. We need to sort things out first."

The junior Rover nodded. "We'll get him settled, and then you and I will hunt down that bastard together."

"Works for me."

Hopkins stepped aside and instructed his men on the move. A minute or so later, they were carrying Theo down the passageway on the tarp. By then, a few of the pub's patrons had gathered on the street.

"Did the Ripper get 'im?" someone asked, deep in their cups.

"No," Hopkins replied, tersely. He tossed the man a coin with his free hand. "Have a pint in his honor, God rest his soul." The rest of the gawkers followed the beneficiary back into the pub to spend his newfound wealth.

Once Theo was in place, she covered him with a blanket one of the agents had scrounged. Hopkins and the others fanned out around the wagon like it was a funeral cortege, their faces grim.

Perfect.

As the wagon began to move forward, Cynda slipped back into Angel Alley and triggered her interface. Hopkins would see to Theo, guard him with his life. It was time to dangle the bait.

CYNDA BARELY MADE it back to her hotel room when her interface started buzzing. The message was from Hopkins, demanding to know where she'd gone.

She ignored it. Instead she logged onto GuvNet.

You find him? Ralph asked.

Yes. Before Ralph asked anything further, she typed, *One down, one to go. Send that message to everyone with an interface, no matter the time period. You understand?*

What does it mean? Ralph asked.

Don't worry about that. Make sure all the TPB Rovers receive it.

That's just egging them on.

I know what I'm doing. Leave my interface open to all incoming messages.

You're acting weird. What are you up to?

Setting the score.

SHE WAS PULLING on the trousers when her interface lit up. Another message from Hopkins. She blanked that one as well. *We're not ready yet, guy.*

Then came the one she'd been waiting for.

Morrisey went down like a girl. I expected better.

Copeland. "I knew you couldn't resist the bait." She triggered the watch so it would project the keyboard on the desk.

Morrisey for Rover One. That's the deal appeared in the air above her watch.

We've got TEM. You have no leverage.

There was a long pause.

Help Guv burn TPB. It's your only chance, she offered.

A longer silence. She began to wonder if she'd lost the connection.

When and where?

"I knew you'd bite." She gave him the instructions.

Come alone or I'm gone, was the response.

Deal. She closed the link, then began to log into GuvNet. Ralph needed to send her a few supplies, including a spare interface.

"You can't possibly believe he's going to turn himself in," Mr. Spider shouted inches away from her ear.

"Ouch! Easy on the eardrums, okay? I know he's not turning himself in. I just need to slap a time band on his wrist and he's in '058."

"You have to touch him to do that."

"I don't think that's going to be a problem," she replied. "He'll want to get close."

"Why are you so sure?"

She eyed her delusion. "I'm the reason the plot failed. As bad as he wants Defoe, he craves payback."

"Get Hopkins in on this," Mr. Spider warned. "You can't do this alone."

"I never intended to."

CHAPTER TWENTY-ONE

Like a military commander, Cynda chose familiar territory for the final battleground: Mitre Square, a poorly lit area in the City of London, surrounded mostly by warehouses. The last time she'd been here was nearly five weeks earlier, the night Kate Eddowes died. The night Cynda had actually seen the Ripper. There was still a stain where the woman's mutilated body had rested, despite someone's efforts to clean it away. Cynda laid a rose in the middle of the dark patch, remembering Kate's laughter.

It was fitting that it would end here.

She popped open her watch. Eleven thirty-two. The constable on duty had just left the square on his beat and would return in about thirteen minutes. If all went well, the site would empty on his next pass. If it went wrong, the Blue Bottle might discover a corpse or two.

Their enemy had amassed an impressively murderous resume, torturing Chris Stone, even trying to kill Hopkins, his own partner. Copeland had shot Defoe and beaten Theo nearly to death. Then just to cap his achievements, he'd tried to implement the fiery annihilation of history.

"Ambitious fellow, isn't he?" Mr. Spider commented from his usual perch. He peered into the gloom, his multiple eyes glowing. "If I were you, I'd hang him from a web, suck his bones dry."

"Too much work."

"Not for me," he boasted.

"Yeah, but he can't see you."

"That's definitely an obstacle," he admitted.

Cynda fidgeted. "Where's Hopkins? He should be here by now." To calm her nerves, she began her preparations. Stripping off her coat, she tossed it next to the Gladstone. The telescoping metal baton went into the back waistband of her trousers and the time band into a pocket. The spare interface was in that pocket, as well. If she was mortally wounded, Copeland would remove it so her body wouldn't automatically forward to 2058. As long as he didn't know about the backup interface, her plan might work.

Another check insured the e-skin patch was still attached her left forearm. If Copeland proved true to form, she'd need that medication to counteract the effects of the Neural-blocker. She set the patch for Hopkins on top of her coat.

Mr. Spider crawled down her arm to read the information on the outside of the patch. "Did you see these side effects? Euphoria, hyperventilation, auditory and visual hallucinations. That's just the short list," he reported.

"None of them are as ugly as being dead," she said, straightening up. "Hopkins? Where are you?" she grumbled. "We're about out of time, guy."

"Maybe he didn't get the message," Mr. Spider suggested.

"I sent it a half hour ago. Guv should have delivered it."

Silence from her shoulder.

"Hopkins wouldn't hang me out to dry," she insisted. "He's come through every time."

"Hopkins did. How about Klein?"

"Don't start with me." She flipped open her interface and gave it a test wind. It lit up. Accessing the messages showed the one she'd sent earlier in the evening, but still no reply.

Spirals of light began to appear in the square, the visual precursor to a transfer. She looked away so they wouldn't blind her. It had to be Copeland. She'd told Hopkins to arrive by foot.

"What are you going to do?" her delusion pressed. "Run or tough it out?"

Her mind told her to run for it. Copeland was too nasty for her to confront alone. Running away would give her and Theo a chance together.

"For how long?" she heard from her shoulder.

She saw the future with startling clarity.

"Copeland won't quit," she said. "He'll come after me. He'll go after Theo. He'll keep killing until he finds Defoe for his masters."

"That's the way I see it."

There was only one way to stop him—send him to Guv.

"It ends here."

Cynda pressed the medication patch on her bare arm, feeling the seal break. The infusion of the neural stabilizing solution burned like wicked fire, making her grimace. She rolled down the sleeve and buttoned the cuff. Almost immediately, her heart rate sped up and her eyeballs began to feel bigger than their sockets.

She executed a particular set of windings on her interface and then buried it under the coat. If she'd gotten the sequence right, it would create an audible recording of that happened in the square. If she died, the interface would automatically forward itself to Guv before Copeland would know it existed. Though it wouldn't save her life, his fate would be sealed.

The transfer effect began to fade. If the watchman at the Kearly and Tonge warehouse was paying attention, he'd just witnessed one helluva of a lightshow.

Cynda studied her enemy. In his left hand was the favored weapon of the Whitechapel killer—a double-bladed amputation knife. The blade was at least seven inches long.

"Pretty low tech," she said.

"Fits the scene, don't you think?" he called back, advancing toward her.

"Toss the knife away. You don't need any more charges when you get home."

"Who says I'm going home?"

"Me."

He cocked his head. "You're one ballsy bitch, I'll give ya that." He gestured with a free hand. "Where's your backup?"

"He'll be here soon."

A shake of the head. "Don't count on it. The message never made it. Time delayed. He'll get it after you're dead."

Just trying to psyche me. Unfortunately it was working.

"Why'd you kill Chris?" she asked, buying time for the medication to work. The way things were headed, the Neural-blocker was definitely on the menu.

"I didn't. Mimes gave him too much chloral hydrate by accident."

"It was an mistake?" she said, her concentration rattled.

Sensing her distraction, he took a few steps closer. "Stone wouldn't tell us where to find Defoe, so I figured if the kid fell off the radar, they'd send you."

Chris was bait?

Copeland edged sideways, closing. "You and Defoe were the only ones who could screw up the plan. I had my orders—deliver Rover One to my employers and you go back home a corpse. Problem solved."

"Why would the Futures work with you?" she asked, moving to the right, like a hand on a clock dial. They were about nine feet apart now. She dug out the baton, letting it open to its full length.

"I'm the guy who gets things done." He rolled his neck and shoulders, loosening up. "I'm amazed you found Morrisey," he said. "How many pieces was he in?"

That didn't deserve an answer. "The Ascendant's dead."

"Doesn't matter. We don't need him anymore."

His right hand came up. A second later, the Neuro-blocker hit her center chest.

Cynda staggered back, feeling it flare through her like a bolt of electricity. She panicked when her breath tightened. Then it eased. The medication was working. Forcing a deep inhalation, she laughed so loud it echoed in the square. *Euphoria.* They'd not been lying about the side effects.

Copeland gaped at her. "How the hell—" He fumbled to reset the device.

"Don't bother. It won't touch me." She beckoned to him again. "Put the toy away and let's head home."

For a half-second, she thought he'd give it another try. There was no guarantee extra hits wouldn't take her out. To her relief, he dropped the device into a pocket. Then he closed the distance between, playfully lunging at her. She jumping backward, overreacting, though he'd not been that close. The medication wasn't helping on that front.

"Work on his brain," Mr. Spider said. "Try to distract him."

"You're not doing very well, Copeland. You didn't blow up London and you can't find Rover One. I'd say your string is running out. You've only got one chance."

"Which is?"

"Come back to '058 and testify about the Null Mems."

Her enemy's face stiffened as he shifted stance. He twisted the blade in his hand, a nervous gesture. "Never heard of them."

"Then how did you know there was more than one?" Her foe's eyes narrowed. "How about Drogo?" she pushed.

"How'd you hear about him?"

"Chris had it his name on him when he died."

A snort. "Probably Mimes. He was always making notes. The kid probably got hold of one. I knew I should have checked his pockets."

"Why did Davies orphan the Null Mems in the time stream?" she pressed, playing a hunch.

"What better way to hide your mistakes?"

She took another step forward, though it put her closer to the blade. In response, it tilted in her direction, a taut line of lethal steel.

"How do you know about the crazies?" Copeland demanded.

"I'm one of them now. Didn't your puppet masters tell you that?"

His expression held, but she saw something flicker in his eyes. A hint of fear, maybe? *Yes.* The mercenary was afraid of her. Of what she'd become.

"That's a lie," he hissed. "You went into Rebound."

"I have the mark on my temple to prove it." She dropped her voice to a near whisper, beckoning with a forefinger like an eager lover. "Come closer, I'll show you."

He shifted his weight to his left foot, telegraphing his move. His right foot shot out, aiming directly for her chest. She forced her arm down, blocking the leg. Using the momentum, she tried to spin toward her opponent, to strike him in the ribs with the baton. It only brought her closer to the blade, which raked across her left cheek.

They broke apart, eyeing each other.

"The geek freak taught you some moves," he said, grinning.

"Among other things," she replied. The air between them began to sparkle and pulsate like a heartbeat. She blinked her eyes, but it didn't help.

"You give me Defoe and I'll make it easy for you," Copeland offered.

"Did you tell Morrisey that?" she asked, wiping the blood off her face.

"Sure did. He didn't listen."

Copeland casually shifted the weapon to his right hand. That changed everything. As if sensing her uncertainty, he began to test her defenses. Jab, move, jab and move again. A moment later, he kicked at her, high. She turned at the last presenting less of a target. The foot clipped her arm.

She recovered, but not fast enough. Another kick, square in the shoulder. The blade moved in and scraped down the metal baton, past her hand, slicing downward. For a second she could feel nothing, then a burning slice as he scored deep into her flesh the length of her forearm.

He rammed his shoulder into her, throwing her off balance. The baton slipped from her bloody fingers, tumbling onto the bricks.

Before she could move, Copeland was between her and the weapon.

His cold laughter echoed off the buildings. "That's better," he said, taking random swipes at her, like an actor in a play. "Where's Rover One?"

"Don't know!" she said, feeling the blood dripping from her fingers and the constant throb of the wound with each heartbeat. "No one does."

"Wrong answer."

When he grew near, she kicked out, hard, striking him in the leg. He danced back with a slight limp.

"Good one. You're making this fun."

Another swipe, too close this time. She kept trying to maneuver so she could retrieve the baton, but Copeland was always in the way.

"Forget it," her delusion urged. "Remember what Morrisey taught you."

At the mention of his name, the ants exploded into life with a throaty yell that nearly deafened her. Cynda moved forward, positioning her hands as she'd been taught. She centered herself, pulling that fury into her soul.

"Too easy," Copeland said. As he moved forward, seeking to press his advantage, she circled her hands. He watched her warily, trying to judge her next move.

When he lashed at her with the knife, she blocked the thrust with her left arm. Curling her right hand into her chest, she formed a fist, then shifted her weight onto her back foot.

At the last second she relaxed, drawing energy from ground. Spiraling it into her body as she moved her weight forward, her right fist shot out, the blow smashing into his chest at heart level. Copeland gave a choked gasp and then staggered backwards, stunned, the knife still firmly in his grasp.

"Bitch," he wheezed. He spat. It was bright blood.

Cynda fell back on instinct. The spin kick seemed to last for a century, a perfect arc of body, mind and ferocious will. Her boot caught him square above the diaphragm. In the stillness she heard an explosive grunt, then the thick snap of ribs. The knife tumbled to the ground with a clatter.

He took one step backward, then two, his face gray. Then he folded.

Cynda kicked the knife aside, retrieved her baton, and then knelt behind him, pulling him onto his back.

Do it! the ants screamed.

Despite the torment in her left arm, she applied the baton across his throat and heaved back with all her weight. Copeland's eyes bulged, his fingers clawing hopelessly at the metal. Feet hammered against the pavement. Time slowed. His face turned crimson, then blue-purple. There was the sharp tang of urine.

In the midst of it all, the scent of orange spice tea came to her, overpowering everything else in the square. She was in the pagoda, watching the sun rise. Theo's resonant voice echoed around her.

In the end, only you can decide who you truly are, what you stand for, what you hold most dear. No one else has that power, Jacynda. No one.

"Ah, hell." Cynda jerked away the baton, her hands shaking so hard it slipped to the ground. Her foe's chest moved like a broken sail, his breathing patchy. She retrieved the Dinky Doc and checked for damage: it was significant. Crushed ribs, bruised heart. The list went on. She let the device do what it could. Cynda hunted through his pockets for his interface. She didn't need the time band—he was too incapacitated to put up a fight. When she found the watch, she executed the windings and then secured it to his wrist. Closing his trembling fist around it, she staggered backward, dizzy.

Copeland's eyes widened in abject terror. He shook his head, trying to mouth words.

"Say hi to Klein for me," she told him.

Chris' murderer vanished in those pinwheels of light the Ascendant had found so compelling: a devil headed home. Guv would take it from there.

This one's for you, Theo.

CHAPTER TWENTY-TWO

It took some effort to adjust the Dinky Doc one handed. Once it was set, she pressed it against her neck and tried to relax. The dizziness evaporated, along with the ache in her chest. The wound would clot quicker now, but she still felt weird. It would take some time for the neural med to dissipate.

When she went to collect the knife, it was gone.

Cynda's eyes tracked upward. Satyr was caressing the blade reverentially.

"Well done. I am impressed," he remarked. "You sure you don't want a job as an assassin? I'm short a couple."

"How long have you been here?"

"Since the beginning." He spread his hands. "I couldn't resist following you. You're so entertaining, Twig."

Her attention remained on the knife. "Is there a new Ascendant?"

"Yes, they elected Cartwright since he cast the first vote. He's a very malleable soul. He'll live longer than most of them."

"What about the rest of the explosives?"

"The previous Ascendant was ever so kind to tell me where they're located right before he met his end. I dispatched an anonymous note to your Sergeant Keats. I would guess that at this very moment the cache is being retrieved."

Keats will be the hero, again. "Thanks."

Satyr nodded. He scrutinized the blade in his hand. "Fine, isn't it? I see why the Ripper liked it. Too unwieldy in my opinion, but then he was a novice."

"Novice?"

"All that hacking. Second-rate," he observed, shaking his head in disapproval. "The mark of a true psychopath."

"This from a guy who cut off Ahearn's balls?"

Satyr looked hurt. "He deserved that. I left him near Traitor's Gate for a reason."

Her puzzled frown made him explain, "He'd always had his eye on Fiona Flaherty, even though he was married. He kept after her. When she threatened to tell her father, Ahearn took his revenge. He followed her back to Effington's house and sold her out to Effington for a few coins. When she resisted Hugo's advances, he revealed her true identity to me."

"So that's why you chopped him up."

A nod. "He betrayed his employer's trust. He deserved what he got."

"But you told the Ascendant about Fiona."

The assassin scowled. "That was a mistake. He promptly ordered me to kidnap her as leverage against her father. I did not approve of that. It was not proper."

"Didn't fit your code of honor?"

When there was no reply, she realized that's exactly what he meant.

The last of adrenalin bled away. Suddenly she felt washed out, like she hadn't slept for months. She was too tired to fight anymore. She just wanted to see Theo.

A triple beep came from her interface, reminding her that the rest of the world was still on schedule. "The constable is due here in three minutes. Does our truce still hold?"

"Certainly, Twig."

Cynda nodded. Taking him at his word, she collapsed the baton. Satyr dropped the knife and gave it a kick; it halted at her feet. She struggled to jam it in inside the Gladstone. Leaving it behind would open up an entirely new branch of Ripper investigation.

"Allow me." To her unease, Satyr stepped to her side, knelt and inserted the knife into the bag. She threw the medication patch inside and he snapped the bag shut.

Without a word, he pulled his handkerchief, then expertly tied it around the wound. It slowly soaked up the blood. "Best I can do," he said. "Looks very nasty."

As she stood, she scooped up the coat. Her interface sat open on the ground. He picked it up and for a moment, she thought he intended to keep it. Surely he knew what it was. Instead, he handed it to her.

"Yours, I believe."

"They're going to need a new female on the Twenty."

"Shouldn't be a problem." She clicked the stem to halt the recording.

When Satyr helped her with her coat, carefully positioning it to allow for her injured arm, their eyes met.

"We're kindred spirits now," he said, his voice curiously mellow. "You were one heartbeat away from murder. Revenge was within your grasp, yet you backed away. You kept your humanity."

"It was very close," she admitted.

"It always is."

As Cynda put the baton into an inside pocket, it thunked against the spare interface. She made the decision in a heartbeat. She tossed the pocket watch to Satyr. He deftly caught it, blinking in confusion.

"You need a Dinky Doc?"

"No. The clueless Rover was so kind as to lend me his."

He clicked open the dial and then looked back up. She had just given him the means to go anywhere, any time.

"They can follow me if I use this," Satyr replied, gesturing toward the interface.

"It's untraceable. When the heat gets too much, go somewhere they can't find you."

He stared at her, confusion etched on his face. She could imagine what was parading through his mind.

"Why?" he asked.

"I'm feeling generous," she joked.

"Tell me why," he repeated, more emphatically this time.

"Because not all monsters are evil."

—

Saturday, 10 November 1888

Alastair looked up when the clinic door swung open. One of Hopkins' somber men stepped inside, allowing a figure to pass. It seemed frail by comparison to the bulky guard.

"Jacynda?"

He was across the room an instant, taking inventory as he moved. She looked unnaturally pale, her eyes hollow. There was a cut on her cheek. Then he noticed how she was cradling her left arm. The fingers on that hand were thickly coated with dried blood.

He put an arm around her waist and guided her toward a chair.

"No. Must see Theo first," she murmured.

"You are in shock and need—"

"Theo first," she repeated.

He gave in and took her into his office, where the patient rested on the cot under a mound of warmed blankets. She sank into the chair slowly, oblivious to anything but him.

"How is he?" she asked, her voice more fragile now.

"Much better. He's warming up, bit by bit. I've stabilized him as much as I can. Your people will have to do the rest."

Jacynda leaned over and placed a kiss on the patient's forehead, then murmured something in his ear. Then she looked up at Alastair.

"Now you can work on my arm."

ALASTAIR CLEARED HIS throat. "Tell me if you can feel me touching each of your fingers in turn," he ordered. He carefully performed his exam, taking care not to hurt her any further.

"They're fine," she said. "How's Keats?"

"Doing as well as expected. I received a note about an hour ago—he's located the remainder of the explosives and is in the process of moving them to a secure location."

Cynda smiled to herself: Satyr had truly come through. "That's excellent news. Will it save Keats' job?"

"Not from his perspective. He's already given the chief inspector his resignation."

"I'm truly sorry to hear that."

The door that led to the parlour swung open as Mrs. Butler pushed her way in. She was carrying a tray of instruments.

"I boiled them as you asked, sir."

"Thank you, Mrs. Butler. Is Davy here?"

"No. Still out sellin' papers. I bet he's making a fortune, what with all that went on today." She looked at Cynda, then at her arm. "Good heavens."

"When he comes back, I need to send him out for some supplies," Alastair explained. "I wasn't anticipating a full house tonight."

Cynda smirked and that earned her a raised eyebrow.

The moment the door closed behind the housekeeper, Hopkins strode in. Once he was sure only the doc was present, he let loose.

"Why did you take off on us?" he demanded. "What the hell have you been up to?"

Alastair started at the oath, and shot him a frown.

Cynda eyed the junior Rover. "I was busy sending Copeland home."

"Home? You caught him?" he blurted.

"Yes." She delivered her own frown. "So where were you?"

"What do you mean?"

"I sent you a message asking you to join the party. You never showed."

The Rover's angry faded. He flipped open his watch, twisting the dial, then shook his head. "There's nothing here."

She pulled her interface out with the free hand and offered it to him. He accessed the files. "I didn't get this." His interface vibrated.

Hopkins raised his head. "No, no, he knew I wanted to be in on the capture." Then he swore. "The message just arrived."

She shrugged one shoulder. "Well, it's done. He's at Guv."

"Copeland's finally ours," Hopkins muttered. Then he smiled. "Thanks. I owe you one. I can't wait to be there for the trial."

Cynda turned her attention to the doc. "So how bad is it?"

"You're very fortunate there is no muscle or tendon damage," he responded. "Still, it will need suturing."

"Then sew it up." She'd already dosed herself with the Dinky Doc. The pain level was manageable.

"You'll have a nasty scar if I do."

She looked down at the long slash. "That's okay." *I want to remember this night for the rest of my life.*

Despite the painkiller, she winced when he applied the disinfectant. Raw acid would have been more welcome.

"That's probably what he's using," Mr. Spider joked. He was positioned on Theo's pillow, feet tucked under him like a housecat.

Hopkins was getting itchy. "What about Morrisey?"

"We'll send Theo home after the doc is done playing seamstress."

"Stop moving," Alastair grumbled.

"Sorry." The tugging on the skin continued as he redoubled his efforts with the needle. Despite the Dinky Doc, it stung, making her eyes water.

"You done yet?"

Alastair glowered in response.

Apparently not.

OBLIVIOUS, THEO SLEPT through her arrangements. Cynda set his interface, clipped the chain to his wrist and placed it in his hand. Then she wound a bandage around it, tying it off so he wouldn't lose contact with the watch. No contact, no 2058. Finally, she gave him a kiss, knowing he'd not feel it. The hole in her chest grew wider.

Hopkins knelt next to the bed. "Klein wants you to stay here, make sure everything's secure. He needs time to settle things down, start proceedings against TPB. If you return now, it'll just muddy the waters."

"What about Morrisey?"

"TPB won't touch him, not in his condition," Hopkins reassured. "Not once they realize Copeland is to blame for all this."

Not all of it. "Did Klein say anything about him?"

"No and I didn't ask. I didn't want to tip our hand to TPB. I don't think they can listen in our interface traffic, but you never know."

She nodded. "I'll stay here until I get the all clear."

The young man gently placed a hand on her uninjured arm. "Thanks. Having Copeland out of circulation means a lot me."

Cynda nodded, too tired to talk. Instead, she rose and moved out of the way as he clicked Theo's watch shut.

10 ... 9 ... 8

"Let's go!" he ordered. Hopkins and the three other Guv agents vanished. The transfer effect began to form around Theo. Then he was gone.

I'll be home soon, now that I have a reason.

"I'll never grow accustomed to that," Alastair said, shielding his eyes from the doorway. "How soon will we know if he made it in good shape?"

"Soon." *I hope.* She gnawed the inside of her lip raw until her interface lit up. *Now you owe me three beers.*

"What does that mean?" Alastair asked, looking over her shoulder.

"It means everything's going to be fine," she whispered.

INTERMITTENT SLEEP, ENDLESS side-hops, the chaos of the last twenty-four hours. They all came to collect their bill. It was a big one.

At Alastair's suggestion, Cynda pulled herself up the stairs to a spare room, tossed her clothes in random directions, then poured cold water into the basin to remove the remaining blood. Once that was completed, she collapsed into the bed. The feather mattress enfolded her like a mother's arms, and she sighed into its softness. Stuffing her interface under the pillow was her last conscious act.

HER INTERFACE WOKE her, buzzing incessantly until it dragged her out of her zombie-like state. Then it went quiet. It started up again, nagging at her like an electronic spouse.

"What do you want?" she snarled, digging under the pillow. "I've done my bit. Go away!"

More buzzing, followed by something that sounded like one of those old British cop cars. The two tones wavered back and forth, sawing away at her nerves.

Cynda hauled herself to the small desk in the room and logged onto GuvNet. As the screen lit up, she groaned and trudged over to the door, locking it and stuffing a sock in the keyhole. Mrs. Butler, bless her soul, might feel inclined to bring her guest some tea at the wrong moment.

The screen erupted into a blur of type. None of it mentioned Theo. Maybe that was a good sign.

Where have you been?

She had no desire to play nice. *Who's this?*

Who do you think? Is your interface defective?

Had to be Ralph. *Interface fine. Rover isn't. No sleep.*

Suck it up. We got problems.

Is TEM okay?

Healing. Hopkins gave us a full report.

So what's the problem?

The screen lit up. *So where is he?*

"He" had to mean Copeland. *Look under the rocks. I sent him to Guv.*

Guv doesn't have him.

That broke her haze immediately. *Transfer at 11:40 or so on 9 November 1888.*
There was a long pause. Too long for good news.

"Come on, guy, this century, will you?" she complained. "I want some more sleep. I've earned it."

"We both have," her delusion added and then yawned. She leaned back in the chair and started to doze when the response came through.

No go. Transfer diverted.

To where?

There.

Anyone else would have panicked. Cynda let out another yawn. The last she'd seen of Copeland, he was no shape to harm anyone. He wasn't going to get better overnight, especially not in Victorian London.

Cyn? Ralph prompted.

I'll look around. "When I'm damn good and ready." Or they could send Hopkins. Why did it always have to be her?

A series of numbers started flying across the screen.

And that meant? she typed blearily.

Coordinates. It's where he landed in '88. Use your interface to pinpoint them.

You can't tell on your end?

Coordinates still wonky here. Can't recalibrate until Guv says it's okay.

Cynda dug around in the room until she could find something to write on, and then made note of the numbers, not quite sure how to store them in the device.

Got them. I'll be in touch.

TEM says to tell you two words: unfinished business. Whatever that means.

She smiled. *Message received.*

Though she'd not been expecting it, the heal shield arrived a few minutes later, wrapped inside a piece of cloth. She immediately applied the shield to her arm. It covered the wound, sped the healing and cut the pain, while looking remarkably like her own skin.

"Thanks, Ralph," she said, tucking her sleeve around the nearly invisible shield. When it finally evaporated the wound would be healed, though the suture marks would still be there. That was okay.

She set the interface to rouse her out at eight in the morning. Until then, she was off-duty.

The coordinates Ralph had given her turned out to be quite specific. London Bridge. As she stood near the railing, feeling the breeze against her face, she checked the interface dial again.

"Another three hundred feet out." Which put the location in the middle of the Thames.

Copeland wasn't stupid. He knew not to transfer into water. That was a death sentence.

"He had no choice, I suspect," someone observed.

Anderson. He hadn't been there a moment ago.

"So how can you just appear in the middle of a bridge without anyone thinking that's weird? Except me, of course."

"You'd be amazed what we humans will ignore," he replied.

She peered down into the water. "I sent Copeland to…" she waved to indicate the future. "Why did he bounce back here?"

"His *future* bosses did not appreciate his failure, so they diverted him. It's a very unpleasant way of dealing with failure."

"That's why he looked so terrified," she murmured. "I figured it was because he'd have to face Klein."

"The Government was the least of his problems."

"Who are those *future* bosses?"

Anderson leaned against the rail, watching a boat glide underneath the bridge. "We're not particularly sure. It's much like here—you can't quite put your finger on who is pulling the strings."

"Why didn't you just tell Morrisey about the coins in the first place?"

"Some things we knew, some things we didn't. As it was, we've done a lot of meddling here, more than we probably should have."

"What sort of meddling?"

He looked over at her. "I was with Inspector Ramsey throughout the Keats' investigation. Though he didn't need much help, I made sure he was aware of any clues he'd missed. I was the one who persuaded the academics to loan you their interfaces, and I convinced the police commissioner to allow you and Morrisey to handle the bombs in the East End."

"That's a *lot* of messing around" she said, astounded. "I thought that was a no-no."

"It used to be, but now we seem to be involved in the time stream more than ever. I can't say I like that."

"We?"

Anderson shook his head. "I've told you too much as it is."

That was fair. "What about Defoe?"

"His mind will never be right again. He must stay in our time. We'll keep him safe."

"Theo isn't going to like that," she protested.

"We know, but there's no other choice. We have no idea why our counterparts want him so badly. Until we do, he's at risk."

Farther downstream, a boat departed from a landing, heading to the far shore.

She had to ask the question. "Is this how my timeline was supposed to fall out?"

Anderson shook his head. "Much like the doctor and the sergeant, your life is now on a new thread."

"It was Chris' death, wasn't it? Things felt wrong from that point on."

Anderson nodded. "His accidental death triggered a time swell that rippled through the stream."

And brought Theo and I together.

She straightened up. "Do me a favor—make sure Defoe attends Adelaide Winston's funeral."

The Future opened his mouth in protest, but she waved him off. "That's not negotiable, Mr. Anderson. That's what you owe *me*."

There was a deep sigh. "I will see what I can do."

"Thank you." Cynda relaxed, gazing out at the Thames. "Why the Armageddon scenario?"

"It was the opening they needed to replace some of the key figures in Victorian politics with shape-shifters. It would have been easy during the upheaval. There are some who believe the Transitives should reveal themselves before 2062. That's a mistake, of course, because it significantly alters history."

"So does London burning like a Yule log. Why not let the shifters come out?" she insisted. "It's going to happen anyway."

Anderson shook his head. "The outcome of the Second World War would not have been to our advantage. They play a key part in overthrowing the Axis powers. If they are revealed now, that would not happen. Changes would ripple upstream." Anderson paused, pitching his voice lower. "It was not a decision we made lightly."

"What about the Null Mems?"

"Those are your problem. We have enough of our own."

"Thanks," she muttered.

"What matters to us is that our foes have lost this round. There will be other plots, though I suspect not in '88. This patch of time is significantly more stable now."

"Lots of good people got hurt," she said.

"Far too many."

Then Anderson was gone.

She leaned against the bridge railing, staring down into the water below. Copeland's new home.

So where will you come to rest?

CHAPTER TWENTY-THREE

Sunday, 11 November 1888
Sandringham Estate

They alighted from the carriage, discomfort translating into organized grooming: shooting of cuffs, straightening of collars, smoothing of hair.

As they waited, Chief Inspector Fisher seemed to be off in his own thoughts. Inspector Ramsey stood next to him, mute, clearly uncomfortable. Keats kept pulling on his collar. Even Alastair was struggling with his nerves. One did not meet the future King of England every day.

"Posh digs," Keats observed.

Ramsey craned his neck upward. "I wonder how many sweeps they need to clean all those chimneys."

"I could retire here," Fisher said, a bit louder. "I wonder if they'd mind if I just took up a few rooms. Probably wouldn't miss them."

More tentative smiles.

"This way, sirs," a servant announced, guiding them forward with gloved hands and a noiseless tread.

They found themselves in a room with an intricately carved minstrel's gallery. It promised grand balls and the sound of gay music.

"Well, gentlemen, our moment has arrived," Fisher announced quietly.

A door opened to admit His Royal Highness, the Prince of Wales. Behind him was a tall, gaunt young man who wore a high collar. As he took his place near the prince, Alastair realized it was the Duke of Clarence, second in line to the throne. The young man's disinterested expression immediately caught his notice.

"Your Royal Highnesses," Fisher said, bowing. All the others followed suit.

"Ah, you must be Chief Inspector Fisher," the Prince of Wales replied.

"Yes, Your Royal Highness. With your permission, I would like to present Inspector Ramsey and former Detective-Sergeant Keats. They were instrumental in preventing the anarchist's attack."

Alastair felt a pang of regret that Jacynda and her Mr. Morrisey weren't here. They'd been as much a part of the effort as the rest of them.

"Good day, gentlemen," the prince replied.

"Your Royal Highness, this is Dr. Alastair Montrose. He assisted us in our efforts. If I may say, his efforts are proving a boon to Scotland Yard."

"I have heard of you, Doctor," the prince replied. "You assist another physician... Bishop, I believe his name is."

"Yes, Your Royal Highness. I am most honored to work with such a learned man... and with Scotland Yard."

"I read your testimony in newspaper, how you determined that Mr. Keats here was not of sufficient stature to have murdered that woman." The prince nodded his approval. "Stellar work, I must say. New ways are upon us, gentlemen. Don't you agree, Eddy?"

His son blinked and then nodded. "Indeed." He seemed bored by the conversation.

"Our enemies are very clever," the prince continued. "This whole affair speaks of dangers the like of which we can only imagine." He eyed Fisher. "I understand you are taking retirement, Chief Inspector. Is there no way you can be persuaded to remain at your post?"

"I am honored, your Highness, but I am ready to hand off the reins and, frankly, I believe Home Office is ready for my departure. Inspector Ramsey will be taking my position. He will do a fine job."

Ramsey shifted his feet, uncomfortable with the praise.

"I am sure he shall." The prince turned toward Keats. "And you, sir, to what will you turn hand to now that you are no longer with the Yard?"

"I have been encouraged to become an agent of private enquiry, Your Royal Highness. In that way, my training will not go to waste."

"Excellent. Miss Lassiter speaks highly of you, sir, and your staunch spirit during the trial bears strong witness to your honor. I shall keep you in mind, lest we have an issue of a private nature that would need such talent as yours."

Keats swallowed in surprise.

At a gesture from the Prince of Wales, a footman bustled up.

"Gentlemen, you have the gratitude of the Queen and the country for your unfailing service. God knows how many would have perished if you had not risen to the call in this time of need." He solemnly handed each a box and an envelope. "A token of our appreciation."

They bowed in unison.

"Might you have time for a whiskey?" the prince asked.

"Well, certainly, Your Royal Highness," Fisher said, astonished at the offer. "We would be very honored."

"Then come along. I just received some fine cigars in honor of my birthday. Let's break them out, and you can tell us about this ordeal. It sounds most hellish."

An hour later, warmed by the excellent spirits, the quartet loosened their collars as the carriage rattled toward the train station.

"It *has* been a week, I must say," Keats observed. "I'm nearly hanged, then almost blown to bits, and then I get to sip spirits with the next monarch."

Ramsey pulled a frown. "Not to speak ill, but I don't think the Duke of Clarence is the brightest hatchet in the woodshed."

"I have to agree," Fisher allowed. "He does not possess his father or his grandmother's intelligence. Eddy is, in fact, quite dull. *Collars and Cuffs* will not be an excellent ruler."

"We get the monarchy we deserve," Keats chided. "If the line had continued through the Scots—"

"Keats!" Fisher scolded.

"It's the truth, sir. The Germans are, well—"

"Not English," Ramsey finished.

Fisher chortled. "I think that's the first time I've ever seen both of you agree on a subject."

"Don't worry, it won't last," Keats assured him. "Not once I begin accepting cases the Yard can't solve."

Ramsey eyed him. "Just mind you don't get in our way, Mister."

"Oh, I'm sure I shall on more than one occasion," Keats chirped brightly, "if nothing more than to get up your nose, *Chief* Inspector. How else will I amuse myself?"

"Ah, good, that's more like it," Fisher exclaimed. "I had thought the world was coming to an end." He gave Alastair a concerned look. "You're very quiet, Doctor."

Alastair's eyes caught Keats'. "A bit too much whiskey, I think."

ONCE THEY WERE alone, and ensconced in Alastair's parlor, Keats broached the subject. "So what's bothering you?" he asked, polishing his medal on a sleeve for the second time, obviously proud of his achievement. "You were pretty quiet on the return journey."

Instead of answering, Alastair slit open his envelope. "Seventy-five quid. Very nice."

Keats checked his. "The same. That'll help with expenses." He put away the check. "What was going on at Sandringham?" he pressed.

"There was one of us *en mirage* with the princes.'"

Keats' eyes snapped up. "Which one?"

"I'm not sure. Could have been one of the servants for all I know."

Keats slumped back in his chair. "A shifter in the royal household. Where else are they?"

"I would expect *us* to be everywhere," Alastair said.

"As you say."

"I'm curious—where is Flaherty now? Has he gone back to Ireland?"

"He's out of the country. Left rather suddenly," Keats replied. "Clancy Moran, as well. They seemed to have come into a bit of money and decided to start over in America."

Alastair eyed his friend. "Did you have a hand in that?"

"Yes." Keats smiled. "Aiding and abetting anarchists. How far the mighty have fallen."

The doctor nodded his approval. "Well done, my friend."

Keats sighed. "Despite everything, Flaherty was still going to blow up the Crystal Palace. He'd heard about that Irish girl who was murdered in Whitechapel, and thought it was his daughter. He believed his enemies had gotten their revenge."

"What kept him from doing it?"

"Someone told him it was Mary Kelly who died. He said knew her, that they'd been together a couple of times."

Alastair shook his head. "I don't know if I ever met her. I might have, at the clinic. I saw so many."

Keats sighed. "I liked Mary. I'd give her money every now and then. She was a nice sort. I didn't know she'd seen me that night in Whitechapel."

"What?" Alastair asked, puzzled.

"Oh, sorry, I thought you knew that. She came forward, after the trial," Keats explained. "According to Kingsbury, she made her statement right before the case was reviewed by the Lord Chief Justice."

"That was a risky for her."

Keats shook his head. "The Irish wouldn't hurt her. Flaherty spread the word that she wasn't to be harmed."

"Then it was the Ripper," Alastair replied. "I had hoped we'd see no more of him."

"I'm not so sure it was his handiwork," Keats said.

Alastair cocked his head. "Who then?"

"I know this is going to sound outlandish, but I think her murder was retribution, a message, as it were. You cross us, we'll destroy you. They couldn't get to Paddy, so they came after her."

"Good Lord," Alastair exclaimed. "What a horrifying thought."

"Perhaps someday, my friend, we'll know the truth of all of this," Keats said, rousing himself from his melancholy. "But first, I must find new lodgings. My dear landlady is pleased at my acquittal, but uncomfortable with my presence. I can't blame her what with all the notoriety. Any suggestions for my next abode?"

"Well, Annabelle's Boarding House is quite reasonable and the food is hearty, but you are accustomed to more space than she offers." Alastair thought for a moment, then snapped his fingers. "I have the perfect place."

"Where? Is it near here?" Keats asked.

"Very," Alastair replied, beaming. He pointed upward. "It's the room you're in right now. You can pay me what you feel it is worth. Mrs. Butler will see your laundry is done and cook your meals as needed."

Keats shook his head immediately. "No need to trouble yourself. I can find another place."

"I'd like the company, my friend, and the income will help as well."

"I see." Keats puzzled on the offer for a few moments. "It *would* be quite pleasant. I've missed our talks."

"Well then, why not?"

"We'd be like Holmes & Watson," Keats said impishly.

Alastair frowned. "I am no Watson, and you are most certainly not Sherlock Holmes."

"Why not?" Keats challenged. "I just helped solve a most baffling case."

"You're smarter than Holmes, for one."

"That remains to be seen. Yes, I shall accept your offer. If you don't mind, I shall move in tomorrow afternoon, if that will suit."

"That will be fine. Mrs. Butler will help you as I shall be out. Evelyn has invited me for tea."

Keats leaned forward. "How's that going?"

"Slowly. We have a lot unsaid between us."

"So don't say it. Just kiss her," Keats urged. "That always does the trick."

"You're sounding more like your old self, my friend."

"Maybe." Rising, Keats tucked away the medal and the check in a trouser pocket. "I just realized—after I move, I shall have to find a case. I've never had to do that before. They just came to me."

"I'm sure you'll be kept busy."

"I hope so. I'm fond of eating regularly." Keats awkwardly stepped forward and offered his hand. "I owe you so much, my friend. Not everyone would want to be associated with someone once accused of murder."

Alastair waited for him to make the connection.

Keats colored in embarrassment. "Oh, I've put my foot it in now. We are birds of a feather, are we not?"

Alastair rose and shook his hand in a firm grasp. "I cannot think of a better friend than you, Jonathon."

"Well, either way, we're stuck with each other," Keats said. As he marched the hallway, he called out jauntily, "Good evening, Watson!"

"Go away, Keats."

—

Monday, 12 November 1888
Scotland Yard

Fisher looked up as Ramsey entered the office. "Ah, there you are, *Chief Inspector*. Congratulations, Martin. I hear it's official."

"Thank you, sir." Ramsey shook his head. "I kept thinking you'd change your mind. Not that it would have troubled me if you had."

"No. I'm ready to go. I may have always been partial to Keats, but I knew in my heart you had the potential for this job. These last few weeks you withstood immense pressure and conducted one of the most thorough investigations of your career. You are worthy of becoming Chief Inspector, Martin. I have no doubt of it."

Ramsey looked away for a moment and then back, his eyes glassy. "It was a damned nightmare."

"One of the darkest I've ever seen," Fisher agreed. "We nearly hanged an innocent man just to keep a sybaritic few safe from public condemnation. That's not why I became a copper."

"What will you do, sir?" Ramsey asked.

"Jane and I are moving to Brighton, near her family. I fancy a house near the water. It's idyllic there. No Home Office toadies or police commissioner watching my every move."

"Your good wife will be," Ramsey quipped.

Fisher chuckled. "Yes, she has already said that I must acquire a hobby, a pursuit that keeps me occupied. She is accustomed to running her own household, and would not appreciate a retired chief inspector's interference."

Ramsey quirked a bushy eyebrow. "So how long will it be before *they* start pulling my chain?"

"Not long. It's been embarrassing for them, what with Warren's resignation and the prince putting pressure on them about Keats. You'll have a lot on your plate."

"Do you think Hulme killed himself?"

Fisher shook his head. "No, but that's one avenue of investigation you should not pursue."

"I don't like the notion that someone can murder a copper and get away with it."

"Or frame one, for that matter."

Ramsey sighed. "Where will I find someone to take my place when the time comes?"

Fisher smiled. "That's your problem, Chief Inspector, not mine. Not anymore."

Ramsey offered his large hand and Fisher shook it earnestly.

"Watch your back, Martin. If you need advice, contact me. Visit me sometime during the next week. We'll dine together. There's a private conversation we must have. You don't know all the players in this game, but I'll tell you what I know. Just not here."

"Does it have something to do with those coins?"

"Those remain a mystery."

Ramsey nodded. "What about Keats?"

"I suspect you and he will bump heads soon enough."

"That I don't doubt," the new chief inspector replied.

"Let me clear out my things and you can move in."

"Take your time, sir. I'm in no hurry. The sooner I'm in that chair, the sooner they're at my throat."

—

"If you would prefer not to do this, I am willing to view the body," Keats offered, clearly puzzled by her reticence. "Just give me a description and I'll see if it's him."

"No. You'll just be guessing," Cynda replied.

"I hadn't expected you to find this so difficult," he noted sympathetically.

"It's not. It's just that … I remember Chris. I had to identify him just like this." Cynda his arm. "If it's him, I'll need a couple seconds alone with the body."

"As you wish."

This morgue attendant seemed a bit more on the ball than the last one she'd encountered. Keats did the talking, explaining how Cynda was looking for a lost relative and that when she'd read the article in the newspaper, she felt the need to view the body that had been fished out the Thames just this morning.

"Who ya missing?" the man asked.

"My cousin," she said, trying to sound suitably upset.

"What's he look like?"

She told him. He heaved himself out of the chair and waved them forward into the room.

The form was covered by the usual gray sheet.

"Ain't pretty, miss. Been in the water a few days. Doesn't do nothin' for 'em."

"I know. Go on."

Keats took hold of her arm as the sheet was drawn back. Cynda winced and wrinkled her nose at the smell. Unlike Chris, who had been found very quickly, this body had been given the full Thames treatment. One leg was at an odd angle, chunks of flesh were missing. The bloating had begun, but the face was still recognizable. A massive bruise sat just below his chin.

She gave Keats a look. He took the hint.

"Who found him?" he asked, leading the attendant a few steps away.

"Couple of watermen. They hauled 'im in."

Alf and Syd, maybe? She hoped that was the case.

Cynda leaned closer. Carefully touching the Dinky Doc to the corpse's neck, she held it in place until she got the post-mortem readings she needed. *Water in lungs.* Copeland had landed in the Thames and drowned like a rat. No matter how hard she tried, there was no sympathy.

"You family, too?" the attendant asked.

"No, I'm an agent of private inquiry," Keats replied.

"A what?"

"Sort of a detective. Did this fellow have any personal possessions on him?"

"Nothin'."

So much for his interface. If Guv wants it, they can send someone else to find it.

"Is he the one, Miss?" the fellow called out.

Yeah, he's the one. "No," she said, turning away, holding a handkerchief to her face, mostly to stifle the smell. She walked hurriedly toward Keats. "I need air," she said, trying to sound breathlessly feminine.

"Thank you, sir," her companion said, dropping a coin in the man's outstretched hand.

Cynda jammed the handkerchief back into her pocket the moment they reached the street. Copeland had met a nasty end, killed for his failure. If no one claimed his body, he was headed for a pauper's grave. She saw no reason to alter that.

✝

CHAPTER TWENTY-FOUR

Tuesday, 13 November 1888
Highgate Cemetery

Cynda carefully made her way down the steps of the carriage, mindful of her full skirts. She could have come by hansom, but in her mind that would not have shown her respect for the woman they would bury this evening. As was proper, she'd chosen the finest black mourning dress with a full veil. It had only taken a quick trip to the venerable Jay's of Regent Street to acquire everything she needed to pay tribute to Adelaide Winston. If nothing else, the Victorians were masters of grief.

"Come back in about an hour," she called up to the driver.

"As you wish, miss," he said, tapping his hat. "Sorry for your loss."

So am I. Though Cynda had only met Adelaide Winston once, it was easy to discern the power the woman held over Harter Defoe. A strong woman navigating the waters of a man's world. She'd been worthy of his adoration.

She took her time walking toward the gravesite, passing mausoleums and gravestones alike. This would be an unusual funeral. Most did not occur at dusk, and few involved a top London courtesan. The funeral notice had appeared in the paper, black-edged, but dignified. Even in death, standards must be upheld.

As Cynda approached the final resting place, she noted only a handful of Victorians present. It appeared most of Adelaide's admirers were more concerned about maintaining their reputations than bidding her farewell. Still, in years to come the occasional bouquet of roses or bottle of sherry might be propped up against the headstone as a token of respect, and of fond memory.

Anderson had kept his word. To her relief, Harter Defoe stood at the side of the grave, his face pale and his coat rumpled. The figure next to him was immaculate: top hat, black suit, black gloves and cravat. The epitome of Victorian mourning. As she moved closer, he tipped his hat in respect.

"Theo," she said softly. *Thank God you're here.*

"Jacynda," he replied solemnly. Their hands briefly touched, then withdrew. To do more in front of Defoe would be thoughtless.

Robert Anderson stood on the other side of the grave and he nodded at her. She recognized a few of the other mourners: Adelaide's butler, for one, and a few other well-dressed women. *Probably rivals.*

The funeral went as any other. The priest spoke of redemption, of God's paradise even for a woman who had tempted others onto the path of sin. As the sun vanished behind the buildings in the distance, Cynda saw no paradise, no redemption—only a man who had lost his way.

Through it all, Defoe remained silent, his eyes fixed upon the grave. When the customary shovelful of dirt plummeted downward, striking the coffin with a dull thud, he shuddered. On impulse, she took hold of his hand, gripping it tightly. He looked at her, confused, before returning his gaze to the coffin.

It was nearly dark by the time the local mourners departed. Cynda looked around for the gravediggers. They were nowhere in sight.

"I asked them to wait until we left," Anderson informed her, divining her thoughts. His eyes tracked over to Theo. There seemed to be tension between them.

"You two know each other?" she asked as she rolled back the veil.

"We just met," Anderson said. Theo didn't reply, but she could tell by the set of his jaw it hadn't been a pleasant meeting.

Wordlessly, Defoe knelt by the open grave, dismantling a rose. Petals floated downward and settled onto the coffin, mingling with the clods of dark dirt, burgundy against brown.

When he was finished, he raised his head, like he'd just caught a scent on the wind. His eyes were lit with that strange fire. It'd had been there as Adelaide had bled to death in his arms, and then at Effington's party.

"You'll help me, won't you?" he pleaded, his voice raw. "I need to get her back."

"She's gone, Harter; we can't change that," Theo told him gently, his words catching on the emotions. "I am so sorry, my friend."

The fire in the grieving man's eyes grew stronger. "Then I'll do it. I can go back and kill him. I can save her."

"That will not work, Mr. Defoe," Anderson replied patiently.

It was only then Cynda noticed the band on Rover One's wrist. She glowered at Anderson. "What is that?"

"It keeps him from shifting. If it wasn't there, he'd go Virtual on us and disappear."

"You told me he's not your prisoner," Theo barked.

Anderson frowned. "He's not. If I recall correctly, you did something similar for Miss Lassiter when she was incapable of keeping herself safe."

Theo bit back an oath.

Thick sobs rebounded off the headstones in the still night air. Cynda held Defoe as he descended into his private hell, her own tears triggered by his. What if it had been Theo in that grave? Would she change history to save him?

Yes.

"I loved her," Defoe confessed between strangled sobs. "We were going to have a house in Paris, a small garden. It would have been perfect." He rambled on, his words gathering momentum. "It can still happen, still be right. I'm the Father of Time. I can fix anything!"

Except death.

"Harter," Theo began.

"I will make it right," Defoe retorted. "I have to. I don't care what happens."

"You can't," Theo said softly.

His friend glared up at him. "You don't want us to be together," he raved. "You're jealous because she loves me, and *no one* ever loved you."

Whoa.

"We should go," Anderson said, opening up his interface.

"No. This won't work," Theo announced. "When we finish here, he comes with me. I'll try to find away to mitigate the Transitive effects and restore his sanity."

Cynda's gut told her that would be a mistake.

"I'm sorry, Theo, but I don't agree," she said. His expression turned to hurt, like she'd stabbed him in the back. "There's too much going on we don't know about. Let Anderson take care of him. He's given us his word he'll keep Defoe safe."

"Why should I trust him?" Theo asked. He spoke in anger, but his eyes were filled with indecision. "You're just guessing these people are on the level. You have no idea."

"Theo, I—"

"Will you trust me?" a voice asked. A figure now stood next to Anderson, clad in navy. She rolled back the light veil.

The woman from Bedlam, the one who had given her the piece of paper with her name on it. This was no shifter *en mirage*. Just in case Cynda had any doubts, the blue arachnid on the woman's shoulder gave her an enthusiastic wave. Her own delusion returned it.

"You look good," her Mr. Spider announced. "A little gray, a little heavier, but it suits you."

He was right. The few wrinkles at the corners of her eyes spoke of contentment.

"Is she for real?" Theo asked, his eyes riveted on the newcomer. "I mean..."

She knew what he meant. "Yes, she is." Cynda shook her head at the newcomer. "I should have guessed it was you at the asylum."

"You should have," her future self chided back, "at least once your mind was back online."

"Why did you leave me there? You knew what would happen."

"We had multiple time threads in play so I had to let them go forward. I knew you were in danger, but I just had to hope you'd survive. For both of us."

"*We* could have drowned in the river," Cynda protested. It seemed odd arguing with yourself.

"It was worth the risk." She turned to Theo. "Harter has to come with us."

Theo's frown didn't diminish. "I don't know what's going on your time, but I know Harter. He needs to be with me."

"It's got to be this way," the future Cynda insisted. "If he stays with you, he's in danger."

"He's my best friend. It is my duty to help him in any way I can."

Her future self lightly drifted across the grass and touched his sleeve. It wasn't an awkward gesture, but one that seemed natural, like she'd done it a thousand times. It was a gesture of respect. Love.

"The danger is not just to him," she said, her voice uneven now. "Please, Theo, let us help him."

His dark eyes turned Cynda's way, pleading for guidance.

Oblivious to the conversation, Defoe was clutching the rose stem, now devoid of petals. He didn't seem to notice. One moment he was grieving, the next maniacal. A mental seesaw.

Theo took a deep breath, bordering on a shudder. "He can go with you." She swore she heard his heart tearing in two.

Cynda knelt next to the grieving man who was staring blindly into the grave. "Come on," she urged him gently. "It's time."

Defoe he shot a look over his shoulder at Theo as they rose. "*He* did this," he whispered, as if sharing a secret. "But I can make it right. I know how."

The mania was growing again. She shot an urgent look at Anderson.

"Harter…" Theo began. It was too late. He was talking to air where his best friend and Anderson had once stood.

Cynda's future leaned closer to him, whispering to him, then a brushed a kiss on his cheek. He murmured something, and she whispered again. Whatever she said earned her a faint smile. After holding their gaze longer than necessary, each of them turned away.

Without a sound, she vanished.

Cynda stared at the empty space, then down at the coffin. Around them she could hear birds settling in the trees, the hoot of an owl. Theo grasped her hand tightly in his, tears forming streaks down his face. He made no effort to wipe them away.

"We should stay…" his voice broke. "until they've buried her."

"Find the gravediggers. I'll stand vigil."

As he strode away across the darkening landscape, a single rose petal floated downward on the breeze. Cynda caught it between two fingers, remembering Defoe's boutonniere. This petal had a fragrance. She tucked it away in her pocket, a memento of a love lost to fate.

—

The silence inside the carriage was unlike anything she'd ever experienced. Part of it was grief. Part of it was uncertainty. The sure knowledge that things couldn't remain the same between them.

Unfinished business.

They held hands, a simple bond of flesh against flesh. It was comforting.

When he placed his arm around her, she pulled off her hat and veil, not willing to relinquish the warmth of his shoulder.

His embrace suddenly tightened. "Why did you confront Copeland alone? You should have left when Hopkins didn't arrive on time."

She turned toward him. "If you didn't want me to fight for myself, why did you teach me?"

"I wanted you to be able to *defend* yourself, not go into battle like some Valkyrie," he retorted.

She liked that image. "Copeland would have found us, one way or another. I made sure he came to *me*, on *my* terms, not his."

"I should have been there with you," he insisted.

"You did your hero bit. You saved thousands of lives. Taking down Copeland was my job."

"It could have gone so wrong, Jacynda. I could have lost you."

He hugged her tighter, gently brushing back a strand of hair. Touching her cheek as delicately as a faint autumn breeze, he leaned close and kissed her. It was a powerful beginning to whatever lay in their future.

When they broke apart he began whispering to her, so quietly she had to listen closely to hear his words over the sound of the carriage wheels.

"Harter was right," he admitted. "I would have been jealous of him if it hadn't been for you." His voice gained strength. "I was not in favor of Chris and you being together. I thought you too erratic, and I told him so. After you were knifed, it all changed. I was there when you arrived. Though you were dying, you clutched your Gladstone like it held the Crown Jewels. What a silly woman, I thought, worrying about a piece of luggage.

"Then I found my nephew's ashes in that case, and realized you'd risked your life to bring him home." He swallowed heavily. "I felt a heartless fool. It made me look inside myself, and I loathed what I found."

She didn't know what to say.

"Every trip you took to 1888 got harder for me," he told her. "By the last time, I almost refused to allow you to leave."

"I would have gone anyway."

"I know. I realized that I couldn't very well spout platitudes about choosing your own path, and then proceed to put myself directly in the middle of it."

"It was the right decision."

His fingers caressed her cheek again. "It could have gone so wrong. I couldn't stand the thought of losing the woman I love. Not a second time."

He put his arms around her, drawing her close. Part of her wanted to say she needed more time, that she didn't want to make a mistake. That would be a lie. Her heart had already weighed in on the matter of Theo Morrisey.

As CYNDA UNLOCKED the door to the hotel room, he trailed in behind her on silent feet. She could feel his apprehension. It matched hers. He set aside his top hat and jacket, regarding her with those dark eyes. Waiting. The moment her hat, veil and mantelet were set aside, she turned toward him.

"Theo..." He wrapped his hands around her waist, drawing her close against him. A kiss on her ear. She shivered at his warm touch. It stirred a greater need. The next kiss was on her lips. She savored it like a fine wine.

A second later, his control broke. Her back was against the wall in a heartbeat, kisses flaming across her mouth, cheeks and neck. She met his desire with hers, hands running under his waistcoat to pull him closer. Nervous fingers worked her bodice buttons, and one by one they opened. His hands glided across her breasts. She reveled in the sensation, spiraling into the stark passion that began to claim her.

"No," he muttered and abruptly stepped back, a flush of color on his cheeks. He took a deep breath. "Not this way. Not for our first time together."

He was right. This was more than just easing the ache. She caressed his cheek. "Go warm the bed. I'll be there soon."

After another deep kiss, he left her alone.

After lighting a gas lamp, Cynda selected a piece of hotel stationary, dipped the pen in the ink and began to write her resignation. Until tonight, her world was time travel. Now, it had expanded to include the man waiting for her in the other room. She would give him the paper in the morning. He'd be sure to protest, but somehow they'd find their way forward.

She heard the creak of a bedspring. Leaving the paper on the desk, she turned down the oil lamp and entered the bedroom. Theo was already in place, covers pulled to his waist, his chest mottled with nearly healed bruises.

Cynda took her time undressing, knowing he was watching. Seduction came in many forms. First she removed the boots, then the hose, making sure he got a good view of her legs. Then her skirt, petticoats and the bodice. That left the onsie with the lace edging, which was about as feminine as she got. She reached for the ribbon ties to remove it.

"No, leave that for me," he said. She shook out her hair and moved closer. "You are beautiful, you know," he confided huskily.

She scoffed, even though she enjoyed hearing it. "You're biased."

"I know true beauty when I see it. Adelaide Winston had it. So do you, now, *and* in the future."

The compliment warmed her cheeks. She never blushed, but she would for this man.

"What did she say to you?"

He placed a kiss on her forehead, brushing back a stray strand of hair. "That if we trust our hearts, all will be well."

Sitting on the side of the bed, she remembered the ring. As she went to remove it, he stopped her. "It's only fitting that you keep it," he said.

"But—"

"You didn't see it, did you?" She shook her head. "You were still wearing it. I think that bodes well for us."

Cynda could only nod, flooded with new emotions that were hard to comprehend. He slid his hands down her arms, pulling her closer. The kiss was beautiful in its simplicity.

"New beginnings are always scary," she admitted.

"For both of us." He had as much to lose as she did. As she crawled under the covers, she noticed his interface was open on the nightstand. "Ah, what's that for? You have other plans for tonight?" she joked.

"No. The night is ours. The interface will dampen any…sounds we make."

Like Defoe's watch had masked their conversation in the dining room.

"Sounds? What did Chris tell you?" she asked, suddenly nervous.

He chuckled, clearly enjoying her embarrassment. "He was always a gentleman when it came to you. I just thought we might embarrass our Victorian neighbors, especially since they believe we're brother and sister."

She'd forgotten that little white lie. "We'll have to sort that out tomorrow."

His fingers deftly untied the top ribbon on her bodice. "That is tomorrow." Another ribbon fell to his fingers. "I am only concerned with tonight." Another ribbon. Then the last one. He gently parted the two halves of the garment. His eyes reflected a hunger, a wonderment that she never thought possible. Curving his hands underneath her breasts, he ran his thumbs across each nipple.

Cynda moaned at the sensation. It had been too long. She'd made love, but never *been* loved. That was what she craved.

Leaning closer, she whispered, "Make time stand still... for both of us."

CHAPTER TWENTY-FIVE

Wednesday, 14 November 1888
Arundel Hotel

It had been his interface that had pulled him out of her arms. The message made him curse: things were starting to fall out with TPB and Guv wanted him home. Pronto.

"I should ignore them," Theo said, frowning. He pulled her back in his arms. She relished the feel of their naked bodies sliding against each other. She could still hear the words he'd whispered in her ear as they'd made love. Their cries of passion as they found their release as one.

I don't want you to go.

Not after last night. They'd savored each other, then rested, then began again. Each joining built the bond between them. A bond for the future.

Now he had to leave.

With a groan, he pulled himself out of bed and began to dress. After he'd finished, she propped herself up and watched as he'd sorted through his suitcase, even though he'd not brought that much with him. He took a great of time folding and refolding his one pair of socks, delaying the inevitable.

She had to make it easier for him. "It's not the end of the world," she jested.

He dropped the socks into the suitcase like they were burning coals. "It is to me. After last night ..." His deep eyes met hers. "I've ... never felt that way with anyone, Jacynda. Not even Mei."

Her heart melted. "I've never felt that way, either." Then she winked at him, hoping to bust through his melancholy mood. "You can welcome me home in a day or two after I settle things here. I promise I won't stay any longer than necessary."

He snapped the suitcase shut and then pulled out his interface. "One minute is too long for me, Jacynda."

"For me as well." She pulled on a robe as she walked toward him. Once in his arms, she delivered a kiss that glazed his eyes.

It took all her resolve to step back. "Now off you go!" she said, waving her hand to shoo him away. "I have other paramours to consider, you know."

An eyebrow arched. "You are too cheeky by half. We'll have to work on that."

She sobered. "Don't let the bad guys win."

"I won't." Then the transfer took him away from her.

The ache began instantly. The bond between them stretched taut.

I'll be home soon. I promise.

She hadn't been lying about the paramours. Well, Alastair and Keats weren't exactly lovers, but she owed them a goodbye. They weren't the only ones: so many bridges to burn. The official story was that she was returning home to New York. She'd need to visit Sephora and Sagamor, see how his lordship was doing. Then there was Davy and his mom, and dear Mr. Pratchett at the bookshop.

It was proving difficult, caught between the desire to go home and the sadness of leaving true friends behind.

As SHE PREPARED for her visit to the Wescombs, Cynda was about to jam the hat pin home when the maid arrived with a calling card.

"Do you wish to meet him downstairs?" the domestic asked.

"No, send him up." Whatever had brought Chief Inspector Fisher to her doorstep wasn't a topic they'd want to discuss in the dining room.

From the moment he stepped inside the door, Fisher was all business, which told her this wasn't a social call. He looked older, more war weary that the last time they'd seen each other. After they'd sat on the couch, he jumped right into it.

"I owe you my most sincere gratitude for saving Jonathon's life," he told her. "I still cannot see how you were able to speak directly to His Royal Highness, or for that matter, convince Flaherty to come forward."

"Sometimes you get lucky."

He examined her closely. "No, I suspect it had little to do with luck."

"How can I help you, Chief Inspector?"

"By being honest with me. I am about to retire, Miss Lassiter. I've had a long career, and though not every case I've encountered has been successfully concluded, this one has. At least, that's the general consensus. I, on the other hand, have a lot questions that have gone unanswered since the moment I first heard your name."

Oh boy, here we go. "What kinds of questions?" she hedged.

"For a start, who you really are and who do you work for? Please, don't bother with the Pinkerton's hoax. I have a friend who recently retired from their service. He tells me that you have never worked for Pinkerton's in any capacity. Neither has Mr. Anderson, nor Mr. Hopkins."

"Checkmate," her delusion called out. "He's got you."

She lounged back on the couch, pleased with this man's astuteness. "What took you so long to work that out?"

"My friend has been quite ill and was unable to answer my enquiries for some time. I received his letter just this morning." Fisher leaned forward. "So who are you, really? How could you possibly know the details of the Lord Mayor's Day plot so intimately? Where do you go when you disappear from the city?"

If anyone deserved the truth, it was Fisher.

When she didn't answer right away, he fluffed up, "Miss Lassiter, it's about time I knew the truth."

Cynda removed the interface from her pocket, setting it in her palm. As she began to wind it, she let him see the display. Both of his eyebrows raised in surprise as the dial lit up.

"You're absolutely right, Chief Inspector. It's about time."

—

Thursday, 15 November 1888
The Crystal Palace

"I'm glad Flaherty didn't blow this all to pieces," Keats remarked, gazing up at the roof of the massive cast iron and glass building. "It's such a marvel. No matter how many times I come here, it still makes me feel so insignificant."

"I must bring Mrs. Butler and her son here. This is an amazing feat of architecture," Alastair said.

Cynda did a slow three hundred and sixty degree turn while Keats and Alastair watched, each with smiles in place. "Wow. It's huge."

"When it was originally built in Hyde Park, it was nearly eighteen hundred feet long and just over one hundred feet high," Keats announced proudly. "Now it's even larger."

"Look at that!" Cynda proclaimed, pointing at a tall glass fountain.

"It was made by a firm from Birmingham and has more than four tons of glass in it," Keats said, this time consulting a brochure.

Victorian ingenuity. Why this time period had gotten under her skin. She'd originally hated it but now it was like a beloved old aunt you couldn't wait to visit. It was the improbable marriage of stuffy manners paired with an indomitable spirit. A spirit that said anything is possible if you put your mind to it.

As she gaped in wonder, people wandered around them. All were dressed in their finest clothes, whether that be a simple gown or something far more elegant. Children laughed or stared in astonishment at the displays.

Alastair touched her elbow. "Is this still there in…?"

She shook her head. "You've got about another fifty years to enjoy it."

"Oh. Perhaps someday I'll bring my children and grandchildren here," Alastair exclaimed.

"I think you're getting ahead of yourself, my friend," Keats remarked.

"How so?"

"I would suggest you bring Miss Hanson first. That way you'll have a better chance of making the other visits sometime down the line."

Cynda giggled. "He has a point. Besides, when you bring those grandkids here, you can tell them your best friend kept this from being destroyed."

"I did, didn't I?" Keats replied.

She held out both arms and they took them, walking three abreast. Cynda couldn't help but notice some of the women shooting her envious looks.

"I'm leaving right after this," she told them. "It's time for me to go home."

"We thought that might be the case," the doctor replied. "You have a life there, a future, one that holds a great deal of promise."

"That wasn't always the case," she admitted.

"I know," he replied. "That's why I'm so happy for you."

"This Morrisey person, does he love you?" Keats blurted.

"Keats," Alastair protested. "That's a very personal question."

"I know, but…"

Cynda squeezed the former sergeant's hand. "Yes, he does love me, and I love him."

Keats tilted his head in thought. "Well then, it will be all right," he proclaimed. He gestured with his free hand. "Come on, I'll show you the Medieval Court. It is very striking."

As they strolled, Alastair mused, "When I look back on it, I have no regrets for how it's fallen out. I still work with the poor, and yet now I truly make a difference."

"Even the future king knows your name," Keats jested.

"Oh, did I tell you?" the doctor asked. "Reuben has arranged for us to go to Edinburgh so I may meet Dr. Joseph Bell. Can you believe that?"

"That's fabulous, Alastair. You'll learn a lot from him." She turned toward the former detective-sergeant. He'd lost the most of any of them. "What of you, Jonathon?" she asked.

"Well, I would have liked to be chief inspector, but that's not in the cards now. As for my future, the jury is still out on that."

"I suspect it will be just fine," Cynda replied.

"I sometimes have my doubts," he replied.

"Excuse me, sir?"

They turned as one.

"Are you the fellow in the paper?" a young man asked, addressing Keats.

"I am," he replied, instantly ill at ease.

"It's him!" the man said to a group of people "It's the man who stopped the bombings!"

There were tentative smiles, and then someone gave a cheer. Others followed. Keats' face went crimson, his eyes darting around in extreme discomfort.

"Excuse me, but my friend here, Dr. Montrose, was involved as well," he informed them, gesturing toward Alastair. "He put himself at great personal risk."

"Don't confuse them," the doctor replied.

Cynda broke ranks with the pair, turning to face them. She began to clap.

"Bravo!" she shouted. Heads turned. People began to gravitate toward the noise. "Bravo!"

"What's it all about?" someone asked. The news began to spread.

Not everyone clapped. Some remembered Keats' face from when he was on trial. Luckily, those who *did* appreciate his heroic efforts made up for those who didn't.

When it was over, Keats was mopping his forehead with a handkerchief.

"How embarrassing," he murmured, his face still crimson. Cynda could see he'd been moved by the gesture.

"Very extraordinary," Alastair remarked. "I shall always remember this moment."

Cynda took their arms again. "You'd better get used to it, gents. The pair of you has just begun to take the Empire by storm."

—

2058 A.D.
TEM Enterprises

The moment the transfer stabilized and she was able to stand, Cynda heaved a tremendous sigh of relief. She was home, not off-timed into the center of a volcano or the Thames at high tide. Given the nature of the people she'd thwarted, either of those options might have become reality.

Ralph was behind the chronsole, waiting for her. His glasses twinkled in the overhead lights. As soon as the pod door opened, he called out, "Hey!"

"Hey yourself," she said. This reminded her of the old days, before it had all gone wrong.

"Welcome back to TEM Enterprises," he announced. "Heard about Copeland's end." He issued a thumbs-up.

"That seems to be everyone's opinion."

Cynda wedged herself in the time pod door to allow the disorientation to pass, methodically going through the Orientation to Place technique. Unlike Guv's chronsole room, this one was pleasant. Artwork on the walls, some sort of flowering vine on a trellis that exuded a faint hint of jasmine. A light piece of Baroque music in the background. Classic.

Like Theo.

Once her head stopped spinning, she made her way to the chronsole, still unsteady. Ralph unwrapped a candy bar and pushed it toward her across the counter. She took a bite, and then frowned. Chocolate just didn't taste good anymore. She ate it anyway.

"I hear you resigned," her friend said. "What's that all about?"

"Theo and I are..." She waggled an eyebrow suggestively.

A pensive frown appeared. "You mean...? You sure that's a good idea?"

"Yes. I'm in love with him."

"Well I'll be damned," Ralph exclaimed. "First time for everything."

She playfully punched him in the arm. He responded with a big hug.

"I don't agree with your taste," he said, "but if you're happy, I'll deal."

They hugged harder.

Fulham sailed through the chronsole room door. "Welcome back, Miss Lassiter," he said.

She grinned. "Hello, Fulham. How are you?"

"Quite well. Your return will certainly help."

She followed him out into the corridor, toting her Gladstone.

"Mr. Morrisey has ordered that you are to see the company physician first thing. He is particularly concerned that your health remains sound."

"Later," she said, rolling her eyes. "So where is our fearless leader?"

"At TPB. It's why I sent the message for you to return at this particular point in time."

Her footsteps faltered. "Is everything okay?" Surely Ralph would have known if it wasn't.

"Going very well. M.A. Fletcher is the new chairman. The boss is there for a meeting. They're trying to get the truth out of Ex-Chairman Davies." Fulham gave her a sidelong glance. "Your presence might do the trick."

"Consider it done."

"I'll arrange a grav-car," he offered.

"No need," she said, turning on her heel. "I'll go the high tech way. Tell the boss to save me a seat."

"That would violate a number of rules," Fulham observed with a wry smirk.

She smirked back, pulling out her interface. "Yes it would, but I have a legend to maintain."

⊹

CHAPTER TWENTY-SIX

2058 A.D.
Time Protocol Board Complex

Her grand arrival in the central hall of the TPB complex shocked a number of bystanders. Once the disorientation passed, she ignored the curious stares and marched over to the gleaming reception counter. The AdminBot behind the counter monitored her every move, sizing her up with electronic precision.

Cynda knew what was coming: a lecture about unauthorized arrivals within a public building, along with a citation of all the statutes she'd just broken.

Before the thing could start, she said, "I'm Jacynda Lassiter and I'm supposed to be in a meeting with Chairman Fletcher. Where is it?"

The thing whirred for a moment, then beeped. "Scan ESR Chip," it demanded.

"Don't have one. Where's the meeting?"

"Scan ESR Chip," the bot repeated, mimicking the bored personality of many human front desk assistants. "No entrance allowed without valid identification."

Cynda leaned over the counter to rap her knuckles on its shiny silver head. "You're not paying attention. I don't have a chip. So where's the meeting?"

The bot chirped and beeped faster now. As the situation deteriorated, she felt her interface vibrate. *Fulham.* As she'd hoped, the watch dial said he'd been in contact with the boss, then told her precisely where to find Theo within the complex. As an aside, Fulham wished her good luck getting there.

Piece of cake. Bots were nothing compared to knife-wielding maniacs or deluded men intent on immolating history. Well, except Sigmund. For a bot, he was cool.

"Never mind," she replied, clicking the watch closed. "I know where I need to go. Have a mindless day."

As she headed down the hall past wide-eyed bystanders, she began to hum *Rule Britannia* just for spite. As she'd anticipated, there was the whir of the bot's wheels as it hurried to catch up with her, spewing warnings nonstop now.

"Halt! Unauthorized intrusion. Return to the lobby immediately!" it chirped.

Cynda turned on a heel and glared at it. Her brother had trashed a couple of these things. How hard could it be?

It skidded to a halt. "Return to—"

"Oh, bugger off," she said, taking a step toward it. Sensing the threat, the bot flew into reverse, nearly mowing down some poor fellow behind it. A red light began to whirl on the top of the thing. It was summoning Security.

Cynda laughed all the way to the room.

To her glee, her entrance was an eye-opener. She was in full Victorian garb, toting a Gladstone bag, and equipped with enough attitude to power a grav-rail station. After 1888, this was nothing. In fact, it was fun.

She slid into the empty chair next to Theo.

"Hello there," she said.

"Welcome home, Jacynda. I've missed you."

Bet you have. She clunked the Gladstone on the floor.

"Lassiter," Senior Agent Klein said. "Quite an entrance. As usual."

"Give it a bit. The front-desk bot is pretty annoyed. It summoned Security."

"Is it still in one piece?" Theo asked in amusement.

"For now." He sought out her hand under the table and gave it a squeeze. She returned it. She'd missed him so much.

Mindful of their audience, Cynda slid her eyes toward the head of the table. "Chairman Fletcher," she greeted with a nod of respect.

"Lassiter," Fletcher acknowledged. "Don't remember your name being on the roster, but I'll add you to the agenda." She tapped on the holo-keyboard in front of her. "I'll cancel the security bots while I'm at it." A few more taps and then she looked up. "I think you know almost everyone else, except for Mr. Randolph."

Cynda catalogued those around the table. Besides Theo and Klein, there was Johns Hopkins, Ex-Chairman Davies and the aforementioned Mr. Randolph. Probably Davies' legal mouthpiece.

"Hi Hopkins," she called down the table. "How's it going?"

"Not bad," he replied, sending her a grin. "You?"

"Never been better."

"Your timing's good," Fletcher remarked. "Mr. Davies is explaining to us what happened in 1888."

Cynda leaned back in her chair. "Can't wait to hear this."

She gave him two minutes. She counted it out in her head. She could do that now that 1888 was right again. And in those two minutes, he'd avoided responsibility with every single word.

"We were solely concerned with returning Defoe to our time. He was out of control," Davies said, leveling his eyes at Cynda. "Much like Miss Lassiter."

"That was the only reason you had your people in '88?" Fletcher challenged.

"Yes."

He'd stepped right in it.

Cynda synced up her interface to the terminal embedded in the tabletop, waiting for the digital record to advance to the precise moment before Copeland appeared in Mitre Square. Davies watched her like she'd just pulled a knife at an ice cream parlor.

Not a bad idea.

She dug out the blade and placed it in front of her.

"What is that?" Fletcher asked, peering at it curiously.

"Amputation knife. They think Jack the Ripper used one like this."

"Wicked," Fletcher exclaimed, smiling.

"Sure is. Copeland brought it to our meeting in Mitre Square."

"My God," Theo murmured. He'd known of her injuries, but not what had inflicted them.

"Copeland?" Davies repeated, as if it was the first time he'd heard the name.

Cynda played along. "The former military jock. He was Hopkins' partner."

"We have a number of sub-contractors at TPB," Davies replied dismissively.

"This one's special. Copeland was involved in the death of Chris Stone."

"I sincerely doubt that. Stone committed suicide."

"No, his death was an accident, but the torture he endured was deliberate."

"Speculation," Davies shot back.

"Not anymore. Copeland was paired up with Dalton Mimes. I watched them drop Chris' body in the Thames the night he died."

"Given your psychiatric history, Miss Lassiter, it might be argued your testimony is of dubious value," the lawyer spoke up.

The ants didn't even raise their collective eyebrows. "I'm not the one on the hook here," she replied, smiling.

"None of this has anything to do with me," Davies protested.

"Let's start with bribery, for one," Klein weighed in. To his credit, he wasn't gloating. "You paid off an employee at Time Immersion Corporation to ensure Stone's body wouldn't be returned home."

"Which meant you knew my nephew was dead before Miss Lassiter found him," Theo pointed out.

Davies frowned. "All right, I wanted him left there. It would only complicate things. But I had nothing to do with that so-called plot in 1888."

"I'll give you that one," Cynda said. "You were too busy hiding your own mess."

"I have no idea what you're talking about."

She leaned over the table, relishing the moment. "Drogo."

Davies' face paled.

"Who's Drogo?" Fletcher asked.

"I think it's best to let Copeland answer that one." Cynda performed the windings. "Pay attention, folks. There'll be a quiz."

It was hard to experience it again, to hear her enemy's taunting laughter and her sharp cry of pain when the blade scored her flesh.

Too close. If she hadn't delivered that punch to his chest, Copeland would have left her mutilated corpse cooling in the night air.

As he heard the battle for the first time, Theo sought her hand again, this time for reassurance. She watched his face grow ruddy, the muscles at his jaw clenching and unclenching.

"Sorry," she whispered. He didn't respond, too caught up in the drama pouring from the interface.

To her ears, her voice sounded thin, but at least it didn't quaver.

"You're not doing very well, Copeland. You didn't blow up London and you can't find Rover One. I'd say your string is running out. You've only got one chance left."

"Which is?"

"Come back to '058 and tell the truth about the Null Mems."

Across the table, the ex-chairman's face went from pale to pasty white.

"Never heard of them."

"Then how did you know there was more than one?"

She and Copeland had bantered and forth, as he'd slowly nailed Davies to the cross for his transgressions.

"Why did Davies orphan the Null Mems in the time stream?"

"What better way to hide your mistakes?"

Then the battle had begun in earnest.

Cynda ended the recording the moment right after she'd bested Copeland. Right after she'd sent him to 2058. The portion of the recording with Satyr was gone now, erased. Reading the holo-manual had proven worth the time.

"Who is this Drogo?" Fletcher asked.

"It's a patient's code name. He was given the Null Memory Restoration treatment to keep him from becoming a serial killer. When the treatment failed, Davies ordered him abandoned in the time stream."

"Wait a minute," Fletcher interjected, swiveling toward Klein. "Is this the NMR thing you told me about?"

"That's it," he replied. Then shook his head. "You put them in the time stream. I never would have thought you'd be that stupid, Davies."

Davies drew himself up. "They had to go somewhere. They're all violent psychopaths. We couldn't keep them here."

Fletcher's face turned the color of her hair. "How many did you transport?"

"If he answers," his mouthpiece began, "that would implicate Mr. Davies in the unlawful—"

"You're damned right it will," Fletcher barked. "How many?"

The lawyer whispered in his client's ear, but Davies shook his head.

"Fifteen," he admitted. "As best as we can tell, there are at least thirteen still alive."

A Baker's dozen of the worst.

"What time periods?" Fletcher demanded.

"We just dropped them where we felt they would do the least damage."

"Least damage?" Theo growled. "How could you possibly think they wouldn't present a threat to individual timelines? To history?"

"Ah, nothing to worry about," Cynda cut in, her voice brittle. "What's a few more Stalins, Rippers or Elizars?"

Davies fluffed up. "The psychiatrist in charge assured us they were incapable of doing any harm, at least to the timeline."

"Walter Samuelson?" she quizzed. A nod. "Let me guess—he became a liability, didn't he?"

Davies nodded. "Walter knew too much. He kept asking to visit Drogo and some of the others. He knew they were in the time stream, wanted to do a follow-up study."

"So you ditched him in '88."

A wary nod. "It was his brother's idea. We used Mimes to lure Walter into 1888. He thought he was going to meet Drogo."

"What was Mimes' payoff?" Klein quizzed.

Davies rubbed his face, his expression hunted. "We promised to hide the fact he'd ever been in 1888."

"So his *Name the Ripper* book would look like actual scholarship rather than complete trash," Cynda deduced.

"That was the deal. He'd make a lot of money off the book and that would ensure he kept quiet."

"You didn't think anyone would notice when Dr. Samuelson went missing?" Hopkins asked, incredulous.

Davies shook his head. "We didn't care. By then, it was starting to fall apart."

Which meant they weren't thinking, just reacting.

"Why did you put one of these people in 1888?" Theo challenged. "You knew how volatile it was."

"We didn't. We dropped him in 1768. He forced a Rover to take him to the nineteenth century."

"Which Rover?" Fletcher asked.

"Some guy named Miller."

Frank Miller. Cynda groaned. *Of course.* The guy was so stupid he made a mud puddle look like a Mensa candidate.

"Wasn't he an old boyfriend?" Mr. Spider chided from her shoulder.

Not for very long. Lesson learned.

"You covered up Miller's bungle?" Fletcher asked.

Davies nodded. "Copeland still had a use for him, so we didn't pull his license."

Bait to keep me distracted. If she hadn't been so disgusted with old Frank, it might have worked.

Fletcher's face was less crimson now. "What have you done to retrieve these crazies?"

"We sent out a couple sub-contractors out. They didn't return."

That wasn't surprising. If any of the other Null Mems had Satyr's cunning, it was a suicide run to go up against these guys.

"We'll take care of them," Klein said.

Cynda's eyes met Hopkins. He'd be right in the firing line, one of the first into the time stream.

Sorry guy.

Fletcher leaned back in her chair. "Here's how it's going to work, Mr. Davies. You're going to tell us about each of these transfers—names, dates, all if it. You understand?"

"The previous government is responsible for this. They dropped this mess in my lap," Davies complained, his forehead damp with sweat now.

"Don't give me the victim routine," Fletcher snapped. "You could have raised a stink and stopped this disaster, but you didn't. You played along and it got you the chairmanship."

"I am not responsible!" Davies bellowed. "I had nothing to do with what happened to Stone or anyone else in 1888, and I shouldn't pay the penalty."

"Someone must," Theo said evenly.

Cynda picked up the knife, weighing it in her hand. As she anticipated, all eyes swung in her direction. "You hired Copeland and he was your responsibility. While you were trying to save your own butt, you became a party to murder, kidnapping, torture...the whole works. You're not walking on this one, Davies. We won't let you. Someone has to pay the piper and it has to be you."

"Why not Copeland? He did all this! Why isn't he here?"

Klein started to chuckle. It was an odd sound, like a cat with a rusty purr. "Copeland's dead. He didn't survive the transfer from 1888. You're the one holding the bag."

Davies' anger collapsed. He motioned to his lawyer and they whispered back and forth earnestly. After some heated discussion, Randolph sighed.

"Mr. Davies will cooperate," he announced, "as long as he is given immunity to future prosecution."

"To hell with that!" Theo roared, pounding the table with his fist. Everyone jumped at his raw fury, including Cynda. "He's got as much blood on his hands as Copeland or any of the others."

"You'll not get the information any other way," the lawyer replied.

Theo's face hardened. She knew that look. A samurai adopts it right before he lops off your head. "Then if we grant him immunity, he's sent Off-Grid. *Permanently.*"

For a moment, she thought Davies was having a heart attack.

"Good God, that's a…a death sentence," the man sputtered. "You know what it's like out there."

"Yes, I do," Theo replied coldly.

"We'll fight this," the lawyer replied. "You can't force him to do this."

"You might be surprised," Klein replied. He gestured to Hopkins. "Get him out of here. We'll talk details later."

As Davies and his lawyer departed, Cynda spied three black-suited Guv agents in the hallway. The guys from 1888. She shot one of them a wink, and his mouth twitched up in a grin. They quickly formed a cordon around the prisoner. She could just imagine what the AdminBot would think of that.

The second after the door closed, Cynda shut down the interface and repacked her Gladstone, eager for a shower and a nap. The adrenalin rush was ebbing faster than she'd expected.

"Who Null Mem'd you?" Klein asked.

She shrugged. "Not everything is clear about that." *Because I don't want it to be.*

Klein shot her a dubious look. "What about this Drogo guy in 1888?"

"I'd worry about the others first."

"Why are you protecting him?" the agent asked.

"Consider it my compensation for this whole fiasco. There are worse monsters to hunt."

"You're not going to tell us, are you?" he said.

"Nothing to tell. The bad guys didn't win this round. That's all that matters."

"But what about the next time?" Fletcher asked, meeting her gaze.

Cynda rose, Gladstone in hand. "Then it'll be another madman's dance."

CHAPTER TWENTY-SEVEN

Saturday night, and the Time Pod was packed. They'd commandeered a table, ordered some beer and pizza. Her former boss seemed to be enjoying himself.

"Far too much," Mr. Spider observed. "He's like a kid out on his first date."

She felt the same.

"Not quite like the Ten Bells," Theo observed with a grin.

"Nothing is like the Ten Bells."

"Why haven't they posted the results yet?" Hopkins complained.

"It takes time," Ralph replied. "Have another beer."

Hopkins gave Cynda a look. She nodded. "Okay, it's on me."

He tapped in the order on the tabletop and then waited for the waitress. At least the Time Pod still used real people, not ServBots. When she arrived, their waitress was clad like someone from Ancient Rome. Cynda didn't have the heart to tell the woman the costume wasn't at all authentic.

It had taken a great deal of time to get Cynda's run report past the security clearances, including Fletcher and Klein's sign-off. In the end, it included all the juicy bits about her saving Defoe's life, preventing a repeat of 1666 and bringing a murderer to justice without mentioning the Futures or the shifters. In a nod for his "cooperation" Davies was left out of it, all the blame falling upon a deceased TPB heavy named Copeland. The run report's glaring holes would give the conspiracy theorists new fodder to chew on.

"This is going to put you on the top," Ralph said confidently.

Or not. The groupies were fickle. They might think she'd sold out Rover One when she'd sent him home with the bullet wound in his chest. That would banish her from the boards forever.

"I'm still in third place!" Hopkins crowed as the reports began to jigger the rankings. He was going to be a handful tonight.

"I'm in ninth," Cynda grumbled.

Hopkins smirked. "Life's a bitch."

"Go ahead, be smug. Your day is coming, buddy."

He guffawed. With Copeland dead, Hopkins was euphoric. He still hadn't learned that the good guys don't always win.

It took some time for her run report to reach the tables and the Vid-Net.

"How about a kiss for luck?" Theo whispered in her ear before giving it a gentle nibble.

"Sure." He planted one her cheek.

She swore he enjoyed being the center of attention. It'd taken some of patrons awhile to recognize him, but once they did their eyes lit up. She knew vid-messages were bouncing around the city with the latest gossip.

Let them chatter.

Theo blew in her ear. It was so damned erotic and so not TEM, the man who used to calibrate window blinds at twenty-three percent.

"I'm still waiting to hear your answer," he whispered.

That was the other thing. The proposition he'd popped on her after one particularly tender lovemaking session.

"I'm still thinking."

"It's a pretty easy decision."

For a time she'd thought he was proposing, he'd been that serious. Instead, it was business: he'd decided he wanted her as a partner in TEM Enterprises. A full partner. That felt weird. She'd always been a worker bee, not a queen, and certainly not *management*.

She was a Rover, first and foremost. It was in her blood.

"I have to be able to travel," she'd protested.

"It's not worth the risk," he'd said as they lay curled around each other, tentatively learning the curves and passion of each other's bodies. The conversation had ended shortly thereafter when they'd found yet another way to make love.

On the plus side, his proposition would solve her issues with dating higher up the ladder. She and Theo would be equals, at the top of the heap. The flip side was that he didn't want her to travel. That was a restriction she didn't think she could tolerate.

Either way, he was going to need an answer soon.

"Here it comes," Ralph said, keying up the report on the table in front of them.

She watched the wall with a mixture of eagerness and dread. Her name had vanished from ninth place. Was that good? Hopkins shot up to second. He shouted in approval. Third place was someone named Madigan.

"Who's that?" Ralph asked.

"No idea," Hopkins replied. "Must be new."

Then T.E. Morrisey's name appeared in the lights under First Place.

"Me?" Theo said. "*Me?*" he repeated, even more incredulously.

"Will you look at that!" Ralph said. "They've never had a non-Rover on the board before."

"I didn't do anything," Theo protested.

"Yes, you did," Ralph shot back. "Cyn's run report included your work in '88, disarming the explosives and all that. You're getting the updraft from it."

Theo shook his head in amazement.

Cynda's name was nowhere on the board. She sighed. Still, Theo's performance in the time stream had been awesome for a rank newbie. He deserved the praise.

She turned to kiss him, whispering, "I'm very proud of you."

Suddenly, Ralph let out a yell. "All right!!"

"Look," Theo said, pointing.

First through fifth place hadn't altered. What had changed was the Emeritus portion of the board. Harter Defoe, Time Rover One, was no longer alone. Next to his name was a new one.

"Jacynda Lassiter," Ralph proudly read, "Time Rover TWO." He leapt from the chair, launching a fist into the air. "Yes!"

"Whoa," she murmured. That honor would never change, no matter the whims of the groupies or TPB's rulings.

The bar erupted into frenzy cheers. "Speech!" someone shouted from the back. Suddenly, this didn't seem like a great idea.

Theo pushed her upward. There were calls for silence, and amazingly it worked.

"I…" She looked at the men around the table. Ralph, her oldest friend, was beaming at her. Johns Hopkins gave her thumbs up. Then there was Theo, his eyes glowing with love and admiration.

She lifted her pint. "To Rover One, wherever you may be. You cleared the path for us so we could follow in your footsteps."

And paid the ultimate price.

When the cheers died down, she turned to the Memorial section. "To Christopher Stone and all the others who've died on this journey. A Rover is eternal, forever traveling through time. Someday we'll all be there with him. Until then…" She blinked away tears. "We miss you, Chris."

There was absolute silence for a few seconds.

"Tales!" someone called. "Tell us a tale!"

It was tradition. No one was truly gone if there was a story to be told.

A man stood. "I remember my first trip with Defoe. He kept me from being speared by a tribesman in New Guinea and becoming a shrunken head. He never let me forget it."

The tables were pounded in approval.

Another rose, a young fellow with sideburns. "My first run was with Chris Stone. He taught me how not to get mugged in 1970 New York."

So it went, tale after tale, like a verbal wake. Cynda sank into her seat, a myriad of emotions flowing through her.

Theo looked wistful. He leaned close. "Just remember, I will be waiting for you at the end of every journey."

He was saying he understood what it meant to be a Rover and would not deny her that freedom.

Cynda's heart melted and she leaned over and kissed him again, touching his cheek fondly. "Even better, come with me."

"What?"

"Why not? You're in First Place. You don't want some youngster like Hopkins kicking you out of that. Come with me. There's a lot to see."

"I can't, not with the—"

"Fulham will watch over things. He's very good at it."

"But—"

"You could go anywhere and meet *anyone*," she said, throwing bait under his nose. "Well, I'd skip the lunatics and the dictators. They're never any fun."

He looked up to his name on the board. She could hear the wheels turning. "Anyone?"

She unveiled the ultimate prize. "Even...da Vinci."

His mouth fell open.

"Oh, that's not playing fair," her blue delusion complained, crawling out from underneath a bar napkin. "You know he's nuts about Leo."

All is fair in love and war.

She'd seen the books in Theo's library, the drawings on his office walls that competed for room with all the Oriental watercolors. Every man had a soft spot and Leonardo was evidently his.

"I hear he's a blast," she added, upping the ante. "Before we go, we'll have to work on your Latin."

There was a lengthy pause. "We'll study together," Theo decided. "We can start now." He pulled her into his arms and kissed her, earning them some harassment from both the spider and Ralph.

Then he whispered into her ear, "Te amo."

That one she did know.

                              ✦

EPILOGUE

1495 A.D.
Milan

Cynda leaned in the door of the villa, enjoying the breeze sweeping across her face. Behind her, in the workshop, she could hear animated voices rising and falling in a waterfall of Latin. They'd arrived the night before, found themselves a room at an inn and after a dinner of wine, bread and cheese, had curled up in the narrow bed. Despite not getting much sleep, Theo had been up at dawn, promising he wouldn't take very long. She knew better. While she had no worries about her lover tainting Leonardo's timeline, the reverse was always an issue.

The sound of sandals drew near. Theo leaned close. "This might be a bit longer," he whispered to her in English. "He has some drawings to show me. I know they'll be incredible." He added a kiss on her cheek for good measure. "You don't mind, do you?"

"No, not at all," she whispered back. "Enjoy yourself."

"Oh, I am," he said, eyes twinkling. "I'll make it up to you later."

Cynda smiled at the thought. After another hasty kiss, he scurried off like a kid who'd found himself locked inside a toy store over a long weekend. It was the third time he'd made such a request. She didn't have the heart to say no.

A donkey cart rolled by, kicking up little puffs of dust. She leaned back against the doorframe. For once she wasn't keen to go anywhere in a hurry. No desire to jump out in traffic, like the daredevil she'd always been. It felt good to be here with him. Her father had once told her that sharing the journey made it more meaningful. Now she knew what he meant.

"I like it here." Mr. Spider hung from a makeshift cerulean web near the top of the doorframe, watching a potential meal buzz haplessly near. "Lots of flies."

Glad to hear it.

Behind her, Theo's voice rose in a flurry of Latin, telegraphing his excitement. He would tell her all about it later in glorious detail after they returned to 2058. A few days rest, and then he wanted to see the Columbian Exposition in 1893 Chicago. From there, they'd go directly to 1889 Whitechapel, their clothes nearly compatible. What would a few months have wrought for Alastair and Keats? What exciting forensic mysteries would the doctor have uncovered? What of Keats' new career? How had he adjusted to life outside the Yard?

Maybe they could all go to the Crystal Palace again. Theo had never seen it. She could only imagine what his analytical mind would make of it.

"Where after that?" the spider asking, winching down on a thread so he could sit on her shoulder. He settled there with a contented sigh.

Cynda spread her hands. "Who knows?"

We have all the time in the world.

THE END

FINAL AUTHOR THOUGHTS ON
JACYNDA'S JOURNEY

Jacynda's journey doesn't really come to end in this book, but it pauses at a resting place, a moment in her life where all is in balance. When I began her story I had envisioned it as sexual romp that I might sell to one of the erotica publishers. That's why all the mention of chocolate and sex to cure time lag. Cynda promptly told me that wasn't going to be the case, she was in 1888 to find a tourist, not get laid. She asserted her authority early and for that I am grateful.

Over the course of the three books readers have long pondered which of the two Victorian gentlemen she might choose as her lover, which one might be her soul mate. Both were worthy. Alastair and Jonathon are wonderful men, each with their own strengths. I could easily see her choosing either one. When Jacynda and Keats nearly become lovers in *Virtual Evil*, I thought she'd made her choice. In some ways she had, but her damaged mind wouldn't let her go there. In retrospect, that was the right decision.

T.E. Morrisey came to be as a tip of the hat to Tee Morris, who introduced me to Gwen Gades, publisher of Dragon Moon Press. The similarity in name is the only commonality they share as Tee is an energetic soul and Morrisey is the Zen Master. I initially wrote Morrisey as a mysterious, almost creepy, boss who pulled strings and manipulated people. The only hint that Morrisey had more to him than just eccentric behavior is when we learn that Chris Stone, Jacynda's dead lover, was his nephew.

We don't hear Morrisey's first name until late in the second book. At that point Theo began to take on a real personality, but wasn't on my radar as Jacynda's choice. There were little "tells" however, that this author didn't see until after the fact. Theo makes his first time travel journey to help Jacynda, because, he said, he couldn't trust the sensitive information to anyone else. Surely there had to be a Transitive in his company he could have sent. He runs interference for her with both Guv and TP, at great personal and financial risk. I finally realized something was up in *Virtual Evil*, when he gently squeezed her arm and called her by her first name as she prepares to return to 1888 after the TPB trial

As *Madman's Dance* unfolded in my mind, I saw their story. Theo's protective instincts kicked in, though he didn't really know why. His respect for Jacynda, and the huge gamble he took allowing her to rebuild herself from within, were turning points for him. His willingness to go to 1888 to be at her side was the final emotional commitment, though he was ill-equipped to survive in that era. In the end, it was Harter Defoe's immeasurable loss that allowed Jacynda to take that leap of faith and finally accept that love could be hers if she was willing to take the risk.

Jacynda and Theo's story is certainly not at an end. No doubt we'll see more of them down the line. I sincerely hope you've enjoyed their journey so far. I know I've loved writing it.

Oh, and Mr. Spider wants me to ask if you might spare him a scone morsel or two. Matchmaking, he says, is very hard work.

Jana Oliver
September 2008

ABOUT THE AUTHOR

Jana G. Oliver

Jana Oliver admits a fascination with all things mysterious, usually laced with a touch of the supernatural. An eclectic person who has traveled the world, she loves to pour over old maps and dusty tomes, rummaging in history's closet for plot lines. When not writing, she enjoys Irish music, Cornish fudge and good whiskey.

Jana lives in Atlanta, Georgia with her husband and two cats: Midnight and OddsBobkin.

Visit her website at: www.janaoliver.com

Photograph by Jennifer Berry, Studio 16

Made in United States
Orlando, FL
05 August 2022

20566180R00215